THE GIRL WHO CANNOT DIE

ALESSA WINTERS

To D. H. Gastelum, for his magic and coin work consultations.
To A Brand New Chapter, for listening to this entire trilogy two chapters at a time
To Allen, who helped me brainstorm, even though this isn't his jam.
To Lemon Creek Breeze In Convenience Store, for helping me with the food questions in

CONTENT WARNING

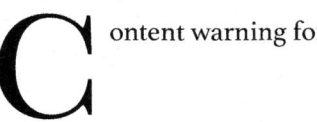ontent warning for body horror and gore.

THERE IS sex in this book, Mom please skip those chapters.

THE FIRST BOOK in this series is "The Girl Who Brings The Dead" and this book won't make much sense without reading it first.

1

Near as she can tell, Terese has died twenty-four times in the last seven months, and she's tired of it.

She's tired of a lot of things.

Like how she still can't control whatever hellish magic that got dumped on her somewhere between being possessed and then un-possessed, like how her body still doesn't process all the normal things like being hungry or being sleepy in any way that she can easily interpret, like how she still doesn't have a place to call an actual home, and like how she's not sure if she's actually spoken to another human in well over three weeks.

She thinks she has. But again, not sure.

Because, see, she's been losing time, and it freaks her the fuck out.

It's different from The Possession, it's far different from the demon that had forced its way into Terese's mind and body and ruined everything, but the part of Terese that's left that still shrieks about her overall health and safety tells her that losing track of time and where she is, is definitely a symptom of something Not Good.

So when Terese finds herself in her favorite safety tunnel, bleeding suspiciously from a wound on her side into the dust of the rock floor, her dog Izzy calmly asleep on the blanket Terese scavenged a while back, and no memory of taking either of them there, she takes a moment.

The area is little more than an abandoned maintenance tunnel for a long-since-forgotten railway company, with crumbling rock walls held up by aged wooden beams. Graffiti decorates wherever a clean enough rock face presents itself, the long ago scrawling of teenagers.

It's also incredibly silent, remarkably mild in temperature, and she can hear anyone coming.

She rests her head against the rock wall, and her skin stretches at the wound.

It's not like she can go get medical treatment. Not when she's had multiple fatal injuries and popped right back up. Not when pain still wracks her bones whenever she moves wrong.

Not when being in unfamiliar places still makes that tickle of panic crawl down her throat.

She stretches her legs out in front of her—huh, she's wearing pants, she could've sworn she had a skirt on last— and prods at the mysterious bleeding wound.

It hurts, of course, pain shooting up from it and twisting around her lungs and her neck, but the skin is already starting to grow back over it and the bone of her rib doesn't look chipped. Like she got stabbed by someone or half-impaled on a metal pipe.

Terese looks up at Izzy, but there's no blood on her dog, so maybe not an attack? While Izzy may just be the laziest large mutt that Terese can think of, she'll try to help if Terese gets outright attacked.

Ruined another shirt, too, by the look of it.

"Alright," Terese whispers, and her voice echoes down her tunnel. "Mystery wound."

Slowly, because gut wounds still fucking hurt even if they don't end you, she reaches to the first aid kit she keeps tucked into a crevice of the wall.

She's learned quickly to keep a medical kit in all of her safety spots because her magic takes her to the safety spots whether she wants to go or not, and some bandages and antiseptic go a long way towards comfort.

Izzy doesn't move as Terese dumps half a bottle of rubbing alcohol on the wound, doesn't move as Terese hisses in pain, and doesn't move when Terese slaps a sterile bandage on the still-seeping puncture.

It's not like Terese meant to adopt a dog, not while she's out here with unpredictable magic and lost time and the penchant for being killed every few weeks. But after seeing the long-haired, filthy dog tied up in the same place for over a week (at least, Terese thinks it was a week) with no food and only a puddle for water, she found herself untying the leash and just...teleporting away.

That's how Terese discovered she could teleport with other things, and after that her life got way better. Because if her nebulous power could teleport with an eighty-pound dog, then it could teleport with a bag of groceries and first aid kits.

The vet she threatened at knifepoint behind his clinic (not her best moment) told her Izzy had no microchip, was severely malnourished, and probably around eleven years old. That Izzy had probably been tied up at that location for close to three weeks.

Terese has—so far—tried to avoid killing anyone since becoming un-possessed, but the temptation had been strong to track down Izzy's former owner.

She doesn't know how long she's sat there, bleeding, but both her butt cheeks are cold from the stone ground and half the blood on her shirt is sticky cool.

"Izzy," she mutters, and her voice is weak, thready, so she must've been dead or unconscious for a while, "Izzy, want to go somewhere else?"

At her name, the dog lifts her head to blink lazily at her.

"Want to try for the park?" Terese says, reaching around blindly for her backpack. It's a ragged, dirty one, but she keeps a few changes of clothes and some food in it, in case her magic decides to teleport her somewhere new. "The park is nice."

Izzy thumps her tail at her, then laboriously climbs to her feet.

The vet said Izzy probably has joint issues because she's a big old dog, but it still makes Terese's throat stick.

Out of muscle memory, trying not to stretch her wound, she pulls out a hoodie and shrugs it over her existing tank top.

The park will be hot, but the dark hoodie will at least disguise any bandage or bloodstain peeking out.

Knowing the routine, Izzy lumbers close, so Terese can grab her collar while keeping a hand looped through the backpack straps.

"Okay, let's see where we go," Terese whispers, and Izzy pushes her snout into Terese's hand. "I'll try for the park."

Because the thing about Terese's magic is that instead of taking her to a location she's thinking of, it takes her somewhere it considers 'safe,' particularly if she's feeling unsafe. Over time, she's found that her magic has picked out five 'safe' locations, and it will take her to one of those at random. So when she teleports, she knows it will be one of those five places, but which it will be is always a mystery.

Now, leaning her head against the cold rock, Terese thinks 'safe'.

There's a moment of gut dropping free fall, before her ass hits damp moss and cool air fluffs her uncombed hair.

She cracks her eyes open to see blackberry brambles and spruce trees.

Not the park. Ugh.

Izzy immediately wriggles out of her grip to sniff around, leaving Terese to catch her breath.

She's next to a long gravel driveway, and a modern concrete building sits squat on the top of the sloping hill, blackberries and ivy growing over the side.

It's the headquarters of those magicians. Whenever they took down the protective wards five months ago, her magic immediately placed this location as a safety spot, and it's intensely annoying.

Last time she encountered the magicians in any real extended way, one shot her in the head and in the chest and it took her a few days of sitting down until she felt entirely right again.

Izzy likes it though, likes sniffing for the squirrels and romping through the underbrush.

And, true to form, they have not attacked her since she started teleporting here, but the mere presence of the magicians sticks uncomfortably in her gut, almost as uncomfortable as the wound.

She knows the demon killed one of them. Maybe two. She saw the horror crossing over the one with the braid's face, as the demon bullshit killing power rushed over her and she dropped like a brick. Heard the yell of the other one, felt the sick satisfaction of the demon enjoying it.

The demon had enjoyed killing whenever she could. Enjoyed ripping people and things apart, from stopping their hearts to bleeding their brains to crushing their lungs, and Terese remembers too much of it.

"Izzy," she whispers, because she doesn't know if the magicians keep any listening spells on their house, "Izzy, come back."

The dog ignores her, crashing through the ivy with her nose to the ground.

Damp moss soaks through her pants, and Terese grips the tree to drag herself up to standing.

Her wound stretches, and she holds her breath to see if it's gonna tear and kill her again, but the already-new skin keeps it in place.

Far in the distance, there's a flash in the sky, and all of Terese jerks.

The Necromancer. Doing some sort of magic, something with her powers.

The demon had wanted the Necromancer so badly, wanted what she could offer, so much so that even the thought of the necromancer now turns Terese's stomach.

She doesn't know why she can still see the Necromancer's power, doesn't know why it still punches through her with awareness and hunger and terror, but it does.

"Great," she whispers, "Izzy, park?"

This gets the dog's attention, and she bounds back to her close enough that she can snag the collar and try to teleport to the park again.

Her feet hit a rough-hewn wooden floor, and it's the cabin in the middle of the European forest and definitely not the park.

Terese doesn't even bother opening her eyes to the cabin, instead thinking real hard for the dry heat and dead grass of Izzy's favorite place.

There's an immediate crunch of brown plants, and Terese lets herself sit down hard before opening her eyes.

Immediately, Izzy sniffs around with enthusiasm, and Terese lets go of her grip on the collar.

The park just might be Terese's favorite, too.

Her magic always zaps her underneath a gazebo, away from prying eyes and shaded from the harsh Southern California sun. It's fenced in, so Izzy can run and socialize with other dogs without Terese worrying, and Izzy always gets magnificently dusty from playing in the dirt. There's water bowls and tennis balls galore, and a corner store right next to it where she can get almost anything she needs, including a well-stocked first aid section and a stunning variety of potato chips. There's a coffee shop a few blocks away that gives out whipped cream to dogs, and Terese finds herself walking there more often than not when they visit.

Terese lets Izzy run around with more energy than she usually has and lets her body sit there and recover. The new skin itches, crawling over the wound, but there's no urgency to the park, no genuine threats. It's not as isolated as the tunnel or the boat, but there's a strange comfort in strangers milling about and not giving her a shred of care.

It's so far removed from the demon possession in the Pacific Northwest. Here Terese can just be a person watching her dog play.

~

AFTER ABOUT TWO hours of roughhousing with younger and smaller dogs, Izzy plops over by Terese's spot in the gazebo's shade with the deep satisfaction of a tired dog.

"Yeah?" Terese says, as Izzy shuffles so her head is in her lap and Terese can scratch behind her ears. Terese's voice is stronger now, and her body feels less shaky, less like she's one bad step away from ripping apart again.

Izzy huffs at her, as if in agreement.

"Do you want some whipped cream or anything?" Terese asks, and Izzy thumps her tail.

Terese climbs to her feet again, and it hurts substantially less, replacing the pain with a gnawing hunger that suggests she hasn't eaten in a few days.

Though it could have just been the glimpse of the Necromancer's power. It's hard to tell.

She digs out Izzy's leash from her backpack and clips it on her collar, because the coffee shop won't let her bring in the dog unleashed, which makes sense even though Izzy clearly hates it, and, with a small bit of fear, leaves the park.

It's not like bad things always happen when she leaves one of the five safety spots, but it sure feels like it, and without knowing exactly when or where she last got stabbed (or impaled), she still fears.

Terese's awfully tired of the fear, too.

2

After a donut and a too-sweet coffee milkshake, Terese's starting to actually feel as normal as she ever does. The bandage is now more annoying than the pulling skin, and the blood on her shirt has dried enough that she no longer notices it sticking to her.

Izzy, with whipped cream still on her snout, leads her on a meandering walk through the Southern California suburb, and the sun is still pleasantly warm through the early evening. The early dandelions of summer peek through the cracks in the sidewalks, and cars zoom past, completely unconcerned with a woman strolling around with her dog. Terese'll have to figure out a place to sleep for the night at some point, but there's always the opportunity to go back to the cabin or try for the boat.

It's almost peaceful.

It's almost peaceful, in the way that Terese never thought she'd ever get to have. She knows she had peaceful moments Before, but those memories are so far away they feel like they belong to someone else, like a movie watched through fogged glass, so she holds onto the rare moments she gets to have now. With the setting sun streaking pinks and oranges over the rows and rows of identical houses and suburban strip malls, there's a beauty to it that is so exquisite it almost hurts.

The demon hadn't paused to look at any sunsets, so Terese does, stilling her feet in her scuffed-up boots, looking up between the two side-by-side buildings of tiny shops. She tucks herself in the alley, leaning against the rough concrete, and Izzy sits against her legs.

She hadn't trained Izzy to do that, but the big dog's solid presence is...nice.

"Good dog," she murmurs, scratching Izzy behind the ears, keeping her eyes on the colors of the sunset. Might as well give positive reinforcement, make one creature's life better, even if she can't do anything for her own.

The sky darkens into purples, and finally deep blues, before Izzy stands up and growls.

Terese flinches, the growl rougher than sandpaper against her skin, and her hand tightens into a fist before she shakes it out.

"Shh," she says impulsively, but Izzy bristles, growling at...

Something.

Izzy's grey muzzle points out towards the entrance to the alley, her teeth bared.

For a few seconds, there's nothing there, and Terese grips down on Izzy's collar, ready to go somewhere else, anywhere else, then—

"Oh, what are you?"

There's a dizzying sound, a motion of something sliding through and then past her, before a shifting, indistinct figure stands in front of her.

Terese freezes. She freezes, her breath stuck in her

throat, her fingers tight around Izzy's collar, her feet frozen against the dirty pavement beneath her.

Light reflects in the figure's eyes, red, and Terese jerks herself back, grabbing towards her magic, and—

"No, don't do that," the figure says, hand cutting down, and Terese can't move. Can't leave. Her magic doesn't take her away, nothing comes to her, her feet stay on the concrete.

Izzy barks, loud, but the figure pays her no mind, taking another step forward.

"But what are you?" the figure repeats, and there's a swirling, dire power to the figure. "Normal humans can't do that, even magicians don't usually teleport."

Terese can't speak, nothing's coming out. She thinks 'safe,' tries to conjure up the thought of the boat, of the tunnel, anything, but nothing moves.

She can't push past the figure, they're blocking the entire entryway, and Izzy bristles and backs up. She can't run, she doesn't think she can climb walls, there's no easily visible magic she can grab and throw at them, nothing.

The figure stills. "I forgot this form scares humans. So few can see." The glowing red eyes slide towards the store next to the alleyway, and a man comes stumbling out of the door, his suit shirt askew, a cheap pocket knife clipped to his belt. "This will help."

The man stares blankly at Terese, standing in the alleyway, his brows knit together. "Did you call for help?" he asks, looking past the figure as if it's not even there. "I thought I heard—"

The figure twists its hand, and the man's neck snaps, a sickening crunch, his head jerking to the side, his knees buckling and sliding out from underneath him.

Before he hits the ground, the figure steps sideways into

the body, straightening out, shaking out his arms as if it's nothing.

A demon.

Terese jerks back, but her feet don't move.

She has seen this before, in the few seconds before The Possession.

In those precious few moments, when the doctor —Dr. Frisse—had reassured her that nothing bad would happen, in those few moments when Terese had been excited, actually excited about the prospects of learning what was to come.

Her feet had felt frozen to the ground then, too.

The demon turns his head towards her, stretching the body's face into a smile, and his eyes reflect the light back at her. "Sorry, I know humans frighten easy." He shakes out his arms again, as if settling into the form. "What are you? You don't feel like a necromancer, spell weavers and alchemists can't see us, and you're"—he waves a hand at her—"astoundingly visible."

"Let me go," Terese whispers, barely more than a breath past her lips. Behind her, Izzy growls, but the demon's eyes never leave Terese's face.

He takes another step towards her, and she tries to flinch back. She tries to move away, but can't. She can't.

"You don't want this," she says, instead, her heart pounding in her throat. "You don't want this, this will only bring you pain."

"You do know what I am," he says, casually pacing in front of her, like he hadn't just killed someone to take a body, like he hadn't just immobilized her. "Interesting."

So he will talk to her. So he's not just trying to possess her, not just trying to grab whatever power she has.

He examines his hands, and the body he had just killed

has neatly maintained skin, clean nail beds, no callouses. Like the act of taking a body is distracting him.

"I can't help you," Terese blurts out, and she doesn't even know what the demon wants, how he found her, anything. "Whatever you think I can do, I can't."

The demon peers at her, and the body's eyes are a light hazel. "I don't know what to think you can do," he says, voice sharp. "Though you certainly think you can do something special."

Again, Terese pulls at her magic, pulls for anything, but nothing happens.

"That won't help you," he says. "I don't want you getting away until I figure out what you are."

"I'm just human," she says, and the man takes another step forward and Izzy barks. "I'm just human, and I'm just walking my dog. Please."

Her voice breaks.

His head tilts at that, and he crosses the remaining space of the alleyway until he's just inches away from her, so close she can smell the cologne still on the body's neck.

She cringes, leaning away, but her back meets a barrier of magic so solid it might as well be a wall. She hadn't noticed him cast anything, she should have noticed that, it should have been obvious.

"You certainly have power," he murmurs, as if she is merely a puzzle to be solved. "It's practically bleeding off of you." His hand hovers over her gut, right at the stab wound. "And you're up and walking around when something like this usually kills humans. There's no healer around, no necromancer nearby, nothing that could bring you back from this."

His hands grip the edge of her shirt, peeling it up, and prods the bandage over it.

Terese slams her hand down and does little else but bat him away.

"Definitely should be dead in a ditch," he says, unfazed. "Call me Daniil."

"Go away," Terese says, and her voice hitches up around her fear, spiraling down her throat and squeezing through her lungs. "I don't want—"

Suddenly, he grabs her by her chin, slamming her against the invisible wall, and Izzy's on the other side of the wall, scrabbling against it, barking and braying.

His fingers are like a brand and he turns her head like a butcher examining a prime cow. "Something's hollowed you out," he says, and slow delight blossoms over his face. "Something's hollowed you out to make space for another and then left you like this."

Terese tries to kick out, but all she can do is jerk a leg. Terror pools in her gut, burning like fire against the wound, and no matter how she reaches for the magic, reaches for something to defend herself, it slips like water from her palm.

"Stop that. It's annoying," Daniil says, but his voice is still delighted. Like she's a prize he discovered. "How?"

She doesn't answer, she can't answer. All words stopped and congealed in her mouth, and she's shaking. Her hands shake, her legs shake, her stomach shakes, everything.

He tilts her chin, contemplative. "Was it another demon?"

When she doesn't answer, he shakes her like she's a doll.

"Yes," she whispers, her voice breaking. "You don't want to. She's dead, she died in pain you wouldn't believe."

"I bet you tell all the demons that," he murmurs, like he thinks he's funny. "Good defense mechanism."

Izzy growls, deep, a noise Terese has never heard from her before.

The grip on her chin tightens past the point of pain. "And with your power," he muses, "any demon inside of you would be unstoppable."

Terese kicks out, jerks her leg, something, anything, to get him away.

It doesn't work.

"What do they call you?" he asks, like this is still a friendly conversation, like she is just as willing a participant as he is. "Do living vessels even get names?"

Something opens up inside of her, like the terror and the horror eats away at her spine until nothing else remains. Until all she is, is a body of fear, roughly shaped like a person. Until even the fear doesn't seem real, like it's happening to someone else, like she's a passive participant, observing the panic from far away.

Terese won't. She won't go back to that, she won't. She won't go back to the pain, to the horror, to the helplessness. To the lack of control in her own body. To being ridden around like she's just a conduit for someone else.

"Fuck you," she snaps, and he blinks in surprise, the fingers tightening ever so slightly. "Fuck you, you don't get me."

"Fine," he says, a grin spreading across his face, mirrored in the shadow self beneath, eyes glinting in the last light from the setting sun. "Let's do this that way."

And with a rush, he peels her mind open like it's a fruit to be consumed, and rushes in.

Terese crumples to the concrete, her ankles giving out, then all control of her knees, and there's too much. There's too much in her mind, like there's not enough space. Like he's forcing his way past her walls, past her agony, past her pain. Like her head will explode, like there's not enough room for both of them, like he'll force her out, force her into a smaller and smaller corner of her brain.

Oh, Daniil's voice says, inaudible in her mind, *oh, you have so much to offer here.*

No.

She flinches, and she can still flinch, and there's something wet on her face and she doesn't know if it's blood or tears or what, but she can move. She can control herself, she can—

No.

"Fuck off," she grits out, her teeth slamming together, almost jarring her jaw loose. Her cheek scrapes against the pavement. "Fuck. Off."

It's her mind, it's her body, and she can push him right back out.

There, crumpled on the concrete, she grabs at something, anything, and forms her fist around a ribbon of magic and twists, shredding it to pieces. The magic fragments out, her ears popping, bright and gold, and the dirt and pebbles float into the air around her body.

The wall of magic behind her shatters, then the concrete and rebar wall of the shop, shrapnel spiking around the narrow alleyway.

And she jerks the magic to her, all the explosions and the power, and pain blossoms around her, but she can't stop, she can't, and—

As fast as it started, the demon's out of her, and back in the man's body, shaking his head like he's disoriented.

Terese tries to push herself up off the ground, but her arms give way. Izzy cowers in the back of the alleyway, as far away as she can get, whimpering.

The golden bubble around them warps, thrumming. Illuminating the blond in the man's hair. In Daniil's body.

"You are powerful," he says, conversational, then smiles, wide and heartbreaking. "This'll be fun."

He stands, then looms over her, blocking out any light from the street, until all that remains is her little bubble, reflecting and casting shadows against his face.

"I'll get you, I'll figure this out," he says, with the flippancy of someone dedicating themselves to winning a sports game. "You can't hide, you can't run, I will always be able to find you." He raps a knuckle against her forehead, and pain shocks down her back, arcing into her legs and trailing to her fingertips. "This will only be a matter of time."

With that, he straightens, adjusting the suit jacket on the body he stole.

There's blood on the white of his shirt. Blood from Terese.

He takes a moment, staring down at Terese, like the sight of her collapsed is a good one. Like it's something to relish.

"See you soon, Terese," he says, and she hadn't told him her name. She hadn't, she hadn't even thought of it, but he got it from her mind. "I won't be long."

With one long, lingering glance, like it takes all of his energy and power to not consume her, he disappears.

3

Everything hurts, and Terese can't move. She can't, she's frozen there, surrounded by her golden bubble, pebbles in the air around her, until a sob tears its way out of her throat and the bubble collapses.

Izzy whimpers, cowering in the back of the alley between a brick wall and a dumpster.

"Izzy," Terese coughs out, reaching her arm out towards her dog. Magic moves around her again, like the absence of the demon brought it all back. Like it never happened. "Come here."

The dog cowers, a trembling mess of fluff and fur.

Her magic creeps along the side of her vision, pulsing with the need to get her somewhere safe, somewhere that's not this, but Izzy's too far away.

Terese grits her teeth and pushes herself up, but her arms shake and buckle underneath her, collapsing her back onto the grimy concrete.

Blood splatters around her.

She doesn't know what's wrong with her, what physical injuries he placed on her, but it's bad. It's bad, and black edges around her vision, and her magic won't let her die without taking her to a safety spot, and she can't leave Izzy behind, she can't —

With another whine, Izzy creeps towards her, close to the ground, her ears back.

"Come here," Terese chokes out, and her magic throbs with the want to take her somewhere else, so sharp it almost competes with the pain all around her. She crooks her hand to Izzy, barely a twitch of her fingers, but Izzy pushes her snout into her palm, whining.

"Good girl," Terese mumbles, then closes her eyes to the black, and lets her magic take her where it will.

SHE LANDS face down in blackberry bramble and against a spruce tree, the bark scraping and tangling in her hair, and there's too much black against her vision for her to care to try for somewhere else.

Izzy whimpers and curls up, tight against her, a brilliant heat of fur and body warmth.

"Good dog," Terese mumbles, and every breath creaks her ribs, pounds against her head. "Good girl."

Then, with one small motion to do something, anything, to shift, to smooth the pain for just a few seconds, she dies.

OF COURSE, it doesn't last.

SHE COMES to with full sunlight hitting her eyes, and Izzy is barking.

"Quiet," she mumbles, but like the first words after dying always are, her voice cracks and wheezes.

It had been night when she had blacked out.

She pries her eyes open, and her eyelashes clump together, sticky. It's bright outside and her head pounds, but Izzy keeps barking, her loping bray echoing around the mountains and the road.

A car idles a little distance away, the low rumble like sandpaper to her brain.

Whatever happened, whatever did this, did a number on her mind, and—

The demon. The demon is out there. The demon tried to get her, and she's just laying here.

She jolts upright, which is a mistake, and she can't see Izzy. Her stomach revolts like someone took a cheese grater to her intestines. She lists dangerously to the side, collapsing all over again.

There's a demon out there that wants her, and she could barely throw him out. A demon knew how to find her, a demon had found her, and—

The rumble of a car comes closer, and Izzy's barking jumps in pitch.

"Help," she whispers, and her eyes barely focus, like her body hasn't made enough blood yet to power both her voice and her eyes. "Izzy, help."

A car door opens, then shuts, and Izzy barks. It's her 'I need something' bark, and Terese can barely see, can't stand, can't move.

With as much power as she can muster, she flops over on her side. She's next to a gravel road, hidden in the underbrush of a giant spruce tree. Blackberry thorns drag at her hair, tug at her dark hoodie.

Hands shaking, she pushes herself up...and blood coats her hands. Dried blood, streaked across her skin and saturated into her clothes, congealed into a giant, sticky mess.

"Aww, aren't you a cute dog," someone says, and Terese flinches, full body. Izzy barks, and Terese doesn't know how long she was out, if Izzy had food, if Izzy got hurt—

If the demon hurt Izzy.

Slowly this time, she hooks a hand on the tree, using it to pull herself up, and everything spins, but she doesn't lose consciousness, doesn't pass out.

And freezes.

The black car, the Mustang that the previous demon that had ridden her had tried so hard to destroy, idles not even thirty feet from her. The magician—the strange one, the one she doesn't remember from Before but shot her when they found her tunnel—bends over Izzy, enthusiastically thumping her on the side.

His black curls hang over his face, and the roots of his hair are lighter, like the color is dyed and growing out. Izzy barks again, dancing away, then dashing back, as if leading him towards Terese.

Three things occur to Terese in rapid succession.

One, this is the magician who shot her. Twice. Doesn't seem like a safe place to be.

Two, she's not sure she could even teleport right now, and Izzy's too far away to grasp without the magician spotting her.

But three, he's one of the *magicians*. One of the ones that didn't seem to know what Dr. Frisse had done until it was too late. One of the ones who had stopped the last demon, had killed that demon and left Terese behind.

"Help," she chokes out again, still so quiet she can barely hear. It's like her ears are stoppered up by something.

Izzy tugs on the man's pant leg, pulling him towards Terese.

"Help," she repeats, and almost topples over, bracing herself on the tree with a blood-streaked hand.

The man stiffens, then straightens, and locks eyes with her.

She knows, she knows she must look like a wreck, but everything hurts and everything throbs and her eyelashes stick together and her knees almost buckle with the sheer effort of remaining upright.

Slowly, the magician lets his hand fall away from Izzy, the color draining from his face.

She doesn't know what she did to him, other than the nebulous 'something'. The one with the braid had told her that much. But if someone, anyone, could help stave off Daniil, it's the magicians who beat the first demon inside of her.

Izzy lets out another bark, crashing over to Terese, then back to the man.

He looks just as gobsmacked as she feels, which solidifies something inside Terese.

"I need your help," she says, and her voice cracks again, "please —"

And that's enough talking for her. Her knees buckle, and she falls.

SHE JOLTS BACK TO HERSELF, jerking her knees up, and she's in a car, and —

"Jesus Christ, you're awake," someone says, too close, too

close.

She hauls herself upright, and the magician pulls the car into a parking spot.

They're in some sort of underground parking lot. There are dead runes written all along the beams, runes that she can tell once held power but no more, and she's buckled in.

She flinches, recoiling away, then twists and faces the magician. "Where —"

Smoothly, the magician pulls out a gun from the glove compartment and flicks off the safety, and it's the same gun he shot her with last time.

In the back seat, Izzy whines.

"Please don't shoot me in front of my dog," Terese blurts out, and talking is easier, much easier.

Her body had some time to recover.

"This will hurt you," he warns, "it won't kill a demon, but it'll fucking hurt you."

"Noted," she says, and she hurts enough already.

"What are you doing here?" He hasn't shut off the car, it's just idling in the underground parking garage, the only car there. "How'd you find us?"

There are plenty of options for what she can say, but nothing that seems entirely accurate or appropriate.

"Why are you covered in blood?" he continues when she says nothing, and Terese lifts her hand up, marveling at it. Blood flakes off of her wrist, and her hoodie sticks to her.

"I was attacked," she says, and the panic jumps against her throat again. "There was a demon, he wanted me, I kicked him out, I can't, I can't, he killed someone, I can't —"

Izzy barks, and it echoes in the car, a din to Terese's ears, and she squeezes her eyes shut.

"I didn't mean to come here," she starts over, and the forced breeze of the car air conditioner feels like too much,

like her entire face is so sensitive that even just air movement hurts. "I was just trying to get away, and the magic
took me here."

"The magic," the magician says flatly.

"It tries to take me to safe places." Again, it's wholly
incomplete, wholly inadequate. "You can help, the Necromancer, you and the one with the braid." His expression
doesn't change. "The one with Zoel; she could help, Zoel
could help—"

He lifts a hand, and she falls silent. Her head pounds
still, and her mouth is metallic, like she had even bled
against her tongue.

Without speaking, he kicks open the door to his car,
then opens the one for Izzy, and Izzy jumps out, dashing
around to where Terese sits.

She doesn't know if she'd be able to walk without
passing out.

Even so, she paws at the door handle, then leverages
herself out of the car, knees shaking. Her pants stick to her
skin, still damp, and they're coated in blood.

Just how injured did the demon leave her?

Izzy pushes up against her legs, trembling.

"I know, girl, I know," she mumbles, then looks up.

The magician watches her, sharp, his brown eyes
missing nothing.

"I don't know what the demon did, but it hurt, and I'm
not...back yet." Again with the wholly incomplete descrip-
tions. "After that sort of...thing...it might take me a few days."

His eyes narrow. "Do you remember me?"

"I know you shot me," she says, leaning heavily against
the car. "The one with the braid said I hurt you, but you
weren't...you weren't there when the other demon was in."

"Oh, I was," he says, and there's a bitterness behind his

voice, cutting through whatever smoothness in his tone. "I was there."

"Well," Terese starts, then blinks at him.

He doesn't look like anyone from before. His jaw is square, strong, his skin a bit uneven. His hair curly, his shoulders broad.

There had only been Dr. Frisse at first, then the one with the braid and the pretty man, before the Necromancer showed up.

"I'm sorry?" she tries, because that is probably appropriate.

He stares right back, and she takes his hesitation to rest against the car, trying to figure out if her legs are any good.

They shake, of course, they'll probably shake until she gets a good meal and maybe a few nights of rest.

"What time is it?" she asks instead, trying to calculate the hours since the donut and the coffee milkshake. At least twelve, probably more like fifteen.

"Roughly around two thirty," he answers, and he still has the gun in his hand, but if she hurt him before, she can't really blame him. "Are you going to attack me?"

"I don't think I can right now," she replies, probably a bit too honestly, and his eyebrows flash up. "No. I don't want...no."

"Comforting," he says dryly. Gesturing with the gun, he points towards a bank of elevators. "Walk that way."

She hesitates, gingerly pushing herself away from the car, wobbling. Izzy tucks herself close to her, almost tripping her, but the rest from the car ride had given her legs more stability than she would have thought.

"Where are we?" she asks as soon as she's safely against the wall and not going to fall over.

Again, the same flat stare. "You mean you teleported

here and didn't know?" He pushes a code into the elevators, and the entire contraption groans, a hideous sound of metal on metal.

The skepticism is warranted.

"I know I was outside Dr. Frisse's compound," she says, casting her eyes down and away with the foul taste the name brings to her mouth. But it answers her question— she's still at their headquarters, still in the same square mile of land in the wilderness outside of Vancouver.

Hopefully still a safety spot.

The elevator doors scrape open, and the magician gestures her inside, and she doesn't think she can do stairs right now, so she steps in.

Izzy shies away.

"Come here," she says, but Izzy just backs up again. "I don't know if she's seen an elevator before. Come here, it's okay."

Izzy's ears flicker up at her tone.

The magician steps around Izzy to join her, and Izzy sits down on her haunches, before creeping low into the elevator and pressing against Terese's legs.

The elevator groans upwards, and instead of focusing on the magician in front of her, she just pats Izzy's side. There's dried blood in Izzy's fur, but not to the skin, which means she must've cuddled against Terese almost all night long.

"I must've dropped my backpack," Terese says, and the magician's expression doesn't move away from icy and hardened. "Do you have any dog food?"

That gets him, and his face flickers for a brief second, almost a hint of pity, before he sighs, heavy. "I have some lunch meat?"

"That'll do," she says as the elevator doors open and Izzy

shoots out into the hallway, faster than her aging joints usually let her.

Wordlessly, he leads her past two giant wooden doors, down a surreally carpeted hallway, past more dead runes and the whispers of magic remnants, and her skin crawls.

The runes were written to keep her out. Written so she would never find the place, never go inside, and now...now they're just bits of paint.

No wonder the previous demon hadn't been able to find them. No wonder they were always protected until they left.

Terese has some giant black holes in her memory the night that the Necromancer saved her, but she knows it resulted in Dr. Frisse's death. And she also doesn't feel bad about that.

But now, with how hollowed out the entire building is, how utterly lacking, a smidgen of pity hits her, too.

She raises a hand to a rune, as if she could caress them back to life, before flinching away at a sudden sound.

The magician opens a door, one of many doors that's all but indistinguishable from the rest of the hallway, opening up to what appears to be a completely normal apartment, with a kitchen and a couch and a TV and a hallway that leads to a closed door.

On the table is a stunning array of little bits of machinery and electronics, all spread out in a taped grid, with a variety of tiny screwdrivers to one side. There's a coffee pot plugged in on the counter next to a mound of chip bags and granola bars, and there's a half-empty pallet of energy drinks next to it. There's a pile of neatly folded laundry on one side of the couch, with a basket on the ground. Across the floor is a giant, fluffy rug, the sort of rug that Terese's mind immediately connects with roaring fireplaces and rich people.

She hasn't been inside someone's living space since...since Before. Since before the demon, at the very least.

Izzy ventures in, sniffing cautiously around the small kitchen.

"I need to make some calls," the magician says, which feels like an understatement, though hope fills her stomach and threatens to choke her. "I don't want blood on my couch, take a shower." Brusquely, he hands her a pair of sweatpants and a t-shirt. "Don't teleport away—I want answers."

Which again seems fair. She doesn't know exactly what she can give him, but...but she's fairly certain the previous demon had utterly ruined the magicians' lives, and she'd want answers in their situation, too.

"What's your name?" she blurts out, in the middle of all the painful domesticity, standing soaked in blood in another person's living space. "I don't...I don't think anyone told the demon any of your names, so I don't know."

His face does this funny thing, vacillating between anger, confusion, and something close to amusement. "Axel," he says, gesturing to himself. "The one with the braid, who you killed at one point and would still be dead if it wasn't for our friend, is named Alette."

"I didn't mean to," she says, which is probably not helpful. "I wasn't exactly the person calling the shots for that."

His face pinches, and he points down the hallway. "Don't get blood on my towels."

4

Terese recoils at her reflection the moment she steps into the bathroom.

Blood streaks down her face from her eyes, and thick globs of it trail from her ears. Her hair is half-matted with blood, and both sides of her mouth had leaked it as well.

"What the hell?" she whispers, leaning close to the mirror and poking at the dried blood from her ear.

It hurts, the deep sensitive ache of a wound that hasn't finished whatever weird healing bullshit she does, and there're bits of tissue mixed in with the blood, bits of viscera.

No wonder her appearance had scared him. It'd scare her, too.

Pulling back her white-blond hair, she pokes at the blood matted against her scalp. There's no obvious open wound, no dents in her skull.

It hurts, way more than it should.

Because, of course, a demon would have that ability. Of course.

And of course he'd be after her.

She leans against the counter, where a stunning variety of skincare products live, and breathes through her nose.

She can't go back to that. She can't.

From outside of the bathroom, she can hear the familiar pad of Izzy pacing a room, and the magician—Axel— speaking to someone on a phone, his deep voice muted.

So she pushes herself away from the mirror, peeling the hoodie off of her. The bandage on her side hangs on, but gingerly removing that shows entirely new skin underneath.

At least that bit of her power still works.

After scrubbing a truly horrifying amount of dried blood off herself and trying really hard not to look at herself in the mirror, she stuffs her hoodie, tank top, and pants into the trash can. She'll have to go someplace to get more of her clothing. She doubts that this outfit will be salvageable.

And somehow, someway, she's going to have to convince the group of magicians to help her. This group that she's apparently all hurt and harmed, even the people she doesn't recognize.

She hasn't had this much sustained conversation with anyone. Not even Zoel, who would kindly check in on her during the first few months.

Dressing herself in the sweatpants and oversized t-shirt, she finger-combs through her pale hair, now thankfully devoid of blood. It's getting longer, so it hangs around her face near her jaw, but it still doesn't look like her. Nothing about her appearance matches the vague idea of what she had before, but at least it's been long enough without the demon that she's gotten used to it a little bit.

And it's been long enough without the demon that she knows when she's avoiding something.

"Okay," she whispers to herself, and if she's going to have

to be social, she's going to have to stop with the talking to herself. "Okay."

The click of the door opening is loud, even to her ears, and Axel abruptly stops talking when she comes into view.

"I'll call back," he promises to whoever is on the other side of the phone, before setting it down on the table with a controlled click.

Izzy wags her tail at her, padding over to push her snout into Terese's palm.

"I tried to feed her some turkey. She didn't eat it," he says, gesturing at an open packet of lunch meat on the table, right in the middle of all the bits of electronics.

"She's not used to strangers." Her voice sounds bizarre to her own ears, saying something so mundane.

"I gathered," Axel says, then levels a glance at her. "You look a bit more alive without your brain melting out of your ears."

That seems like an accurate description of what happened, so she doesn't correct him, instead sitting down at the other chair at the table.

Immediately, Izzy rests her head on Terese's lap, giving her the biggest puppy dog eyes ever.

"Okay," Terese says to her, picking up a slice of the lunch meat and handing it to her dog, who gobbles it up. "I think it's been...fifteen to twenty hours since she ate. I think. Who knows how long I was unconscious."

Axel looks like he's about to reply to that, but sits back, crossing his arms. And then immediately uncrossing them to tap against his leg, some sort of nervous tick.

She makes him nervous.

She swallows past that, sitting back as far as she can, giving Izzy another slice of meat.

"Alette and Zoel are up in Alaska, fixing a Ley Line," he says, after too long. "They won't be back for at least a week."

She knows that the previous demon had killed some people up there, but she's not entirely certain where.

"Haines?" she ventures a guess, trying to match the vivid memory of the demon killing a scholar in deep snow with an actual location. The demon hadn't taken to looking at sign posts or reading maps. "Or Hyderburg?"

"Hyderburg," he says, and if he hadn't been tapping his fingers, he could've been mistaken for a military interrogator. "Lyra and Melekai can be here tomorrow."

Her stomach drops, and she stares at the grid of electronics so she doesn't look at him.

Because if anyone would have the motivation to harm her, it would be Melekai. The demon she clashed with while being possessed, and somehow got resurrected into the body of a human. The being who had been so protective of his necromancer that he fell in love.

Conversely, if anyone would want to prevent her from having a repeat performance, it'd be them.

But the idea of seeing the Necromancer again turns her stomach, once with the gut churn of hunger and once with horror.

"I doubt they want to see me," she says, and Izzy whimpers against her leg.

"Oh, they want to," Axel says, sharp. "They want to make sure that you won't hurt them, no matter what."

Her stomach flips again at that. "The Necromancer can control demons, right?"

He nods, impassive.

"Then can she put something on me to stop another demon? Or to control him if he tries? Or stop me from..."

she trails off, unsure about where to go with that sentence, then rubs her face with her hand.

Her entire face hurts.

"I know she had a trick," she continues, finally pulling herself together. "I want her to use it on me." Her voice breaks, her throat twisting around and stopping her words.

The trick had hurt when the demon was in her, and she doesn't know if it'd still hurt without.

"I'm sure Melekai will have opinions," he says, grimly smiling, before the brief expression vanishes. "I need some more information from you." He sits back, leaning his chair over until he can grab a notebook from the kitchen counter, twisting a pen around in his fingers with a flourish. "Or, rather, Melekai and Zoel need information, and I just want to know what the fuck is up."

"I don't know," she blurts out, useless. "I was walking my dog, and the demon found me. I wasn't...I wasn't doing anything, I was just watching the sunset and—"

Izzy whines, cutting off her words, and she takes a big gulping breath, then another, as Axel just watches.

"I don't know if it was chance or if he was looking," she finishes lamely. "I don't know how much he saw in my brain. He got my name without me telling him. He...he stopped me, so I couldn't run, I couldn't teleport, so Izzy couldn't get to me, he could tell I was stabbed, and-and- and he could tell that I had been possessed before, he said I—"

Axel holds up a finger, his brows drawn up, and she falls silent.

She's trembling, she realizes, her fingers twisted tightly in Izzy's long fur, but her arms are shaking like she's shivering, like she's been plunged into cold water, and it brings tears to her eyes, blurring her vision.

"Stabbed?" Axel asks, finally. Like that's the applicable part of the conversation.

"I had been stabbed, uh...sometime yesterday, I think," she says, and her voice warbles. "I was midway through feeling better."

His eyebrow raises, and the expression is so familiar. "Stabbed."

"It's like...it's like when you shot me," she says, and her voice is still hitching. "I get better."

He leans forward, the notebook forgotten on the table, and his eyes are wide.

"So in one day, you got stabbed, then you walked your dog, then got your brains melted by a demon." He rubs his face, eyebrow still curved up. "Okay, no."

"No, what?" she asks, as he pushes himself to standing, crossing over to his fridge and pulling out a water bottle. His motions jerky, he throws open his cabinet before tossing a protein bar on the table.

"Eat that," he commands, and his voice is even shaky. "You're going to eat that, drink this"—he holds up the bottle of water, for emphasis—"and then we will continue."

He sits back down with a huff, leveling a glare at her.

Terese freezes, blinking owlishly at him.

"Eat it," he says again, and slowly, she reaches for the protein bar. "I don't know how the hell your bullshit works, but you can't answer questions if you're passed out. Eat it."

It still feels like a trap, but she peels off the wrapper, taking a bite. It tastes like something between chalk and hot chocolate mix, and her throat is raw from...from probably screaming...but she chokes it down as he glares.

"Where do you live?" he asks, after she's managed to consume most of the deeply unpleasant protein bar.

"My magic has five spots it'll take me it thinks is safe," she says, taking a swig of the water to wash down the chalk.

Finally, Izzy flops over to her side onto the fluffy carpet, as if she had been waiting for Terese to eat as well.

"No, that's not an answer," he says, and he's sticking his jaw out, like this is deeply irritating to him. "Do you have a home?"

Slowly, she shakes her head.

"So for the past"—he checks his watch, overly showy —"seven or so months since we dealt with the demon, you've been homeless, bouncing between magic location to magic location?"

She nods, and it's horrible.

"You put yourself into positions where you get stabbed, you have a dog that completely depends on you, and you don't have anyone to go to except the people you almost killed for help." It's a condemnation, and she doesn't like it.

"Zoel's helped, some," she says, prickly.

He rests his chin in his hands, all fury and self-contained fire, and it's almost overwhelming in its intensity. "What about your family?"

She shuts her mouth with a snap.

"Friends?" He ventures when she doesn't answer. "Colleagues? Coworkers? You didn't exist in a vacuum before."

She might have well had.

"It's not exactly like I have that knowledge easily available," she says, which is almost certainly not what he's asking for. "When I tried to track them down, they..." She shrugs, and the motion hurts her head, sending a spiral of pain rocketing down her back. "Either I remembered the wrong people, or the demon did a better job at changing my appearance than I thought."

He stares at her, and she really wishes he wouldn't, so she scowls right back at him.

"I need to make some more calls," he says, finally, voice horrifically neutral. "Don't teleport away, sleep on the couch if you need to." He grabs his phone off the table, then stalks out of the apartment, closing his door with a loud click.

Izzy raises her head at the noise, then rests it back down again. She's still dusty from her play in the dog park, and there's still dried blood in her fur, but she looks so content on the carpet that Terese can't find it in herself to try and move her so she can get clean.

"That didn't go well," Terese whispers to her, and Izzy thumps her tail against the fluffy rug.

HOURS LATER, long after Terese curls herself up on the couch, the apartment door opens, and she floats back to consciousness.

Her stomach drops in terror at that moment, when the fabric against her cheek is unfamiliar and the air rustles through her hair, but she keeps her eyes shut and her body as still as she can.

Izzy sleeps near her, the soft sound of dog snores audible, as a person moves around the small space.

A clink of keys against a table, the shuffle of someone taking off shoes, all while trying to be silent.

Terese's heart pounds, but Izzy would surely growl if a demon had walked through the door. Izzy would have woken up. Izzy went crazy before, in the alleyway, and she would go crazy if Daniil showed up here.

Instead, the other person curses under their breath, then shuffles past her, down the hallway. Axel, the magician. Not trying to wake her up, but carefully stepping around the couch, padding to the other door at the end, then closing it softly.

Terese exhales when nothing else happens, pushing herself up to sitting on the couch.

The apartment is lit only by the clock on the microwave in glowing blue numbers, telling her it's so far into the middle of the night it's early morning. Izzy lays sprawled out on the giant fluffy rug, bloody fur dark in the dim light, but looking content, her sides rising evenly and easily.

Despite herself, despite the overall coziness of the enclosed walls and the softness of the couch and the small whirr of filtered air, Terese shivers.

She sleeps no more that night.

5

Seven AM finds Terese sitting on the fluffy rug on the ground, back against the softness of the couch, and Izzy's head in her lap, when Axel emerges from his room.

She can't see him from the angle she sits on the floor, but the awareness of him blooms against her mind, before it sounds like he abruptly turns to the bathroom. Like she's too much to handle before anything else.

Terese's head still throbs, but it's a dull throb, more akin to a day in the sun without enough water than the racket it had been before. An exploratory pushing against her skull and ear found it still tender, but a sort of new-tender, like this body piece hasn't learned to protect itself yet.

She hadn't bled anymore during the night, which is a relief.

She'll have to find a better source of food than just lunch meat for Izzy and a way out the building so she doesn't make a mess on the carpet, but Izzy is all too content to sleep against what is probably her new favorite rug.

"Lyra and Melekai will be here in about an hour," Axel

says, exiting the bathroom suddenly, and she flinches. "You don't understand how early this is for them."

"Is that a warning?" she asks.

He crosses the room in three long strides, pulling open the fridge and extracting an energy drink. There are dark circles under his eyes, but his curls are neatly combed, with a care that rests uneasily against Terese's mind.

He had said he had been there. He had acted like he knew her.

She had been puzzling over it for the last hour, after her mind got bored with obsessing about Daniil and the nebulous danger of staying here.

"Might as well be," Axel replies, leaning against his counter, jangling his foot, before he levels a glare at her. "What's your breakfast order?"

She just narrows her eyes at him.

"They're bringing food. What's your breakfast order?" he repeats, like he thinks she just didn't hear him.

"You really think they're going to want to give me food?" Terese points out, and Izzy lifts her head briefly at her tone, before settling back down.

"I think Mel will want to throttle you. I think Lyra's going to be horrified if she doesn't bring food," he answers, and that needles at another memory from the demon.

A memory of standing in the snow, feet so cold they ached, and the Necromancer asking leading questions, like she was going to give in and help the demon. A memory of a gnawing, all-consuming hunger rising with each word, until Terese had tried screaming, had tried screeching to the sky, but nothing left her throat.

The Necromancer had looked at the demon as if she pitied it.

"Did you call him Mel?" Terese asks, instead of sitting with the memory. "I can't imagine he likes that."

"Oh, he hates it," Axel says, conversational, and she doesn't trust it. He's being too kind, too casual, and even considering the early morning, it feels wrong. "Food order?"

Still feels like a trap. "I'm not picky."

He levels a glare at her, and she faced down a demon the day before, so she just stares right back.

"Fine, you're getting an omelet," he says, finally, and she can't help but feel like she won something as he taps that out on his phone. "I'm not dealing with Lyra's sad face because of you."

"Tell her to bring something dead," Terese says, working a bit of dried blood out of Izzy's fur. "I want her to do that trick."

"You're a joy in the morning," he says, again too casually. "Mel's unsure if it would work." His eyes flicker up to hers before continuing on his phone. "You look better today. Less like you're going to pass out."

"The more time since I died, the better I am," she says, and his face goes blank, blinking at nothing. "I'll be fully better in a few days."

"Nifty trick," he finally settles on, an unhappy twist to his mouth, before he levels another stare at her. "They're going to ask for details," he starts. "Mel is going to ask a lot of questions about this new demon, about what you can do, and it will not be friendly."

She doesn't deserve friendly.

"Lyra's usually nice, and her niceness might get him to slow down, but you took her little brother as a hostage before, so she just might not."

Terese nods, because the demon had been so excited when they'd realized that the Necromancer had such an obvious weakness. Had a way to get her to come out, no matter what.

It had always been a stupid plan, but the demon hadn't listened when Terese tried to scream about it. That there'd be no way the Necromancer would come alone, not when she'd so carefully gathered allies and friends.

But smart plans hadn't been the demon's forte.

"I need to take Izzy outside, before," Terese says, and Izzy thumps her tail with her name.

"Don't teleport," he interrupts, and she falls silent. "We've spent the last seven months looking for you, don't teleport away now."

She strongly suspects he wouldn't be able to stop her, but also...refusing orders like that would probably do very little to convince them to help her, so she nods again, climbing to her feet.

He leads her, energy drink in hand, through the hallways, until they reach a small solarium with a few obviously patched windows and a very unusual pattern of magic.

She lets Izzy sniff around the dirt pathways, meandering herself where the magic obviously used to lay. The sun is barely up, but it's already warm in the greenhouse, under the sparkling glass panes.

"Did someone...really disrupt the magic here?" she asks, nudging the dirt with the toe of her boot. "Someone not me? I've never been here? I think?"

"That's what they tell me," Axel says, which pushes at her mind again, and she pulls her attention onto him, the mental equivalent of prodding at a loose tooth.

Under the bright light of the morning sun, she's no closer to actually recognizing him than before, but without the pounding panic behind her eyes, there's a bit more logic leaking its way into her brain.

There had been Dr. Frisse, Alette, and the pretty man before, and Axel had made no mention of another guy. Nor had Axel done any magic, anything, despite living in a magical bunker and presented with someone who may as well be his worst enemy.

And he said he had been there.

It doesn't fit neatly, so she keeps that bit to herself.

"Glad to see something going wrong that I didn't have a hand in," Terese says, instead, after too long of a pause.

The dread around Melekai and the Necromancer's imminent judgement sits poorly in her stomach, but the need for something resembling help thrums in her veins.

Axel doesn't speak much as he leads her back through the compound, like the brief trip had exhausted the strange friendliness of before. Like he's back, remembering all the hurt she caused, all the hurt from under the demon.

The need to run itches underneath her skin, at odds with her logic. The irrational, horrible idea that facing Daniil just might be better than dealing with facing all her past actions.

With each step, she tries to breathe in confidence in herself, to breathe out the idea that she's just as complicit in that demon's actions.

It's hard. It's hard, with the ever-present creep of certainty that if she had just tried harder, she could have stopped something, anything, from happening.

Instead of heading back to the apartment, he stops at the giant wooden doors. "Do you want to leave the dog at my place?"

Her immediate gut reaction is a nausea wave of no, but she swallows past that. "Is...is there going to be anything that would be harmful to her?" she asks, and her voice is smaller than she wants it to be.

"Oh, no, nothing like that," he says easily, "I just don't want to see what Mel would do if a dog charged at Lyra in defense of you."

Terese glances down at Izzy, who sits heavily on the carpet in front of the doors, panting from just the short walk from the solarium. "I've never seen her charge," she says, and everything feels too dire. Like this should be a straightforward decision, something a normal person would have no issue deciding.

"Well, that's simple," Axel says with a loose shrug, pushing the door open.

Inside is a grand conference room, with mahogany tables and far too many fancy chairs.

The air reeks of a sinister sort of magic, something beyond the realm of spell weavers or necromancers, of demon or human, and she raises an eyebrow as she steps inside. It feels like the opposite of natural magic, the opposite of the magic up in the greenhouse, the opposite of the magic in all of her safety spots.

It does nothing to her, besides leave a foul taste on her tongue. Izzy doesn't react, instead sniffing along the table.

Axel nods at her, like she passed some sort of test. "Have a seat," he says. "This might take a bit."

She picks the chair furthest away from the door, and Izzy climbs into the wheeled chair immediately next to her with a humph.

Axel just raises an eyebrow, taking his own chair and propping his feet up on the table, and silence descends on the overlarge room.

It's suffocating. It's suffocating, pushing all the air from her lungs like she's a tube of toothpaste, but she just breathes

The door flies open, and in strides Melekai, all long lines of fury and barely bridled anger, and Terese flinches.

His gaze slams into her, sizing her up and immediately finding her wanting.

He looks human, with none of the distortion of a double self of a demon, and he's even added glasses to his face, like the body he had picked had poor eyesight.

Terese wonders what Daniil would find wanting with her body.

Izzy doesn't even lift her head at his entrance.

"If you hurt her, I'll kill you," he says, and Terese knows exactly what he means.

"That apparently won't work," Axel says, still leaning his feet up on the table. "You kill her, she just pops back up."

Melekai doesn't even look at him. "Doesn't matter, you hurt her, I'll kill you."

"Understood," Terese says, and it's fair. If she could find someone, be able to protect them, keep them safe, and have them love her back, she'd do the same.

"You lay one finger on her, one bit of unneeded contact, and I'll hurt you far more than you've ever been hurt."

This she doubts, after the previous demon and whatever Daniil promises, but she nods. She'd threaten herself, given the opposite position. "Just don't touch my dog."

At this, Melekai falters, his eyes flickering over to Izzy, like he hadn't even noticed the giant fluffy dog curled up in a chair right next to her.

And she sees the mental calculation, one she felt so many times from the previous demon that possessed her. The risk-reward weight on what they want versus the consequences if they pursued that specific line of action.

"Deal," he says, and that must be the influence of the

Necromancer on him. Any other demon would have refused that.

Or who knows, maybe being human softened him.

"Can she do her trick on me?" Terese asks. "Stop any demon from possessing me?"

"Doesn't work like that," Melekai says, deeply and obviously skeptical. "Unless you're actively demonic"—he glares, a furious smolder—"then it would be useless."

"Did you bring the breakfast?" Axel asks, still lazily, and she doesn't understand him, she doesn't. "Or is this just the intimidation time before the food time?"

Terese and Melekai briefly meet eyes in an age-old 'can you believe this' moment. She wouldn't let herself eat with a treasured person, either. Not without vetting. Not without some threats.

Not without finding out all possible dangers.

And here goes the full disclosure. "I don't know what the previous demon left behind," Terese says, and Melekai twitches, like he wants to strike out but stops himself. "I know I can do things that normal humans cannot."

"Which is the pop back from the dead thing I told you about," Axel says, and despite the casualness of his tone, his eyes are sharp. "Mel."

"What else?" Melekai asks, crossing his arms.

"Teleportation, though not well controlled, shredding magical lines, seeing demons without the dead bodies." She ticks off a finger with all of them, the lump in her stomach growing. "The same wave or bubble magic the previous demon did, but I try not to because it pisses off Zoel and he has to fix it."

She had done it back in the alley, and she'll have to figure out a way to tell Zoel without going back to show him.

Or what would happen if a police officer stumbles upon

it and the probably extreme amount of blood left in the middle.

Melekai and Axel glance at each other, like they're trying to communicate something silently, something that she's completely unable to pick up and understand.

Which makes sense, though the dread grows in her stomach, twisting and warping around in some unholy amalgamation of pain and nausea, and her magic thrums, once, in a threat to teleport her somewhere else, before she tamps it down.

Asking for help is not the time to run away.

She doesn't know which of these powers Daniil had noticed, didn't know what he thought he could access, but the last demon had been ecstatic, had been thrilled, at the toolset laid in their hands.

"Where do you feel hunger?" Melekai asks, finally turning back towards her.

"I...don't?" Terese says, voice lilting upwards. "I mean, I notice if I get dizzy, or..." Unable to control her impulses, she glances at Axel, as if he would know how to put in words what she's thinking, but he's rubbing his face, like she didn't give the right answer. "Back of my throat, I guess. Like I'll choke if I don't have something."

"I don't like it," Melekai interrupts, speaking to Axel. "We have no guarantee it's not the demon Terese in a human body."

"She wouldn't ask for help," Terese retorts, before stopping herself.

"I don't think a demon would adopt a dog," Axel mutters, head in his hands.

"I adopted a cat," Melekai says, like that solves the problem.

"No, Lyra adopted a cat, and you imprint on anything

that likes her," Axel replies, before waving his hand at him. "No offense."

"That demon wouldn't sit here and ask for help," Terese says, and outside of her control, something close to desperation leaks in. "That demon would try to manipulate you or try to blow up the other one."

"You don't think showing up, covered in blood and begging for help, is manipulative?" Melekai asks sharply. "You don't think isolating out a young human man and using a dog to gain his trust isn't exactly what a demon would do?"

"I didn't isolate him, I teleported here by accident," she says, and the dread is growing deeper and deeper. "I want help, I don't want to hurt anyone."

"Mel, it's okay," from the grand doors, speaks the Necromancer.

Before she can stop herself, Terese glances up. The Necromancer is holding a bag of takeout, her face wrinkled up in something resembling frustration.

And she's...so bright.

Power radiates off of her, glaringly brilliant, cutting through the fog in Terese's brain and slamming into her.

Immediately, hunger wracks Terese, choking her out, clawing up her throat in an overwhelming wave of need, then terror, then dread.

It's too much like the demon. It's too much, the all-consuming longing that drove the last one to insanity.

6

Before Terese can do anything else, before she can process anything, she's screeching her chair back, recoiling away from the table, bringing her arms up to block her face, away from seeing the Necromancer.

Silence falls on the room.

"Well, that's interesting," Axel says, sitting up straight and finally taking his feet off the table.

"I'm not going to hurt you," the Necromancer says, and even her voice holds the promise of pain, of too much power, of all the memories that Terese would rather forget.

Terese cringes back, and Izzy lifts her head from the chair.

"What are you seeing?" Melekai snaps, and it's not helping. "Tell us, now."

"Mel, she's scared." Again, the voice cutting through everything. "She's scared and...you're hurt?"

Without even being able to see her, Terese knows the Necromancer just took a step closer, and Terese holds a hand out, as if she can keep her further away.

"Don't!" she manages, and the Necromancer stops, thankfully. "Don't come near me."

There's a moment where they collectively all hold their breaths, and Terese forces herself to stay still, to not move, to not do anything.

"I don't...I don't want to hurt you," Terese chokes out past the clawing in her stomach. "I didn't know...I didn't know I'd..."

"I'm glad you don't want to harm me," the Necromancer says, and there's amusement in her voice, something gentle. "You're...very hurt."

Terese ventures a glance up. Everyone is watching her with some variation of concern or anger on their faces, and it's horrible.

Melekai crosses his arms, like she's fulfilling all of his predictions.

"I'm not, I'm better," Terese says, and the horrible hunger twists into nausea, so she looks anywhere else besides the Necromancer, her eyes settling on Axel.

He raises an eyebrow at her.

"Most of the blood vessels in your brain are burst or bruised," the Necromancer says, almost marveling. "You should be dead, or unconscious, or in a coma."

"She was bleeding out of her ears, mouth, and eyes yesterday." Axel ticks the symptoms off, but he keeps the eye contact with Terese, throwing her a lifeline so she doesn't have to look at the Necromancer. "She was pretty messed up."

With a rustle of plastic bags, the Necromancer sets the takeout on the table, and Terese can't imagine eating physical food right now.

"You're also close to starvation," the Necromancer says, matter of fact. "How long has it been since you ate?"

She blinks at Axel, like she could communicate that way.

"I gave her a power bar last night," he says, like he got the message. "She said she was unconscious for around fifteen hours before that."

"Why would you feed it?" Melekai says, and Terese flinches.

Axel breaks the eye contact to roll his eyes at the former demon. "Because she was having a panic attack in my kitchen."

Melekai rolls his eyes right back.

"Well, we brought breakfast," the Necromancer says, and thankfully she doesn't come closer, pushing the bag towards Axel on the table. "Another demon, you say?"

And once again, all eyes are on her. Izzy laboriously climbs out of the chair, to sit next to Terese, plopping her head on Terese's lap.

Even her dog could tell how fucked she is right now.

"He...found me and tried to possess me, like the last one," Terese says, letting her hand fall onto Izzy's fur. "Said it would give him power."

"How'd you stop him?" Melekai asks, and his voice is careful, like he's trying very hard to not be rude, so she lets her eyes flicker to him.

"I shredded the magic and created one of those waves on myself," she says, once again frustrated by the lack of terminology she has. "Like the one the previous demon did to...to Alette."

Axel nods. She got the name right.

"He said...he said he was going to figure me out, so he could have me," she says, forcing it out. "I don't want that. I don't think you guys would want that, either."

The words hang in the air, before Axel sighs, pulling the food bag towards himself and pushing one of the takeout containers towards Terese.

"The last one tried to end the world," Terese continues, words tumbling from her mouth, like she can't help herself. Like even her vocabulary is outside of her control. "And this one killed someone in front of me just to talk to me."

"So you death bubbled yourself?" the Necromancer says, and Terese's eyes slide over to her, out of her control. She's sitting next to Melekai, her chin in her hand, intent. "That's intense."

"I didn't want to go back," Terese says, taking another deep, dragging breath, and the hunger, the clawing need, recedes. "I don't."

AFTER AN EXCEEDINGLY AWKWARD BREAKFAST, where Terese can't taste a single thing in the omelet and tries not to watch as Axel, Melekai, and the Necromancer whisper about her.

She lets her mind wander away, away from them literally deciding her fate, away from everything that could go wrong.

Her mind does this sometimes. It's different from the losing track of time, but her mind sometimes tries to shield itself from all the bad, from all the things she should worry about.

In the early days, when she had still been reeling from the possession and the injuries and everything else, her mind did it a lot more. Compulsively thought of other things, only surface level aware of the things going on around her.

Her mind settles on normal things. Things she needs to do, things she needs to gather.

She'll need a new backpack, purchase more food for

Izzy. Some more clothes, another jacket and hoodie. The cabin safety spot is running low on non-perishable foods; she should buy some more and cycle through her spots until she ends up there.

Maybe stay there, hoping that Daniil can't get to her there.

Her mind shies away from thinking about the demon before skittering back, like someone poking at a sore tooth.

She doesn't know if her spots will remain safe. For all she knows, he could try to get her in this compound, and nothing could stop him.

They should rebuild their runes. Put up whatever protection that's needed. Teach her how to do it so she can fortify something.

There's a lull in the whisper fight, and Terese looks up to find the Necromancer watching her, like she's waiting for Terese to say something, to do something.

Terese lets her eyes flicker away.

"I'm going to step outside," the Necromancer says, calculating, and her voice is far too kind, far too understanding for what hell Terese put her through. She pushes herself up, wincing a bit, like sitting there hadn't been friendly.

Immediately, Melekai's hand is on her elbow, supporting her, and the Necromancer leans just enough that it's noticeable.

A moment passes between them, something tantalizingly quick, before Terese averts her eyes again.

No wonder Melekai threatened her.

But the Necromancer steps away, and Melekai lets her, as easy as breathing. As familiar, too.

The moment the grand wooden doors close behind her, the weight abruptly lifts off of Terese, and she doubles over in the chair, forcing out a breath.

"How did you let her live?" she blurts out, and it's the wrong thing to say, the wrong thing to do when she's asking for help. "How did you stop yourself?"

"Self-control," Melekai says, and worse, his voice is understanding. "I'm a fair bit older than you."

Tears prickle at the edges of Terese's eyes, dread filling her veins. "I don't want to hurt her."

"So, some demonic sensibilities," Axel says, and she squeezes her eyes shut. "But not personality or drive."

"I don't..." She lets herself trail off, and, head still on her lap, Izzy gives a little whine.

"You don't get to be alone with her," Melekai says, and the implications are staggering, but she nods. "No matter what, you don't. You don't want to hurt her, so keep one of us between you and her at all times."

It's way too kind.

"Did the demon, the one who found you, give you a name?" Melekai settles back in his chair, and she doesn't know how anyone could look at him and think he's a normal human.

"Daniil."

"That's useless," Melekai retorts. "Might as well have said his name is John Doe."

"So you can't help?" Terese asks.

"We don't know if we can help," Axel clarifies, and it's better. Just a little bit, and a tiny ribbon of hope worms its way among all the despair. "But none of us really want to face you with another demon possession anytime soon."

Melekai nods along, his arms crossed over his chest.

"Zoel might have some idea "—Axel starts, and Melekai scoffs—"and Alette is amazing with research."

"And I actually know demon abilities," Melekai interrupts. "And will tell them if they're wrong."

The Necromancer pokes her head back into the room, and the wave of terror and hunger mixed crashes into Terese all over again, but she blinks through it, weaving her hand through Izzy's fur instead.

Melekai nods, like she passed a test.

"What do I need to do?" Terese asks, and her own voice sounds weak to her ears. "I'll do anything."

"I think you need to heal," the Necromancer says, and her words stick in Terese's mind. "If you face him again"—fear wells up in Terese—"then you need to not have an actively bleeding brain, and maybe gain a few pounds."

It's as terribly unfamiliar of an ask as anything else, but Terese nods, looking down at Izzy.

"I still think we should keep you as weak as possible," Melekai says, which is more of what she would expect. "Keep you locked up in a box that nothing could get into."

"Can you do that?" Terese asks, honestly curious. "That might be a solution."

Wrong thing to say, and both the Necromancer and Axel blanch.

"That's not...that's not a solution," Axel says, rubbing his face. "That's torture until we solve a problem."

Again, Terese and Melekai lock eyes in agreement on how unreasonable they're being.

"I just want to avoid possession," she says again. "If you find a way to kill me where I can't be brought back, that also works."

Once more, Axel and the Necromancer look horrified.

"I'm not down with murder," the Necromancer says, and she's said that before, Terese is sure of it.

"It's not murder if it volunteers," Melekai says, almost gently, to the Necromancer.

"Let's not with the murder," Axel says, as if he's forgetting that he shot her before he knew she could come back from that dead. "At least until there's no other option to, you know, stop the end of the world."

Murder suggests a person, and Terese still isn't quite sure she counts as one of those, so she shrugs instead.

The Necromancer's mouth tugs into a frown, and she squints at Terese, and the attention is almost too much. Like she can see through all of Terese's thoughts, see through all the bullshit and the fear.

"Don't go off alone," she says, finally, and whatever mental gymnastics she did to get there, it's lost on Terese. "Wherever you go off to, keep one of us with you. Axel"— she turns to him, and there's almost something like leadership in her tone—"get her set up so we can keep in contact. I assume you don't have a phone right now?"

Terese has a vague memory of being utterly obsessed with a phone Before but handling them after just left her devoid of emotion. "Haven't needed one."

"And Axel said you were homeless?"

At this, Melekai looks away from her, like this is the one insignificant detail that he can't ignore. Like everything else, he'd be able to shrug away, but the lack of a place to call home is the end of his patience.

Terese doesn't really want to rehash all of that again, not with the anger Axel showed last time, so she shrugs.

"Okay, yeah, you're staying here," the Necromancer says, and Axel makes a wordless noise of denial. "Don't or I'll tell Alette."

That shuts him up, and there's a dizzying amount of backstory, a vast amount of interplay and relationships that feel just out of Terese's grasp. Like if she reaches, she'd be able to understand, but now, with a pounding head and the pit in her stomach, she can't.

Izzy whines in the back of her throat, redirecting Terese's attention back down.

"I need to get food for her," Terese says, trying to put as much force of personality into her voice and probably missing the mark. "And some clothing, if I'm going to stay here."

AFTER ANOTHER BRIEF ARGUMENT, where Terese tunes them out and tries not to think about all the implications of all of this, Melekai and the Necromancer disappear down into the basement of the compound, down where apparently Dr. Frisse kept a library for research.

Leaving Axel and her in the large, foul-smelling conference room.

There's an unhappy tilt to his mouth, but not one directed at her, instead scowling out at the grand room, with the heavy wooden tables and the clean carpet.

And Terese's done her share of staring sadly at walls, so she just pets Izzy's head in her lap, and the dog is content to let her, closing her eyes.

"Do you have money?" Axel asks finally, the words pulled from him.

"Some," Terese says, pulling her mind back to focus. "The...the previous demon put a bunch in a bank account." And she's come to after losing time with a few piles of hundreds in her lap more than once, but she's not going to say that aloud to someone who's rightfully unhappy about helping her.

She once used a stack to stay at a hotel for a week and a half, but the entire thing just felt creepy, like she was under surveillance while there. She noped out of it and hadn't gone back.

"Okay," he says, springing to his feet with way more energy than she would think possible after sitting down for so long. "Let's get you set up."

Getting Terese set up involves leaving the compound, and the moment the Mustang crosses the property line her skin crawls with the sudden realization she's leaving safety.

In the back of the car, Izzy whines, curled up tight.

"What if the demon comes for me while we're out?" Terese blurts out as they drive down a long, bumpy gravel road. "Can you fight him?"

"Nope," he says, popping his 'p' sound. "Most I can do is cause him a bit of pain with the spelled gun. But to be fair, the only one of us who conceivably could is Lyra. Maybe Zoel."

And wights can't fight demons. The entire idea is fairly preposterous, but she keeps that to herself.

"The magicians tried to explode the previous demon," Terese continues, breezing on past that inaccurate statement. "That pissed it off, at least."

Out of the corner of her eye, she watches him. Sees how he responds to the statement.

His mouth just twists before he smooths out his appearance. "That didn't work."

She files that away, more proof in the small, growing collection.

The road turns to pavement, then to a highway, and it's been so long since she's actively been in a car that she catches herself staring out the window.

"Maybe you," he continues, and it's a fresh douse of icy water down her spine.

"I don't know, the Necromancer thought fighting him gave me brain bleed," Terese says, watching as lush green trees filter by.

She knew the magicians had been remote, but not this remote.

Without even looking at him, she can tell that he glances at her. "Lyra," he says, deliberately, "can tell how someone's body is fairing. Part of her abilities, she does a quick scan and can tell all the strange places you're injured, and she's just getting better at it."

"Is that what that was, a scan?" Terese asks, as the sunlight filters through the branches of the trees, speckling the car window with brief glimpses of brightness. "Is that why it was so much?"

Again, the side-eyed glance. "Possibly."

She lets herself fall silent again, watching as they pass the first car she's seen this trip, and Izzy gives a muffled, sedated woof at the other car.

His phone rings and he curses under his breath. "Say nothing, don't make a sound, we know nothing about you," he instructs Terese, who raises an eyebrow right back before he pinches the phone between his ear and shoulder. "Yes, Gurlien?"

Terese lets herself watch as annoyance, frustration, pity, and dislike flicker across his face, as his jaw tightens, and his eyes pinch together.

"Still no word from the College on that," Axel continues, after a lengthy diatribe from the tinny voice on the other side of the phone, and Terese wants to flinch away, but takes the moment to analyze it.

The demon had been skeptical of the College, then furious, and the anger had bled into Terese, so even the mention makes her reflexively angry, but she never actually knew what they did.

So no reason she should react now, not without further knowledge.

"Nope, still no sign of her," Axel says, his eyes flickering to Terese. "Not a sign since the cave."

Oh, it's someone looking for her. It's someone looking for her, and it's someone untrustworthy enough that Axel feels the need to lie to them.

Interesting.

She tilts her head at him, and he shakes his head.

"I don't care who you thought you saw, I don't think it was her, you've thought that tons of times now and you're always wrong and—" He takes the phone away from his ear to glance at it. "Look at that. He hung up on me. Pity."

"Do I need to be worried?" Terese asks, more curious than anything.

"Probably not," Axel responds, finally returning both hands to the steering wheel. "They've been looking for you just as hard as we have with hundreds of times the manpower and resources and they never found you."

"Why would they look for me?" A horrid thought occurs to her. "Did the demon piss them off? I know she was angry at them, but never actually specified why."

"Oh, I don't know, definitely part of the whole killing off most of the magicians on the west coast and then destabilizing the magic in the area, definitely that," he says, aiming for sarcastic and hitting it square on. "They didn't approve of Dr. Frisse."

"Good," Terese says, and he straightens, like her words shove a steel rod down his spine, and his mouth shuts with a click.

It's a dark silence, until he pulls into a large outdoor shopping center, with a stunning variety of the big box stores that Terese usually avoids.

"Clothes, pet food, or phone first?" he asks, pulling her out of her quiet contemplation of the horror of interacting with so many people.

She leans her head over to him on the seat rest, and he's drumming his fingers nervously on the steering wheel.

"Clothes," she says, pointing at the smallest of the stores, one that looks primarily geared towards cheap clothing for women. "Establish a respectable visual presentation, then move onto critical tasks that require people to take you seriously."

"Right, obviously," he says sarcastically. "How could I have thought differently?"

"The demon would go to the cheapest shop, buy an outfit that looked good enough to go to the next most expensive shop, then work its way up," Terese continues. "If you go into a nice store with bloody clothing, they report you. You go into a store like that"—she points again—"Then you don't get bothered."

"How many times have you had to do that?" Instead of horror, though, there's honest curiosity.

"Three times with the demon, about five since getting unpossessed," Terese says, then slowly opens the door and lets Izzy out of her seat. The dog dances out next to her, preening in the sun, until Terese clips the leash on her.

Izzy promptly sits on Terese's feet in protestation of the leash.

Axel watches her, leaning against his car. "You said you had access to money. Why not just rent a place?"

Her magic would definitely not feel very safe doing that, but she doesn't exactly want to go over all of that again, so she ignores him in favor of coaxing Izzy back up, then heads towards the smallest, cheapest store.

It's clearly some sort of fast fashion, the sort of shirts that are paper thin and will disintegrate after just a few washes, so she grabs a tank top and pair of pants without even trying them on, pays, and is back out in under five minutes.

After a quick change in the bathroom, she rejoins him outside in clothing that actually fits her, instead of just a band shirt and sweatpants.

Dread still drips down her back every moment she's somewhere unsafe. Like her very body can tell there's a giant ticking clock over her head, one that she can feel in her very core.

Of course, there's nothing malicious outside.

Axel raises an eyebrow at her, but she just unties Izzy's leash

"Thanks for the clothes," she says, shoving the bag with his sweatpants and band shirt into his hands.

He shrugs in return, then follows her as she heads to the pet store. Izzy's tail perks up the moment she realizes where they're going. By now, she knows what this means, and knows that she can absolutely manipulate Terese into buying some treats for her.

"You've never had to reinvent yourself, have you?" Terese asks, keeping her eyes on Izzy.

"Nothing as severe as a possession," he says sardonically. Which, fair.

"It's a handy skill," Terese says. "I never know when I might need to run."

She doesn't know why she is telling him this, but the words just sort of seem to fall from her mouth.

He just gives her another unreadable look and swings the door open to the pet store for her.

"Where does somebody like you even get a dog?" Axel asks, as she breezes right towards Izzy's food.

Teresa doesn't feel like explaining that to him, so she ignores it instead, letting Izzy sniff enthusiastically at the row of bags.

"I can't figure it out," he continues, still watching her, and the back of her neck itches. "A lot of this adds up, but not the dog."

Terese doesn't think a lot of her life adds up, but she will not dispute any credit she can get.

She grabs Izzy's favorite bag of food, and without even pausing, Axel grabs the bag out of her hand, holding it easily on his shoulder.

"Hey," Terese says without any heat.

"Brain bleed, remember?" Axels says. "You can bet that Lyra is going to be checking on you, and if I let something else happen to you, she's gonna be mad at me."

His frown only deepens when they leave the store, but it's not directional. More of a pondering frown, like the world has given him something that deeply puzzles him.

But before she steps into the phone store, he gives her a sidelong look, and somehow, without even needing to be told, she knows to pause, her hand inches away from the handle.

"Yes?" She pokes, as Izzy thumps her tail against her leg.

"This might require more...concrete of a persona than other places," he warns, "I'm not sure how established you are in terms of ID that matches your bank account, but they will stop you if they don't match."

Her hand hovers to her pocket with her wallet. "They match," she says, as neutrally as she can. "They're not my name but they match."

He sighs, then rubs his face. "Is the ID believably you?"

"The demon used it," she says. "Put money into it, obsessed over it, and used it on ridiculous things. I figured I deserve to use it, too. I used it to get a hotel, once."

"Good enough," he says, though there's a wrinkle in his forehead. Like this entire thing is genuinely annoying.

The inside of the phone store is busy, busier than the others, and the press of the crowd pushes Terese back as she tries to avoid running into people.

A clerk with a wide friendly face waves them over, and it's a whirl of setting up information that Terese mostly blanks out from and Axel pokes at the different phone accessories in the store, before wandering back over to her when it's time to pay.

His face changes, however, the moment she digs the card out of her pocket.

It's not her card, she knows that, but the demon had used it enough and ensured enough money was in the account at all times, and Terese didn't have to think terribly hard before she concluded she should be allowed to use it.

But the store clerk takes it without even blinking, so it must not be that much outside of a social norm, just enough of one that it shocks Axel.

Soon enough, she has a phone tucked into the pocket of her new jeans and a stunning number of boxes that hold things they say are important, like 'chargers' and 'headphones', and Axel looks like he's about to vibrate out of his own body by the time they leave the store.

"Want to tell me why you have one of Dr. Frisse's old cards?" he asks as soon as he strides out of the shop with her.

She juggles the bag of things enough so she can untie Izzy's leash, mulling over it.

Izzy sniffs the bags, and Terese holds still enough to let her. "I didn't know her by any other name besides Dr. Frisse."

His eyes narrow, and, suddenly she wonders if this is going to be the thing that stops all help.

"Joyanne Jyotshi was her married name," he says, finally, after too long with Izzy sniffing her bags. "Knew her well, did you?"

It's an odd conversation, one that speaks volumes of things Dr. Frisse must not have told him, and her magic pulses, once, threatening to teleport her away.

And if he didn't know, not exactly, about Frisse's involvement, Terese isn't sure how to say things.

"Not entirely sure," she settles on, wrapping Izzy's leash around her hand, as if that could keep Terese in one spot. "Based on the whole vengeance thing, I think the demon knew her better."

He doesn't buy it, she can just tell, but instead of anything witty or any immediate judgement, he just broods the entire way to the black Mustang, broods as they pull out of the parking lot, until they are well on their way down the freeway.

"Don't tell Alette you have her aunt's card," he says finally, fingers drumming on the steering wheel. "Not until I figure this out."

That suggests even more family relations, so Terese just closes her eyes against it. "Will she refuse to help me?"

"It has much more to do with me trying to prevent her from getting upset," he says, his eyes flickering to her for the briefest of seconds before back to the road. "She doesn't need any extra grief."

The highway passes in a blur around them, and the day has been so much already.

Her throat closes up as they leave the highway, lumbering down the road she now knows leads towards the headquarters, and the impending doom just gets worse.

In the backseat, Izzy gives a small, high-pitched whine, barely audible.

Terese turns in her seat until she can scratch Izzy on the top of her head. "Hey, hey, it's okay."

Izzy just hides her head under her paws, like everything —the drive, the leash, all the new people—just became suddenly too much.

"If I disappear, I'll come back," Terese blurts out, keeping her fingers in Izzy's fur. "The magic just takes me somewhere."

"You say that as if it's separate from you," he says, and her spine chills. It's not at his words, it's not, but there's something there, something that's wrong.

She shivers, even though the sun is warm on her skin. "It gets scared." It's wholly incomplete, wholly wrong. "I don't know why, I don't —"

He flicks the turn signal on, then coasts to the side of the road. There's no one around, no other cars, just the two of them and the woods.

"Give me the phone," he says, holding his hand out, and she stares at him. "The one we just bought. Give it to me."

Slowly, like if she moves too fast the air will choke her, she pulls it out of her pocket.

"We spent too long looking for you," he says mildly, typing away at her phone, fingers moving so fast. "I'm going to turn on location sharing, so even if you disappear, we know where you are."

"You can do that?" she asks, craning her neck to look, the curiosity cutting through the illogical terror.

"Easily," he says, though his lips thin. "So if your 'magic' gets spooked, we will know." He taps away at the phone, a ghost of a frown between his eyebrows. "I'm also putting my phone number in there, and Lyra's and Melekai's, so if it's an emergency you can call."

She sits, watching him as he fiddles with the phone in the air-conditioned car.

Before, she probably had this. Had someone to call in case of something going horribly wrong, but the idea is as foreign as the lump in her stomach.

"I end up dying like twice a month," she warns, as he hands her the phone again. "It's annoying, but not really an emergency."

"Jesus Christ," he says, flippant. He shifts the car back into drive, pulling back out to the road. "You must be real fun at parties."

And the only actual party she knows for a fact she's experienced is the one she crashed to kidnap the Necromancer's brother, so she just says nothing in response to that.

Izzy whines again softly, and the hair rises on Terese's arms.

"I have a theory, though, one that I just can't wait to sic Alette on," Axel says, back to the casual conversation that is as surreal as it is out of place in her life.

"And?" Terese asks, suppressing yet another shiver. She had been fine when the car was stopped, but now it's like they're on a road towards certain doom.

"Yeah, I'm not gonna tell you until I figure it out, though," he continues, light.

Terese opens her mouth to respond, but then three things happen.

One, in the back seat, Izzy growls, a deep noise from deep inside.

Two, the words leave her mind like they've been blown away like puffs of dandelions in a breeze.

Three, somewhere deep in the back of her brain, in the part that's been peeled open again and again, Daniil's voice whispers.

I see you're trying to hide.

A gasp presses its way out of her, so small it's almost a squeak, and she can just blink once, twice, before she skyrockets into the black.

8

The first thing Terese is aware of is Izzy's head on her lap. There's a familiar huff of breath, like Izzy thinks she's being unreasonable with something, but still wants to be close.

She's on a couch, the cushions plush underneath her thighs, she's sitting up so straight her back aches, like she's been in that position for hours. There's a strange taste in the back of her throat, acrid like panic.

Like she forgot time again. Like time has passed, and she is none the wiser.

She blinks her eyes—they were open, but until she did so no light registered in her brain—and she's back in Axel's apartment, her feet on the fluffy white carpet and her fingers twisted in Izzy's fur.

At the table sits the Necromancer and Melekai, heads bent towards each other, murmuring, and the kick of hunger is lesser than before. It's still there, gnawing at her stomach and her throat, but far away. Axel rests in a chair tipped backwards, his feet on the desk with the grid of electronics, a coin flipping in his hands in an idle motion.

It's an intimate moment, of her former enemies in a state of relaxation, one she's sure she's not supposed to see.

Izzy huffs against her, so she gentles her fingers.

Last thing she knew had been Daniil —

She forces herself to exhale, forces her body to be slow with it. Her lungs comply, fully in her control.

Her head throbs, still, but no fresh injury. Nothing to show a struggle, nothing to belie any injury or horrible fight.

As if the words in her mind had been simply that.

She glances around again and finds Axel's brown eyes watching her.

He raises an eyebrow silently. He's uninjured, too. No sign of fighting off a demonic presence.

"You back?" he asks, voice dangerously mild.

She nods, still not quite trusting her voice to speak. She can tell she didn't die, at least not painfully.

Melekai's head snaps up. "What happened?" he demands, and the Necromancer rests a hand on his arm. "What happened and what made you leave?"

Terese looks to Axel. "Did I teleport away?"

He shakes his head. So Melekai means metaphorically.

"I thought—"

And the Necromancer turns her attention to Terese, along with all of her focus and all of her intensity, burning through her resolve and her willpower.

"Nope," Terese blurts out, jolting to her feet and dumping Izzy from her lap. She sways, her legs cramping—she must've been sitting in one place for too long—before she all but dashes to the one other room in the apartment she's been to, the bathroom, and closes the door with a click.

It's no better in there, either, so she slides against the door until she's sitting on the cold hard tile.

There's a sudden silence outside the door, before Melekai says something, just out of the edge of her hearing, the Necromancer's quieter voice just underneath it.

If this is to work, if she is going to be staying here, getting their help, she'll need to adjust, she'll need to get used to it, but she squeezes her eyes shut.

Daniil had tried again. Had found her mind, had pinpointed it over an unknown distance, enough so he could speak to her with unerring accuracy, and she hadn't been able to stop him.

And now, she's sitting on the floor of a bathroom, and her hands are shaking.

There's a quick knock against the door, a rap of knuckles against the wood. "You okay?" Axel asks, muffled through the door.

"No," she answers.

"Fair enough." His footsteps recede from the door, mercifully leaving her alone.

She stares down at her hands, at her pale skin and the freckles along the back of her knuckles, and searches her mind. Looks everywhere for something, anything, that could be a demon hidden away.

She comes up blank, of course, but she hardly knows her own brain these days, so it's not really a surprise.

A loud beep echoes through the small bathroom, and she flinches before digging out the brand-new phone from her pocket.

THE CREEPY ONE (5:22 PM): Sorry for scaring you.

Terese blinks at this, her brain skipping it, shying away from it, before she taps out a response.

TERESE (5:25 PM): Who is this?

The motion of typing, of her thumbs moving against the

slick glass of the phone, is familiar. Natural. Like she's supposed to do this.

Then she immediately shuts her eyes in embarrassment. Of course it's the Necromancer. She has common sense and can piece these things out.

THE CREEPY ONE (5:26 PM): Lyra. Sorry, I had been scanning you for the last two hours and you didn't react, so I didn't think.

So she lost at least two hours, and Terese mulls over that fact, staring blankly down at her phone. Two hours, and she didn't teleport away or obviously hurt anyone.

She's never had people around she could ask about when she loses time.

Flipping through the phone, she quickly finds the contact, changes it to read THE NECROMANCER instead.

She has obviously had a phone before, all of this coming way too easily to her.

TERESE (5:31 PM): Three questions. 1. How long was I out? 2. What did I do while out? 3. Can you tell Melekai the demon tried to contact me and spoke in my mind and how do I tell if it's gone?

There's something a bit easier about typing it, instead of speaking. Something clinical, where she can see the words and know them to be true, but not rely on her voice to get things across.

It cuts through the panic.

From the other side of the door, Izzy whines, the same high-pitched noise she makes if Terese does something without her, so Terese reaches the doorknob and cracks the door just enough for Izzy to snake through the crack, then shuts it again.

Even that brief gap is enough time to hear the urgent voices of the three outside.

Izzy curls up on the tile next to Terese, even though it's cold, and she'd be far more comfortable on the fluffy rug outside.

"I'm okay," she whispers, and Izzy's tail thumps against the floor.

THE NECROMANCER (5:33 PM): What did he say?

TERESE (5:33 PM): Just that he knew I was hiding. It was silent—in my mind—like how the last demon spoke. Ask Melekai how do I know he's gone?

THE NECROMANCER (5:34 PM): I saw no demon in you. I checked.

She checked.

Terese squeezes her eyes shut, and Izzy huffs against her side. Out of everyone in this world, the Necromancer could check. Could spot the difference. And if Terese didn't react violently when she had lost the time and the Necromancer scanned her...

She presses the heels of her hands against her eyes, in some vague hope that the pressure would solve whatever tangle of emotions she's feeling, but it doesn't.

TERESE (5:37 PM): Thank you.

It seems polite to thank her, after all the hell Terese had put her through.

TERESE (5:38 PM): If he can locate me, you should probably leave. A demon would immediately turn to you.

THE NECROMANCER (5:38 PM): I can defend myself.

It makes a certain amount of logical sense, in the last eight months, that the Necromancer would develop tools and tricks to fight off threats. That she would partner with Melekai for his knowledge, for whatever was left with his demon protection over her.

But skepticism crawls over her skin. If Terese can sense her from miles upon miles away any time she performs the barest minimum of magic, then a demon with centuries of experience and the drive to explore must.

THE NECROMANCER (5:40 PM): If I promise not to scan you, do you want to come out and talk to us? Everyone has questions.

It sounds like the worst sort of torture, to face yet another interrogation, when her hands are still shaking, and her mouth still tastes like panic.

She makes herself take a deep breath, to see if she can still her fingers, and Izzy leans against her.

Too many things had happened in the last few days, and the cumulative weight of them sits heavy on her chest. She hasn't spent this long in the company of another person since the demon, and she's not even sure she'd count the demon as company.

But even she knows that asking people to help means working with them.

THE NECROMANCER (5:48 PM): Mel and I are going to pick up some food if you need more time.

Now, this is worse, because they're being kind.

"Ugh," Terese whispers to the cold tile of the bathroom but waits until she can dimly hear the sounds of the door closing to the apartment, before pulling herself up along the wall.

Izzy springs to her feet, tail wagging, like this is what she's been waiting for all along, then sticks her nose at the crack of the bathroom door.

"You're the one that wanted to join me in here," she mumbles, but opens the door anyway.

True to her word, the Necromancer and Melekai are gone, leaving just Axel, still precariously balancing his chair on two legs, staring up at the ceiling.

Terese hovers, hand still on the bathroom door, unsure of what to do.

"Thanks for not teleporting away," Axel says, still tilting his chair back. "Though a warning for the catatonic creepiness would have been nice."

"I didn't mean to," Terese says, but lets her feet bring her forward, until she stands awkwardly in front of the couch.

Izzy immediately flops over onto the fuzzy white rug with the deep satisfaction of an old dog finding a comfortable spot.

"I gathered." Finally, Axel rights himself in the chair. "Any other surprises?"

"I don't know," she answers, and that, at least, feels honest. "I've never known what I did when I lost time."

She sweeps herself over to sit on the couch, and it's at least comfortable, and she buries her face in her hands.

"How common is it?" Once more, it's the mild voice, the one that makes the hair on the back of her neck stand up.

"I don't know," she says, still hiding her face. "Not the most common. Usually not twice in the same two weeks." She could tell he's watching her, even without looking up, the awareness sharp on her mind. "I don't know what I do, I don't know how I react, I just wake up and I'm in a different place than I was before."

"Well," he starts, tapping his fingers against the table. "You said nothing. You stopped talking, even when asked direct questions. You stared straight ahead. You didn't interact, not even when your dog was howling. You followed me out of the car, but like a robot."

She blinks up at him, lifting her head. "Why would someone stab me when I was like that?"

"What?" he blurts out.

"Last time when I got stabbed. I had lost time."

He stares at her, then up at the ceiling, as if asking for help. "Right. You also got stabbed."

"It's good that I didn't hurt anyone," she says, small, and he pauses in his drumming of his fingers. "Why are they being so nice to me?"

"You can ask them that," he points out.

"That sounds awkward." Still, Terese makes herself sit up, pushing her hair away from her face, like that could make her more respectable. "I'm not exactly the most gifted in human interaction these days."

He blinks at her. "Is that a joke?"

"A little?" At his silence, she shrugs, and that just reminds her that her back is stiff. "It's not like I talk to anyone."

He levels her with another look, and she doesn't know how to interpret it still, so she just stares back. "Of course," he says, sarcastically, "you've just been huddling alone in caves for the last few months while scores of magicians look for you, somehow evading all of us."

"You two found me," she points out, and she knows, she just knows, that she's missing the point of the sarcasm, and it needles under her skin. "And shot me. That wasn't fun."

He rubs his face. "Yeah, I thought you were attacking Alette."

Which is fair, so she nods and gives him that one. "But for most people, my magic would get scared and take me away the moment it thought I was in danger. Didn't work with you two, but it means I didn't really have extended conversations with anyone besides the store clerks."

"Well, if you want a tip, don't immediately run into the other room when someone makes you uncomfortable," he says, tenting his hands. "Ask Lyra to stop, and she will."

She files that away in her mind, nodding.

"Mel can be a dick, but if you tell him that, he changes the subject. Alette can be..." he trails off, and for a few seconds his face shuts down. "Secretive and intense with her questions, but she's at least aware of that and tries to hold it back."

"And she's with Zoel, who will fight anyone who's being a threat," Terese interjects. "As long as she's with him, I don't have to worry." Zoel had made that clear, at least. "I asked him, after you shot me."

His brain seems to skip off of that before he visibly pulls himself back on topic. "Point is, don't be scared of us."

It's a nice thought, and easy to comprehend when it's just the two of them in the room, without the hate of Melekai and the intensity of the Necromancer in front of her. When she doesn't have the outward physical reminder of what she did, of how many people were hurt by her.

"And you?" she asks, because he gave her no cheat sheet for him.

"What?"

"What do I do if you're...too much?"

"You could just tell me?" he says, his face scrunching up. "I'm too much for most people."

She doubts that. "The Necromancer and Melekai left just to be nice, didn't they?"

"Absolutely," he answers.

"They realize that's almost worse, right?"

"Not at all," he says, cracking a brief smile. It's a hell of a lot better than the grim tension that she had seen so far, but it melts away before she even has a chance of understanding it.

Instead, it fades to a complicated look, something halfway between cunning and feigning casualness, and immediately, she recognizes the look. The demon before had seen it, only on the face of the pretty alchemist working with Dr. Frisse. She doesn't know if she's ever seen anyone else with that expression, and it burns through her memory.

The demon had bought the casualness, thought it exploitable, no matter how much Terese had raised mental alarms at it.

Probably why the pretty alchemist had caused so much physical damage to them, at almost every interaction.

Terese swallows, blinking and looking away. She doesn't know what exactly the demon did to Axel that could cause him such a dramatic change in appearance, but whatever it could be is...not good.

The small, contrarian part of her, the part that screams to stop taking responsibility for everything, reminds herself that it could've happened after the battle with the demon, but she doubts that.

"I would think I would be the face of their nightmares," she says, nudging Izzy with her feet and getting another dog huff for it. "I could understand if they're less than friendly." She includes him in that thought but doesn't give it words.

"Don't worry, Mel won't be," he says, still with the cunning. Like he's figuring something out about her. He hums wordlessly in the back of his throat, resuming the drumming of his fingers.

She should definitely feel threatened by the expression, she knows this, but instead she just sits back against the couch, letting herself enjoy the silence without the Necromancer and Melekai.

"Do you know what brings you back?" Axel interrupts, after a few blissful moments of silence. "When you lose time, what brings you back?"

She has theories, of course, but nothing concrete. "Seems random, most of the time."

The cunning look just sharpens, and she remembers that the demon had thought Alette had been the smart one among them. "Hmm."

9

The conversation with the Necromancer and Melekai passes in a blur of hunger and fear, but Terese doesn't leave, even when every fiber of her being thrums with the need to teleport away.

It's inconclusive, whatever it is, and when the two of them leave, Melekai's scowl is more thoughtful than combative.

It doesn't quite ease the fear inside of her that this might be impossible for her to avoid, but it's further away. Like it would be hard for Daniil to reach inside the compound and pull at her.

Terese waits until she can no longer feel the brilliance of the Necromancer's magic against her senses, then turns to Axel. "How safe is this place?"

"It kept you out," he says mildly, though his eyebrow raises. "But a lot of the runes are dead now."

Which isn't exactly the answer she had been hoping for, but she pushes herself up to standing, nervous energy bleeding through her.

Izzy lifts her head at her motions before slowly climbing to her feet.

She's had too many panic attacks for the day, and everything still feels raw.

"I'm gonna take Izzy to the greenhouse," she says, knowing she sounds anything but casual as the exhaustion seeps into her voice. "Then where can I sleep?"

She knows it's not the normal time that people usually head off to sleep, but she suspects that proper circadian rhythms weren't exactly her thing even before she was possessed.

He stands, and they wordlessly walk down the hall with the dead runes to the solarium. She knows, she just knows, that she's not worthy of the trust to wander around freely.

It's a strange sort of beauty, despite the setting sun and the taste of tension in her mouth. The sky glows pinkish at the horizon, with the promise of a truly spectacular view if they wait longer.

"I think Daniil found me because I stopped to watch the sunset," she blurts out, as Izzy sniffs around the lines of roses and half-dead orchids.

"Are you one of those people who says things whenever they feel awkward?" Axel says, and while she doesn't have interpersonal skills, that feels insensitive.

"I think my filter for talking to people is gone," she says, deliberately choosing not to be insulted.

"Could be entertaining," he says with a shrug, shoving his hands in his pockets, like he's about to dance out of his skin. "I'm going to venture to guess you'd be uncomfortable staying in Dr. Frisse's old apartment."

"Good guess," she says, unable to stop herself from making a face.

"And I'm not putting you in Alette's space. She's far too

picky about how things are," he muses. "Other than that we have medical cots and we have couches in the small library."

"Library," she says immediately.

HER MIND MAKES the connection that the library is the size of a school classroom, though she does not know exactly the reason for the conclusion, as she sets up a bowl of food for Izzy and curls up on one of the many couches.

There's a dead rune right next to the couch, halfway between a nightlight and a reading lamp.

It's a simple one, hastily scrawled, like someone had etched it in frustration, and the frustration shines through, even through its deactivation.

Gently, like it'll bite her, she lays a single finger against the rune. For a second it does nothing, before it flickers underneath her touch, glowing softly.

It's a warm glow, nice and low, soothing in its own right, banishing the shadows of the harsh overhead light.

It's almost, almost peaceful.

It's certainly silent.

"YOU DON'T EXPECT me to buy this, right?"

Terese gets hurtled out of sleep, the lights are bright, she's not in any of her places, she's not—

With a gasp, she bolts upright, and there's magic around her, magic she can grasp. She grabs at it, two greedy handfuls, pulling it towards herself, and—

Sitting calmly in the chair across from her is Melekai.

She stares at him, hands full of magic that could almost certainly end him, and he just stares at her right back.

So she forces herself to exhale, to let the magic bleed away. "You woke me up."

"Completely intentional," he says, with a bored affectation. "I don't buy this at all."

Izzy's still asleep on the carpet next to the couch, breathing evenly, and if Izzy's not barking, then she should be safe. Should.

"Is this where you threaten me more?" Terese says, shaking out her hands, and her heart calms down a little.

This, she understands.

"Sure," he says with a shrug. "If that's effective."

Because despite the human body, despite everyone treating him like just another one of them, everything about his personality is demon. Is exactly like the one that possessed her, is exactly like the one hunting her down.

"Does the Necromancer know you're here?" she asks, pushing her chin-length hair away from her face.

He shakes his head. "Her and Axel think I'm doing research in the basement."

She lets herself pause, lets herself think, and her magic is calm. No intense need to leave, to teleport away, despite the shock at being awoken like that.

"Okay," she says, finally. "Go ahead."

His eyebrow twitches, like he expected more of a fight.

"Daniil spoke to you, then left you alone?"

There's the familiar panic crowding her throat at the mention of him, but she swallows it down.

"Near as I can tell."

He gives her a flat, unamused look.

"I blacked out," she says, because that's an important

part of the story. "I blacked out and don't know what happened next."

"Convenient," he says. "The moment you might have something actionable, and you don't remember it."

Which, fair.

"I'm more frustrated by it than you," she points out. "It's my brain that gets tossed around."

He nods, as if conceding that point. "You've done a good job of appearing helpless. Axel's buying it."

"I'm not trying to appear helpless. Your little group is the only reason the first demon is gone." Izzy raises her head at her tone before giving an unimpressed look to Melekai. "It wasn't planned."

He tilts his head, and it's such a pure demon movement that for a moment her head spins with dizziness.

"If you're going to threaten me, can you just do it?" she asks, pushing through the vertigo. "I agree to your terms and all. I'm not going to touch the Necromancer, I just want to not go through being possessed and almost ending the fucking world again."

"If Lyra dies because of this, I'll tell him where you are myself," Melekai says, voice deathly quiet.

She swallows past that as her magic pulses through her, but she grips the couch tight with her fingernails so she remains in place.

"You should leave," she says. "Take her somewhere the previous demon wasn't aware of, because if he gets me, he'll find out about her and know where you two live."

He nods, and of course he's probably considered that. Probably had ideas and backups in his mind, probably had since the first day he woke up as human and unable to defend her himself.

"It'll probably happen," he says, and a chill goes through

her spine. "If he can speak into your mind without being present, he has his claws in you already."

She flinches, she can't help herself.

"It's only a matter of time before he figures out how to break into those places you consider safe, to possess you despite your fighting," he continues. "Once a demon has their mark on you, they'll always know where you are, always know how to find you, you will always be present in their awareness."

This pokes at something in her brain, a memory from the first demon, looking at the Necromancer in a convenience store. The demon had been furious that someone else was being so selfish in keeping their grasp on the person in front of them.

"Like how you did to the Necromancer?" she asks, and his glare sharpens. "The last demon could tell."

"Yes," he says, voice clipped.

Her initial gut reaction is to panic, to spiral into herself, but she takes a big gulping breath instead.

"Lyra and Axel don't realize it," he says, after watching her deal with that for a few minutes. "They're both moral, upstanding people. They'll try to help anyone, even if it gets them hurt. Even if it's someone like you."

That seems accurate according to her limited knowledge of them.

"Lyra still wakes in the night with terror because of what you did," he says, painting a picture of an emotional connection that she can only dream of, "and sees your face threatening her brother. Axel has been obsessed with finding you since you disappeared, to get some sort of justice for what you did to him, and now you play helpless to him and appeal to his pity."

She nods, and her eyes sting.

"And they're still going to help." Finally, he sits back. "Think of that when you run back here."

"Can it be stopped?"

"The easiest way to cut off a demon from their toys is to kill their toys, burn their bodies," Melekai says. "And they say you won't die."

She shuts her eyes, as if blocking out the sight of him will block the meaning of his words.

Izzy huffs, shifting next to her until she's sitting up, and Terese feels the often-familiar weight of her dog putting her head on her lap.

"So we figure out the way to kill me," Terese says, after the moment stretches on too long, opening her eyes again to stare down at her dog.

"Lyra and Axel won't," he says, but his voice is solemn. "I'll work on it."

It's so close to a promise that she exhales, heavy, out of her nose.

"Thanks," she says.

"Or kill the demon," he continues, almost flippantly, "but we both know how difficult that is."

He pushes himself up, just as dramatic as every other demon she's ever encountered.

"It's already eleven AM," he says, and it's such a switch of subject she blinks. "Lyra will make noises at you if you haven't eaten yet, don't upset her."

And he swings out of the room, leaving her on the couch.

She waits just long enough for his footsteps to fade away, before she doubles over, hugging Izzy to her chest.

Izzy wiggles at her, yawning, making the grumpy noise of a dog who just wants to sleep and is wholly inconvenienced by Terese's dramatics.

SHE MAKES HERSELF SIT THERE, getting her breathing under control, so an hour probably passes before she changes into one of her extra shirts and wanders her way back through the building.

Her footsteps bring her to the grand ballroom, stinking of a horrid lack of magic, before she hesitates.

Voices, yelling, from behind the closed doors.

She pauses there, holding as still as she can, barely even breathing.

One of them is Axel, that much is obvious, even after such little time she can pick out the timber of his voice.

The other is male, higher pitched, hovering on the edge of familiarity, but she makes herself walk past, until their voices fade.

It's far more labyrinthian than she remembers, without Axel as her guide, but after a brief trip to the solarium for Izzy, she meanders past the dead runes. Past the rooms that smell distinctly of strange magic, past small reading nooks and places that seem closer to medical rooms, until she finds herself in a makeshift kitchen.

There are three separate coffee machines, a toaster, and a pantry full of snack-type foods, a curious relic that suggests way more people once inhabited this place.

She grabs a prepackaged muffin for herself, poking disinterestedly at the coffee machine, Melekai's dire words still bouncing around her head.

The kind thing to do would be to run. To leave the Necromancer and Axel alone, so Daniil doesn't drag them into it. To stock up on supplies and go to one of the remote safety spaces, camp out until the demon figures her out enough.

Because then, if he takes her, she'll be far away from anyone she could hurt.

Terror shivers down her spine at that, and she's too much of a coward. Too scared to just wait for that end.

Her phone beeps, and Izzy gives her a brief glance.

THE HANDSOME ONE (12:03 PM): You still alive?

She squints at it, then opens up the contacts on her phone.

All the numbers are under nicknames. The Handsome One. The Nerdy One. The Grumpy One.

It wasn't just the necromancer that Axel put in under a nickname. Now there are four people she barely knows under pseudonyms.

TERESE (12:04 PM): Who exactly is this?

THE HANDSOME ONE (12:04 PM) Axel.

TERESE (12:05 PM): Of course. I am still alive. Did not die in the middle of the night to my knowledge.

THE HANDSOME ONE (12:06 PM) See, that sounds like a joke, but I don't think you're kidding.

Briefly, ever so briefly, a smile flickers to her lips before it vanishes under the weight of Melekai's words.

TERESE (12:09 PM): Nope, not joking. I can usually tell.

THE HANDSOME ONE (12:10 PM): It's the usually that gets me.

TERESE (12:10 PM): Same.

She marvels at how familiar it is, the very act of texting someone like this. Of not feeling the incredible weight of her interactions, the pressure to be normal.

Instead, the phone does it for her.

THE HANDSOME ONE (12:11 PM): Alette called with some ideas a bit earlier. How open would you be to experimentation?

She waits for the panic, for the guilt to start at Melekai's words, but it doesn't immediately strike her.

It should. It was, after all, Dr. Frisse's experimentation that got her into this entire thing, and Axel is one of her prodigies.

TERESE (12:15 PM): What do you have in mind?

"Old fashioned rune circle and some bronze paint," Axel says, breezing into the small kitchen, like he knew where she had been all along. "It's how we neutralized the first demon—I want to see if it neutralizes you."

"I like the phone," she says, mulish. "A bit easier than talking to people."

"Oh, you're one of those introverts," Axel says, shredding the plastic package of the muffin. "Old people are gonna hate you."

She squints at him, trying to decipher if it's a joke or not, then moves on. "I think I had one before the demon," she says, poking at the phone. "At least, it's easy to learn, which suggests that."

"Well, you're our age, so if you didn't have a phone, it'd be downright weird," Axel says, leaning forward and grabbing the phone from the table. "Did you know it had a camera? Here."

He flips it over, then aims it at Izzy, who ignores him, then turns it back to her.

"See? Now you have a picture of your dog."

Terese cradles the phone, and knows, somehow, that she's going to be really fucking annoying with this, so she aims the camera at Axel, catching him mid-bite of the muffin.

"Hey," he objects.

She ignores that in favor of tying it to his phone number, then sets the picture of Izzy as her background.

"Is everything okay?" Terese asks, shyness dimming her voice. "I heard yelling earlier."

Axel's face is blank for a few seconds, before he shrugs. "Just Gurlien being an ass. He wants me to turn on Alette, I won't, but I can't kick him out permanently, so every few weeks we get together and yell over each other until we both feel better. It's great."

She squints at him, because great isn't how she would describe such an encounter.

"But seriously. Circle of trapping, what do you think?"

"I don't remember much of that day," Terese says, setting her phone down on the table. "But that pissed her off."

"Good," Axel says, sitting down at the card table with her, leaning down to pat Izzy on her side.

Izzy doesn't react, except for a brief glance at him.

"But she could still strike out," Terese says, blinking rapidly, as if that could help her memories come back. So much of the night had been coated in panic, so much of it inaudible over the demon's screaming. "She just couldn't leave."

"Exactly," he says, reaching one of his long arms over and grabbing another prepackaged muffin for himself. "We put you in one, see if you can teleport out, see if you can do anything, and it could give us a starting point."

She doesn't see the starting point, but with the grimness of Melekai's conversation, she grips onto the hope, onto the idea that there could be something else, anything.

HE LEADS HER, the Necromancer, and Melekai to the edge of the property, and it's close enough to the nebulous barrier of what her magic considers safe that the back of her neck tingles.

Izzy follows them along, sniffing contentedly at the forest

There's a flat concrete platform with a circle and an x painted in the middle, and her mind immediately supplies the phrase 'helicopter pad' even though she's not entirely certain she's ever interacted with one of those before.

Scuffed-up spray paint in gold and bronze mark up the concrete, evidence of past magical attempts.

"This won't work," Melekai says as they survey it.

It's brilliantly sunny out, and there's sweat at Axel's hairline. "You're just a pessimist."

"Where's the property line?" Terese asks, instead of looking directly at Melekai and the Necromancer, even though she's acutely aware of both of them watching her.

Though thankfully not scanning her.

"Your magic can't possibly care about legal ownership boundaries," Melekai says, toeing the traces of the past magic attempts with something resembling contempt.

And he's right, but she's not about to quibble with the logic of her bullshit.

"Dr. Frisse—Alette now—owns about a few acres more in this direction," Axel answers. "Past that is just state forest."

"So it's not related to the legal ownership boundaries," Terese says, and doesn't miss the grin flickering on Axel's face.

"Alette's going to have so much fun with you," the Necromancer says, not unkindly, before taking the proffered spray paint bottle from Axel.

Again, Axel's face flickers, briefly going sour, before he pastes on an immediately fake smile. "Yeah, obscure rules that have no reason and need to be figured out, she'll have so much fun."

Terese raises an eyebrow at him, but the other two don't react to that, with the Necromancer starting to spray paint shaky runes, and Melekai closely supervising.

The gut kick of hunger, at the Necromancer so obviously using her abilities, knocks Terese in her chin, but she just turns towards Axel instead of watching, blinking rapidly.

It's simpler to avoid the Necromancer's gaze outside. To let the brilliance of the power wash in the other direction, but that does not mean it's necessarily easy.

"That bad, huh?" Axel says, tapping his fingers against his thighs.

She doesn't exactly like admitting that, so she keeps silent.

"How's the headache?"

This causes her to pause, to evaluate. "Better?" It's more of a dull ache, easily ignorable, so she prods at the sensitive bits behind her ears, and barely gets a pang. "Not bad."

"And the stab?"

"That's...that was better like the next day," she says, flinching when the Necromancer calls on a particularly bright bit of magic, visible even though she's facing the opposite way. "Stab wounds are the easiest."

"Of course they are."

Izzy slithers between the two of them, leaning heavy against Terese's leg, so Terese thumps her on the side with the vague hope of distracting herself.

"In terms of getting back upright, it goes stab wounds, suffocating, blunt force trauma, gunshots"—she gives him a significant look—"then the weirder stuff."

In terms of distractions, his smile works wonderfully. "You might have to keep this all a secret from Alette, she might try to dial in exactly how long this all takes with observable results."

Terese screws up her face at the thought, before flinching again at a spike of magic. "Do I need to be here for this?" she asks, dipping her voice down.

"Yes!" Melekai calls from across the circle, even though Terese thought she had been whispering.

It frays at her patience, like strings tugging away from the fabric that is inside her, so she scowls at the ground.

"I think she's almost done," Axel says, bouncing on the balls of his feet. "What's the weirdest way you've died?"

It's too weighty of a question for the bright sunshine, but she scratches Izzy behind the ears as she thinks.

Her own deaths haven't been something she's ranked, not really, other than the quick judgement of 'worse or better than usual.' Seems almost too morbid to dwell on.

Another spike of magic through her awareness, and contemplating death is suddenly more preferable.

"Gonna assume you don't count the time when she"— Terese jerks her thumb at the Necromancer—"ripped a demon out of me, right?"

"You were breathing after that," he says, brow wrinkled, "Alette checked."

"Fairly certain I died." Waking up in the hospital had felt like death, at least. Like death and terror and the sudden drop of exhilaration that she didn't have the demon inside of her. "Why aren't you doing this, instead?" She points towards the circle, where her back is still turned. "Alchemist magic would be better than this."

Axel stills, and her heart drops because he has always been in motion. Even in the memories with the demon controlling her, the pretty alchemist had always been moving, every line of his body kinetic.

But instead, he is as still as stone, his face carved from the very concrete they stand on.

"You don't know?" he asks, his voice deathly quiet.

"No?" she says, though her heart pounds and her magic thrums, as if this question has put her in danger.

He says nothing, just regarding her, still.

"Did I do something?" she blurts out, before she can stop herself, "I think the demon changed your appearance, something, but did I —"

"You think she changed my appearance?" Something sharper than sarcasm whispers its way into his voice.

She's not sure where she misjudged. "I've figured out that you don't look the same, but you're the alchemist from before, the pretty one. You have the same mannerisms and the same way of standing." Izzy makes a disgruntled noise, so Terese looks down at her, instead of at the chilling still-ness of Axel. "I don't remember much of that day, but I know she changed my face, so I thought she must've to you."

"Hmm," Axel says, and it's far less than friendly.

"I'm sorry?" she says, and her voice tilts up, outside of her control, and she hates it. "I don't know what it was, but I'm sorry."

Finally, he exhales in a huff, shaking out his hands, but the motion is back, and something inside of her unwinds. "I'm not talking about this," he declares, and Terese finds herself nodding as quickly as she can. "But you're up."

He jerks his chin towards the circle, and despite herself, Terese turns.

10

The circle flares brilliant gold, burning against Terese's eyes until she has to squint.

The Necromancer stands on the other side of the circle, ablaze in power, every line of her etched in light.

Her mind overlays the image of the circle Dr. Frisse had trapped her and the first demon in, at the terror of that moment. Of the chill in her bones, of the wind whistling through the meager jacket, of a sharp pain behind her ribs.

Of snow and slush underneath her boots, of the demon shrieking in terror and pain. Of Melekai's face, intent on ending her. Of the Necromancer, gripping her arm and peeling her apart, bit by bit.

Terese shivers again, despite the summer sun.

"What do you need from me?" she asks, and her voice is smaller than she'd like.

"Step on in," the Necromancer says, and despite the power there's a smile on her face, an easy exhilaration. "Let us know if it hurts."

"It's not going to hurt," Melekai says to the Necromancer,

an almost automatic reassurance. "At most it might feel weird and she might want to sit down."

If anything, she can trust that Melekai would not let her do something that would distress the Necromancer, and if the Necromancer doesn't want her to feel pain, she can trust this.

So, despite the lump in her throat, she strides over the spray-painted lines.

There's a whisper of pressure against her sinuses, like the sensation right before it rains after being cloudy all day, but nothing stops her chest or spikes pain in her nerves.

Immediately, Izzy dashes forward to be with her, but Axel catches her by the leash, and Terese stops short, turning and looking back.

Axel bends over and pats Izzy's side, but Izzy quivers, her ears back. "Best to keep her out, some magic is weird in animals."

It's something Terese knows, intellectually, but it hurts more than the throb in her head.

Izzy whines, a small noise that raises the hairs on Terese's arms.

"It's okay," she says, and her dog hunkers down, tail between her legs, at the furthest the leash will allow. "I'm okay."

Izzy clearly doesn't believe her, but Terese keeps her eyes on her dog as she slowly backs towards the center of the circle.

Axel crouches down next to Izzy, scratching between her ears, but she pays him no attention.

"Aww, okay, I need you to do some magic," the Necromancer says, and Terese jumps. "Nothing big, nothing dangerous, just something small."

Something small.

Terese breathes past the sinus pressure and flexes her fingers. Most of her magic weighs heavy on her, large or reactive or dramatic or actively harmful to everything around her, and she doesn't want to cause a disruption here.

With the lightest of grips she can manage, she pulls some magic close to her, twisting it in her hand like its nothing more than a string.

It pulses, glowing gold to match the circle, visible.

"Zoel will be here in a few days, right?" she asks, feeling the magic in her hand. It's smooth, like it had been at this place for so long, used to being manipulated for these types of circles.

"Why?" Melekai asks, immediately suspicious.

"Because most of what I do is destructive, and I want to make sure he'd be able to fix it," Terese says, rolling the magic between her fingers before lifting her eyes to Axel. "I have no desire to make things worse."

"Yes, he'll be here," the Necromancer says, elbowing Melekai gently. "Alette can also clean up a lot of the messes, especially on her own property."

Terese nods, mostly to herself, then gently rips the strip of magic in her hand as if it's a delicate piece of paper.

The rough concrete underneath her feet dents, pebbles stirring, and her ears pop, but the brilliant circle around her holds.

"That's small?" the Necromancer asks, impressed.

Like Terese's magic is impressive.

"Okay," Melekai says, and his voice is more analytical. "That's good."

"It is?" Terese asks, and her hair stirs in the surrounding wind. The demon had always loved the sensations around causing that amount of damage, of the strange reversal of gravity inside of the bubble.

After all this time, Terese doesn't mind it as much.

"It means if we get you in here and neutralize the demon, you can still fight," the Necromancer says, shifting so she leans against Melekai.

From inside the circle, the Necromancer doesn't shine as brightly, and it doesn't cause the dagger inside of her.

"Interesting," Melekai says, voice thoughtful. "Teleport away."

She twists to look at him.

"I want to see if it'll trap you," he continues, more pondering than not, "or if you have to be actively possessed."

The beginnings of a plan worm their way into her mind, and she releases the magic with a flick of her palm. "And Izzy—"

"The dog stays here," Melekai interrupts, and the Necromancer makes a wordless noise of confusion. "We need to make sure she comes back."

Terese has only teleported without Izzy twice since she rescued her, and Izzy gives a warbling whine at the words, like she understood the former demon's statement.

"I'll come back," Terese says, her voice barely audible past the roaring in her ears, before she forces her eyes to look up at Axel.

Axel nods, like he understands what she's putting in his hands.

"It may take me a few minutes," Terese says, with more confidence than she feels. "It's not terribly under my control."

"Comforting," Melekai snarks, then gets elbowed again by the Necromancer.

Izzy whines again, and Terese closes her eyes and thinks of safety.

At first, her magic doesn't budge, giving her a pang of

confusion because she's already safe. She's safe. The demon can't get to her in here, and Izzy's here, so why would she ever try to leave?

After a few moments of prodding at her unwilling magic, though, cool air puffs over her face, and she opens her eyes in the tunnel.

Across from her, on the rough-hewn rock wall she stares at each time she teleports in, written in big red letters, is:

YOU CANNOT HIDE FROM ME

She stares at it, her heart jumping and her fingers trembling, and tries to teleport away. To go somewhere safe.

But her magic protests, just like before. Still thinks it is safe.

Still thinks she's safe.

Panic spikes through her mind, sudden and sharper than any knife.

"No," Terese whispers, then drags in a shaky breath. Whoever did this isn't here, she's not actively in danger, she can pause and think.

Loud underneath her silencing spell, her phone beeps, and she jumps.

THE HANDSOME ONE (1:30 PM): You're in Southern Washington, right? The tunnel?

Her belongings are strewn around, the spare bag of clothes slashed open, red paint spilled all over them, ruining them. The paint still glistens wet, like she had just missed it.

It could be regular teenagers. It could be a homeless person, acting out in a space they think they won't get punished.

Or it could be Daniil.

It could be Daniil, slowly finding all the places she lives, everywhere she's stayed, and leaving them ruined. Taking her little pockets of safety, the little pockets of peace, and showing her how he could still reach out and touch her.

Or it could be teenagers.

So she snaps a picture of the rock wall, then focuses on somewhere, anywhere else, that is safe.

Her feet land on the rough wooden floor of the cabin, and it's completely untouched, so she takes a moment to grab an extra backpack with Izzy's toys and some more clothing, then teleports again.

Back to underneath the spruce tree in the blackberry bramble, next to the gravel driveway of the headquarters.

There's still a spot of dried blood and clumps of tissue where she had laid dead for fifteen hours.

But the entire place smells like spruce and pine and nothing like the stale dust of the tunnel, so she tilts her head upwards, towards the squat building.

TERESE (1:32 PM): Back on your property, on the edge. Walking up.

With a deep breath, she shoulders her backpack. Her fingers tremble on the straps as she pulls them tight, then tromps up to where she thinks the helicopter pad is.

Her mind skitters away from the paint, from the lump in her throat. Her magic wouldn't take her somewhere unsafe like that, somewhere that had been so violated, and so specifically.

If he could get there, track her down to that one spot, then he could find her here, at the headquarters.

Her footsteps still, on the gravel road next to overgrown blackberries, the fruit just beginning to grow.

She wouldn't be able to go anywhere. She'd be relegated to such a small part of her mind again, just to scream in agony.

Breathing hard out of her nose, not even stopping her

hands from shaking, she adjusts the backpack, and continues the climb up the hill.

THE HANDSOME ONE (1:35 PM): Did it dump you on the road?

TERESE (1:36 PM): Yes.

Shortly enough, she can hear the oft familiar sound of Izzy tromping through dense underbrush and gets greeted by Axel almost jogging down the gravel road, Izzy straining on the leash.

Behind him, at a much more reasonable pace, are Melekai and the Necromancer. His arm is thrown around her, a casual comfort that does nothing to help the fear in her chest.

"Your dog doesn't like it when you leave," Axel calls the moment they get into easy hearing distance, letting go of the leash.

Terese crouches down, letting Izzy bound towards her, and her dog crashes into her with all the finesse of a toddler. "I'm okay," she whispers into Izzy's fur, as Izzy tries to be a lap dog right there on the gravel road in full sunshine. "I'm okay, I'm here."

"See, that's almost adorable," Axel says, and there's a light in his eyes, like she actually did something good. "You went to southern Washington, then to...Romania?"

"Is that where that is?" Terese asks, taking a moment to shove her hair out of her face, only for Izzy to sloppily lick the side of her cheek. "It's not near any town or anything, so I never found someone to ask."

"Well, you confirmed some stuff for us," Axel says, as Melekai and the Necromancer draw close.

"Your circle didn't work on me," Terese says as she unloops her backpack, unzipping it and offering Izzy her favorite squeaky toy. "And someone's been in my tunnel."

Izzy immediately chomps down on the toy, and the ensuing noise causes all three of them to visibly pause.

Melekai's the first to recover. "What do you mean, someone's been in there?"

"You need more food," the Necromancer interrupts him, and Terese gets the barest of flashes of terror, as she obviously scans her for a split second. "You're about fifteen minutes away from a sugar crash."

Terese climbs to her feet, offering Melekai her phone with the picture, and all three of them crane their necks to look at it.

"Could be nothing," Axel says, first. "The tunnel isn't exactly blocked off, anyone can access it."

"And paint is pretty rudimentary," the Necromancer says, before looking back at Terese. "Food. You need it."

"It's what I would do if I wanted to unsettle you," Melekai says, handing her the phone back. "Get you nervous until you make mistakes."

"I'm already nervous," Terese says. "The tunnel is supposed to be safe. How can it be if he could get in?"

"If it is him, that's at least in Zoel's territory," Melekai says, overly casual, and Terese has been around enough demons to know when they're faking something, and she cranes her neck over to look at him.

"What exactly does that have to do with it?" she asks, and Melekai looks away, out at the moss growing on the old spruce trees, instead of at her. "You and I both know that he can't face a demon."

He avoids her glance.

The Necromancer prods Melekai, then starts walking back up towards the Headquarters.

"We got in," Axel says, and his brows are raised, but he tilts his head for her to follow the Necromancer.

"And before this, you two were the only ones to ever threaten me in one of my spots." Terese pats Izzy's side to prompt her up so they can walk back. "Come on, apparently I need food."

Izzy's ears perk up at the mention of food, as if she hadn't been fed already that day.

"Magic burns more energy than you think it does, most likely," Axel says. "Alette's gonna try to figure out what makes a place safe. If you have an answer, it'll make it easier."

He's still wooden around her, like he's forcing the friendliness that seemed so easy before, and even though she deserves nothing like it, she misses it.

And worrying about that is a lot more comforting than obsessing about the paint.

ONCE BACK AT THE HEADQUARTERS, back in Axel's small apartment, the Necromancer watches as Terese chokes down one of those awful power bars with a scowl. Izzy flops over on the fluffy white carpet, the squeaky toy gently held in her mouth.

"I don't feel like I'm hungry," Terese says, as the Necromancer tosses her another one. "I ate this morning, I'm fine."

The Necromancer levels her with a glare, but Terese's dealt with demons, so she just stares back.

After the circle, looking at her is still less awful, and she doesn't know how long it's going to last, but it's nice. Makes the world less hostile.

"I dunno. Lyra knows what she's talking about," Axel says with that fake casualness that makes her hair rise. He's texting someone, with the air of someone who's only half paying attention to the conversation.

"Just because you have lived unhealthily, doesn't mean you should," the Necromancer says, and Melekai gives her a bare-teethed grin. Like he enjoys this part of his partner. "And magicians are more powerful when they're healthy."

"There is nothing healthy about me," Terese says, prickly, and that draws a smile from the Necromancer. "And I don't see why I need to care about that now."

Melekai snorts.

"Alette wants to see the pic. Can you send it to her?" Axel asks, still not looking up from the phone. "She'll show it to Zoel."

"Did you put her under a weird name in my phone?" Terese asks, crossing her arms and not touching the power bar.

"Absolutely," Axel drawls, then taps on his phone again. "Here, I'll create a group chat."

In unison, three phones beep in the room, and Melekai sighs, put upon. "I'm not going to check it."

"Didn't think you would," Axel says breezily, but the two of them grin at each other, like it's an old joke.

Terese pulls her phone out of her pocket, suddenly aware of the friendship around her. That even after everything, even with Melekai literally being a former demon, he managed to make friends.

THE HANDSOME ONE (1:53 PM): This is the official keeping track of Terese text chain.

THE NERDY ONE (1:53 PM): Thank you. Terese, can you send the picture?

"Is that Alette?" Terese asks, but sends the picture anyway.

"Yes, that's Alette," Axel says. "She's way smarter than any of us."

Terese doubts that. Axel's shoulders are slumped ever so slightly, and there's a frown tugging on the corners of his mouth.

The demon had thought they were inseparable, never seeing one without the other, but here Axel is, subtly unhappy whenever Alette is mentioned.

"Would it help if we gave you actually good food?" the Necromancer asks. "Instead of just the granola bars?"

"Hey, they're good," Axel retorts.

"They're really not," Terese says. "Fast food is better."

"Fast food is better than most things," Axel replies, then winks at her. "You want fast food, we can get you fast food."

"I'm not going out there," Terese says immediately. "He found one of my spots —"

"—He *may have* found one of your spots," Axel interrupts. "We don't know yet."

The more Terese thinks on it, the more it seems like he did, but she lets him win that one, sits there as the magicians debate over the different ideas of food and what is good for her.

And tries to not despair.

11

Their idea of food is an outdoor cafe with large awnings to protect from the summer sun, and Izzy settles at her feet. Melekai and Axel bicker the entire way there, with the Necromancer chipping in, but Terese just rests her head against the car window for the ride.

Whatever dulled the spike of the Necromancer's power has made the car ride bearable.

"The key after expelling a lot of magic is to have about as giant of a meal as you can stand," Axel says, sitting next to her as Melekai helps the Necromancer into her chair. Axel's face has settled into that cool distance again, and a small part of her hates it.

It's beyond strange to be sitting across from her former enemies. From people she would have sworn would never help her.

"I'm not hungry," she points out, looking over her shoulder after a disinterested waiter drops off a few menus. The cafe is horribly exposed, anyone walking by could watch them, and her skin crawls.

"Yeah, that's not what I said," Axel says, picking up the menu.

She sighs, glancing at the menu. It's a horridly extensive collection of food, and none of it seems familiar.

"Think of it this way," Axel starts, still avoiding looking at her, "you'll be better equipped to take down any threats if you've eaten."

"And, you know, feel better," the Necromancer says, exasperated.

"Seems fake," Terese says, and gets rewarded by the barest hint of a smile from Axel. "I hardly know what any of this is."

Axel's eyebrows do a funny thing, like he can't figure out what expression to make, before they settle on amused. "If you don't decide, I'll just order for you, and I'll get the most ridiculous thing they have."

"Deal," Terese says, tossing the menu back down on the table.

He gives her a grin, almost playful, and she doesn't know if she's ever been looked at like that, before he makes a show of examining the menu.

Melekai sits back, and for the first time, he almost seems amused.

"Any food allergies?"

"I mean, if I die from food poisoning, it's not like it's going to be a big deal." Terese shrugs. "I don't like salads."

"Yeah, I'm not getting you a salad," he says, theatrically arching an eyebrow before folding the menu back up.

"You should get her something spicy," Melekai grouses, and it's so normal, so far removed from their discussion that very morning.

"I've eaten spicy foods before," Terese interjects, then pauses long enough to think. "Wait, had you not?"

"I didn't eat before eight months ago, of course not," Melekai shoots back, crossing his arms.

Axel grins, sharp and mischievous. "We had a great time," he says, and the Necromancer coughs uncomfortably. "Got to introduce him to all sorts of things."

It's another small trauma, one she added to the group, by simply changing Melekai's very nature.

The thought sits heavy with her as Axel waves down the tired waiter and makes a show of pointing to something on the menu instead of saying it aloud.

But Axel turns back to her with a smile, and she doesn't want to have that disappear.

"You are either going to love this or hate this," he says once the waiter swings away with their orders.

"Most food isn't worth that strong of emotion," she points out, "awful protein bars notwithstanding."

"I like those," he says loosely, before reaching under the table to scratch behind Izzy's ears.

Izzy huffs, then rearranges herself so she's out of his reach, and the Necromancer laughs at the expression on Axel's face.

"She's not used to other people," Terese says. "I think she'd been abandoned when I found her."

She doesn't know why she said that. It's almost too much of a confession.

"See, that just makes it sadder," Axel says, but he's at ease, leaning back against the chair. "I dare you to tell me one detail about you that's not sad."

"Hey," Terese says, but still feels a smile creeping over her face. "I'm not possessed."

"That doesn't count," the Necromancer interjects.

"Sure it does," Melekai responds.

"We're gonna have to find more than just that," Axel

says, with enough confidence that Terese believes him for one shining moment.

"Izzy likes the dog park, whipped cream, and sleeping in the sun," Terese says, "and I get to give her that." The group around her goes silent, like she's actually said something worth listening to.

"Okay, that's good," Axel says, like he's encouraging it, drawing it out.

"And you?" she asks, somehow hoping she can lead it to an opening for her to apologize without being an awkward weirdo. "You all have good things?"

The three of them stare at her, like she honestly took them by surprise, and Axel opens his mouth, then closes it several times before managing to speak.

"My rent is free," he starts, "I have a shit ton of knowledge that most people don't, I can fix things, my best friend is happy for like...the first time in her life, I actually have a guy friend for once who's hilarious—"

"—Do you mean him?" Terese interrupts, pointing at Melekai.

"Hey," Melekai says.

"It's amazing to see how bad you are at being a human," Axel says. "It's the most awkward thing in the world and it makes me laugh. And Lyra finds it endearing."

"It's true," the Necromancer chips in with a grin. Melekai rolls his eyes at her, but they're both smiling, something soft. An expression Terese never thought she'd see.

There's a light in Axel's eyes, like the mere act of him talking about his friends brings him joy.

"I'm alive," Melekai says, and there's only a trace of irony in his voice. "Human bodies aren't too bad."

"Rude," the Necromancer says. "Um, it's like I'm getting a degree in magic with none of the student loans."

And the moment is broken by the waiter swooping back with a giant plate filled to the brim with food. Of waffles topped by fried chicken topped with...eggs? With a sauce?

She gives Axel an accusatory glare.

"I told you, weirdest thing on the menu." He smirks, getting his exceedingly normal plate of a burger and fries.

"Oh, that's not bad," the Necromancer says as the waiter gives her a sandwich, before she looks deliberately at Terese. There's none of her usual scanning, and her magic is still dulled, but Terese steels herself to not flinch, just expecting the intensity.

The waiter swoops away, leaving Terese feeling like she's all of a sudden under a microscope.

"So," the Necromancer starts, "what do you remember?"

Terese glances at Axel, but he's too busy making a show of batting away Melekai from stealing one of his fries. She knows he's paying attention, but at least wants plausible deniability.

"I assume you mean from when I was possessed?" Terese asks, buying herself a little time to figure out why the question makes her so uncomfortable. "Most of it."

There's a brief slice of a scan from the Necromancer, like it slips from her grasp, but it evaporates just as quickly, leaving Terese wide-eyed.

"Then do you know how she found me?" the Necromancer asks. Next to her, Melekai briefly glances to her, before back to Axel, an obvious check-in before an equally obvious giving the pretense of privacy.

It's not the question Terese expects. "Um," she starts, taking a bite out of the monstrosity in front of her to find the answer, then pauses. "This is actually good?"

"Told you," Axel says smoothly, then gives her a cheeky

grin, and it's almost as good as the food. "We just need to give you weird food."

"And not those protein bars," Terese says. "She felt you inspect the bubble, then went searching. She didn't stop walking or teleporting until she found you, and when you don't sleep, you can cover a lot of ground."

"And my brother?" the Necromancer asks, completely ignoring her food. "How'd you find him?"

This sounds like the question that she really wanted to ask and, at least, it's easy to answer. "She spied on you and heard you mention him," Terese replies, staring at her food instead of at the too-eager Necromancer. "She asked me what a brother was and why it mattered. I told her it was a stupid idea, I did, but she went ahead and went after him."

"You could communicate with her?" Melekai cuts in, because of course they were listening and not actually ignoring them. "That's not possible."

Izzy sits up underneath the table, putting her head on Terese's lap, and she's not sure if it's because of the fried chicken or because of her sudden spike of anxiety.

"We didn't communicate well," Terese says, scowling at him before she realizes she's still relying on them to help her. "Mostly it was just her talking out loud and me trying to scream at her."

"Sounds disorienting," the Necromancer says, shrewd. "She didn't know what a brother was?"

"She was remarkably stupid," Terese says, and it shocks Melekai to a short bark of laughter. "She wouldn't think things through, she would do whatever her first instincts were, and then swear up and down that the result she got was what she wanted."

"Good to know we got outsmarted by a dumb demon," Axel says, and there's the hint of something sharp behind his voice, but when she glances up at him, he just shakes his head.

Something for a different time, then.

Again, the small slice of the necromancy power, and Terese flinches.

"Sorry, sorry," the Necromancer says with a sigh. "I've spent the last six months learning how to scan everyone, how to absorb all that information, and now you're..." She trails off, picking up her sandwich. "Sorry."

"Why are you being nice to me?" Terese blurts out. "You should be so angry, all the time, and you're giving me food and apologizing. I...I all but upended every bit of your life, I hurt your brother, I briefly killed you"—she gestures at Melekai—"and now you're just a regular guy, and..." She looks up at Axel, abruptly losing steam, the words evaporating from her mind faster than she can think to say them, and she flounders. "It doesn't make sense."

Axel just holds her eye contact, another little lifeline.

"The more I hear, the more it just sounds like you were a victim as well," the Necromancer says, and her voice is kind again, and that's worse.

Terese sighs, as if that could make the frustration bleed away from her body, but it does little, so she scratches Izzy behind the ears instead.

"I still think we should lock you in a box," Melekai grumbles. "Don't look at me for being nice."

"Thanks," Terese says, aiming for sarcastic and missing it completely. "That helps."

∾

DESPITE ALL THE NICENESS, later that night, she paces down the long hallway between the solarium and the library, her magic thrumming that she should leave.

Not that she's in any danger, just that they've remained in one spot for too long and leaving means safety. Leaving means no one will find her. Her head aches with the injuries from just a few days before, and that's not helping.

Izzy tromps next to her, good-natured, despite Terese's twitchiness.

Her footsteps take her to the door she thinks is Axel's apartment, and she hesitates, like her brain takes a moment to breathe between thoughts, and before she can stop the impulse, she knocks on his door.

A few moments pass, and she seriously considers teleporting away and then back just to move, just to get out, before the door cracks and he gives her a guarded, wary look.

"What?" he asks, voice neutral.

And that certainly is the question.

"Is there somewhere outside I can walk?" she asks, which seems close enough to what she needs to know that she runs with it. "I'm not leaving, I'm just..."

"One sec," he says, ducking his head back inside the apartment, and emerges with a sleek leather jacket.

"You don't have to come with me." The words fall from her lips, pricklier than she intends.

"Oh, that's easy. I don't trust you not to run yet," he says flippantly, tossing the words between them like a bomb. "Running off would be bad, I want more answers, it's a nice day out. Two birds, one stone."

"That would be three birds," she informs him, and his lips twitch, almost into a smile.

He leads her out another door, and a small part of her

marvels at how many entrances and exits the squat, ugly building has, before the magic pent up inside of her unwinds with a snap at the fresh air and sight of trees.

She sighs, her shoulders dropping at the sudden lack of tension against her spine.

"Get stir-crazy?" he asks, dry, as she takes a few steps out onto the mossy loam.

"The magic does," she says, tapping her sternum. "Then it drives me crazy until I go somewhere else."

He looks up to the sky, where clouds now threaten rain but don't follow through, as if that can help him understand. "Magic doesn't work like that. It's not...it's not separate from a person."

"Yes it is," she says mulishly, watching Izzy sniff through the underbrush.

"You might be unpracticed at controlling it, or it's following a subconscious thought instead of your actual will, but it's still an intrinsic part of a person."

She throws him a look, and he's scowling at the forest.

"Not if I didn't have any until a demon possessed me," she says, trying and failing to not sound like an asshole. "I don't think I teleported everywhere before then. I certainly didn't come back from the dead before."

"That one might be inaccurate," he says, pointing at her like he caught her in something. "Unless you had a catastrophic accident or something, how would you know?"

Terese rolls her eyes, but he has something close to a point.

"There must've been some reason you could get possessed, my money's on that," he continues, and her stomach drops.

He still doesn't know it was his own Dr. Frisse.

She shivers, even though the muggy air is anything but cool.

"I mean, maybe," she says, neutral, even though it feels like a lie. "But the point is, all of this"—she waves at herself again—"is outside of all my control."

"Which means you can learn to control it," he says, bouncing on his toes, and it's like a switch has been flipped, turning him from sullen to excited, and it's a bit like whiplash. "Lyra never knew how to control it until like eight months ago, it used to make almost everywhere annoying and 'taste like death.'" He makes quotation marks with his fingers. "Now she can do all sorts of things with it, including being in a hospital where people are dying and it doesn't, you know, hit her over the head."

"Wait, the Necromancer hadn't been trained before that?" Terese asks, some small part of her getting drawn into his energy, into his curiosity.

"Not at all," he pauses, a funny look on his face. "You can call her Lyra, she doesn't have a title."

Terese's mind skitters away from that, and she shakes her head. "That's just weird," she says, and they walk down the gentle slope of the hill. "The demon had troubles with her name, and it's like...stuck in my head that way."

"What was the demon's name?" Axel asks, and he's opened up too, while walking outside. Like the motion and the movement smooth a restless part of him as well.

"Terese," she says, eyeing him. "At least, pretty sure."

His face does a funny thing, where it's caught between amusement and horror, before settling on firmly skeptical. "Are you saying you call yourself after the demon?"

"Not like my name is, you know, readily available." She knocks her knuckles against her temple and immediately regrets it, pain spiraling down her back and through her legs. "She stole a lot from me. I get to steal stuff from her."

"That's fucked up," he informs her, like she didn't already know. "You should have your own name, at the very least."

"Sure, if you can figure it out, I'm game," she responds, again back in the prickly, too-exposed state of mind, before she sighs. "It's not that pathetic, I swear."

"Right," he says, wary. "Just an incredibly depressing thing, where you don't remember your name and call yourself after a being of incredible power who ruined both of our lives."

"And now her name is mine, and all she is, is a dead demon," Terese says, sharp. "I won that battle, I get to take it."

"I guess," he says, before he crosses his arms, watching as Izzy crashes through some blackberry brambles after a squirrel. "Still dark. Still fucked up."

"Still my decision," she retorts, and her magic pulses once, as if sensing her mood, and she sighs, steeling herself to be a bit kinder and a bit more polite. "Sorry."

He shrugs, but the corners of his mouth tug downwards. "Thank you for getting me, instead of just disappearing," he says, like an olive branch, and she takes it he accepts the apology. "Mel will probably have ideas on how you can control all the magic, he's the one who trained Lyra."

"Pretty sure I'm not a necromancer," she says, aiming for a joke, but it falls flat.

"No, but you have the death bubbles, and you come back from the dead, so it's not...not necromancy adjacent. Like, if Lyra is a healer type, you'd be a combat type."

She shudders. She can't help herself.

"Not that you have to fight," he hastily adds, obviously seeing that reaction. "Just figuring you out."

"Also pretty sure Mel absolutely does not want me to have any more abilities than I already have," she points out, and he nods, giving her that one. "If I ask him for training, he will say no."

"And probably punch me for telling you to ask. Do it, it'll be funny."

"If it was possible and I could have none of this bullshit, I would," she informs him, and his face twists for one brief second, before his mask snaps back on. "But I just get this restlessness and magic that doesn't cooperate and...creeping death powers. It's not fun."

She takes a deep breath, trying desperately to tamp down her temper, and he says nothing, letting her breathe and get herself under control.

It takes longer than she would like, and they circle back towards the giant squat building. But when he's holding the door open for her and Izzy, there's something calmer inside of her.

12

After a few days of skirting around each other, Terese finds herself staring up at the ceiling of the library in the middle of the night, at the dead runes scrawled well beyond her reach.

The little nightlight rune glows merrily, like all it had needed was her touch.

Izzy snores on the rug next to the couch, her little doggie huffs filling the room.

The paint in her tunnel bothers her, like an itch beneath her skin. She doesn't know how the magic determines some place is safe; she doesn't know the reasoning, but the fact that someone obviously broke it disquiets her.

"I'm not going to get any sleep, am I?" she whispers aloud to the room, and Izzy doesn't budge.

Slowly, she pushes herself up to sitting and the rune grows brighter, like it could tell her intentions.

The previous demon didn't let her sleep at all, rendering her chronically conscious throughout all of it, and even now, sometimes her brain forgets how to sleep. Forgets that she's not currently under attack, forgets that there's not a big demon presence inside of her stopping her from falling asleep.

It happens less, the longer she's been unpossessed, but it's still fucking annoying, especially because she can't completely blame it on the demon.

Careful not to wake Izzy, she slips her feet into her shoes, then pads out of the library. She hadn't been locked in; if they get upset with her she could always just say she's going to get some food or something.

Or something.

Wordlessly, she trails her hand along the long corridor, and the runes flare to life in her wake. Runes for comfort, for warmth, for a bit of light. Runes Alette should have repaired, or Axel, or the Necromancer, and it sticks out in her mind that they hadn't.

She pilfers a bag of chips from the kitchen, but the restlessness just seeps deeper into her bones. Her magic doesn't want to leave, doesn't want to go somewhere else, but the buzzing in her blood does.

Somewhere deep in the recesses of her brain, there's a dim memory of her pacing a pattern in the ratty carpet of a small house, and a voice telling her to walk it out, but no matter how much she pokes at it, it gives her no other context. Just suggests that she's always been like this, always needed to move around and walk around.

Her steps take her to the grand ballroom with the giant mahogany doors, and she pushes them open, just to stand inside in the darkness for a few moments. It still reeks of a toxic magic, like too much antiseptic, like someone upended a bucket of bleach on the carpet and didn't let it air out.

It's unpleasant, and she doesn't know why any magician wouldn't have changed it yet.

So she leaves, lets the doors close behind her with a click, and continues pacing along.

She passes Axel's apartment, and no light seeps out from underneath the door. Probably asleep, like a normal person. She could try to text him, try to text one of the others, but she doesn't know if they'd welcome the interruption from an insomniac like her.

In times like this, she had usually aimed for the dog park, with the suburban sprawl around it and the always open convenience stores and coffee shops. Places where she could walk to and find other humans, see other people just as awake as she is.

Runes glow bright underneath her fingertips, flaring up at her touch. If she wanted to, if given the opportunity, she could bring this entire place back, restore it to whatever glory it previously had.

If they even wanted that.

The carpeted hallway slopes downwards, and she walks by a room that sparks brightly of necromancer magic. Like the Necromancer had experimented in that room.

She avoids it.

Instead, in the seemingly never-ending hallway, a bit of light peeks around a corner, the yellow sodium glow of a lightbulb, not a rune.

Her footsteps still.

She doesn't know who else could be here. Even if she's seen no one else, that means nothing, she's only been to a fraction of the sprawling headquarters.

If they wanted to keep her a secret, they most likely would have told her.

Her curiosity gets the best of her, and slowly, she moves forward, as if she could grant her footfalls silence as she turns the corner.

Nearby, there's a door cracked open, light pouring from it like mist upon the water. There's no noise besides a mechanical clacking, as if someone's messing with a screwdriver.

Terese exhales, as if breathing out could calm the sudden pounding of her heart. She's not supposed to be doing this, not supposed to be still in a hallway, listening to the tiniest of sounds from an unknown room.

Despite that, she pushes herself forward, into the warm glow of the light, until she can see through the crack in the door.

Inside is a controlled detonation of mechanical chaos: there's a grid taped onto the padded floor and each section has a separate bit of machinery, there's a wall full of screwdrivers and wrenches and tools all neatly categorized, and in the middle of the floor sits Axel.

His back is to her, but she thinks she could recognize the curls in his hair anywhere. He's messing with something in his hands, the source of the clacking noise, but the line of his shoulders is tense.

"Are you okay?" Terese blurts out before she can stop herself.

He jerks, dropping the screwdriver, then turns to look at the door.

"Why are you awake?" he asks, and he has a magnifying loupe over one eye with a little flashlight attached. "It's like two AM."

He didn't banish her away, so she leans against the door-frame, even though she doesn't have a good answer for that. "Sometimes I don't sleep."

He flicks up the loupe to rub his eyes before peering at her. "Of course you don't."

"What are you doing?" Terese asks, sitting down so she's

at the doorjamb, ready to leave in case asked. There are no runes in the room, but she'd hardly call it devoid of magic. Instead, the magic seeps softly from the items, old, like they hadn't been touched in too long.

Which is bullshit, because there's one in Axel's hand right then.

There's even a full car engine in the room, neatly in its place in the grid, and it too weakly glows.

"Fixing things," he says, almost surly, holding up the item. It's halfway between the old bluetooth headphones— she doesn't know why she thought of that—and the ear protection from a baseball helmet, and the magic from it is thin. Reedy.

But familiar. It has Axel's own brand of alchemy all over it, tasting the same as the explosions he lobbed at her during the possession.

His eyes are red, like he's the one that needs to sleep instead.

She's not about to tell him to use magic, not after how the discussion earlier went, but it seems like it would be an easy fix.

"Then why are you upset?" she asks, even though it's a horribly invasive question to ask. But the words are pulled out of her, like something just as horrible would happen if she didn't ask.

He pauses long enough to give her an evaluating look, then shrugs.

"It's not working too well," he says, gingerly setting it on the padded ground. "Why don't you sleep 'sometimes'?"

It's her turn to shrug. "I don't think I ever slept well," she says, letting her fingertips play with the edge of the padded foam of the room. "Before any demon, before any weirdness, I think I just always...paced around."

"Glad to know not everything about you changed," Axel says, taking off the loupe and setting it next to the earpiece. "It's depressing to think otherwise."

"Yeah," she agrees, because it is. "You?"

He sighs, and for a brief second she fears she over-stepped, but he just runs his hand through his curls, completely messing them up.

"It's a bit weird," he starts, before falling silent, tilting his head up to look at the ceiling. Like the words he means to say are written up there, like he could find guidance.

She trails her fingers on the padded foam. It's rugged, showing its use, as if it's been here as long as the building has. Has been put through a lot of wear, but still functional.

"I don't think you realize how hard we were looking for you," he says, instead of continuing the sentence. "It's been months. And then you just...show up. And you need help." He trails off, and she gets the distinct impression that he's struggling to find his words.

"Zoel knew when I was in his territory," Terese points out, and Axel shuts his eyes in frustration.

"And he and Alette chose not to pursue you," he snaps out. "And never gave me a reason."

It speaks to a rift, one she doesn't fully comprehend, so instead she just nods, as if that could help anything.

He shakes his hands out, as if ridding himself of an impulse, and gives her a smooth-looking smile that does not reach his eyes. "It's a lot to take in."

"If I thought I would get as...warm a reception...I prob-ably would have tried to contact sooner," Terese says, and it feels weak to say, too honest. Too revealing. "But I couldn't imagine a world where I wouldn't be...shot on sight."

He looks at her, sharp. "Is that a joke again?"

"A little."

Axel rubs his face again, like he should really go to sleep, but instead they're having this conversation. "I still don't get exactly how much control you had when you were possessed, or how it happened, or how much to blame you are, but the fact that it seems like none makes all the searching feel real shitty."

She hugs her knees to her chest, weighing on both hands whether she should feel hurt. "I'd hunt me down, too."

"Not helping," he says, but it's without heat. He picks up the earpiece again, starts to fiddle with it, still without magic. "It's just weird, and I don't know what to think, so I'm doing anything I can do to not think." He gives her a sideways grin that she does not buy at all.

She watches him as he pops open a panel on the earpiece, a scowl on his face. He's not using magic. It'd be so easy with magic, and it grows a pit in her stomach, at the thought of what the demon possibly did to him.

What she did to him.

"Did she block your alchemy?" she asks, after the sodium lights buzz on for far too long. "Is that what...is that how I hurt you?"

He shuts his eyes, like he's visibly collecting his patience in order to not snap at her.

"Melekai says I did something, something bad to you," she continues, then desperately wishes she could stop. "And the demon changed your appearance, and I don't remember, and—"

"You didn't block it, you took it away," he interrupts, then rubs his eyes, not looking at her. "You, the demon, whatever."

She takes the moment to look at him, really look at him, find some evidence of that.

"The demon didn't change my appearance. I did, for years, with my alchemy. She took it away." His hand spasms. "My entire life, everything I've ever worked for, gone." He smiles reflexively, and it's not convincing. "But hey, not dead, just useless."

"I don't think so," Terese says, and he snaps his head up to look at her, wounded. "I mean, you don't feel like you have no magic, and if the demon knew how to do that, she would have done that with Dr. Frisse ages ago. First thing, probably."

He just stares at her, his brown eyes wide.

"You still...look, feel, sound, whatever, like you have power," she continues, words falling from her mouth, "so I don't think it's gone, she would have gone around doing that instead of killing people."

"Jesus Christ, just stop," he bursts out. A muscle ticks in his jaw.

She shuts her mouth, staring back down at the edge of the foam, and the silence stretches on, interminable. She can wrack her brain all she wants, but she knows there will not be an answer to how she should respond to him, there will not be a thing she could say that could make it better.

"I could help fix the ear piece," she finally ventures, and he doesn't look up at her. "I think I see where the magic faltered."

Abruptly, he sets the earpiece down on the foam, jerking up to his feet. "Go ahead," he says, then breezes past her, out the door and down the hall.

Which, fair. She would do the same to herself if she was in the same position.

His footsteps fall on the hallway, until the heavy sound disappears, leaving her under the buzzing lights, alone.

She takes a moment to close her eyes and thud her head

against the doorframe. "Smart," she mumbles at the empty room. "Real kind and nice."

Taking care not to step on any other piece of equipment in the grid, she crouches next to the earpiece, poking at it.

It's easy to see where the magic flickers, what it's intended use is, how Axel's alchemy changed it and imbued it. There's an intent, to make it hear things not audible to the unenhanced ear, to hear words spoken by magical beings...

Demons. He had made this so he could hear demons talking.

She rests her fingertip over the delicate wires, over the hard-plastic casing. Probably for when they coordinated with Melekai, before he was human.

It's a smart bit of magic to use such a ubiquitous piece of machinery. Something already designed to pick up signals and translate them to audible noises, and it feels clever.

Most of the alchemy from others she saw while possessed had been...stately. Boring. People obsessed with turning things into gold, turning rocks into things with value, and very little of tweaking something to be more functional.

It must drive him crazy to not be able to do it right now.

Her brain skitters away from the idea that it's a permanent change for him, that she could have—however unwillingly—caused so much damage to change the course of his life so drastically.

So instead she lets her eyes flutter shut and pushes a little bit of power into the earpiece, just enough for the spark of the wires to connect again.

The earpiece gives a loud squawk, startling her, before falling silent, the blue light on the side glowing serenely.

If she took so much away, at the very least, she could repair a few things.

In the grid next to it is a modified pair of glasses, streamlined and tech-y and incredibly nerdy, giving off the same intent as the earpiece.

Obviously to see demons. Though he'd look like an absolute geek wearing them.

The magic is weaker on it, less complete. Like he hadn't quite finished tweaking it near the end. She takes a few moments of puzzling over it, to figure out exactly how the magic connects, before she can bloom the connection back into place.

SHE LEAVES the glasses and earpiece by his door on her way back to the library.

13

S
he wakes up on the floor of the library next to the couch, back aching, and has a split second to stare up at the ceiling and wonder before there's a small knock on her door.

She contemplates getting up, but Izzy's curled up in a ball next to her and she's actually asleep. "Yes?" she calls, resting back on the rug.

Instead of answering, the door clicks open, and Axel pokes his head in, then falters.

She just tilts her head and stares at him, unsure of what he's going to say after the previous night.

"Why are you on the floor?" he blurts out.

"I was asleep?" she answers, and Izzy thumps her tail against the ground at her voice.

"It's...well after noon." Still, Axel steps in, sitting on the over chair across from her and flipping a coin between his fingers. "But why the floor?"

"Wasn't sleeping on the couch, thought it worth the try," she says, and the inside of her mouth is dry, like she slept the entire time with it open, and she makes a face at the taste. "Obviously it worked."

"We can order a bed if you want it," he says, brows still drawn up. "I could bring in a cot, or —"

She pushes herself up to her elbows, and her hair sticks up, hilariously frizzy. "Did you need me?" she asks, hoping to cut off another spiral of him feeling guilty again.

"Alette has some ideas," he says, making a face at her he probably isn't conscious of. "And you weren't replying to texts."

Her phone is on the side table, next to the glowing rune, and she sure as hell didn't hear it.

"Okay, ideas," she says, pressing her palms into her eyes. "Ideas are good."

She swipes the phone off the table, thumbs it open.

THE NERDY ONE (8:21 AM): How experienced are you with Ley Lines? Zoel says that, in theory, you may hide yourself with the use of a minor one.

THE NERDY ONE (8:49 AM): He stresses "if you are careful."

"I don't think Zoel would want me near any major magic lines. I damage them."

"He just wants to get some readings today," Axel says, eyebrows still raised.

"Wait, are they here?" Terese asks, sitting up straighter. "Can we see him—"

"Not yet," Axel interrupts, and her shoulders slump down. "One or two more days, then they'll be in town, but I'll bring Alette's materials."

With that in mind, she hauls herself up, and Izzy huffs. "Are there protections?" she asks, running her hand through her hair in an attempt to get it to cooperate. It doesn't work. "Has he put something there to stop any demons?"

"Zoel also told me to tell you to not hide away in fear," Axel says, and Terese scowls at him. "Said that he thought you'd try to bunker down in one place and refuse to leave."

It's fair, as she had done exactly that for most of the first few weeks after she got unpossessed, but a low blow.

"Survival mechanisms aren't fear," she retorts, then fetches Izzy's leash from where she hung it on a bookshelf.

"He said, and I quote, 'sounds like something someone who is afraid would say'," Axel recites, and she squints at him. "He told me you'd give an excuse."

"And your Alette is dating that," Terese says, grabbing her jacket. "Or sleeping with, or something, I don't know."

"Something like that," he says dryly, but he's still wooden, like he hasn't quite forgiven her for her intrusive questions the night before. "It's about an hour's drive."

THEY GET about three miles onto the freeway before Terese has to close her eyes to stop herself from spiraling into a panic attack.

"Which Line are we going to?" she asks, keeping her eyes shut, the slow rumble of the Mustang helping.

"Right, because you know all of them," he says.

She cracks an eye open to look at him, but he's watching the road. "Probably not all of them," she says. "I have no delusions of omnipotence."

"Yeah or else you wouldn't ask so many questions."

It stings a bit, so she closes her eyes again and lets herself drift off.

It's not true sleep, not really, but she springs back to awareness when the Mustang pulls into a park, the slow vibrations ceasing.

Axel doesn't even look at her as he gets out of the car in one smooth motion, so Terese takes a moment to blink away the nap from her eyes.

They're in a parking lot, the asphalt broken and scarred, next to a crumbling building with dead concrete and exposed rebar.

She's been here before.

"Really?" she asks, swinging out of the car and leaning against the roof. "The gas station?" It smells damp in the drizzle, like molded concrete dust.

Slow, Izzy climbs out of the car, and Terese takes the moment to clip on the leash.

"Zoel wanted a line they've cleaned up," Axel says, shielding his face from the drizzle. "I wanted to take you someplace where if this goes weird, you're not going to cause any additional property damage."

"Thanks," Terese says, and Izzy shies away from the pile of concrete, like she can sense the demon in it.

The building is half-rotted away, like whatever magic had been poured into it soured the very foundation, and a few spare sparks of unhappy magic crackle over the exposed edges. It tastes foul in the back of Terese's throat, acrid.

"Alette cleaned this one," Terese says, and his face twitches, like he already knew that. "She's gotten better."

Instead of answering, Axel pops open his trunk, pulling out a military grade bag, then—

Fits the glasses she repaired onto his face.

They are incredibly geeky, even beyond what she had thought when holding them, transforming the usually handsome Axel to someone who would be more at home at an engineering college.

He looks instantly younger.

"Wow," she says, before she can stop herself.

"What?" he protests, then looks past her at the rebar. "Oh, that's what they meant by sparks."

"They work that well?" Terese drifts closer to him, peering at the glasses. "I didn't think they'd show all magic, just demon-y things."

"Demon-y things," he deadpans.

Magic flickers across the glass, faster than she can track, but it doesn't seem to faze him. The few drops of drizzle that land on the glass sizzle off.

"So anyone, regardless of how magical they are, could see through those?" Terese asks, almost reaching a hand up to touch the glass but stopping herself before she gets too weird.

"That was the idea," Axel says, adjusting them on his face. "You got to me before I could finish them."

"And Alette...just didn't finish them?" She squints at the magic across the lens. "It should've been easy for her, she seems very competent."

He sighs, put upon, and Terese makes herself step away, get out of his personal space. "She's not tech-y," he says, instead. "I tried to explain to her, she didn't follow. Zoel's magic doesn't work like that. Lyra has no clue about any magical theory, and Mel scoffed."

She stares at him, looking past the glasses to his brown eyes.

"So something that could've actively helped you these last...however many months...and they just said no?" she scoffs.

"It's not like you asked for help," he retorts, then shakes his head. "Not the point."

Her estimation of Alette drops, but still, she turns back to the sparks and the rebar, evaluating.

There's the obvious crater where the demon had tried

her death bubble on the Necromancer etched into the tile, though covered in moss and dust and mist. There's broken glass everywhere, rusted out chunks of metal that once were shelves, and the bare remains of what used to be walls.

Izzy flicks her ears back, and Terese hands Axel her leash.

"She shouldn't walk in there, it's bad for her paws," Terese says.

Izzy gives her such a betrayed look, crouching down and tucking her tail between her legs.

"Yeah, I know," Terese says, crouching in front of her dog and scratching under her chin. "Here." She offers Izzy a treat she had squirreled into her pocket before leaving.

"Didn't feed yourself but took the time to get treats for your dog," Axel grumbles, but all his attention is on the sparks, his eyes alight.

Unless something big happened, this had to be the first glimpse of magic he's had since she —the demon—took it away.

"She has more anxiety than me," Terese says, and he snorts. "What, she does."

"How many panic attacks have you had this last week?" Still, he reaches down to give Izzy a pat on the head, to which Izzy studiously ignores.

"Bit close to the Necromancer's house for me to be doing magic, don't you think?" she asks, scowling at the very visual reminder of the demon's attempts. Her hair slicks to her head in the rain unpleasantly.

"They're not home," Axel replies, digging in the military bag and unrolling a strip of spell weavers' linen.

Terese sticks out her arm automatically, and Axel rolls his eyes before wrapping it around her wrist.

"I see you know how this works already," he grumbles,

loosely tying the linen on with some string. "Alette swears she'll be able to figure stuff out from this."

"I'd believe it," Terese says, flexing her wrist and watching the whisper-light linen shift against her skin. "She wove raw Ley Line into one of these, that's not exactly an easy feat to pull off."

"Yeah, she's leveled up a bit lately," he says, and again, there's a bite of heat behind his voice, and now Terese agrees with it.

Terese shakes her head to banish the thought—it wouldn't exactly be smart to be pissed off at one of the magicians trying to help her—then offers the sparks a critical eye.

"The demon was insanely stupid here," she offers. "Not that she was ever terribly smart, but she looked at the Necromancer with all of Melekai's claws in her and thought it was an acceptable risk."

Instead of answering, Axel just re-shoulders the military-grade bag and nods for her to go forward.

So she takes the step, into the vague remnants of the sparks, where she once held down the Necromancer and tried to kill her.

The cracked tile clinks underneath her boots.

"Alette's going to ask you all sorts of questions about how conscious you were," he warns, eyes flickering with the glasses, as a spark snaps at her ankle.

Izzy whines.

"Easy, I was conscious," Terese says. "It's okay, puppy, I'm okay."

"Puppy," Axel marvels.

"Every dog is a puppy," she says, crouching down and resting her hand against the dead rebar.

Another spark tickles against her palm, light and frothy, before circling her wrist and vanishing into the linen strip.

Even as grumpy as she may feel towards her, Alette clearly prepped the linen to do exactly what it's doing.

"She wanted to know if it's hurting," Axel says. "The more descriptive you are now, the less you'll have to answer later."

"It definitely doesn't hurt," Terese says, and there are still a few pennies on the ground, from where the demon had exploded the till.

Another spark winds its way around her ankle, then races up to her wrist, almost playful.

"That's good. It gave Alette a concussion the first time she went in," Axel says.

"Concussions aren't that big of a deal," Terese points out. "Give me a day and I'll be fine."

For a split second his lip twitches, like he wants to smile but doesn't want to give her the credit, which makes her want to dig her heels in, keep quipping at him, until the wooden stiffness between them is gone.

It's wholly irrational, so instead she just nudges a penny off a bit of tile, as if that could release the sparks, but there's no elucidation in the bits of mold and rubble.

"How long do you need me here?" Terese asks, lifting her eyes to look at anything but him. "Did she give a set time?"

"Not particularly, but now that we can at least confirm that you aren't gonna be thrown around, try some magic." He adjusts the glasses, fingers tapping nervously against the frames.

Which makes sense. He hasn't seen any of her magical bullshit since he lost his powers. Trauma and all that.

"You can take them off, if you want," Terese offers, and he scowls.

"Why would I want that?" he retorts.

Deep in the remnants of the building, something shifts, drawing Terese's attention like a hook in the cheek.

"Did you do something?" he asks, puzzled, and her eyes snap to him. "I saw a spark, but then nothing, and—"

Terese twists to look behind her, a glimmer of light or something, then.

Then.

Izzy raises her head and howls.

With a flash of something she feels in her chest more than sees, on the other edge of the perfect circle of broken tile and crumbling rebar, appears Daniil.

His face is the same, still the hapless handsome businessman with a pocket knife tucked in his belt, and flecks of blood still decorate his collar, now brownish from age, and he curves up an eyebrow at her.

And Axel's right there, holding Izzy's leash tightly.

And she has a choice, in this crystalline moment. She can get away, teleport herself away so fast Daniil cannot follow.

But leave Axel and Izzy behind.

"Fuck," Terese blurts out. With the magic still in her grasp, she drives a wedge into the ground between her and the two of them, sending them tumbling back and away, and—

"Enough of that," Daniil says, and the magic withers away from her hands. Like she never had any to begin with.

She reaches towards something, anything, but there's nothing there.

Izzy barks, muted by whatever barrier she put up, and there's a wordless noise of confusion and pain from Axel.

"Get out of here," she says, not willing to take her eyes off of Daniil, who's standing so still.

He's watching her just as intently. Not moving, just there. Paying no attention to Axel, no attention to Izzy, just her.

And horror wells inside her, bubbling up from her stomach and encircling her throat. Because now she can't just get away, she has to make sure they get away, make sure they leave, all without alerting Daniil, and—

Daniil takes a step closer to her, and she flinches back, her spine hitting an iron wall of power.

"I found such marvelous things," Daniil says, and his voice is still horrifically normal, horrifically human, and terror drips down her back with the rain. "The closer I looked, the more signs of you, spread across the globe."

Out of the corner of her eye, movement. Izzy scrabbling along the leash, lunging, and Axel scrambling away, deeper within the wrecked Buggees.

"Evidence of you snuck in between stones in a cave, traces of your power, death still crawling beneath the soil, as clear as day coming from you."

He takes another step, and her feet are frozen to the ground, like the very broken tile and concrete have cluttered over her and grown.

"And here you are, experimenting with spell weaving, like you have to stoop that low, Terese." He reaches out, snagging his fingertips against the linen strip, unraveling it from her wrist until it flutters to the wet ground.

She cringes away, as far as she can, but it's not far enough.

He draws the hand up her arm, and his skin is warm. Like a normal human, like the body he's in still breathes.

He hasn't possessed her yet, hasn't tried to peel open her

mind, which means he hasn't figured it out yet, so she swallows down her fear.

"You don't want me," she says, and her voice breaks, right in the middle. "You don't want me, you'll go crazy, I'm not worth it."

His eyes are light, like this is fun. "Someone else tried," he says. "They tried with you and only half succeeded."

Deliberately, watching her face like he could decipher a mystery, he steps closer, well within her personal bubble, until there's only him and an overwhelming nausea of demonic...stuff. Nature. Power. Whatever.

Izzy barks, a horrific snarling sound, and any moment now, he's going to turn, going to look at them.

She doesn't think she can dissuade him, but all she needs is enough time for them to get away.

The body in front of her has hazel eyes, and the lines around them suggest he smiled a lot.

"Care to tell me what the other one did wrong?" Daniil asks, like he's asking her for a recommendation for a restaurant. "Make this a lot less painful for both of us."

"She thought she could," Terese says, voice shaky. "It's not possible, not without pain."

"To take a living vessel, maybe."

He thinks he can kill her.

Abruptly, she relaxes, outside of her control, her spine unwinding with a snap.

She can't run, she can't do anything, so she stands there, arms loose, eyes refusing to focus on anything. Like she's a passive participant in the conversation, observing from over her own shoulder, unable to say or do anything that could change the outcome.

Izzy howls.

"Now, naturally, after last time you should be dead, or

yelling gibberish in a hospital, with what you did to your brains." He knocks his fist against her forehead. "The fact that you're not says something truly, truly interesting."

She opens her mouth to respond, but no words come out.

He's going to kill her, he's not going to succeed, and then he'll try again.

There're wisps of magic, the sparks crackling back over the rebar and concrete, but he pays them no interest.

One flicks around her ankle, a promise of something, but not enough. She can see it's not enough, just how she can see Daniil staring at her, waiting for a response, like she can see the mist around them both and the wreckage of the gas station and how she should fight, she should scratch and claw and something, but her arms hang loosely and her gaze lilts to the side.

"What are you looking at?" Daniil asks, a frown settling over his face. "You should only look at me."

The last demon had hated it too, when attention drifted away, but Terese's mind shies away from it, shies away from even thinking of that time.

There had been so much adrenaline before, and now she feels nothing.

Faster than a whip, he lashes out, grabbing her by the chin and wedging her up on the wall, slamming her back against the brilliant fiery pain.

"You should only look at me."

She drags her eyes up to Daniil's, like they're heavy, heavy burdens for her to carry.

She can't see Izzy from this angle, can't see Axel, can't see the car, and her ears are too full of the magic and the crackle of sparks for her to tell if they drove away. Or if Izzy's still barking.

She hopes they're gone.

"What's wrong with you?" Daniil breathes, then, with a shake, snaps her neck.

Pain shocks its way down her back, spiraling down her body and she gasps; she tries to gasp, but nothing happens, nothing connects, and—

Black crowds into her vision, faster than it should.

She's had her neck snapped before, it's not fun, but this is different, there's something different, she can still feel his fingers digging into her chin like a brand.

Let's try it this way, he whispers, so only she can hear.

He crowds his way into her brain, slicing through any defenses she could have, in those moments where her blood suffocates itself and her brain sends signals nothing can receive. As her legs give out and her arms dangle, as her eyes slump, as the words she wants to scream drain away.

Dimly, so dim as if it's far away, she can hear yelling. Someone is yelling, and she can't tell who.

Don't pay attention to them, Daniil's voice whispers into her mind, catching her waning consciousness and dragging it back, until all she can feel is the prodding into her brain. Just the ghostly fingertips, poking and peeling away everything that makes her herself.

She tries to mouth something, anything, but her lips don't move, black seeping into her vision. Her eyes are still open, they're staring up at the gray mist in the sky, but she can't focus, she can't—

No, you don't get to fall asleep.

She's dead, after all this time she knows how to tell when she's dead, but her awareness doesn't go away, keeping her there, like he has her consciousness in his fist.

I want you to feel this.

Terror jolts into her once more, but she can't move, she

can't breathe, all she can do is lay there crumpled against the fractured tile.

He roots around in her mind, leafing through her experiences and her knowledge like it's a book to be read.

Pain wracks its way down her body, and she can't move, she can't react, she can't flinch, but it gives him pause.

Is that what you meant, he asks, honestly curious. The curiosity bleeds between her mind and his, twisting in her emotions. *This pain?*

"No," she moans, her lips moving despite the air not passing through her lungs.

It doesn't take long to recover from a snapped neck. Last time she was back and conscious—if disoriented and unable to walk for a day or so—within a few minutes.

I don't think you'll get that long.

She gasps, the air dragging up and across her back, blossoming across her nerves and her skin and her throat, as with a snap her spinal column connects again.

He looms over her again, suddenly out of her mind, but his eyes are intent.

"You are such a puzzle," he says, his fingers playing over her chin, and every sensation is a fire against her, bright angry lines of agony.

He tilts her head up, and the still-healing bones grind together, and all she can do is breathe. Tears leak out of her eyes, but she can barely blink, so they just blur her vision until he warps and fuzzes.

Another spark of magic nestles its way against her arm, where she lays flopped on the concrete.

His hand on her chin gentles to almost a caress, and it's worse, much worse, than just holding her in place. He runs his fingers over her jaw, like an artist evaluating a piece for a sculpture. The pads of his fingertips whisper light against her skin, her cheeks, before dipping into her still open lips.

If she could move, she would bite down, but he trails the hand down the front of her neck instead, over the sharp pain of the break and rests his fingertips against her clavicle.

"Taking you apart will be fun."

A new sort of horror bubbles up, twisting and consuming her.

He turns her chin to the side, evaluating, and her eyes land deeper in the Buggees.

On Axel and Izzy.

They're trapped, and Izzy huddles behind Axel, ears back and quivering. If they could get over the partially broken wall, then skirt around without Daniil seeing them, then maybe —

Axel's still wearing the glasses, his eyes wide behind the flashing magic, and he starts when she looks at him. His mouth forms words, but there's nothing reaching her ears.

He needs to run, but all she can do is blink, slow, at him, her vision blurring. He's reaching into the bag, as if there's something he can do.

Still over her, Daniil touches the space right behind her ear, where her brains melted the last time, then prods it, hard.

Terese gasps, her blood pumping again, and it hurts. It fucking hurts to be conscious through this, and black crowds around her sight before abruptly clearing again.

A second spark, larger than the other, crackles into her hand, and Daniil hesitates, just a moment, and Terese uses the only motion she can make, a twitching of her fist, to shred the magic apart, turn it on herself.

The bubble detonates around her, popping her ears, and the tile stirs around her, already abused by this once before.

It's small, barely anything, but the demon in front of her recoils, just enough to be noticeable. His fingers fall away from her skin and it's a blessed, blessed relief.

"You shouldn't be able to do that," he says, and he's still within her bubble, the golden threads shining in his hair. "You should be whimpering on the ground."

She is, but he's ignoring the small noises wrenched from her throat.

He crouches next to her, and he's blocking the view of Axel and Izzy, and she can no longer see them.

There's a smile curling over his lips.

"How about this," he starts, then, with a vicious, violent movement, slams his elbow down on her temple, rocketing her into black —

— and then immediately back out of it, hauling her up by her chin, bones grating against each other in her neck, severing her spinal cord once more, peeling her mind open again, and —

With a bang so loud she hears it through her teeth, Daniil's head snaps back, black blood spraying over her.

He drops her, and she clatters to the ground, pain so sharp it's almost hope.

The pressure against her mind evaporates, shocking in its sudden lack, as her cheek rests on the cold tile. She's not breathing, not at the moment, consciousness buoyed above any darkness.

Another bang, vibrating through the floor, and black blood blossoms on the body in front of her, a gunshot punching a hole straight through the cheap white shirt.

Her head lolls to the side, and Izzy cowers behind Axel, who stands there, the bespelled gun in one hand and the leash in the other, aiming just how he did when he shot her in that tunnel all those months ago.

Daniil looks down at her, blood trickling down his face, then back up at Axel, and, in one quick moment she recognizes as cowardice from practically every other demon, disappears.

With a crash, the wall he slammed up falls, and the bubble around Terese dissipates, pebbles falling around her almost like an exhale.

She tries to drag in a breath, but nothing moves, her brain firing off in the wrong direction. Her magic is suddenly back against her chest and thrumming with panic. Izzy dashes over to her, ears back, dragging Axel by the leash.

Her lips part, somehow, but no air passes, as Izzy thrusts her snout into her hand and with a puff of air and the crunch of dried grass, they're no longer at the Buggees.

14

"What the fuck?"

She can't react, nothing's working, nothing's moving. Her heart's not beating, her lungs aren't drawing air, her nerves firing off in every direction, alternating her between crawling cold and fiery heat.

Hands pull her up, the motion scraping the bones in her neck together, and she tries, she really does, but can't stop her head from drooping over to one side.

"Terese." In front of her, face blurring into view, is Axel, and her heart gives a single thud at the sight of him. Not enough to actually start again, but something. "Terese, can you hear me?"

She can blink, somehow, so she does.

He looks away from her, and her eyes can barely track the motion.

"Where are we, what do I do, are you okay, what—"

Izzy whines, high pitched, and presses against her side, a mass of trembling fur, but she's here, she's safe. The demon didn't get to Izzy, and—

She gasps, her lungs flexing in one long, brilliant spasm of pain, and Axel's hands grip her arms tight.

She's sitting, her legs crumbled underneath her, and they're in the little pavilion at the dog park in Southern California. Sun streams down around them, and dogs bark happily on the edge of her hearing.

"Okay, okay, uh, that's good, I think. Where are we?"

His words swim around her, and whatever blow to the head Daniil gave her must be worse than she thinks.

She shuts her eyes, as if she could will herself into falling unconscious, until the worst of all of this is done, but her heart pounds, sudden and erratic, so loud it drowns out anything from her ears.

"Hey, no, don't pass out," Axel says, and she opens her eyes again out of sheer protest. He's crouched next to her, the military surplus bag at his feet. "Okay, uh, blink twice if you understand me?"

She strongly considers not out of stubbornness, but blinks twice. A shudder makes its way down her back, crawling in her skin, and the hands on her arms loosen.

She should apologize to him. While she still has the chance.

Axel sits down, cross-legged, in front of her, and he still has those ridiculous glasses on, though the runes stay motionless on the glass. Inert, like they're just waiting for something severe enough to kick back up.

"Okay, blink once for no, two for yes." This is a farce. It's a farce and she can't believe this. "Do you need medical help?"

She blinks hard once.

"That's good, I think."

Her lungs flex again, and she gasps a big gulping breath,

and pins of pain spiral down her body, like it's not quite ready for her to be alive yet.

Being unconscious for this is far better.

"Do you know where we are?"

She blinks twice, and her eyes burn, so she shuts them.

"Again, okay, good, uh," his voice trails off, and he's bewildered, she can just tell.

He takes a deep breath, the type that people take when they're scared but trying not to show it, and she hears him rummage in the backpack.

"So you said you need time, before," he starts, before scooting himself until he's sitting next to her. "So...we wait?"

She opens her eyes to blink twice at him, and he's watching her.

"Okay. We wait."

It's hot out, in this summer in Southern California, and the wind is harsh against Terese's skin, but he unfolds a hoodie from the bag and, carefully, wraps it around her shoulders.

Another shudder spasms through her chest, and the whites of Axel's eyes are fully visible.

From the bag he pulls a bottle of water, a first aid kit, a protein bar, and, somehow, a little travel pillow, the inflatable type that makes Terese immediately think of airplanes. He tucks the pillow in between Terese's shoulder and her head, on the side that wasn't bashed by Daniil.

Her neck creaks, and she's not sure if it's her bones or what, but the weight of her head against the pillow is far less than before.

He tears open an alcohol swab from the first aid kit and gingerly moves aside her hair, each touch blisteringly hot against her skin, before dabbing it on her temple.

She flinches, completely involuntary, but she's moving,

bit by bit. Still not breathing, not fully, and each moment stretches on in suffocating silence.

"Okay, I'm fairly certain you got your neck broken twice, don't be a baby about antiseptic wipes," he says, and she manages to twitch her eyes to look up at him.

His touch is feather light, but somehow it still stings, more than it should.

"I don't know how much time," he says, musing aloud, "but it's probably better to not be in public bleeding from your head if you don't want nosy onlookers."

She knows this, but knows he's saying it way more for his own benefit than hers.

"Also, don't really fancy being accused of murder if someone calls the cops," despite his light words, his fingers tremble, and he takes a moment to steady his hands before wiping away some more blood. A lot more blood than she had thought there would be.

She hadn't even realized that Daniil broke the skin there.

Izzy shuffles herself so she's pressed up closer to Terese, so she has Axel on one side of her and her dog on the other. Braced between them, like the two of them could protect her.

"And it's fucking freaky to have someone just sitting there with blood on—"

With a snap, her spine connects itself again, and she jolts upright with a gasp.

It hurts, it fucking hurts, but she draws in breath after fiery breath, and Axel sits back, eyes wide behind the glasses.

She coughs as her nervous system kicks back in and all the nausea from the pain makes itself known, so she doubles over.

"Okay, does that mean you're back, or—"

She tries to answer, but just coughs again.

Izzy lifts her head, then laboriously climbs to her feet, pushing her nose into Terese's face.

It takes her a few minutes of choking on air before she sits up again, and her entire body shakes at the effort.

"I'm okay," Terese croaks out, and her voice breaks in the middle. "I'm okay."

"Uh, hate to state the obvious, but don't think you are," Axel says, but he helps her lean back against the pavilion wall. "Here."

He holds up the water bottle for her, and there's no way she could drink something, not with the nausea roiling through her.

It fucking hurts.

"I'm usually not..." She waves her hand, nebulous, and each motion sends pinpricks of sensation down her entire self. "Conscious for this."

He blanches, before setting the bottle down in easy reach, and sits back against the pavilion as well. He's quiet for a few minutes, as Terese closes her eyes and focuses on pulling down air and, bit by bit, quelling the nausea that threatens to upend her.

"Where are we?" he asks finally, and there's a quiver of fear in his voice, and she hates she did that to him.

"California," she says, blinking her eyes open and looking out at the dog park. "One of the safety spots."

"Right, California, never teleported there before," he says, too fast. "Easy teleport back or do I need to look into plane tickets?"

She ignores him for a few seconds, long enough to clench her hand into a fist, then unclenches it, testing the motions.

"I need some time first," she says, her voice cracking and wheezy. "A few hours, something—"

"Right, yes, take what you need, got it," he rambles. "Few hours, not that bad, I always wanted to go to uh"— he checks his phone, obviously checking a map —"Altadena?"

He's scared, he's terrified, and now that she's not covered in blood, he starts to shake, tapping his fingers against the side of his leg like that could save him.

"Always wanted to shoot a demon with an untested piece of weaponry and then get teleported, that was a trip."

She makes herself take a deep breath, and pain still swirls in her stomach and her neck. Carefully, she prods the wound on the side of her head, and black sparks against her vision at her touch.

"Yeah, there're bits of your skull visible," he says, still too fast, his words tripping on themselves on their way out of his mouth. "There's too much blood, your neck was all wonky, and I'm in fucking California." He drags his own hands through his hair, and there're flecks of blood on his skin. "I saw a demon, and —"

With a huff, Izzy stands again, then shoves her nose into Axel's face with the air of someone fed up.

Axel's mouth closes with a click and, hands still shaking, he gently pets Izzy's head.

"Stop panicking," Terese says, with a little more strength behind it this time. "She'll stop when you stop panicking."

Izzy eyes her, like she can't believe she has to do this, but stands there and lets Axel pet her, until his breathing is a little less frantic.

"Is your dog a therapy dog?" he asks finally, as Izzy shuffles away from him to curl up next to Terese again.

"How would I know?" Terese asks, her mouth bone dry,

but she's not sure she can lift a water bottle yet. "She was abandoned."

She leans her head back against the wall, and her vision swims.

Daniil had tried again. And probably would have succeeded, eventually, after killing her again and again and refusing her the ability to actually not be present for that sort of thing.

She swallows a lump down, and it hurts, forcing its way past the spot he broke her neck.

But now she needs to recover. She can't just sit here for forever in her dread.

"There's a convenience store over there," she starts, and there's no way she can go, no way for her to make herself stand up, not yet. "They have hats that could hide the...the skull pieces."

"Jesus Christ," he says, and Izzy lifts her head with a sigh, like she's going to have to comfort him again and is not in the mood. "Okay, hiding skull pieces, good plan. Anything else?"

He bounds to his feet, all jangling energy.

"Potato chips and something cold?" she asks, her tone lilting up in a way that just reminds her of horrid weakness.

There's no real guarantee that Daniil won't find her here, either.

"You just...you used so much energy, I think you need more than potato chips," he says, but he leans the bag against her, so she can pull from it if she needs, and strides away fast, like the speed could help him not freak out.

Next time Daniil would be prepared, and he would remember that Axel had shot him.

She breathes out hard from her nose, and Izzy shuffles until her head is in Terese's lap.

He would remember and would use it against her. Use the protection of Izzy, use her trying to delay, something, as a tactic.

"Fuck," she mumbles, and the words are mealy against her mouth, and she makes a face.

She's awake way faster than she'd normally be from a head injury, and it fucking sucks. Nausea still holds her in its claws, and shivers still race down her body, sparkling into her toes.

And she scared the shit out of Axel.

A small part of her immediately disagrees with the statement. It's the demon's actions that scared Axel, not her own, but the thought evaporates pretty quickly. Axel, who helped her wipe blood off her head, and who she insulted just the night before by being too intrusive, who's now buying her food. Regardless of whose actions it was, he had been scared because of her.

Her eyes blur together, and Izzy licks her hand.

"I'm okay," she mumbles again, and Izzy's just a dog and shouldn't be able to give her such side eye, but she does. "I'll...I'll be okay. Go play."

Izzy turns and looks out at the dog park, at the distant barking, before back up at Terese.

"No, it's okay, go play," Terese says, with only a bit more conviction. She doesn't know when she'll be able to come here next, and her dog deserves some joy. "I'll be here. Go play. Park."

At that word, Izzy's ears perk up, and she stands, shoving her nose into Terese's face once more, before ambling off into the grass and dust.

Leaving Terese sitting there once more, eyes stinging, everything awful and painful, but somehow miraculously unpossessed and alive. She doesn't know if her luck will hold.

Still, if she leans her head against the tiny travel pillow, she can see Izzy play with another dog her size, and her heart beats—if still erratically—and the sun is warm against her face.

She's still shuddering, her body kicking bits and pieces of it back into functioning, and being awake for it blows, but she blinks through the tears and just hugs the hoodie closer to her shoulders.

After not very much time at all, she sees Axel cross the street from the convenience store, juggling two large plastic bags in his hands, talking fast on the phone. Which makes sense, that he'd check in with the others at how disastrous their attempt at measuring things was.

Thank god that the Necromancer and Melekai were nowhere near.

Axel has to hang up the phone in order to open the gate back up to the dog park, and a few dogs bounce over to him before dashing away again.

"Still amused that a dog park is a safety spot," he says, once he drops the too-full plastic bags. "Did you find it before or after Izzy?"

"Before," she croaks out, then makes a face at her voice.

"Yeah, here." He sits, cross-legged, next to her, pulling out a ginger ale soda from the bag, and condensation glistens on the plastic container. "I didn't know if by cold you meant soda or..." From the bag, he reveals a small container of ice cream with a flourish, then a plastic spoon.

"I meant soda," she says, strangely touched, before carefully opening the ginger ale and taking a cautious sip.

It bubbles in her stomach, but after a few seconds of

waiting, it does nothing else, so she takes the proffered spoon.

As if waiting for that motion, he pulls out two large bags of chips and a container of nacho cheese, then a giant chunk of beef jerky, two more water bottles, a bag of assorted candy, and a prepackaged and sad looking sandwich.

"From what I could tell"—he taps the glasses folded up in his pocket—"coming back from the dead takes a lot out of you."

She's not sure if it's a joke, but she tears the plastic off of the ice cream container anyway, and he pulls out another spoon from the bag.

The short walk and solving a problem clearly did him good, as there's less jarring anxiety rolling off of him in waves.

"I'm sorry for prying last night," she says, after a few silent moments of eating ice cream in the summer sun. "I shouldn't have."

His face shutters briefly before he sighs, shaking out his hands and relaxing more against the pavilion wall. "I probably shouldn't have snapped at you."

"Eh," she says, taking another sip of ginger ale, and she's going to need to keep it everywhere if it does this good of a job with the nausea. "I kinda deserved it."

He rolls his eyes, and it's so close to the friendly motions he had with Melekai and Lyra that her chest aches. "Thanks for not leaving me when you teleported, I think."

"I will one hundred percent admit I didn't think about bringing you along," she says, and he cracks a smile at her, "just that I needed to get out of there and I don't do that without Izzy."

"Fair." Silence falls between the two of them, before he opens the bag of chips and the nacho cheese. "So. Demon boy is just as terrifying as Alette said he would be, but also way more cartoony than Melekai ever sounded."

"Cartoony?" she asks. "Didn't notice that."

"I developed the earpiece pretty quick so I could hear Mel when he was still, you know." He waves his hand. "He just always sounded slightly annoyed with everything. This one, Danny, you said? He just sounds like someone trying to be a supervillain, but they don't have a good writing team."

"Daniil," Terese corrects, moderately horrified, but a smile tugs at her lips anyway.

"Yeah, him. Leans heavily into the evil talk." He hands her a chip. "Someone that stereotypical we have to be successful against. Easy."

"Easy," she repeats, dumbfounded.

"The more focused they are on being evil, the less smart they are in their plans," Axel continues, like this is at all a logical conversation and not a blatant ploy to make her feel better. "It's a rule."

"Naturally," she drawls, and takes an offered chip. "Clearly that's how you won against the last one, not sheer luck in finding an actual necromancer." The salt of the chip clashes with the ice cream, but not in a way she terribly minds. "Do you always get ridiculous food at convenience stores?"

"Here," he says, pulling out a neon green baseball cap with an outlandish picture of a cartoon bird on it. "Hide the skull bits."

She fits it over her head, and it smarts against the wound, but she blinks through the ensuing wave of nausea and sips the ginger ale instead.

"That looks ridiculous on you," he says, but it's friendly, almost teasing, though his eyes are sharp. Like he's waiting for a critical piece of information from her.

"I'll be okay," she says, almost impulsively, though a thread of shame worms its way through her. "It just...I take a bit."

He doesn't immediately react, instead taking a few more bites from the ice cream, mulling over his words.

"I don't know what you expect from yourself," he starts, "but you literally got your neck broken and your head bashed in, and now you're talking and eating food. It's pretty freaky."

He's right, so she just looks out at the dog park, where Izzy's flopped over into a patch of dust, rolling around on her back and getting it all in her fur. A shiver winds its way down her back, but it's almost an afterthought, some remnant of her spine still connecting.

"Handy, I guess, if you're dealing with a homicidal demon, to just bounce back," he continues, giving her another chip, then digging into the bag of candy himself. "You got that hurt and you still had enough of a mind to save my life. Do I want to be home right now? Very much so. Would I rather wait it out and eat the finest of gas station foods until it's safe to do so? Absolutely."

Sensation blossoms into her feet again, and she extends her legs, flexing her ankles in her boots with a grimace.

"Usually when I break my neck, I am conscious pretty quickly, but it takes me a while before I can do anything."

"The fact that you have a usually really creeps me out." He settles back deeper against the pavilion, until they're shoulder to shoulder, and if she leans a little more, she could tilt her head against him. "I let everyone know what happened, where we are. Alette will have many questions, I think Mel will as well, and Lyra wants to know if you're okay. I told her I could see parts of your brain."

"Can't wait," she says, then shuts her eyes against a

shudder of pain spiraling down her legs. "I would much rather sleep through this."

"I have Advil in my bag," he suggests. "Though I'm not sure it'd do anything to help skull bashing and neck snapping."

"Somehow I doubt it," she manages, and her voice is reedy. "The previous demon once tried a shit ton of morphine, it worked for like an hour then we got a hangover and withdrawals."

"Horrifying," he says, like he's commenting on the weather.

The ice cream and nacho chips lay heavy in her stomach, but not unpleasantly so, as the sun slowly sets over the dog park and Izzy flops back over to them. It's a companionable silence, where Axel's just idly texting on his phone and she can let her eyes unfocus out onto the dying grass of the dog park.

It's almost, almost, peaceful, and before she realizes it, her eyes have slipped shut and she falls asleep.

15

Terese awakens with a jolt, and it's fully dark out, the only light from the street lamps and the neon signs in the window of the convenience store.

Izzy's fast asleep, her head on Terese's lap, snoring and twitching in dreams, and Axel's eyes are closed, his head tilted back against the wood of the pavilion. The rest of the ice cream is melted in its container. His legs are stretched out, long in their skinny jeans, and there's a sprinkling of freckles across his nose, like the sun brought them out, barely illuminated in the neon from the store.

She's certain he didn't have those before, when he changed his appearance, but is glad to see them now.

It's quiet. It's so perfectly quiet that she can hear the brief breeze in the dead grass. Her temple hurts, now a dull pounding that she can feel in her teeth and less of the all-encompassing pain of before.

She lifts her head from where it had rested half on the travel pillow and half on Axel's shoulder, and tests out her hand, closing and folding all of her fingers before extending them again.

They all work, with no prickles or hesitations.

Izzy lifts her head, blinking slowly at Terese, so Terese scratches her behind her ears, like she's clearly begging for.

"You hungry, girl?" Terese whispers, and Izzy thumps her tail, then looks hopefully out at the coffee shop, green sign barely visible from the park.

Terror immediately shuts Terese's throat at the idea of leaving the safety of the fenced area, so she shakes her head.

"I didn't think there was anything I bought that'd be good to feed her, sorry," Axel says, and she jumps.

He's watching her with those brown eyes underneath his lashes, obviously not asleep at all.

"And by the time I realized it, you were asleep, and I thought it'd be better to let you than leave you alone without warning." He stretches his arms over his head, a nice, long, easy motion, like he commonly sits still for hours in a dusty dog park after closing.

"I think I can teleport now," she says, and her mouth is dry, but it's the normal dryness of sleep, so she takes a sip of the now-flat ginger ale. "I'm glad I could sleep, I thought..."

"What, that he took that for forever?" Axel says, lazily gathering the remaining snacks into a leftover plastic bag. "I doubt it."

She caps the ginger ale, adds it to the bag, and Izzy laboriously climbs to her feet, still pointing her snout at the coffee shop.

"If I get possessed, shoot me with that gun," Terese says, and Axel's eyes are wide again. "I mean, obviously I won't die, it's okay."

"There are...so many things wrong with that," he says, but settles back into the pavilion.

"I mean, don't get trigger-happy, but even if you suspect something, it's not a bad idea."

"One of these days, we're going to have to talk about your self-preservation instinct," Axel says, good natured, and she wrinkles her nose at him.

"Had you ever...teleported before today?" Terese asks, instead of acknowledging how correct he is.

"Nope," he says, with a half-smile, handsome in the shadows of the neon lights. "First time for everything."

"Well, this might take a few attempts to get back to your home," she warns, using the pavilion to haul herself up to her feet. She wobbles substantially less than usual, and she blinks at herself for that, before dismissing it. "I don't so much control which place. It's frustrating."

"I am almost certain Alette will try to teach you." He stands, stretching and popping his back, and his curls are flat. "So we have the park, we have that tunnel, that place in Romania, and..."

"And a boat in the middle of an ocean, but I rarely end up there," she says, clipping on Izzy's leash again. "Mostly it's the tunnel or your headquarters."

"I've been wondering, when did that happen?" Axel asks, and the hairs on her arms raise. "That can't have always been a thing, we absolutely would have found you before."

"When Alette and Zoel dropped the wards, right before the line in Washington broke," she says, then grips Izzy's collar and holds her hand out to him.

He gives her such a blank look that she waves her hand at him for him to take.

"I can't teleport something unless I'm touching it, or something it's touching," she says. "Sorry."

"No, just...you've been teleporting to my front yard for months and we never noticed?" Still, he holds his hand out to her. "How the hell were you that sneaky?"

She ignores him in favor of grabbing his hand and thinking about safety. The nerves in her hands smart, like they aren't fully connected yet and processing everything all wrong.

"Like I said, it may take a few tries."

There's the familiar pull, before her feet land on the rough-hewn stone of the tunnel, and Axel jerks his hand out of hers, then half staggers to the wall, leaning against it.

The paint still adorns the wall, now dried and peeling, still displaying the haunting words.

"You weren't kidding," Axel says, his voice muted underneath her silencing spells.

"It can take up to five or six tries, it's inconvenient," she says, watching as Izzy sniffs at her ruined bag of clothes. "I could aim for one of them, but it just interprets it as the idea of 'safe' and dumps me at random." She readjusts her grip on Izzy's leash, then holds out her hand again.

He raises a finger. "Give me a sec."

She shrugs, using the opportunity to form a fist, then release it, testing out her reflexes. Nothing sparks against her awareness, besides a lingering tingle.

Her legs still hurt, her head still throbs, but she's in far better condition than she should be.

"So we literally shot you here and your magic still thinks it as safe?" Axel says, rapping his knuckles on the stone of the walls. "How do you explain that?"

"I don't." Terese shrugs, nudging one of her ruined bags with the toe of her boot to see if there's anything worth saving. "It didn't take me back here for a few weeks, though."

"Weird." Still, he takes a deep, steeling breath, then holds out his hand. "Okay, let's try this again." His hand is just as blisteringly warm, sending sparks of sensation up her forearm.

Back at the park, in the same place they just left. Izzy perks her ears up, looking over to the coffee shop.

Axel huffs out a laugh, poorly disguised, bouncing on the balls of his feet, as if that could help him regain whatever the teleportation took from him.

She doesn't even bother to warn him before trying again, and finally, they're back underneath the giant spruce tree in the blackberry bramble.

This time, she lets go of Izzy's leash and Axel's hand, and Izzy sniffs around, sedate. Like she's been to the bramble enough lately to not be ecstatic about the fresh smells.

Axel shakes out his hands, and his eyes are still wide. "I'll have to figure out a way to get my car later, won't I?"

"I won't go back there," Terese blurts out.

"Fair enough." They start the slow tromp up to the Headquarters, lit only by the mottled light of the moon. "I'm sure I could get Alette to take me tomorrow. She'll be in town, unless another flight delay happens."

Alette means Zoel, which means someone who actually knows about her strangeness and might shed some insight into how to help. And as much as he is a rather overbearing idealist who protects everyone, he might actually have an idea on how to discourage a demon from his territory.

And as much as he gets comically disappointed at her life choices and how she deals with the vague things she calls emotions, he's pretty damn kind.

"Is she still mad that I killed her?" Terese muses, before catching herself and shutting her eyes in embarrassment. "I mean —"

"Jesus Christ, you're so awkward," he says, but it's light.

Teasing. "Angry? Probably not. Traumatized? Probably. Wants to pry into every detail about you? Certainly."

"She understands I don't even know all the details of me, right?"

"I mean, the entire idea of someone not immediately dissecting themselves to understand every minor aspect of their own psyche is almost certainly foreign to her," he says, as they turn the corner on the long driveway and the squat headquarters comes into view. "But I'd say she probably can guess."

Something inside her pulls her to hesitate, like what is bubbling up could only be told while outside, with the moonlight dappling in his hair and blurring the shadows around them.

"Does she know it was...mostly her aunt? That tied the first demon to me?" At the hitch in her tone, Izzy circles back, shoving her nose in Terese's hand.

Axel looks back at her—he hadn't noticed she stopped —and regards her for a long second, and she doesn't know what he sees in her under the moonlight.

"We...didn't have hard proof," he says, as if he's choosing his words with the finest of care. "We found vague research that suggested it." He shoves his hands in his pockets, and for a long moment he's still, stiller than she thinks she's ever seen him. "We didn't know."

"We—the demon and I—figured that out pretty quickly." His shoulders relax, as if her words calm some sudden fear. "You two would've been absolutely stupid to do some of the shit you did if you knew."

The woods are whisper quiet, barely the hint of a breeze rubbing the branches together.

Finally, he turns away. "Thanks," he says, and probably aims for sarcastic but misses it completely.

They resume the trek up, and even though the shadows are deep and her head is heavy, there's something lighter in her step.

SHE WAKES the next day with a thudding pain in her temple and blood still matted in her hair, so she hunts down a shower right outside one of the experimentation rooms, then jams the neon green hat over her still-wet hair. The clock on her phone reads early afternoon, so she feeds Izzy before attempting to find the kitchen again.

It takes a bit of wandering, with the labyrinthine halls and the sound dampening carpet and the fluorescent lights buzzing overhead, but Izzy tromps sedately next to her, and it's as close to peace as she can get while her head hurts this much.

The moment they get to the door she's fairly certain is the kitchen, Izzy pauses, giving Terese an obvious look, her ears up.

"What?" Terese asks, but Izzy just blinks up at her. It's not her danger signals, she's not distressed, just blinking her dark eyes up. Like she's expecting Terese to be upset, but not critically.

With that in mind, Terese pushes the door open, and the sharp edge of necromancy slices into her for a brief second, before abruptly cutting off. She stumbles, catching herself on the doorknob, the gut punch of power twisting her stomach.

Inside, huddled over a pot of tea, sits the Necromancer and the one with a braid. Alette.

"Sorry," the Necromancer says, her face pale, "instinct."

Terese shakes her head to clear it, but the motion just hurts.

Smoothly, Alette stands, and Terese can't tell if it's in greeting or in preparation to strike out.

"You are still hurt, though," the Necromancer continues, scowling down at her tea. "You shouldn't be conscious."

Terese blinks away from looking at her, instead meeting Alette's eyes.

Alette is tall, beautifully polished, and slender, and all this time she's spending with Zoel lends her the air of someone not quite human anymore.

And Terese had killed her.

They had spoken a few times, back when it seemed like the aftereffects of the demon's actions would end the world, but not since then. Not since Alette all but ran off with Zoel, crisscrossing the coast to repair all the little breaks that Terese caused.

"Where's Axel?" Terese blurts out without thinking.

The Necromancer and Alette exchange a glance, and there's a conversation there, in a language she can't quite grasp.

"He's picking up his car with Mel and Zoel," Alette says, and the golden rims of her glasses reflect the harsh light of the kitchen. "They'll be back in a few hours, most likely."

Terese nods, turning away from the blistering power currently huddled over tea, staring blankly at the array of prepackaged food.

None of it looks good, but Izzy leans up against Terese's leg in some solidarity.

If that had been Izzy warning Terese of the Necromancer, then Terese better learn to pay more attention to it.

"I didn't know Melekai could drive," Terese says, to the

cabinet. She doesn't want more plastic covered muffins, and power bars are right out.

"He's learning," the Necromancer says. "It's a process."

It's all so horrifically awkward.

"Is there another kitchen? I could go there, I didn't mean to interrupt," Terese says, still staring at the food. There are some energy drinks, she could grab one of those then go back to the chips in the library from the day before.

"You can stay," Alette says, and her voice is so very careful, like she's balancing between fear, anger, and friendliness. "I just got in about an hour ago, we were just catching up."

Izzy presses harder against Terese's legs.

"I didn't know you had a dog, what's her name?"

Terese knows Zoel knows, so she finds it hard to believe that Alette didn't have that information, but she can at least read when someone is trying to start a conversation. She grabs the closest thing to her —a box of salty crackers— then sits on the chair furthest from the Necromancer.

"Izzy," Terese says, and her dog perks up at her name, before sitting next to her, her head in her lap. "I don't know why that's her name, but I call her that."

Again, the exchange of glances from the two women, and it grates on Terese's nerves.

"Terese," the Necromancer starts, and Terese looks to her before she can stop herself. "Can I scan you?"

"No," she blurts out.

"You're...you're obviously hurt. Again. Axel said Daniil smashed you around pretty badly, and I want to make sure he did nothing lasting."

"I'll recover," Terese says, as fast as she can. "I'll recover, I always do."

"I have a theory," Alette says, and the fact that she

already does sits poorly with Terese. "If he already knew that it wouldn't kill you, then the actions he took are deliberate and moving towards weakening you." Alette exhales, like she's nervous as well from the conversation.

"He just broke my neck and bashed my head," Terese says, and her mouth is dry, but she makes herself choke down another cracker. It tastes like sawdust. "I've dealt with those before."

Alette's eyes are sharp, and it's so close to Axel's expressions that it's obvious that they grew up together. "Is it the scanning or the privacy invasion you're objecting to?"

"Scanning," Terese says automatically.

Again, the exchanged glance.

"Do you need to be restrained for it?" Alette asks, and nausea wells up in Terese again, so she sets the box of crackers down on the table. "If you're worried about striking out."

Terese stops herself from snapping out her immediate gut reaction, instead twisting her fingers in Izzy's fur and making herself think. Making herself slow down.

The idea that she could miss a step in what Daniil is trying is, rightfully, terrifying. That there could be a tactic besides just hurting her, besides just causing her to die, somewhere in the back of his mind. The previous demon had been so bad at conniving, bad at making plans, and Terese didn't like to think about what could happen if she actually encountered a smart demon.

So. Honesty.

"Scanning me like that provokes the same hunger instinct as the demon had towards you," she starts, and the Necromancer nods, like she understands that. "It's very overwhelming and I feel like I'm going to drown."

"Interesting," Alette says, like it's academic.

"No, it's not interesting, it's distressing," Terese says, then closes her eyes and breathes through her nose as Izzy whines. "Why is Axel mad at you?"

Alette's eyebrows flash up and there's a hint of vulnerability, and the Necromancer sits back, something like an astonished smile on her face. Like the question is so awkward it's almost funny.

"He gets all wooden and upset whenever you're brought up," Terese continues, and she knows, she just knows, that she should accept whatever help they offer, but the question needles under her skin. "He doesn't talk bad about you, he calls you his best friend, but he's upset."

"That's a rather long story," Alette says, after a horrifying polite pause, and her brows are drawn down, like this hurts her too. "We had some miscommunications recently."

The Necromancer snorts, and it's probably the most Terese has liked her this entire time.

"Well, whatever it is, talk to him about it, it's weird and he gets sad." Terese grabs the box of crackers again, determinedly chomping down on one.

Alette grips her cup of tea tightly, before consciously relaxing, the smooth mask fitting over her face again.

Something tells her it's a bit more than a miscommunication, but even Terese knows prying further won't exactly get a sympathetic response.

"I have some questions," Alette starts, and the Necromancer snorts again. "Is there a time I can sit with you and go through them?"

It feels like an olive branch, to ask to set up a time, and as much as she doesn't want to, Terese nods.

"So you really teleported Axel to Southern California?" the Necromancer asks, leaning forward and resting her chin in her hands. "With a broken neck and a concussion."

"I'm not sure you'd call this a concussion," Terese says, dry, but appreciating the lifeline. She takes off the neon green cap, then parts her hair where the wound is, and both of them flinch back. "It doesn't feel great."

"No wonder he freaked out," the Necromancer says, but she's grinning, and this strange, conspiratorial conversation lessens the pull of knife=sharp hunger.

Terese fits the cap on her head again. She'll have to figure out a way to wash the blood out, but in the meantime, it's almost comforting.

"Thank you for getting him out of there," Alette says, overly formal. "I'm glad he wasn't somewhere that a demon could find him."

It once again suggests a strange friendship between the two of them, one definitely marred by more than just a misunderstanding.

But at least Alette is just as torn up about it as Axel is, and some of the hard ball of dislike softens inside of Terese.

"Teleporting is about the one thing I can do that's easy," Terese says, extending the small bit of data about herself like it's another olive branch right back.

"Zoel mentioned," Alette responds, and Terese vividly remembers that she needs to report her destructive magic as soon as possible.

"I tore up the magic in three places," she immediately says, and Alette blinks, as if almost startled. "One in an alleyway a few blocks from the park—sorry, Izzy, not now—one on your helicopter pad—"

"I repaired that one already," Alette interrupts.

"—And one in the gas station store. Again." Terese takes a deep breath, then absorbs Alette's words. "Um. Thanks."

"If we catch them early, they're not difficult," Alette says, "so we appreciate the heads up."

The three of them descend into a silence that is slightly less awkward than before, but it still prickles under Terese's skin.

"Seriously, I can tell you're in pain," the Necromancer says after a long pause. "Is there something we can do?"

It's a different way of looking at it, and Terese just stares down at the crackers in her hand.

"Even if it's not going to permanently kill you, the pain is distressing, and I'm not even the one feeling it." The Necromancer sits back in her chair, a thoughtful scowl on her face. "Can I text you about that?"

"Yes please," Terese blurts out. "Do you know if they're safe? Getting the car?"

Again, the exchanging of a glance, and there's a hint of a smile in the Necromancer's eyes. "Fairly certain."

16

Still, Terese finds herself antsy and pacing the depths of the compound, before stumbling upon Axel's workshop, still set up in a grid.

She doesn't know how she could retrace her steps, but she steps inside, into the soothing lull of soft magic, familiar and quiet.

Izzy curls up in the doorway, and nothing could get past her, providing a strangely safe barrier to the outside world. Not that there is anything that would try to get to her in there, not really, but it's nice. Not like an aging dog could actually protect her from any of the things that hunt her.

But she feels safe from so few of things that she doesn't want to poke at it too hard until the sensation is gone.

The magic around her is broken, but she doesn't want to intrude on everything he's doing, so she just leans against one of the foam walls, knees pulled up to her chest, and stares at her phone.

He doesn't owe her an answer, or checking in on her or anything, but the worry gnaws on her inside.

She's still not used to worrying about someone who's not Izzy.

Finally, after taking far too many deep breaths, she taps out a quick message.

TERESE (3:21 PM): Everything okay with the car?

The response is almost instantaneous.

THE HANDSOME ONE (3:22 PM): He marked it up like your tunnel, but it'll run.

TERESE (3:22 PM): I'm sorry.

THE HANDSOME ONE (3:25 PM): Mel and Zoel are making sure he didn't track it otherwise.

THE HANDSOME ONE (3:26 PM): I'm totally gonna make you help me re-paint it.

She smiles, almost reflexively, down at the phone.

TERESE (3:29 PM): What did he write?

Because any message, no matter how distressing, could be vital. Could be a clue into his mindset, into how she can avoid him.

Though all her instincts tell her the only way to avoid would be to never poke her head out from a safety spot ever again. Just remain holed up and huddled away until he figures how to breach even those places as well.

THE HANDSOME ONE (3:31 PM): Nothing important.

She raises an eyebrow at the phone, because even she can tell when someone is avoiding an answer, then flips over to a different contact on her phone that reads THE GRUMPY ONE and types there.

TERESE (3:32 PM): What is on the car that Axel's not telling me?

There's no answer, so she just rests her head against the wall again, as if that could stop the thudding in her skull, and contemplates everything.

The Necromancer wants to help with the pain, but even

after her initial gut reaction to scoff at her, Terese can't see a viable way to help it. And past that, there's not an easy way to communicate it, to give words to the pain and how ubiquitous it can be.

There's a reason the last demon slowly went insane.

Her legs ache, in the odd way they sometimes do after she's died of a neck injury. It's not a genuine pain, more akin to many tiny prickles inside her skin that are so small they morph together into one homogenous discomfort.

Terese had once tried to read a biology textbook after teleporting near a library, but there was little that she could actually glean from it. Not very many people had ever recovered from any of the things she routinely goes through, so the research is limited.

THE HANDSOME ONE (3:40 PM): Mel said he will not answer your text.

THE HANDSOME ONE (3:40 PM): Didn't say what it was, but that he will not answer.

TERESE (3:41 PM): Call him a coward for me.

She doesn't think he will, but hopefully it draws a smile to his face. He helped her so much the night before, the least she could do was get him to smile.

After everything about her, after everything she did, it seems like the smallest that she could do. After putting him in danger once more, just by being around him in a place Daniil could access—

She shuts her eyes, and her head spikes in pain from the stress.

Daniil.

A part of her wants to shuttle her mind away, turn her focus elsewhere, think of happier things, but as if her thoughts summoned it, the full weight of what happened presses against her.

Tears well up in her eyes, but the pain chases them away.

THE HANDSOME ONE (3:45 PM): How's your head?

It's amazing how something so innocent as a text could jolt her out of an impending panic, so she blinks away the blurriness.

TERESE (3:46 PM): Gross enough to make Alette and the Necromancer flinch.

THE HANDSOME ONE (3:47 PM): I should have taken a picture to really gross them out.

THE HANDSOME ONE (3:52 PM): Glasses are good for active magic, not on anything left behind, so Mel and Zoel are taking this one.

THE HANDSOME ONE (3:53 PM): I can see Zoel without him tiring himself out, so he's happy. Not that he's ever actively sad or shows any emotion besides being nice to people.

Terese worries at her bottom lip, looking out at the room full of softly broken magic, and debates how guilty she should feel, and only comes away with the answer of 'somewhat'.

TERESE (3:55 PM): I don't think I'm an alchemist, but I can try to make them work that way?

THE HANDSOME ONE (3:55 PM): Now I'm curious. What did you know about any magic before Dr. Frisse went supervillain?

It's a stark flippancy, after the vulnerability of the night before, and she squints down at her phone, as if it could parse out the emotions of the man sending her the message.

Also, complicated answer. Dr. Frisse had explained some, done some flashy tricks, to get her to agree to it in the first place, but even right until the first time she saw the demon, she had been sure it was some sleight of hand.

She frowns at herself, at the sudden surety of the memory. It's not something she had actively tried to recall, so she's not sure it had been lost, but the image of Dr. Frisse making a wallet disappear, then re-appear in the other hand, flashes through her mind.

TERESE (3:59 PM): Unclear.

Izzy lifts her head to look at her, ears up, before settling back down again.

TERESE (4:00 PM): Is it safe for you to be out there? It could be a trap.

THE HANDSOME ONE (4:00 PM): Melekai has said many times, and Zoel has insisted many times, that it's not.

It feels unsteady, the idea of him out there, after he injured Daniil. After the demon now knows him, knows he's a threat, or at least someone helping Terese. Makes him another target, another problem.

The smart thing to do would be to run.

She shuts her eyes again at the intrusive thought.

It would be so much smarter to run. Not smart for her long-term survival, not for her staying unpossessed, but for everyone else. Make Izzy stay behind, leave behind the phone, the new clothes, anything that could be tracked back.

Leave Axel behind.

But with the ache in her legs and the pounding in her head a too-vivid reminder, she's too much of a coward to leave her best chance at avoiding all this.

Hours later, Axel leans against the door to his room of broken magic, and Terese just tilts her head to look at him. Izzy shuffles out of his way, but otherwise ignores him.

There's a profound sense of relief sitting somewhere in her chest at the sight of him.

"Did you randomly fix something?" he asks lazily, but there's some tension behind his eyes. Not at her, she can tell that enough, but something.

"Not this time, not all of it is obvious what it was for," Terese says, pushing herself up to standing. "Last thing I want to do is try to fix something the entirely wrong way. I'm not an alchemist."

"Nice hat," he says, and her hand drifts up to the brim of the neon green ball cap.

"It's better than just open head wound for everyone to see," she says, pulling it off and parting her hair to show him.

As opposed to the Necromancer and Alette, he just leans in, peering at her scalp. "That's not your brain, is it?"

"No, just skull, I checked. Last night it might've been brain."

"Did I antiseptic your brain?" Axel asks, pulling aside a bit of her hair to get a closer look, and he's close, so close her heart kicks up a notch. "Shit, will something happen?"

"If I lose any more memories, I'll be pissed," she says, and it startles a laugh out of him. "I think I'll be fine. I once dumped a bottle of rubbing alcohol on a slit throat and nothing bad happened."

He pauses, leaning away enough to give her a look, and she fits the hat on again. "You're not joking?"

"Nope. Would not recommend."

"No, you're shitting me." Still, he's smiling, half out of a horrified amusement and half out of a strange sort of marvel.

"Not in the least. It was super gross."

"The car's okay," he says, obviously changing the subject,

but a simple trip wouldn't have taken hours. "Melekai's antsy. He doesn't like any of it. Zoel says he couldn't find any trackers, but he put some sort of Wight spell on it so that it functionally doesn't exist on the magical spectrum or something. Seemed theoretical."

"Good," Terese says, brushing her hands off. "What did he write on it?"

"You know when people ask a question and there's no way they'll actually feel better knowing the answer?" he says, giving her a crooked smile.

She just shakes her head.

"Right." He gestures for her to follow, and the moment she leaves the room with the softly broken magic, she misses it. "Alette try to talk to you yet?"

"And the Necromancer wanted to scan me, but don't tell Melekai," Terese says, falling into stride with him. He's not that much taller than her, but enough that keeping up is almost, almost difficult with her legs still not entirely back. Izzy follows at a slightly more sedate pace, content.

The runes flare up as she walks past, and they're ones she's already brought back. Axel doesn't—or can't—notice.

"Yeah, well, Mel worries." He gives her a sidelong glance from underneath his lashes. "He said you saved my life twice yesterday."

She doesn't expect any credit from Melekai, so she lets herself absorb that, as they step through the hallways and end up at the bank of elevators. Izzy shies away but takes far less convincing this time.

"I don't think you can call it saving a life if I'm the one that got you into it," Terese says, as the doors to the elevator shnick shut. "And I'm fairly sure only once, and then you saved me, so we're equal."

Another sidelong look, like he's not buying it. "If you feel bad about the car, I'm going to tell Alette you want to talk to her about the magical recharge rate of your powers."

"That's not fair, I've never recorded or measured anything," she says, a smile tugging at her lips. He's trying to preempt her, trying to stop her from freaking out, she can tell. And it's kinda working.

"Oh, she'll help with that and then you'll never hear the end of it." The elevator opens to a deeper parking garage than the one they usually walk through.

It's dimly lit, the concrete rougher, and past gold paint smudges against the blacktop. The pillars cast long shadows, the lights weaker than the other one. The air chills, so close to her underground tunnel, that for a split second her head swims with dizziness, but she pushes onwards. Izzy whines once, before leaning up against Terese for strength.

At one corner, however, ablaze in magic, is Axel's Mustang, and she raises an eyebrow at it.

Wight magic mixes with spell weaving, as well as something tantalizingly close to Necromancy but isn't, all glowing and dancing along the car.

And the black paint is almost entirely covered in scrawling, red paint and scratches, jerky letters too small to see from far away.

"Well," she says, then shakes herself loose. "When did you need it repainted?"

As an afterthought, she notices Melekai, the Necromancer, Zoel, and Alette standing near the car, hanging back. Watching her reactions.

Almost like she has an audience.

"Yeah, we wanted to see if you could find anything demonic on it, too," Axel says, resting his hands on his belt loops, face twisting. "None of them could, but..."

"Yeah, yeah, makes sense."

It doesn't feel like the horrific power that Daniil gives off in spades, doesn't taste like any of his motions, but she doesn't trust that.

Stilling herself, she tilts her head, reaching for the nebulous cloud of power inside of her. It's rarely something she stops and thinks about, instead relying on gut instinct, and this takes a different mindset.

The Necromancer curses under her breath, but Terese barely spares a thought for whatever she notices.

It's clear, even without all the scrawling and the paint, that a demon touched the car. There're scrabbles around the handles, along every slashing mark, and even on the tires.

There's even a wisp of a hint that the previous demon hit it, along the trunk, and it sours Terese's stomach, too familiar.

But all marks are just that—marks. Left behind by anger and frustration.

"You already checked it out?" she asks, lifting her eyes to Zoel. It's far too easy, and if she needed to track someone's location, she'd absolutely leave something on the car.

Zoel nods, simple. While he's lesser than a demon, he should be able to catch most traps and evidence.

"And you?" She tosses a look to Melekai, squinting past the brightness of the Necromancer to focus on him.

"Looked for all the normal spots." Melekai crosses his arms, and there's a funny look on his face, one she can't decipher. "No tracking I know of." And he'd know a lot.

"I found no lingering spells, human or demon or otherwise," Alette says, and even though Terese didn't ask, its good information. "No additional twisting of the magic in the area, nothing that could catch on the car and bring it back here."

"That's...beyond stupid of him," Terese says, peering at the car, then steps closer, until the words become legible.

The first words she recognizes are 'SHE'S MINE'. The next ones are 'YOU DON'T GET HER'.

Same handwriting as the tunnel. Variations of the words, scratched on the finish of the car, deep into the metal of the body.

This wasn't a message meant for her.

Axel's still standing next to her, tapping his fingers against his leg, and when she meets his gaze, his face is serious.

"Like I said, you wouldn't like it," he says with a shrug. As if it's something to shrug about. As if flippant words could mask how much danger he's in.

"No," Terese says, something tugging in the back of her mind, and she takes a moment to recognize it as anger, and it takes her breath away.

She's thought she's been angry since getting unpossessed, but those vague emotions burn away like spiderwebs in the face of this. She's wanted justice for people treating Izzy poorly, she's wanted people to leave her alone, she's felt pain and frustration she thought was anger.

Not like this.

She tears her eyes away from Axel, to stare unblinkingly at the car. Still no obvious demon trap, still no way of tracking it down. Just a message for Axel.

"He doesn't get to say that to you," she murmurs, even though everyone is staring at her, like they're waiting for her response.

"Oh, this is nothing," Axel says, even though it's clearly not. "He's just trying to scare you."

"I really don't think he is," Terese says, but something settles inside her, something rock hard and ugly and vicious.

"This isn't meant for me. If it was, he would have tracked it. Melekai," she calls to the other side of the group, and he nods, like he had expected to be asked about this, "this wasn't to scare me, was it?"

"If it was, it'd be a trap, and it's not," Melekai says, and they lock eyes, briefly, both of them understanding what she's trying to convey.

Axel shifts, uneasy, before running his hand through his curls. "So he's just trying to scare me. Great. Big whoop. Also not a big deal, dealt with demons before."

It tugs at the chunk of emotions inside Terese, so she stills herself, takes the moment to process what exactly she's feeling.

She should be scared, and some remote part of her is, that Daniil so obviously feels possessive over her. That he would be angered enough by someone else defending her, to track down and write threatening words.

But mostly it's just anger. It's indignation, it's a burning, uncomfortable fury.

"I'll kill him," she offers to Axel, and he wrinkles his face at her. "He doesn't get to bring you into this."

"It's a car," Axel says, but he's not upset, he's perplexed. "It's a car, and it's just surface damage anyway. It got smashed worse when you—the other demon—hit it before. I can repair this."

"That's not the issue," Terese responds, and the words seem tantalizingly close, what she wants and needs to make sure he understands, but they elude her. "He doesn't get to threaten you."

His brow furrowed, he looks down at her, really looks at her, and she stares right back, as if she could figure out how to get this ball of anger and ugliness into the open.

And in front of her, his eyes soften, like he gets it. Like he understands the awful inside of her and isn't turned away by it.

"Doesn't erase the fact that he did," Melekai says, and it breaks the moment, shattering the fragile little connection like its nothing, and the rage almost spikes at him instead. "Fact is, now he knows about you, and will probably not react well if he sees you again."

Axel's still looking down at Terese.

"So we kill him," Terese says, and, almost uncomfortably, the Necromancer chokes down a laugh. "You all have done it before, we just need to do it again."

And standing under the dim lights and the broken concrete of the subterranean parking garage, she believes it.

17

Alette ends up putting a demon trap around the car, identical to the one that her aunt put up around Terese, and they leave the car there overnight, alone in an abandoned floor of the parking garage, still marked to all hell.

Melekai and the Necromancer leave, stating they'll go stay somewhere else. Which is smart—better not to tell her where their secondary home is, she shouldn't know. If this all goes wrong, they deserve a place to run to.

After many reassurances, Zoel and Alette drive off, probably to the apartment the spell weaver keeps, where she saw a break. Terese would want Zoel to stay, to catch up with him, something, but...

But her hands shake with tamping down on the rage and the words choke in her throat, so she merely follows Axel back up to the elevator bank, silent.

It's not until the elevators open back up and they're striding down the long hallway, does Axel speak.

"Do you want to go get drunk?"

She doesn't want to look up at him, but she does, and her eyes catch on his.

"I mean, you look pissed off. I just had a demon try to scare me. I need a fucking drink. Do you wanna come?"

She weighs his words against her rage.

"Yes."

Izzy elects to fall asleep on the giant fluffy rug in Axel's apartment, and they take an unfamiliar car parked around back, a lumbering SUV type. They're both silent as Axel drives them to a small town nearby, before parking in front of the most nondescript strip mall ever.

He doesn't speak as he holds the door open for her, and inside is a grimy, seedy bar, where her shoes stick to the floor and the entrance smells of stale smoke. Flickering neon lights provide the only illumination, and it's relatively empty, a few grizzled looking men stooped on the stools at the bar, and a disinterested bartender watches a baseball game.

"Hey, Blake," the bartender says, barely looking up at Axel but lifting his hand in greeting. "Haven't seen you in a bit."

"Been busy," Axel replies, then shifts his attention to Terese. "What do you drink?"

"Anything that doesn't taste vile," Terese says, "Blake."

"Two shots of vodka and two whiskey cokes," Axel says, tossing a card on the bar.

The name on the card even reads Blake.

"Nice hat," the bartender throws to Terese, and she narrows her eyes at him until he turns around and mixes the drink.

There's a garish painting of a pirate boat on one wall, complete with parrots and a carved female figure with her nipples out. It's so obviously in bad taste, so obviously tacky, that a previously unknown small part of her loves it.

She marvels at that sensation, so at odds with the anger, and holds it. Maybe the person she was before the demon loved bad art, and she just hadn't remembered it yet.

It's nice to think of something like that. That she could have had preferences so mundane to be about stupid art.

They tuck themselves into a corner at a small standing table, their backs to the wall, and nobody pays them a shred more attention.

"Blake?" Terese asks, as he hands her one of the shots. They clink the glasses together before downing them at the same time.

Terese isn't sure she's ever had good vodka before, and this certainly isn't anything decent either.

"Did you think my parents would name me Axel?" he asks, after coughing once from the vodka. "No parent would name their kid Axel."

"Huh," she says, the burn of the alcohol quenching a bit of the burn of the rage. "Never thought of that."

"Legally changed it over a decade ago. Still keep a bank account under that name if I need," he says with a shrug, like he's almost uncomfortable with it. "This place never met the Axel that I was, so to them, I'm just Blake."

She understands the want to disappear into a crowd, to not be noticed. To not stick out.

"It's nice to have someone not just look at you with pity sometimes," he continues, and she gets it. She gets it, somewhere deep in between the pit of her stomach and her spine. "They have no idea of a magician named Axel, so there's no need to be him for just a bit of time."

"Yeah," she says, because saying nothing isn't an option. She picks up the cocktail, staring at the ice in it. "You're right, Axel is a ridiculous name."

"I'm a ridiculous person, most of the time," he says, now clinking the cocktail glass against hers.

She can't inherently disagree, instead taking a sip. They're standing so close, around the table with their backs to the wall that their shoulders touch.

"Most of the time..." she starts, then trails off, unsure where she's going, the anger twisting and turning into confusion, and that's far less preferable. "Most of the time I don't think I miss who I was before."

"Yeah, that's still a giant question mark for us," he says, but good natured.

"It's not that I don't remember it, not exactly, it's just..." She waves her hand at her head, as if that would help. "Doesn't feel like me. It's easy to not think of the details of someone that's not you."

"Dark, but I'll bite," he says, and when he takes a sip of his drink, the fabric of his shirt touches hers.

"So yeah, I could go looking for clues, try to reconnect with people I know, but there's no point. I'm not the person they might miss, I barely pay any attention to my memories with them. It's like a movie I saw once, long ago, and the details blur together."

The demon had loved to go to movies, in the beginning, before the pain grew to be un-ignorable. Would teleport from one movie theater to another, without breaks.

Terese isn't sure she's thought of a more apt analogy.

He nods at that, then waves to get the bartender's attention. "We're gonna need four more shots, and an order of nachos," he says, like he needs to be drunker for the day.

Which, fair, he got threatened by a demon and there's no way for him to defend himself.

The anger spikes inside of her, and she takes a large gulp of her drink.

They're silent for a few minutes, until the kitchen brings out a hefty plate full of chips, chili, spicy peppers, and the same fluorescent yellow cheese as the dip he gave her the day before.

"Sure we don't need ice cream to go along with it?" Terese asks, and gets rewarded with a sideways smile as the bartender sets down two more shots in front of each of them.

"I could've gone weird and tried to order the, uh..." He peers at the menu painted on the side of the wall next to the tacky painting. "The deep-fried jalapeño pickle poppers with ghost pepper sauce? But I like the nachos."

They click the shot glasses together again, and the vodka burns a little less this time.

Unless she counts the demon—and she doesn't—this just might be her first time getting drunk with another person, and something about it settles well inside her stomach.

"Don't tell Mel I took you here, he thinks this is our hangout place," Axel says, after a few moments of silence. "He gets weird about stuff like that."

"Noted," Terese responds, and Axel takes a deep breath, like he's working himself up to something, something that needed two shots of vodka and a plate of food for support.

So she lets him stew in that, lets him get his energy from whatever he needs.

The vodka's spread warmth to her fingers and the tip of her nose, and it's not terribly unpleasant.

"Why'd you react that way?" Axel blurts out, after a few

more minutes of them silently eating. "I thought for sure you were just gonna be scared, not...not all angry."

The hairs on the back of her neck rise, but she breathes hard out of her nose instead of reacting any other way.

The words come easier to her than they probably should.

"Because he gets to threaten me, he gets to try to scare me, he doesn't get to threaten you."

"That makes no sense," Axel says, but he's looking at her, directly at her, even though they're standing so close. "If I was trying to scare someone, I'd absolutely go after the people around them."

"Yeah, I expect that. I thought he was gonna kill Izzy that first...first time..." A brief spike of terror blanks out her mind, before she shakes her head, getting herself back under control. "Look, as a demon, it's totally logical for him to hurt the people around me to manipulate me. That's obvious, right?"

At his nod, she pushes onwards.

"But this was meant to scare you," she says, "and that's not fair. He had no intention of that getting back to me, or else it'd be a trap."

He mulls over that, brown eyes down on the plate instead of her. "It's a kinda insane possessiveness, if you ask me," he says, and for a second, she thinks he's referring to her actions. "To threaten someone just because they were with the person they wanted. Lots of crazy ex-boyfriend energy there."

It's a more appropriate metaphor than he thinks.

"Demons think of everything in terms of things they can have," Terese says bitterly, and he blinks back up at her. "He can't have you."

"Glad you think that," he says, the sideways smile back,

but it's halfhearted. "Still don't really want a demon jealously chasing after me."

"I'll kill him," she says, with the same sort of rage and conviction as she felt looking at that car. "It has to be possible. He doesn't get to go after you for the sake of going after you."

"I mean, I like that more than you asking to be locked in a box," Axel says, turning so his body is tilted towards her instead of the table, and her entire face feels warm, the anger and the alcohol mixing and raising the temperature. "I certainly like that more than you just running for the rest of your life."

There's something underneath his words, something dangling out of her grasp.

"I don't know how, not yet," she admits, shyness spreading through her chest. "It might just be wishful thinking. I couldn't stop one demon, I might not be able to stop this one."

There's an undercurrent to her thoughts, one leading to fear and panic, but she keeps her head above the water, eating the nachos with the radioactive cheese and drinking a pretty awful whiskey coke.

Everything's easier to believe with Axel. Just being around him offers her some sort of buffer, some sort of upswell of confidence. Next to him, she believes she could do almost anything, and it's quite frankly terrifying.

"I thought he was going to really hurt you," he says, still tilted towards her.

"He did break my neck," she quips, but it doesn't soften the moment.

"No, like, really hurt you. Harm you. Do something lasting." He takes a swig of the drink. "Mel said you could have run right when he showed up. Zapped yourself away, left me alone with your dog, not put yourself in danger of getting possessed again, and not have to put up with the whole..." He mimes the motion Daniil had made on his own face, the running of the fingers over his chin and mouth. "You could have just saved yourself."

"I couldn't do that," she protests. The neon from the bar cast long shadows over his face, catching the light in his eyelashes.

He's not the smoothly pretty alchemist she saw through the demon's eyes anymore, but he has his own strange sort of beauty. Stronger, rather than polished.

"You could have, and you didn't." His hand grips the glass tight, and if she didn't know better, she would think he's scared now.

Something's scaring him. Here, in a neon bar with a tacky painting and two shots of vodka and a plate of nachos, something is frightening him.

Her magic doesn't pulse, she's not in danger, nothing. There are no threats, no strangers looking askance at them, everyone minding their own drinks and the baseball game.

"Hey," she says, and reaches out and touches his elbow, right where his sleeves are rolled up, and his skin is warm, too. "You're okay, I'm okay, he cannot get to you, I'll stop him, I promise." She might not be able to stop him from taking her, but this...this she can do.

His eyes briefly close, and he ducks his head, clearly taking the moment, and she lets him. Gives him a space to feel whatever he needs to feel, heaven knows she needs a lot of those moments, too.

It settles something deep in her, too, that she won't let Daniil take this. That there would be things she would do first, before letting him hurt Axel, and it doesn't sit well with her, but she pushes those thoughts aside.

"Terese, you are literally the face of all of my nightmares," he says, and she doesn't flinch back, because it's fair, though a small part of it stings. "And now you're...here. Saying things like that." He rests his hand on her arm, a mirror image of how she's touching him. Before, she had thought his skin warm, but this almost burns.

Again, something is lurking in his words, something she can only partially grasp.

"You're here, having shots of vodka and making jokes about nachos and wearing that ridiculous hat." He taps the hat with his other hand, like a blessing, and she smiles, impulsive, up at him.

She shouldn't be smiling. Everything about this is serious, an incredibly soul-searching conversation, but still.

"Yeah, well, you're here too," she says. "You could have left me, run away from Daniil, took Izzy and got away, but you stayed so you could shoot a gun and really piss him off."

"Yeah," he says, "I guess I am."

They remain motionless, under the neon lights and the baseball game and the tacky painting, and Terese isn't sure she breathes.

Before he tilts her hat up, leans down, and presses his lips against hers.

She stills, her chest catching.

At that moment, nothing is real. The pain in her scalp, where the skin still itches in its newness. The lingering ache in her legs, where the nerves are still misfiring. All of it. Gone. The neon lights and the tacky painting and the plate of nachos. Gone.

Just the single sensation of the kiss. Of the pressure of his lips, of his hand against her arm, his fingertips curling around her elbow. Each motion a gentle, beguiling force, inexorably drawing her down and against him.

He tastes like the vodka, like the burn of the anger, and the sweetness of the soda.

Before she can stop herself, before she can even think, to parse out what every sensation might be, she's winding her hand in his curls, pulling him closer to her, pressing her body against his, opening her mouth to his.

He responds by holding her close, an arm tight against her lower back, a small sound in the back of his throat, born from an insistent need.

It's like drowning, but instead of terror and suffocation, just a joy, bubbling up behind her breastbone.

But...

He breaks the kiss like the air is drawn out of him with a gasp, pulling back. She can see the white of his eyes.

Her eyes have never been wider.

They stare at each other, as all the noise swoops back against her ears. The din of the televised baseball game. The grumbling of the bar patrons, the flickering in the neon light, her shoes sticking to the floor.

"Um." He recovers first, blinking fast. "Uh."

Two blotches of red color his cheeks, right underneath his freckles.

She doesn't know how to respond, what to say, so she just stares at him, her heart pounding.

"Probably not a good idea while we're drunk," he says.

"Yeah, definitely," she blurts out. Her eyes catch on his face, like she can never look away. "Not a good idea."

"Yeah," he says, pulling back a bit more and running his hand through his curls, completely mussing them up. "Um."

She tugs the baseball cap back into place, and her hand shakes in time with the thudding of her pulse.

"Have you kissed anyone since?" he blurts out, then covers his face with his hand. "I mean—"

"Not since," she says, turning her body to face the table by sheer force of will alone. "Unless I did while I lost time."

"Right, cause that is a thing that happens," he says, looking down at the table as well, still shell-shocked.

Like he shocked himself as well.

Terese's knees are unsteady, and she's not sure if it's the vodka or the broken neck or the physical contact, so she leans against the table.

And a little against him, shoulder to shoulder.

Without even asking, the bartender brings over two glasses of water, and Axel immediately downs his. Terese takes much more cautious sips, having downed too much water before and had adverse outcomes back when she first became unpossessed.

"This isn't your first time drinking since, is it?" Axel asks, and there's a strange sort of hope in the back of his tone, like he's hoping he hadn't done something wrong, that he didn't make some giant mistake.

"Absolutely not," Terese says, and his lip twitches the slightest amount. "I have money from a dubious source. I can teleport whenever I want. I had just gotten out of the worst thing that ever happened to me. Of course I drank some." It had only taken her three really terrible hangovers to decide to dial it the hell back, but that's beside the point.

"Yeah, you're right, stupid question, I would get fucking drunk too," he says, his words too fast.

"I don't think any of you realize I was a mess for like the first few months," Terese says, and again, the barest hint that there might be a smile, somewhere, and now she wants to dig in her heels and bring it back. "You think I'm at all normal now, you should have seen me then."

"Really don't get the normal vibes from you very much,"

he says, and he's slowing down, his words returning to their normal cadence. "You did try to attack Alette in a cave."

"She attacked first," Terese responds, and there it is, the smallest of amused smiles, back at her, and her stomach flops all over again.

It's not a comfortable silence, with a strange electricity humming underneath the surface of her skin, but the awkwardness bleeds away, leaving a gaping, vast expanse of potential in its wake.

"Was that your first kiss since?" Terese asks, because she can't keep her mouth shut for the life of her on a normal day, and now her cheeks still hurt from smiling and her nose is bright red from the vodka.

"Oh hell no," he says, and it startles something in him, almost an embarrassed laugh. "I mean, it's not like I went around mashing face with anyone around, but my life was... really in a weird flux for a bit, and I definitely..." He waves his hand, as if that can fill in the blank. "Yes."

It's a nonsensical conversation, and he's leaning against her side just as much as she is him.

"Do you need me to teleport us back to the compound?" she asks, because despite everything else, she still remembers hordes of warnings about drunk driving from school. "Get the car later?"

This time, his eyes are a little wild, before he reads something from her expression and calms down. "Is it safe to drunk teleport?"

"I mean, I've done it before," she says, wrinkling her eyebrow at him and his strange reaction. "Probably safer than drunk driving."

He holds up a finger, and she falls silent as he obviously processes. "Yeah, no, not comfortable with that yet."

THEY END up chatting at the bar for almost another hour, the tension never leaving the room, before making it safely back to the compound way late into the night.

She has never felt the weight of being the only two people in a place so heavily before.

Izzy thumps her tail on the carpet the moment they reach Axel's apartment, before laboriously climbing to her feet and leaning against Terese for pets.

"Just might be the longest we've been apart," Terese says as Axel hangs up his jacket, and there's a strange look on his face, one that tightens the butterflies in her stomach. "I... thank you."

Whatever it is he expects her to say, it isn't that. "What?"

"I feel better," she says, scratching Izzy behind her ears and getting a blissed out smile from her dog. "Not as...upset. Angry. Something."

He opens his mouth, as if to say something sarcastic, but no words come out for far longer than is usual for him.

Izzy prods Terese towards the door, in a clear signal she should take her outside, breaking whatever spell had been placed over Axel.

"Good," he replies, unsteady, like her words had taken the carpeted floor beneath his feet and tilted it strangely underneath him. "Good. I'm glad."

They stand there, with Izzy prodding towards the door, and she can see the hesitation in his stance, from his grasp on his jacket, from his still mussed curls, as if he's unsure if he's trying to talk himself into doing something, or out of it.

She gets that a bit too well, so she offers him what she hopes is a small smile, gesturing down at Izzy. "Goodnight?"

"Yeah," he huffs out with a sigh, "goodnight."

18

Terese hasn't been hungover in about three months, and it does not mix well with her head injury.

Or the neck snap.

"Ow," she mumbles, pressing the heel of her hands into her eyes, as if that could fully block out the light from her little rune.

Izzy sighs from the carpet next to the couch, and she's not what woke up Terese. It's something else, but blinking doesn't seem to help her eyes feel any less gummy.

Too close to when her brain got melted for her comfort.

It's not terribly fair, she decides, with her back on the couch cushions and a blanket still over her feet, that she has all these healing abilities and can pop up from the dead, but a normal hangover takes fucking forever to go away.

Izzy sighs again, and Terese drapes her hand over the side of the couch to rest her hand on her long fur.

Logically, she knows that days like when she visited the dog park with its coffee shop and espresso milkshakes right nearby are the best way to get rid of one of these, but even the idea of going somewhere outside the safe walls of the compound fills her with dread.

She pops her eyes open.

She hadn't felt this dread the night before. Had left without a shred of fear, without all the skin crawling terror of leaving a safety spot, but today...

The mere thought of stepping one foot outside drips adrenaline down her spine.

"Okay," she whispers to the small library, now fully awake and still fucking hungover. "It's going to be one of those days."

Her phone beeps from the side table, and that's what woke her up, so she flails her hand blindly to grab it, pulling it over and curling up on her side to prop it on the couch cushion.

THE NERDY ONE (10:02 AM): Are you awake?

Terese spares a thought of why the heck Alette would want to know, before she sighs.

TERESE (10:04 AM): Unfortunately.

THE NERDY ONE (10:04 AM): Great, meet me at the downstairs kitchen in a few minutes.

Nothing sounds worse.

THE NERDY ONE (10:05 AM): I'll make sure the espresso machine is working.

Some things sound worse.

Terese quickly changes clothing, and she's clammy, but she splashes water on her face and finger combs her hair before cramming the neon green hat on her head again.

It's tacky, it's bright, but she would fight someone if they tried to take it away.

She goes through the motions of petting Izzy, of taking her to the solarium, of blearily staring out at the wind and broken glass and wrecked magic of the room, before, heart pounding, she strides back inside.

Her hands are even shaking, out of some detached fear that doesn't even make sense to her.

She's had days like this before, where there's no room for anything but fear, but panic, and they're always awful. Always leave a foul taste in her mouth, until all she can do is curl up in a ball and wait it out, until her brain stabilizes itself with whatever nebulous chemicals it needs, and she can function normally.

It has nothing to do with the hangover, with going out the night before, or...

Or her making out with Axel.

Her foot hesitates, almost missing a stair, mind blanking out for a brief, blissful second, before autopilot kicks back in and a fresh fear worms its way through her bones.

When her brain is like this, it's always looking for new fears.

He had been drunk, too, and probably regrets the kiss, if she had to place money on it. Face of his nightmares, he had said.

Awfully hard to take that at anything beyond face value.

She can't trust her instincts when she's like this, she can't trust her immediate thoughts, so she takes a deep breath for herself before opening the door to the kitchen, Izzy plodding slowly behind her.

True to her word, Alette sits primly at the little table, a perfectly poured shot of espresso at the other seat. Every part of her is polished, from the gleaming braid down her back to her pristine jacket with the gold threads to the magic practically dripping from her fingertips.

Terese shakes out some kibble for Izzy, to avoid looking at Alette.

"What, did you go untangle another mess last night?" Terese mumbles, flopping down into the chair in one disorganized motion.

"How could you tell?" Alette asks, like she's a morning person.

Terese eyes her, trying to gauge if it's a trick question, but everything sounds like a trick question when she's like this, so she moves on. "Lots of magic on you," she says, trying not to sound surly but almost certainly failing.

She pokes at the shot of espresso and it seems safe, but still, the crawl in the back of her throat stops her from just chugging it immediately.

"Do you need water?" Alette asks, which if she looks like she needs water, then she almost certainly does, but it doesn't help the mood.

Instead of saying anything, Terese jolts herself up to the fridge to grab an omnipresent water bottle, then a single pack of chips.

On the table, next to Alette's very practical cup of tea, lays a neatly stacked pile of linen strips, and an obvious needle case next to it.

It's the same needle case she saw through the demon's eyes many times, and her heart rate spikes just at glimpsing it again. Even in a place where it's so obviously not a weapon, even when it's presented like a tool, she just remembers the fiery lines of pain encircling her, doing anything to stop her.

Alette's a lot more powerful now, and that doesn't help.

"Sorry the last reading got spoiled," Terese says, cracking open the water bottle. "New demon wasn't so fond of that idea." That the water was sealed helps, and it's stupid that it helps.

"We still retrieved the linen," Alette says smoothly. "Learned several interesting things."

"I don't like the sound of that," Terese responds, before she can help herself, and Izzy perks up her ears at her tone, so she sighs, sitting back down again. "What did you find?"

"Zoel thinks he's approximately eight hundred years old," Alette says, and once more, Terese can't think, can't breathe, but it passes. "Not usually in his territory, so he doesn't know him directly, but he's asking around."

"Last demon was a young, stupid idiot, so that doesn't bode well," Terese says, scowling at the inoffensive espresso shot.

She will feel so much better once she takes it, but the fact that it's just out in the open stops her, and it grinds against her mind.

Alette blinks, as if she's filtering Terese's words through her brain and trying to decide what is worth replying to, and Terese lets her, eating a chip instead.

"Axel said you had problems with food?" Alette asks, gesturing towards the bag of chips.

"I don't have problems with food, I just forget to eat," Terese says, prickly. What else had Axel reported back about her? What other details did he think he needs to share?

Which still makes sense, of course. She had, after all, been their enemy for so long, she wouldn't blame him if he had a file created of her, of all her oddness, of everything she's said.

Still stings.

"That's a problem with food, still," Alette says, still cautious, and Terese hates it. Hates the kids' gloves, hates the careful skirting around anything about her. Even if she deserves it.

Which she does. She had actually killed Alette, had seen her life end, and here she is, being bitchy towards her.

"I guess," Terese allows. "Axel still asleep?"

"Oh, yes, he sleeps for ages after he gets drunk," Alette says, sitting back, and is immediately less intimidating and more like a person. "I wouldn't expect anything out of him until...two PM or something."

It's an insignificant fact, but Terese takes it, hoarding it away, before realizing the implications.

So Alette knows they got drunk the night before, and is still sitting here, expecting Terese to get magically read. So Axel told her some, possibly abbreviated, version of the night before.

Terese can't decide if she should be offended if he told her about the kiss or not, but definitely knows she doesn't want to ask and volunteer that information.

"Must be nice," Terese says, with an unhappy twist of her stomach.

"He will also want a cup of really bitter coffee and to take a walk outside in the shade," Alette continues, and Terese isn't sure if she's giving her a hint or if she's reading too much into it. "Maybe some toast."

There's a toaster on the counter behind her, but Terese refuses to be so obvious and twist to look at it.

After clearly waiting for Terese to do or say something, Alette sighs, picking up a strip of linen and unrolling her needle case.

Again, her heart rate spikes and terror grips her around the throat, but she stills herself.

"Axel cares a lot," Alette starts, pulling out a curved golden needle that sings with power, "and would help anyone in need, but"—she raises an eyebrow at Terese, meaningful—"doesn't get attached too easily."

It's the same needle that Alette had brought into her tunnel, the same needle Alette had repaired a fucking Ley Line with, and now she's using it on a strip of linen.

Then her words catch up to Terese, and she blinks.

"I haven't seen him get attached quickly in over a decade," Alette continues, laying out the linen in front of Terese, and Terese dumbly sets her wrist on it, brain too distracted by Alette's words to panic about this, too. "I don't know what is going on in his mind right now, but it's not his normal way of reacting to people."

Fingers deft, Alette wraps the linen around Terese's thin wrist, a quick, assured motion she's done many times before.

"He said I was the face of his nightmares," Terese responds, slow, her eyes on Alette's sure stitching.

It's almost—almost—like a restraint, but Terese breathes through her nose. She still has all of her abilities, she could still teleport away, she could still twist the surrounding magic, weaponize it.

"Smooth," Alette says, and there's the barest hint of sarcasm in her voice, a blink and she'd have missed the inflection.

The linen stitches closed, and terror climbs down her throat, choking her out, and her own magic pulses with the sharp need to go somewhere, anywhere, but this little kitchen with the coffeemaker and toaster and perfect little shot of espresso in front of her.

The string in the linen glows bright, vivid gold, cutting through the sterile fluorescent lights.

Izzy whines, a small noise in the back of her throat.

Alette looks up, sharp. "Whatever you're doing, stop it."

"I'm not doing anything," Terese grits out, then squeezes her eyes shut, taking a deep breath, then another. "Sometimes my brain is weird and gets scared and it's picking this right now."

"Oh," Alette says, and as if it's that simple, tugs on the string and unravels it in one smooth motion, until the linen falls back to the table. "Why didn't you say that?"

Terese stares at her, until Alette lifts her head and looks at her. "Because I'm trying to have you guys help me, not make it more difficult?" she says, then rubs her face with her hand.

Her face even hurts.

Alette sits back, holding the linen strip in her hand, and Terese knows enough about spell weavers that she can probably still get information from the strip, even with how brief it was in contact.

"I'll be okay later," Terese says, and it prickles at her, something close to shame. "Just my brain...not today. It does this."

Alette just gives her another sharp look, like she can read everything in Terese's expression in an instant, before she wraps her hands around her cup of tea. "So this is what Mel means by 'obviously traumatized'." Her voice isn't unkind. "Your brain chemistry isn't processing the world in a typical manner, so instead of reacting to everything around you like everyone else, it's interpreting things as threatening."

It's a lot of words to say she's anxious, but Terese nods, scowling.

"Did it do that before?"

Good question. Great question, to be honest.

"Not like this," Terese says, then forces her hand to grab at the shot of espresso, to sip from it.

It tastes great, of course.

"I think, I think I would get worried about mundane

things, stress about class work, about performances—"
Until the words fell from her lips, Terese hadn't connected
that performances were something she cared about, but
even a split second of consideration turns up plenty of
vague memories of standing on a stage "—But not...not
feeling like this." Then, once more, her brain catches on to
the statement. "Wait, Melekai called me traumatized?"

"Well, yes," Alette says, and wrinkles her nose. "He's not
wrong?"

"Obviously," Terese says, grabbing the bag of chips
again. "I thought he wanted me gone."

"He's way softer than that," Alette says. "He doesn't like
the idea of you, but..."

"Nobody does," Terese quips. "I don't like the idea of me,
either."

Alette doesn't respond, her perfectly shaped brow
furrowing, as she sips more of her tea, like Terese's joke falls
flat.

"Zoel trusts you," Alette says, finally. "Trust that you
won't do anything to intentionally hurt us, and that helps
Melekai, I think."

"Glad of that, at least," Terese says, and the fear is still
there, in the back of her mind, lurking. "When you showed
up in my cave with that needle, I thought he had given it to
you to kill me."

It's clearly Alette's turn for her brain to skip.

"That's why I ran," Terese says, and the conversation has
skipped so many places, it's hard for her to track down
where it got off the rails. "Seems foolish, in retrospect."

This gets Alette to crack a smile, and Terese isn't entirely
sure that she or the demon ever saw that expression, and
she immediately looks far younger and far less severe.

"Well, what do you do on days like this?" Alette says, as if she has a spreadsheet of every topic of conversation.

"Pick my most isolated spot and sit there until it goes away?" Terese shrugs. "Not much I can do."

"Hmm," Alette says, cryptic.

TERESE SITS long enough to finish the bag of chips and the espresso, but Alette disappears into the bowels of the compound with the strip of linen in her hand.

Even thinking of the car isn't enough to spin Terese into anger instead of this fear, so she pulls her knees into her chest, still on the chair in the kitchen, and breathes.

It doesn't help much, it never does, but she lets her mind wander, lets it pick apart the conversation, the hints and seeds Alette offered to her.

Of course she knew that everyone else most likely discussed her, but the raw knowledge of it prickles more fear.

Even though Melekai had suggested she needs help, instead of getting kicked out. And Zoel still trusts her to not hurt people intentionally.

And Axel doesn't get attached easily.

She mulls on that, finishing the water bottle, and mulls on the vague shape of emotions inside of her, the ones that exist somewhere beneath the fear.

It's obvious that he cares for everyone around him, that he could care for her, stopping her from panicking and giving her food on the first night, even though he had threatened her with a gun less than an hour before.

It's obvious he doesn't like it when people around him

are upset. How he tried to smooth things over with Mel, tried to offer her comfort when she's distressed.

And she's not sure if she could pinpoint a moment where that concern and care turned into something looser, a bit more freeing and fun, but somewhere it did.

"Huh," Terese mumbles to the empty kitchen, then turns that same, fear-fueled introspection onto herself.

The idea of something happening to him immediately sours her mouth, immediately twists something inside her stomach deeper than her gut, but she blinks through it. Of course she would fear that, that's logical. Everyone would fear something happening to one of their only friends.

But even she knows everyone doesn't have the tightness in their chests when looking at someone, not like how she does with Axel.

"Well, fuck," she mutters, then turns and looks at the toaster.

19

———————

Terese times it well, so when Axel all but stumbles into the kitchen, bleary-eyed and curls askew, she's figured out the labyrinthine coffee machine and brewed an exceptionally dark pot of coffee.

He blinks at her, like she caught him doing something he shouldn't, before visibly shaking himself back together and making a direct line for the toaster.

Izzy twitches her ears at him as he steps over her.

Alette knew what she was talking about.

"Did'ya sleep well?" he mumbles, not looking anywhere but at the toaster.

Something unwinds in her at his words. Like her mind needed him to come into view before it let go of the tiniest of the anxieties.

"Until Alette texted me," Terese says, sipping from her own cup of coffee. It had required a ton of sugar and cream to make it drinkable for her, but her mind complained a hell of a lot less with a drink she made with her own hands instead of someone else's. "She's a morning person, isn't she?"

He nods, face not really moving until the toaster pops up, then pours himself the biggest mug in the kitchen. "Since we were kids." He flops down at the table with his dry toast and bitter coffee.

He, frankly, looks like shit. Circles under his eyes, hair undone, and instead of his normally stylish jeans and well-tailored shirts, he's in a scrubby pair of work pants and a loose band shirt.

And the tight feeling in her chest doesn't go away, even when he's like this.

Fuck.

Not a great time for it, for her brain to decide to work on developing attachments to other people, when a demon is after her and she's reliant on them for help. Not a great choice for it to be someone she hurt so horridly and for it to be someone who once shot her in the head.

She sighs into her coffee cup, as her mind grabs onto the idea of Daniil after her and holds on tight, going off spinning in that direction and leaving her all but helpless to watch herself obsess over it.

It's far more fun to think of Axel, as fraught as that might be.

But she can't count on Daniil just biding his time while she wrestles with such frivolous stuff as emotions and feelings and drunken make-outs. Can't count on him not actively planning, waiting until she shows some vulnerability or chink in her armor and rushing in.

And maybe she and the previous demon had watched too many movies, because all she can think of is that she has a giant gaping one right at this very moment, sitting across from the table from her, hungover as shit.

"Do you want to go on a walk?" Axel mumbles, still into his coffee cup, and Izzy bounds to her feet at his words.

TRUE TO ALETTE'S PREDICTION, he leads her into the thicket of the trees, where the sun doesn't so much shine as trickle down in a mottled shade. There's a winding path, barely wide enough for them to stand side by side.

Blackberries perfume the air in the summer heat, and birds call off in the distance.

Axel says nothing, just sipping his coffee and staring at the world with the air of someone resigned to his fate. Izzy happily plods along, sniffing at every bush and tree.

These sort of walks are good for big dogs like Izzy, and Terese had always meant to take her on them, but always stopped herself.

A part of her brain spins off in fear that she's been a bad dog owner to Izzy, before she shrugs in on herself, watching Izzy in her happiness.

"Sorry if Alette was too much," Axel mumbles, after a good fifteen minutes of them walking in forest-filled silence. "She can be intense."

"That's a good word for it," Terese says, before she can stop herself, then sighs. "She was harmless."

"I woke up to three texts about how she scared you?" he says idly, but his eyes are brighter, a bit more alert, after such a short walk. "Then one that says you have anxiety. Which..."

"Ha," Terese says. "The term she used was, I believe, traumatized."

The corners of his lips twitch up.

"But yeah, magic didn't really like the whole scanning stuff, thought I was being attacked even though I wasn't," Terese continues, the same fear that she had to keep silent around Alette pushing her to divulge everything to Axel. "It was awkward, and I definitely think I offended her, but I mean...she used that needle to connect a broken main Ley Line. It's terrifying to see that so close to my wrist."

He nods, as if he finds nothing crazy about her premise. "I couldn't see it, but Melekai still gets twitchy whenever she pulls it out."

It's a bit of vindication that at least someone else has the same fear, even if the other person is a former demon.

The path bends, turning them more towards the gravel driveway, before Axel tilts his head to her, leading her further into the brush instead of the full sun, down a barely visible game trail.

Izzy practically prances on it, tail held high, and Terese is going to have to comb through her fur to get all the burrs and twigs out.

It takes only a few steps to get deep enough where the road vanishes from view, the established path far behind them, and the sounds of the forest hiding any other evidence of mankind.

A part of her tries to count her steps, so she can get out if they get lost, and she has to remind that part of herself that she can teleport and it doesn't actually matter if she ever gets lost.

"Don't be surprised if Alette still gets something useful from the reading, she's good like that," Axel warns her, like it took the extra path and time for him to find his words. "But seriously, get comfortable telling her to stop, or else it'll be nothing but questions."

Telling someone that outright seems beyond foolish at the moment, and she's inclined to agree with the fearful part of herself regarding that.

The path widens abruptly to a rock outcropping. Vines and moss twist over the craggy surfaces, leaving them soft and blurring the edges. The largest has a crack tracing down the edge, jagged and new, as if something powerful had shaken the land and split them apart.

Giant spruce trees reach overhead, dangling branches over them, shading the stones, and Axel approaches the rocks without fear, sitting down on one and sipping from his coffee.

"What happened here?" Terese asks, tentatively approaching the split, running her fingers over the rough edges.

"Don't know, noticed it a few months after the line went, possibly something to do with that," Axel says, stretching his legs in front of him. "Alette doesn't know about it, I didn't care enough to bring her here to confirm anything."

So this is a private place for him, one he doesn't bring people into, and she lets her fingertips fall from the broken stone.

And he brought her.

"Zoel could probably tell me in a moment, but then he'd know my hangover spot, and I like him fine, but he gets weird about nature."

She could have told him that many times over, but it almost goes without saying for Wights. "He was definitely disapproving of my wards on the tunnel."

Birds chirp overhead, and she pokes at the rock a little more, something about it not letting her just sit there and accept it until she understands it more.

He lets her, just drinking more of his coffee and staring out at the dense forest around them.

"I don't think this was me?" she says, finally. "I mean, I never got this far into your land, but unless you blame me for all the breaks, I don't..."

"Nah, if it's anything, it's Gurlien. He's the one that

messed up the stuff here," Axel says, and the muted light is...nice. Peaceful. If she could relax her brain enough to enjoy it, it'd be fantastic.

She nods at him, not so much agreeing as acknowledging that she received it. "He did the solarium?"

"Yep." Axel stretches out his long legs again. "Right before everything was...bad."

She believes him, but continues exploring the little clearing, half out of curiosity and half out of the furious need to make sure it's safe.

Of course it's safe. Of course he wouldn't take her somewhere dangerous when he is just as hungover as she is. He saved her from the demon, he wouldn't drag her into peril while taking a walk on his own property. Izzy wouldn't be rolling around in the damp moss if it wasn't safe.

Still.

"Did you know Frisse had a daughter?" Axel asks, after watching her pace around in silence for a few more minutes, sipping his coffee.

That stops her dead in her tracks. "What?"

"Our reaction too," he says, shrugging. "Found out about her after Frisse died. Alette never knew about her own half-cousin."

Many things chase their ways through her brain, so she just stares at him.

"Near as we can tell, she's completely normal. Raised by her dad, got a check from mom every month in the mail, has no idea about all of...this." Axel waves his hands at the surrounding woods, towards the compound up the hill. "Alette still hasn't gotten up the guts to talk to her. To tell her things."

A wire worm of hurt winds its way through Terese's

stomach. "Why didn't she do this" —she waves at herself —"to her, then?"

"Fuck," Axel says, which perfectly encapsulates how Terese feels. "Who the fuck even knows. I don't. Frisse sure didn't have any maternal instinct to say otherwise, that's for sure."

Terese stares at him and tries to figure out if she should be offended. Be angry.

Not at him, but facing the exhaustion of being angry at Dr. Frisse for one more thing is daunting.

"Wow," Terese says finally, "she didn't even tell her own niece?"

Axel relaxes, just a hair, and she gets the small thrill of knowing she chose wisely. That choosing to not hold the anger closer than she's holding his estimation. "Her own niece who she raised, I might add."

"Wow."

She falls silent, resuming her pacing.

"Did I cause this?" he asks, after a few minutes filled only with birdsong and the rustling of the wind. "With yesterday?"

"Cause what?" Terese asks, pausing in her scanning of the trees to glance back at him.

"You're pacing around like you're being chased by bees," he says, his hands tight around his coffee mug, "and you're jumping at every sound."

"No," she says, as fast as she can, as if that could make him understand it quicker. "Sometimes this just happens, nothing to do with anyone or anything."

It's weird to explain it twice in one day, after so many months of existing with it.

He nods, a thoughtful frown adorning his face.

"That's what Alette meant by trauma," she supplies, "mind just is afraid, and I'm stuck with it for the day."

"Do you want to talk about it?" he asks, and her stomach drops in terror.

No one has ever asked that, and her skin crawls at the idea of someone knowing that much about her, all the little inner bits of her mind, all her paranoias and thoughts.

"Whatever it is you're afraid of, whatever"—he waves his hand at her, nebulous—"thing is going on in your mind, do you wanna just...say it? Get it out?"

Putting it into words takes her a moment, but he's patient, just watching her.

"I have...never. Done that before." She resumes pacing, everything too much to remain still. "Never spoken about any of it before. Just always stayed alone on days like this."

His kind gaze, still hungover and unkempt, doesn't leave her. "Well, now you don't have to."

Her foot hitches in its pacing.

"You don't have to be alone, if you don't want to."

It's too big of a statement for her hungover brain, in the dappled light of the forest, but she lets herself dwell on it. Makes herself dwell on it.

She doesn't have to be alone.

He's here, even though she's pacing, even though adrenaline spikes through her body and she's twitching at every unfamiliar noise. Even though she snapped at Alette, even though they kissed the night before, even though she caused him so much harm.

"Maybe...maybe I'll talk about it when I'm not...actively in it," she says haltingly. "Not right now, it's too much, but maybe after."

He nods, like that's a straightforward answer. "Fair enough, so we distract you," he says, like it's easy, setting the coffee cup down on the stone and digging into his pocket. "Ever see a magic trick?"

"I can literally explode things," she says, and gets rewarded by a smile. "I teleport and I come back from the dead."

"Not like that," he says, pulling out a large coin from his pocket, showing her as if she would know what it is.

It's definitely not any currency she knows.

"I'm talking tricks," he continues, flipping the coin in his hands in a smoothed, practiced motion. "Things anyone could do, if they learned. Things to shock people, to confuse them, because what I'm doing shouldn't be possible."

Between one word and the next, he closes his hand, and when he opens it again, the coin is gone.

She gives him a wary glance, but he grins at her, wide and charming, then flips his other hand over to reveal the coin.

"So, sleight of hand?" she says, as he flips the coin between his fingers again, drawing closer.

"Exactly." She's watching, but still, the coin disappears before reappearing in the other hand, without them touching. "Make people think they understand where the coin is"—he flicks it in the air, glittering, before catching it —"and then subvert the expectation."

She sits down on the rock next to him, foolishness still settling in her bones, but she's willing to indulge him if he honestly thinks that coin tricks will help.

The traitor part of her mind tells her she'd indulge him in a lot more, regardless.

"Then how do you do this?" she says, skeptical, and he turns to face her, sitting on the rocks, and begins to explain.

∿

IT HELPS, a little bit.

~

THEY RETURN to the compound with a text from the Necromancer that suggests a breakthrough in deciphering the car.

"Still not a trap," the Necromancer greets them as they walk into the underground parking garage, Izzy tucked between them, "but definitely something."

When her eyes flicker to Terese, there's the same instant brief cut of hunger and power, before it evaporates, giving Terese a somewhat dumbfounded look.

"Not a trap is good," Axel says, though his mouth twitches downwards when he sees the state of his car.

The Necromancer closes her mouth with a snap, raising her eyebrow at Terese, before obviously moving on.

"But he left a signature," the Necromancer continues. "Terese, this'll be bright."

"Thanks," Terese says, strangely touched that she gets a warning, then turns away from the car, her eyes landing on Axel instead.

Of course.

"Wait, I want to see this," Axel says with some sort of childish glee, fishing out the magicked glasses from his pockets. Somewhere along the line, his hangover appears to have vanished, which is more than a little unfair.

The brilliant gold dagger of power still rockets through the room, reflecting on Axel's face, the glasses crawling with runes until it disappears.

Terese flinches, of course, unable to stop herself, her chest seizing, until she forces herself to exhale.

It takes a few seconds.

But when it subsides, she forces her legs to turn her back

towards the car, and a warping black thread, almost glowing, draws itself between all the lines and scrawled on words.

And it tastes immediately of Daniil.

Terese swallows down the fear, the immediate gut horror of seeing that there, and her magic pulses, sharp, in response to the threat. The obvious threat, the exact power of the person threatening her, here, right in front of her.

"Yup, that's him," Axel confirms, with a quick glance at her. "Definitely the same guy."

"Exactly," the Necromancer says, and Terese isn't quite getting what she's aiming for. "But now we have a bright, perfect example of what his magic is, how it's constructed, and how to track it."

How to track him.

How to track him, instead of the other way around. Instead of however he's finding her, they could go to him, make the first move.

Find him instead.

She almost teleports away right that instant.

"What about stopping it?" Terese asks, after a few moments of staring blankly at it and focusing all her energy on not disappearing.

"That's significantly more difficult," Melekai says, and Terese had been so focused on the Necromancer that she completely missed him, lounging in a camp chair. "But more possible with this."

He stands, stalking towards the car, and every movement of him is so obviously demon that Terese breathes out hard through her nose and faces Axel, instead.

"Much more possible to get a warning," Melekai continues, completely oblivious to Terese's almost breakdown, "or set our own trap."

Axel reaches out and touches her elbow, and she just about jumps out of her skin.

"That's good, right?" Axel prods, clearly aiming for Melekai but still keeping Terese's gaze.

"It's a start," Melekai says, grim. "Now it's all about designing a trap to keep him."

TERESE ESCAPES as soon as she can back to her little library, curling up into a ball on the couch, poking at her phone with a desperate sort of horror.

TERESE (4:00 PM): If I disappear I'll come back, I promise.

THE HANDSOME ONE (4:01 PM): Do you want to take the gun?

Izzy whines, deep in the back of her throat, and Terese dangles the hand over to pet her.

"I'm okay," Terese whispers, tangling her fingers in her dog's long fur.

Izzy is well in need of a bath, after the dust of the dog park and the mud of the moss, but it's incredibly difficult for Terese to care about that.

It's not a horrible idea, if strange, to think about arming herself with something so concrete as a gun. Even a bespelled gun.

TERESE (4:06 PM): About 80% certain I've never shot a gun before.

THE HANDSOME ONE (4:07 PM): I can teach you.

THE HANDSOME ONE (4:08 PM): Normally I don't let anyone touch it before doing a class with me, but if you misfire and hit yourself, I'm oddly unconcerned.

Terese snorts at her phone, and Izzy raises her head at the noise.

THE HANDSOME ONE (4:10 PM): Seriously though, be safe. We don't know where he can get to you.

And that is the only reason she isn't already at the tunnel, or the cabin in the middle of the woods, or at the boat.

She sighs, letting the phone drop to her chest and staring up at the ceiling.

THE NECROMANCER (4:11 PM): Can we chat?

Terese thinks about sitting up at that but grabs the blanket from the foot of the couch and hauls it over her. It doesn't quite help, but the weight is comforting.

TERESE (4:12 PM): Do you mean in person because I'd rather not.

THE NECROMANCER (4:13 PM): Lol.

THE NECROMANCER (4:13 PM): So you know how demons form attachments to people? Like me and Mel?

TERESE (4:14 PM): If you say Daniil did that to me, I'm gonna cry, fair warning.

THE NECROMANCER (4:15 PM): Well, a little, but Mel said he already warned you about that.

THE NECROMANCER (4:16 PM): But are you meaning to do that to Axel?

Terese sits up bolt upright.

TERESE (4:17 PM): I am not a demon.

THE NECROMANCER (4:17 PM): Obv not, but a lot of your power is, and it's doing that.

TERESE (4:18 PM): Fuck.

THE NECROMANCER (4:19 PM) Lol.

THE NECROMANCER (4:20 PM): I am NOT telling anyone because you do not need any more complications in your life.

Terese debates feeling grateful, but the mortification is too strong.

Izzy lets out a huff before climbing to her feet and sticking her head in Terese's lap. Because even her dog has opinions on her emotions and shit.

"Ugh," she whispers, then finally gives into the thudding of her magic and lets it swing her away.

Instead of the tunnel, she finds herself on the wooden floor of the cabin, and Izzy wriggles out of her grasp to stick her nose where Terese hides her treats.

The teleportation doesn't help the stuck emotion in her chest, but Terese lets Izzy's energy push herself up to puttering around the cabin.

It's a vacation home to some rich couple that has only visited once while Terese has been teleporting to it, instead keeping itself in a thick layer of dust. Floral curtains hang over the windows, and a remarkably ugly couch squats in the living room.

There's a functioning stove and running water and electricity, but it's bitterly cold in the winter and the wind whistles right through it at night.

TERESE (4:32 PM): At the cabin, still safe.

THE HANDSOME ONE (4:33 PM): Pics or it didn't happen.

She snaps one of Izzy, already climbing on the ugly couch, and sends it.

THE NECROMANCER (4:34 PM): Did you run away because you were uncomfortable????

Terese decides to ignore that one, instead wandering from room to tiny room in the cabin, grabbing one of the many grocery bags she's left there and grabbing some of her extra clothing.

THE HANDSOME ONE (4:41 PM): And here I thought
Lyra had bad interior design.

Izzy stretches out with a dog warble, her paws reaching
from end to end of the couch. Terese rarely stays the night at
the cabin on account of all the wind, but it's useful to hide
stuff away. The rich couple hadn't even opened the door to
the other bedrooms, let alone any of the dressers and
closets.

And then she feels it.

A growing pressure, small, at the base of her skull.
Something sharp probing, poking at her awareness, and she
stills.

It's dark beyond the dusty curtains, but even freezing
doesn't stop the search, as it crawls around her mind like a
spider picking through a web. Dark and vicious and oh-so-
familiar.

Daniil.

She doesn't breathe, doesn't move, her knees locked in
place in the guest bedroom of the cabin.

It presses harder, before vanishing.

"Fuck," she blurts out, then dashes back to Izzy on the
couch, all but falling on top of her and squeezing her eyes
shut.

Her magic doesn't want to shift away, not immediately,
but she crams her willpower against it, until she and Izzy
crash down onto the ground underneath the spruce tree
and into the blackberry bramble.

She huddles there, waiting for the power again, gripping
Izzy's collar tight as Izzy wriggles and whines, but nothing
reaches out for her mind.

But even her cabin hadn't protected her. And she had
never been in danger there before.

20

S he spends the rest of the evening huddled in the library, thank you very much, and when she falls asleep, she dreams of spiders and awakens covered in sweat and Izzy blinking plaintively up at her from the ground.

A cold shower does little besides make her shiver, and by the time she makes her way down to the kitchen for coffee, all that's left is a sinking doom.

But also, she ate nothing besides the single bag of chips, and she has a sinking suspicion that if she doesn't, then the Necromancer would absolutely call her out, and nothing sounds worse at the moment.

At least her mind isn't rejecting any food that isn't prepared by her, which is already an improvement over the day before, though now it's back to the refusing to think of anything as appetizing.

Maybe Alette's right. Maybe she has a thing with food.

Almost before she can think, she has her phone out in her hand again.

TERESE (10:21 AM): Want to pick out a ridiculous food again?

She's not sure if that counts as flirting, or if she just wants to see him. Nevertheless, her heart kicks it up a notch when she sees him typing back.

TERESE (10:22 AM): I promise to teleport us all away at the first sign of danger.

"I'm down," Axel says, breezing right in and going for the pot of coffee she already brewed, and her heart unwinds at the sight of him. "It's Saturday, that's prime brunch day."

Izzy pauses in eating her kibble to glance up at him, barely, before continuing to eat.

"How was Romania? Did you feel better?" he asks, sipping his coffee and raising an eyebrow at her. "See, I'm trying to figure out what actually helps and what is just magical mumbo jumbo, and so far all I got is explaining magic tricks."

Terese opens her mouth to respond, to tell him of Daniil and the conversation with the Necromancer, before she just sighs.

"That bad?" He pours the coffee directly into a thermos. "I'll pack the gun."

THEY SIT in a tiny little outdoor booth, all but squished up together with Izzy underneath the table, and the knowledge that the demon-spelled gun is safely inside a normal looking knapsack next to Axel helps.

What helps more is the press of Axel against her side, and she's aware it's ridiculous but not so ridiculous that she's going to stop herself.

She pays him no mind as he orders, instead letting her

mind wander and her vision blur, until all there is, is the sensation of him leaning against her as well.

"You still here?" he asks mildly after the waitress drops off two coffees piled high with whipped cream.

"Yeah," she says, muzzly, before shaking herself loose and grabbing her spoon. "Sorry."

"Just making sure it wasn't the creepy catatonic," he replies, but thankfully doesn't move away from her as she scoops off the whipped cream and feeds it to Izzy. "That's adorable."

"It's her favorite."

Obviously copying her, he scoops his whipped cream and offers it to Izzy, who promptly ignores it.

And another bit of her defense cracks.

"Daniil tried something, but it wasn't successful while I was out and then I hid in the library the rest of the night," Terese says, all in one breath. "The Necromancer is still so goddamn spooky and Alette was giving me hints on how to help your hangover and I ate only a bag of chips yesterday."

He blinks, obviously caught off guard.

"So yeah, it was a bit too much for one day," she says, as he watches helplessly. "I'm glad about the gun."

He stares at his coffee, wide-eyed, then, telegraphing his movements, puts his arm around her shoulders.

She shivers once at the contact, then leans in further against him.

"Yeah, bag of chips wasn't enough," he says. "Lyra continues to be the spookiest person I've ever met."

It's a bit of grace that he's not immediately talking about the demon.

"I've seen her bring two people back from the dead now, and I'd be okay never seeing it again," he continues, and she leans her cheek against him. "I still think Alette needs therapy, and she was only dead for fourteen hours."

Terese can only imagine that Alette would vehemently deny the need.

"Lyra once looked at me and told me she could tell I only slept for an hour and then stubbed my toe and all Mel did was laugh."

"Having a demon train a necromancer is all sorts of insane," Terese says, refusing to move from this strange half hug, half cuddle he has her in.

She knows she probably had this Before, but the vague memories pale compared to the actual sensation.

"It's not like Alette or I had any sort of practical knowledge," he says with a shrug, but he's getting into a storyteller mode, his shoulders straight, his lips cocked in a half smile. "And it's not like we were gonna stop him, he was practically going batty from not doing anything."

His hand idly plays with the edge of her sleeve, one of those idle little motions he's always making, before he takes a deep breath -

And immediately gets cut off by the waitress dropping off the food.

This time he got her an omelet doused in chili and topped with avocado, with a large side of fried potatoes.

"They had nothing truly weird," he says, as if she is anything less than befuddled by the amount of food.

"Probably still better than just a bag of chips," Terese says, allowing herself one more moment of pressing up against him before pulling away to grab her fork. Then, because he's given her enough grace, "I don't know what Daniil was trying to do."

They gave him a pile of waffles with fruit draped on top,

and he remains silent as he digs in, waiting for her to continue.

Which is fair.

"It was pressure against my mind, but not...not how it is when he's in front of me. He didn't speak, instead poking around."

"Have you ever seen the movie Jurassic Park?" Axel asks, and when she shakes her head, continues. "There's a bit about one dinosaur being smart enough to test new locations in an electronic fence. Once they knew one place wouldn't work, they'd try another."

"And this way didn't put him in danger of being shot," she says, then makes herself pause and try the chili omelet.

It's good, of course. Almost unfairly, with the direness of their conversation.

"And not causing brain bleed, probably," Axel says, which almost seems beside the point. "So he's trying new things. Good info to have, we'll check with Mel and see if he has some theories on what will be next, and prep for them. Easy."

"Easy." She marvels at his confidence.

"We have Mel, who will know more about tactics than anyone else. We have Lyra, who is goddamn good at detecting weird demon things."

She detected whatever the heck Terese is doing to Axel, after all.

"We have Zoel, who's able to pick apart problems with an eye on the big picture, we have Alette with all of her research and frankly disturbing amount of power, and we have you, who's survived this before and thrown him out twice now." She's not sure how much of this bravado is false. "I'm not sure you could put together a better team." His face twists, ever so briefly. "Outside of maybe the demonologists at the College, but they're...not likely to help you, and even then Mel will know more."

It's a nice thought, hidden behind everything else, and he leans over to knock shoulders with her.

"Are you ever not optimistic?" she asks, but still, finds herself smiling at him.

"Nah, anything else is depressing."

They're silent for a few moments, eating, as Terese ponders all he just said, and worms of hope weasel their way inside of her.

"The big question is how he found you," Axel continues, gesturing with his fork, "and for that I think we need Lyra's help."

GETTING the Necromancer's help entails asking her to scan Terese, which Terese is not okay with. Thankfully, they had waited a day, giving Terese enough time to will herself up, to trick herself into thinking it might work.

Later that evening, there's a knock on the door to her library, even though the door is left open, so she props herself up to look, plopping her phone onto the side table.

Axel leans against the doorjamb, all faux suaveness that is completely betrayed by his foot jangling against the floor.

Izzy pays him no attention, snoring softly on the rug.

"Yeah?" she asks, sitting up, and she's not blushing, but her entire face still feels warm.

"You weren't asleep, right?" he asks, like he's about to vibrate out of his own skin with energy. "I mean, I saw you on your phone —"

"Yeah, I'm good." She nods him in, and Izzy wakes just

long enough to give him an entirely unimpressed look, before laying her head back down.

"Great, yeah, I figured," he rambles, plopping himself onto the overchair across from her. "I just hadn't seen you for the rest of the day and wanted to...make sure I didn't like...over step or something."

She wrinkles her nose at him.

He sighs, and he's tapping his fingers against the arm of the chair, fast. "Look, I kissed you while drunk, that's not a terribly cool thing to do, and I was cuddling with you, then you weren't hanging around."

She blinks at him, glancing down at Izzy, then back up at him. "I didn't mind any of that," she says, with the itching feeling in the back of her mind that this is something that means something to Axel, and she shouldn't discount it.

So she leans forward, directing as much of her body language to him as possible, as he taps his way to hopefully feeling better.

He gives her a blank look, and it's the look he seems to give her when he's desperately trying to figure out what to say but coming up empty.

Which is almost funny, in some small part of her mind. He talks so continuously, so easily, that him dumbfounded is endearing.

Because these are the things she finds endearing now. Of course.

"Axel," she starts, and he jolts to meet her eyes, "I can blow things up. If I didn't want you to cuddle with me I'd stop you."

"Okay, yes, good point," he says, and a hair of the manic energy leaves him. "I just...I know you need our help, you're trying super hard to work with us and have basically been amazing and constantly trying to do whatever we need…and I don't want to be creepy about it."

It's her turn to give him a blank look.

"I don't want to take advantage of you trying to not be possessed," he says, and she'd be good without ever seeing that look on his face again.

And what he's trying to say slowly leaks through her brain, filters through her ears until it makes sense.

She could take it two ways, easily. She could take him as being a genuine person and having a small freak out about consent and about what she wants, or that he's trying for an easy and gentle way out of whatever they're crafting.

She knows which one she prefers.

The stirring in her stomach knows which one she prefers.

"I'll make you a deal," she says, and his eyebrows raise. "I promise to tell you if you do something I don't want you to do, if you tell me when I'm completely missing whatever the hell conversations are about."

"Deal," he says immediately. Like he didn't even have to think about it.

"Okay, cool, what's this conversation about?" she asks, and he cracks a smile. "'Cause I'm not sure if you're trying to apologize or just make sure I'm not mad. 'Cause I'm not mad?"

"Not being mad isn't…isn't enough for me?" he says, like he's also struggling with the communication, which makes her feel a bit better, then he sighs. "I like you. I like you and I'm pretty awkward about it, and don't want to come on too strong too early if it'll scare you away."

"You are the least awkward person I know," Terese responds.

"That's because you know about five people," he retorts,

and they share a quick, mad grin. "Look, I know I come across as a lot."

She shakes her head.

"Literally every person I've ever dated said I am. And I like you too much to not want to be careful with that."

She sits back, and warmth uncurls around her spine, but she gives herself a moment to think. To process what he's saying, to respond with what she really thinks, instead of the first thing that pops into her mind.

And he fidgets in front of her, like he's the one that needs to be nervous.

"Well, I have no clue if I've ever dated anyone," she starts, and gets a smile in return, which was the goal, "but I'd imagine I'd get some really strange comments in return, on account of all the..." She gestures at all of herself. "But yeah, I'll tell you if you're too intense, or too much, or whatever, if I ever think that."

He nods, like he's absorbing the information, too.

"Are you asking me to date you?" she asks, because she's mostly sure but not entirely, and that's not exactly something she wants to misread. "Because there's a homicidal demon after me, I'm not sure how much dating I can do."

"Dating might be a weird way to describe it," Axel says, finally looking like he's settling into his skin, his hand tapping less on the chair. "Seeing each other?"

"Making out?" Terese suggests.

"Wooing?"

This makes her smile, and he grins at her in return.

"I'm okay with something like that," Terese says, and her face is warm, but there's pink in his cheeks as well.

◠

THE NEXT DAY, all those good feelings evaporate in the face of the nerves of actually getting the Necromancer's help.

"I still think we should tie her up for this," Melekai grouches, as they walk into yet another room with padding on the wall. Deep scorch grooves adorn the walls and ceilings, scorch marks that taste of young and uncontrolled magic.

Terese doesn't entirely disagree, but even she knows how impractical it is. "I can teleport. I don't think tying me down will do much."

Her heart pounds, though, at the idea.

"It just means you'll teleport somewhere, still tied up," Melekai snaps back. "Ask me how I know."

The Necromancer gives him a sideways smile, and with that, Terese is absolutely not going to ask how he knows.

Axel coughs up a laugh, and now she is one hundred percent certain he caught that too. He's wearing the glasses she fixed, and despite everything, they still make him look incredibly young.

"Tying up isn't necessary," Zoel says, looking directly at Terese with the stare of someone who knows entirely too much about her. "We can restrict her."

Terese doesn't know how he knows that, and it grates against her mind.

"And I promise I will do nothing to hurt you," the Necromancer says, which again, isn't the problem and isn't what Terese is afraid of. "And I'll stop the moment you need me to."

"No, don't stop until you get all the information," Melekai interrupts. "She can deal, getting answers is more important than comfort."

As much as her palms sweat and her head thuds, he's

right. As much as she doubts that this will do anything, he's right.

"Should the...killable humans wait outside?" Terese asks, jerking her thumb at Axel and Alette. "I don't want to pull up a death bubble and catch them in the wave."

"Thanks," Axel says.

There are way too many people in the room, with just the six of them, and Izzy sadly warbling outside the closed door.

"You won't pull a death bubble," Zoel explains, still infuriatingly calm. "There's no strip of magic in here big enough for you to do so."

It doesn't help, but she knows when she's stalling.

"And I can help if you do," the Necromancer says with way more cheer than is appropriate. "We've established they won't hurt me. I can bring people back, it's no big deal."

"No big deal," Alette repeats, dryly.

"It's a little bit of a big deal," Axel says, but he's bouncing on his toes, full of energy and something close to joy, at the idea of fixing this, and Terese can't find it in herself to disappoint him, to crush the optimism.

Which, again, fuck.

Terese takes the moment to shove her hair behind her ears, before leveling the Necromancer with as steady of a gaze as she can muster.

"Okay, go for it."

And with a quick nod, she does.

Immediately, everything is alight with a furious, furious blaze of pain and hunger.

Terese gasps, the air pressed from her lungs, her legs jerking outside her control, flinching back. It's too much, it's so much, and—

Oh, what is this? In her mind, Daniil speaks. *What—*

The Necromancer twists her hand, cutting his voice short. "Not right now," she speaks, her voice clear, but the knife's edge of pain and terror remains.

It's different from the pain and pressure of the demon forcing its way into her. Instead of something crowding into her brain, pushing her into a smaller and smaller bit of her mind, it's like all the space she could exist within is full of fire, large and ever growing.

"Easy," the Necromancer whispers, and it's like there's no one left in the room, just the two of them.

Somehow, somewhere, Terese's hands close around two fistfuls of magic, like they could protect her. Like her entire being is working to stop this threat in front of her.

The Necromancer tilts her head at Terese, and she's way more powerful than when she had previously dealt with the demon. She's way more powerful, she's way more controlled.

She could cut Terese down in a second.

Terese shakes her hands out, releasing the magic, and black spots edge along her vision.

"This isn't hurting you, you're just thinking it's hurting you," the Necromancer says, and the edge of her mouth turns down into a frown. "And...there."

The power sears into Terese, into her mind, picking at one particular place, and—

21

Terese doesn't so much wake up as get slammed into consciousness, and she jolts upward with a gasp.

"Oh, hey, it's okay," Axel's voice says from somewhere close by, and she twists.

She's on the couch, she's on his couch with the fluffy rug and the table with the grid, and he's sitting next to her, with Izzy splayed out on the rug in front of them.

She must've been curled up, tight, and for how long, and—

Izzy raises her head and gives her a sedated woof.

"Um," Terese says, and her mouth is dry, like she had it open the entire time she had been out, so she shakes her head to rid herself of the feeling.

Her brain jostles uncomfortably.

He sets down the screwdriver and the electronics he had been fiddling with on the table, eyebrows raising.

"You fainted," Axel says casually, as if it's easy. "Lyra apparently poked your mind where possessions happen, whatever that means, and you fainted clean away."

"I passed out," Terese says, testing out her voice. It's normal.

"No, Lyra was pretty clear you fainted," Axel says, and she peers up at him to find him grinning at her. "Said it was 'clearly out of fear' and not any of the hundreds of other things apparently weird with your brain."

Terese considers denying that she was afraid, but it seems fairly silly of an action to even attempt.

"You've been out for about..." He makes a show of checking his bare wrist. "Ten minutes. Lyra feels absolutely horrible for scaring you, Mel's considering taking her somewhere secret because apparently it scared him as well, Alette is running tests on the room, and Zoel is...somewhere. Probably with Alette. Maybe off being mystical."

She absorbs it, giving herself the space to think for a few minutes, to feel something besides abject panic.

"I've thought Melekai should take the Necromancer somewhere else for most of this," she says, still piecing her way through whatever emotions she's having. "Daniil noticed, he..."

"Spoke in your mind, Lyra told us," Axel finishes for her once she trails off. "Lyra thinks he tracks you when you use any power. Alette thinks he's just low key monitoring you at all points and noticed the necromancy and thought it neat. I think he's trying to wig you out and is just choosing wisely."

None of these sound particularly good to Terese, but she makes herself breathe out of her nose until her hands stop shaking.

The best is tracking when using her power. She'll avoid it, tamp it down, everything, unless it's an emergency, even if the need to go elsewhere drives her insane.

Worst is the idea that he's just...there. Lurking in her mind, reading all her thoughts, deciding when to strike.

Absorbing all of her emotions and feelings and impulses until he can use them and twist them to his will.

"Did I hurt the Necromancer?" she asks, finally.

"Nope," he says, leaning back against the couch, and she just doesn't know how he could be so blasé. "Though to be fair, she was absolutely rocking you."

"Glasses show you much?" she asks, filtering her reactions to that statement.

She's very okay with the idea of the Necromancer being able to shut her down, to her surprise. Leave one less part of her life a wild card, less of an uncontrollable factor.

Even if she'd pop back up, someone able to even temporarily stop her is good. Especially someone who shows the care that the Necromancer has for everyone.

"Got a light show," he says, and his eyes are sharp, like he's picking up on her mental gymnastics. "Alette's right, necromancy is terrifying."

Terese agrees, and obviously the part of her hind brain that passed out does as well.

There are many things, all crowding into her mind, things she wants to say. She wants to ask about the tension behind his eyes, about why he brought her here. She wants to push herself up, find the Necromancer, apologize for some vague idea that she did something wrong.

She wants to beg her to cut out the part that could get possessed, whatever that means. Wants to ask Alette what she finds, ask Zoel how he would restrain her. Wants to create plans, reinforce protections, take the data and run with it until they have some place she can hide and be truly safe. Wants to strike out against Daniil, from the well of anger and protection still dwelling inside of her, from the threats to Axel.

Wants to never go anywhere else besides this couch with the fluffy rug.

"Hey," Axel says, and rests his hand along the back of the couch so his fingertips brush her arm and startle her. "You okay?"

She blinks at him, pulling herself back with both hands. "Oh yes, just had my brain scanned by a death wizard and had a demon try to yell at me at the same time. I'm peachy."

As she hoped, a smile tugs on his lips. "Dare you to call her a death wizard, Mel will try to fight you."

"And you said she doesn't do combat," Terese says, giving her head another shake to clear it, then pushes herself up to standing.

Her legs wobble, then abruptly dump her back on the couch.

"Maybe not with the standing for a bit," Axel says, though his face twists. "She said your body dumped...pretty much all of your adrenaline at once."

Instead of responding, Terese just rests her head against the back of the couch, then turns to look over at Axel. "I've been shot in the head and still walked it off, this is ridiculous."

"Yes, this is what's ridiculous." There's a gentle look in his eyes, something belying some concern, something close to affection, and for a single moment, it's more terrifying than the necromancy scan that someone could look at her that way.

And yet...here he is. Concerned about someone fainting, when that person can't die. Caring enough to take her someplace else, someplace more comfortable, give her the chance to wake up without being surrounded and overwhelmed.

Someone who touches her arm as if she is a fragile treasure.

She has no words for what's bubbling up inside of her, and that grates against her nerves. Like she should know how to be precise with this, how to describe this in great detail, but all she feels is...soft. Something more tender and vulnerable than newly grown skin, like it would just take the smallest of pushes to hurt.

And there is so much she should do, so much she should try to nail down before something worse happens, but she lets the silence settle over her like a blanket, lets herself relax into the knowledge that her body doesn't want her to move, either.

In front of her, Axel's eyes flicker to her lips, then back up to her gaze.

It's different than the charged moment in the bar.

For one, anything that happens, she can't contribute to alcohol, and her heart thumps at the idea that he could choose to kiss her like that without it.

Also, it's just them. Just the two of them, no other patrons, nobody at the door. No loud music, no neon, just the buzz of Axel's lights and the small sounds the building makes and the cacophony of her thoughts. Thoughts pressing her to speak, filling her mouth with words to say before vanishing them to the nether.

And his eyes don't leave hers.

She's a mess. There's no part of her that's not a mess. Magically, personally, situationally, all a mess. There are so many reasons he should look away, why he should clamor for any way out of it. Nobody would blame him for softly disengaging, nobody would bat an eye if he went back to coldly helping.

It sends a pang through her chest, almost as painful as an actual stab at the thought.

It's dangerous, some sort of traitor part of her whispers. It's dangerous for him, with a rogue demon hunting her down, who'd threaten anyone else who'd have a part of her. It's dangerous, for who is she to guess that she's going to have her sanity for terribly long. Who is she to know if she won't be possessed in another week, another month, and doomed to the pain and agony until she loses herself?

But his fingertips are gentle against her arm, and now they've been silent for far too long, and her lips part.

"May I kiss you?" he asks, his voice low, and it almost takes her a moment to understand his words. "I didn't ask, last time, and I should have."

And to that, she hardly has to think, leaning upwards and pressing her lips against his, not even waiting for him to act.

He makes a small noise of surprise in his throat, and she wants to memorize it. Memorize all the sounds he could make, keep them deep in a hidden part of herself, one that no demon and no mind reader could ever reach. Memorize the feel of his skin against her fingertips, as she cradles his chin towards her, the rough rasp of the hint of a beard.

Of his arm snaking its way around her waist, holding her in place on the couch. Of his other hand, bracing against her upper leg, so her head tilts back with the force of his kiss.

It's all glorious. It's all glorious, and it's all hers. Every brief sensation against her skin, every nerve firing inside of her, all hers.

He breaks the kiss, only to press his mouth against her collarbone, then in the crook of her neck, and she gasps against him. It's simultaneously not enough and too much and nerves she didn't even know about spark up around her.

She drapes her arm over his broad shoulder as he kisses

his way up to her ear until she's sure he can feel the pounding of her pulse against his lips.

For a moment, as he kisses against her jawline where Daniil had gripped her, her magic thrums with a panic to get away, before he pulls back so he can see her face.

She gapes at him.

"You didn't like that," he says, tapping his finger against the spot, "just right there, right?"

"Right," she repeats, her voice unsteady.

"But this"—he leans back down, kissing back down her neck—"you do." His lips trace the words against her skin, and she wants more of it. Wants more of her skin open for him to touch, to kiss, to explore.

It's heady, wanting someone to actually know these parts of her.

"Yes," she breathes, tangling her fingers in his curls, arching her back into him.

Another small noise is wretched from his throat, and she can't believe she's the one doing that to him, and pulls back just enough to capture her lips with his once more, teasing them apart, pushing her further against the couch until all that exists is the two of them, in that moment, with her hands in his hair and his hand on her thigh, until—

In unison, both of their phones beep, and they both jump.

There's a split second where they blink at each other before the phones beep again.

"Why?" Terese asks, voice just a little plaintive, and Axel coughs out a laugh.

It's just as strained as she feels.

"Probably"—he clears his throat, sitting back, and his eyes are wide—"probably checking in. You...you did pass out like twenty minutes ago, and..."

His gaze catches on her lips before he visibly shakes himself.

"Did you already tell them I woke up?" she asks. "If they don't know, we can go right back." Her logic is impeccable.

Another one of his small laughs, and she's going to horde those noises most of all, before just her phone beeps.

With that distance, the same cunning, calculating veil falls over Axel's face, and it just makes her heart pound more.

"I say we see delay this"—he gestures between the two of them—"until we see what they have to say and we can get alone and be left alone."

"Will they stop bothering us if we don't check?" Terese asks, but she too sits up, brushing her hair back from her face, his planning fitting into her mind with something close to anticipation.

"Not likely," he says, so she blinks a few more times, then grabs her phone from the table.

GROUP TEXT:

THE NERDY ONE (11:13 AM): How is she doing, Lyra says she should be awake by now.

THE NERDY ONE (11:14 AM): I would like to ask some questions about my hallway.

Then, in a solo text to just her:

THE NECROMANCER (11:14 AM): I'm sorry I scared you!!

"You're right, she feels bad," Terese says, and even her voice sounds strange to her ears, but she shows the phone to Axel anyway.

He gazes at her for a split second longer than the moment would call for, before he glances at the phone. "What does she mean by hallway?"

GROUP TEXT:

TERESE (11:16 AM): I'm okay, just disoriented.

It beeps to Axel's phone as well, and he huffs out another laugh.

"What?" she says, still fiddling with her hair, as it feels woefully mussed. "It's accurate."

THE NERDY ONE (11:20 AM): Feel up to coming back?

He smiles at her, actually smiles, and once more her heart flips.

"You know," he starts, springing to his feet with way more energy than she feels, "when you first showed up covered in blood, this is not where I expected it to go."

It's a thought she's had many times by now, but it's gratifying to hear him say it.

"If I had thought it'd be like this, I would have stayed at that goddamn hospital," Terese says, then pushes herself up, and her legs wobble. Despite her best efforts, she lists to the side, and Izzy lifts her head and whines.

"Woah, hey, you okay?" Axel reaches out, catching her by the elbow as she braces herself on the table with the tape grid.

"This is ridiculous," she informs him, blinking rapidly and trying to evaluate herself.

Shaky legs, stomach is turning over, and mouth feels dry. She's walked around on worse many times, and just passing out from being scared shouldn't hold her back too much.

Though her face still burns a brilliant red from the kissing. But that's unrelated.

So she huffs out an exhale, then stands straight, focusing all her concentration on supporting her legs with her magic. "I'm okay."

"Here," Axel says, letting go of her arm—her skin misses him, immediately— to hand her a power bar. "I know, I know, but it'll help and get Lyra off your back."

They're silent as they get themselves together, and Izzy pads with them as they make their way back to the room with the padded walls and the scorch mark on the ceiling.

It reeks of necromancy, now brilliant and furious, and Terese flinches the moment she strides into the room.

But the Necromancer's shoulders slump in relief when she sees her walk in.

"I am so sorry," she blurts out, and Melekai sighs, before putting his arm around her shoulder. "I did not think you would actually faint, I—"

And Terese feels a bit more like herself, so she waves her hand. "It's okay, I think."

It must be obvious what happened, it must be written all over her face, but they all act as if nothing did.

Izzy leans against Terese's legs, though, like she's scared she'll be banned from the room again, so Terese idly scratches behind her ears.

There's a moment of silence, as everyone waits for everyone else to speak, and even Zoel looks awkward. Terese didn't even know that he could look awkward.

"What did you find?" Terese asks, after nobody speaks and the room fills up with the quiet. "You stopped him from talking to me. What else?"

"I didn't stop him from speaking, I just made it annoying for him," the Necromancer says, gesturing for Terese to sit down directly onto the foam. "It's a half measure, and he'll probably try again."

"He will," Melekai says, grim.

Axel rests a hand on the small of her back, interrupting the swell of panic and slamming her back down to earth.

"But what I want to know," Alette interrupts, and both Melekai and Axel roll their eyes then grin at each other, "is why half the runes from the elevator to the grand ballroom are reactivated."

Where Terese trailed her hand, all those times ago.

Thankfully, all attention turns to Alette, who doesn't have a single hair out of place.

"They're not re-written, so I know it's not one of you two being sneaky," Alette says, gesturing to the Necromancer and Melekai, "and, quite frankly, Terese...can you even do that?"

"No," Melekai interrupts.

"Or do I need to worry about someone else coming in?" Alette finishes, fully ignoring Melekai with something that belies practice. "They're all benign, right now, but since the demon can speak to her in these walls, what else can he do?"

"We would have noticed—" the Necromancer starts.

"No, it was me," Terese interrupts, then has the split second of panic again, at getting kicked out, at being abandoned, before she shakes it off. "It wasn't Daniil, it was me."

Of course, everyone looks to her, and she has to steel her spine to not take a step back.

"That's not something you can do," Melekai says, like he has a full knowledge of all of her powers instead of just the summary she's given them. "The last demon was shit at runes and couldn't break any of them down, much less reactivate ones written by a dead person."

Alette tilts her head thoughtfully, however, and this isn't how Terese expected any of this conversation going.

"I can stop it, I can put them back, it was just..." Terese trails off, because how can she explain it. Depressing? Distracting? Weird? "They should be fixable by all of you, it was just...touching it and they came back. Why are we talking about this, what about what she found out?" Terese points to the Necromancer.

Again, the long silence as everyone stares at her with the creeping sensation that she did something horribly wrong, and Axel's hand drops away from the touch on her back.

A quick look to him shows the cunning expression right back over his face.

"Terese," Alette starts, and she is not going to like where this is going, "I think we need to talk about what exactly you can do."

22

Alette leads them to a basement Terese hadn't seen before, deep in the bowels of the building.

"I shouldn't be here," Zoel murmurs to Terese, once they reach a collection of runes obviously disintegrated by something chemical. "If you bring these up, they could trap me."

It's among the first times she's actually gotten to speak to him since he came back and talking to him always makes her feel like those first few weeks—small.

"Is it a Wight thing or a demon thing?" Terese asks, taking the steps slowly with her still slightly unsteady legs.

"Both, really," Alette says from in front of them. Axel trails behind the group, hands stuffed in his pockets, the cunning look still over his face. "These were the ones enacted by my aunt to keep everyone—and everything—out. Unfortunately"—Alette gives Zoel a look, and it's unreadable to Terese, but Zoel responds with a soft smile—"it keeps out allies just as much as it does enemies."

With a nod to Alette—and only to Alette—Zoel disappears with that whiff of natural magic that somehow still astounds Terese.

When Terese teleports it just tastes like demons.

"So don't pull them all back, got it," Terese says, as she makes it down the final stairs, and Izzy sniffs around cautiously. Somehow, her dog knows how to give wide berth to the disintegrated paint runes.

Chemicals are such an odd way to bring down runes, and she throws Axel a look.

"Did you take these down?" she asks, and he raises an eyebrow, and somehow, he's reached a conclusion, and something's changed, Something has changed in between the quiet moments they had kissing and walking down to these runes.

He nods, though, and he doesn't look displeased, just calculating.

"It was an emergency," Alette informs her, as if Axel needs defending, "but the rest of the runes broke when we took them down."

It's obvious why, at least to her eye, the magic dead behind the erased paint, dead in a way the still intact but inactive runes upstairs are not.

They're complex, in a way that hurts Terese's mind, layered on top of each other so they obfuscate meaning.

When the demon had first explained to Terese what runes are, through intense frustration, the demon called them numbers, numbers that did things, and the more complicated a combination or formula, the larger the reaction.

This, however, looks like trigonometry, when Terese can only really understand basic algebra.

"Well, the demon would have been impressed," Terese says before she can stop herself, then sighs, "I mean..."

"No, it's pretty complicated," Alette says, an undercurrent to her voice. "There's a reason I haven't been able to bring anything back."

Axel still says nothing.

"So, what, do you want me to just..." Terese waves her hand at it. "Try to put it back? I can't fix things that are that broken."

"Well," Alette starts, delicately, but it's more intense than it should be, and the hair rises on the back of Terese's neck, "what can you do?"

"In here?" Terese glances around, until her eyes fall on a small rune unsplashed by the chemicals, just devoid of power. It's tiny, obviously crafted for comfort and not utility, though it's difficult to tell exactly its use.

"What I want to know is where you got your knowledge from," Melekai speaks from behind them, almost startling her from her concentration. "The last demon was shit at this."

"The last demon was an idiot," Terese replies absentmindedly, "the last demon thought attacking people was a good way to get them to help her."

"Fair enough," Melekai says, but skepticism still lingers in his voice.

"And this won't summon Daniil?" Terese asks, fingers reaching towards the rune but hesitating, millimeters away. "You said—"

The Necromancer and Alette exchange a glance, one she doesn't quite understand.

"I feel confident—somewhat—that he won't appear right now," the Necromancer says, sitting on the base of the stairs. "Not for maybe a day, at minimum." Melekai drifts over to standing next to her, and she leans her head against his leg, comfortable in the contact.

Terese narrows her eyes at her. "So can you just do that over and over again, whatever you did?"

"No," Melekai interrupts when it looks like the Necromancer is going to nod. "Only at a point of contact, and I'm not...I would like as little exposure of you to another demon as possible." The last words were spoken down to his partner, and his voice is a hell of a lot more tender when aimed at Lyra.

"Right," Terese says, nodding, her eyes slipping over to Axel. "Makes sense."

She is still the one endangering them, just by existing near them.

But Axel said she didn't have to do this alone.

"The point is, he's going to be very uncomfortable if he tries right now," Alette says. "So if it were the case that he finds you from your powers, which I still don't buy"—the Necromancer snorts at that—"then this would be the safest time to do this."

Her legs still shaky from apparently fainting earlier, Terese exhales, then presses her fingertips to the rune, prodding it back to life.

It flares up, sharp against her awareness, then fades to a manageable glow, something soft, warming the bare wall around it, the cold bleeding away from the unforgiving concrete.

A warming spell, simple, yet almost incomprehensible in how beautifully and masterfully it had been written.

As much as she hates Dr. Frisse, Terese admires the way she wrote the runes. Such obvious talent, such obvious power, wasted on the woman who ruined her life.

Izzy worms her way between Terese and the wall, sitting down and thumping her tail, and Terese vows to write a similar one wherever Izzy ends up sleeping the most.

Almost immediately, Alette steps close to the rune, peering at it with the same intensity Terese remembers being turned onto her whenever they encountered each other. "Interesting."

"Hardly," Melekai scoffs, and his distaste is almost soothing in its predictability, before he turns to Axel with a jerk of his head. "Axel, a word?"

Axel raises an eyebrow at him from behind the bespelled glasses, and Melekai just raises it right back, before following him out, leaving all three of the women staring after them.

"Is that...normal?" Terese asks after the sounds of their footsteps fade up the staircase.

"Sorta," the Necromancer says with a shrug, but her eyes are sharper than the casualness suggests. "Mel...isn't the most subtle person, but he enjoys talking to Axel when he's uncomfortable because Axel isn't judge-y."

"And he thinks I am," Alette finishes.

Terese doesn't terribly disagree, but even she knows better than to say that.

"Most likely, he noticed something he thinks might be upsetting, and he wants to run it by Axel before just saying it out loud," the Necromancer continues, stretching her legs out in front of her. "Half the time when this happens, it's really harmless and adorable."

Terese locks eyes with Alette at that, because Melekai is not someone she would ever call adorable, even in a human body.

From the look of it, Alette agrees.

"But he didn't grow up human," Lyra says, "and he's still learning when to actually say stuff or not. I'm used to him just...saying shit, but..."

"He was so very awkward at first," Alette finishes,

cracking a small smile before turning back to the rune, "I don't care. This is still interesting. And no demon contact?"

"None," Terese says, but the abrupt exit still sits against her mind, and the room seems lesser without Axel in it.

Maybe Melekai had noticed what the Necromancer had just a few days before. Maybe Melekai wanted to warn Axel away.

"Theoretically," Alette says, "reinstating a rune by someone else is massively difficult, and takes a lot of power, but it barely seemed to affect you."

"Is that why you've let everything remain dead?" Terese asks, jerking her thumb up the stairs. "Because you have enough power to do it, you could."

"Power yes, finesse no," Alette murmurs, deftly pulling out a needle—not the curved golden one—and tapping it against the bare concrete next to the rune, in some sort of obscure test. "I was always mediocre in runemaking."

"Mel's teaching me, but I didn't even know other magicians existed until a year ago, so it's a bit of a learning curve," the Necromancer says, but she curves an eyebrow at Terese. "You okay?"

"Yes," Terese replies automatically.

"'Cause I'm not scanning you, but you still look peaky and your face is blotchy."

Her face is probably blotchy from the aborted make-out session with Axel, and she blushes further at that.

The Necromancer's eyes widen, like she picks that up, but Terese gives an obvious glance to Alette, who's still inspecting the rune, to not let her in on that secret.

Not that Alette wouldn't find out from Axel himself, probably, but still.

Suddenly, the Necromancer grins, and it's a smidgen too close to the previous demon's nightmares. "I can't wait until we deal with this threat and we can go have a girls' night or something," she says. "The three of us, without the guys, and we can just hang out."

Alette looks just as startled as Terese, and Terese has a hard time imagining the scholar being relaxed in anything.

"Thanks?" Terese offers, as that seems like the thing to say. "Awfully optimistic there."

So many people are being optimistic about her, and she just doesn't know how to think.

ALETTE ENDS up making her renew several small runes in the basement: one for increasing airflow, one for warming underneath carpet, one for stabilizing electrical currents, and finally, one for an alarm of anyone teleporting onto the property.

"Now, it's probably going to go off anytime you go off somewhere, or Zoel, but—"

"—But it might for Daniil instead," Terese finishes, watching as the spellweaver taps something into her phone, as if she can tie in the runes back to technology, which honestly spins Terese's mind. "And we can make it so it recognizes Zoel, easy."

Izzy has long since flopped over against the warming rune on the concrete wall, but she thumps her tail at Terese's tone.

"We might get it narrowed down to just demons," Alette says, not looking up. "Still might trigger for you, but still useful. Want to give it a test?"

Her stomach drops at the thought, but she shakes out her hands instead of immediately saying no.

"Good of time as any to test," the Necromancer says,

stretching her legs out in front of her. "Daniil's going to be hurting and won't want to engage, you can try somewhere then pop on back."

"You are massively overestimating my control on where I go," Terese says, which is easier than denying them. "It's not really predictable."

"Take one of us with you?" Alette says, still focusing on the rune. "If you're scared, you can even grab Axel's gun."

Terese is sure as hell not going to teleport anywhere with the Necromancer, and Alette is too involved in reading the rune, so her stomach flops, for a different reason, and she pulls out her phone.

TERESE (12:56 PM): Do you want an espresso milkshake?

∼

IT TAKES A LITTLE LONGER, and Alette's still sketching out notes in her notebook with a fountain pen tipped in gold, before both Melekai and Axel come tromping down the stairs.

There's a strangely blank look on Axel's face, but his eyes light up when he sees her.

"Espresso milkshakes, huh?" he says, though a tension runs through his body and he taps his fingers against his legs.

"We reinstated the teleportation alarm from when Aunt Frisse got paranoid about that. We want her to test it to see if it activates for her," Alette clarifies. "She's a bit spooked from earlier so we thought it best if she doesn't go alone. I'm needed to read this on this end."

"And Lyra can't go with her," Melekai interrupts, as if they'd all forgotten, and Axel rolls his eyes. "I'll go."

Terese stares at the former demon, but he crosses his arms and scowls right back.

"What?" Axel says, wrinkling his brow at Melekai. "Why—"

"Maybe I haven't teleported in eight months and maybe I want to do that again," Melekai says, bland, and Terese doesn't buy it one bit, and all of her hackles rise. "I can read runes coming back in. It'll tell me what exactly it's reacting to, and you"—he levels a glare at Axel— "can help here."

Terese and the Necromancer glance at each other. Something tells her that this wasn't just a normal discussion with pals.

"That could work," Alette says, thoughtful, as if she didn't pick up on the gaping hole in the conversation there. "You have a better understanding of alarms like that than Axel does."

"Exactly," Melekai says, with almost a hint of smugness. "Do you want me to bring you back a milkshake?"

"Sure?" the Necromancer says, her voice lilting up in a clear question. "Terese, where exactly is the milkshake shop?"

"Altadena, apparently," she says, and Axel shoots her a quick grin, "next to the dog park."

At the words, Izzy bounds to her feet.

And now, Terese has a choice. She can refuse, dig in her feet, until Melekai explains what he's after, or...or she can trust that he won't actively hurt her somewhere where he'd have no way of getting home and risk upsetting the Necromancer.

She glances to Axel, though, and he's watching her, still. "I'll bring you back one, too."

Without waiting for him to answer, she clips Izzy's leash

on and grabs Melekai by the shoulder, teleporting them away.

Her feet hit the floor of the tunnel, and Melekai shakes off her grip.

"I take it this isn't the dog park," he says, cool.

"I don't control it, I'll get there eventually," Terese says.

The words are still there; the paint peeling off in giant flecks, but still disorienting, and Melekai studies them with almost the same intensity as Alette would. Izzy flops over in her favorite little spot, where a dusty blanket still lays.

"Is this to threaten me more?" Terese asks, after a few moments of heart-pounding silence.

"Do you know what you're doing with Axel?" he asks, not looking at her. "Because he's my friend now. I don't want him hurt."

It's not what she expected him to say, so she takes a moment to think.

"I don't want him to be hurt at all," Terese says, choosing to take his words literally instead of what they suggest. "You could have told me that back there, without the weird tele-portation thing."

He glances at her, and it's strange, still, to see someone so obviously inhuman in such a normal-looking body. "When I first met him, I almost killed him, because he had the temerity to grab Lyra to pull her away from a bit of danger," he starts. "Every time someone looks at her, every time someone brushes against her, it's the same fury and confusion and knot of awfulness that came with that first encounter with him."

Oh. So they're talking about that.

"I don't know what I'm doing with that," she admits, her face burning, grateful for the dim light of the tunnel to hide it. "I didn't know I was until the Necromancer told me."

He crosses his arms again. "It was different when I was... not this," he says, and it's such a matter-of-fact statement it takes her breath away. "I could react how I wanted, very few consequences. Now...it's different when we're human. It hurts them if we react like that, it upsets them if we behave like demons."

"I'm not a demon," Terese says, but it sounds more like a plea than a statement.

"So I," he starts, and he's very deliberate in his words, "have to concentrate really hard to not give in to those instincts. Because it upsets her."

The bare bones outline of what he's trying to say ekes into Terese's mind, and she sighs, rubbing her face.

"Can we at least have this conversation over espresso?"

It takes her four more tries to teleport to the dog park, and Izzy wriggles from her grasp the moment she does.

There's still a bit of browned blood against the pavilion, right where she rested her head back less than a week ago.

It had been less than a week ago.

Melekai looks around at the dog park, at the sheltered space they appeared in, at the multitude of dogs playing and running around in the dirt, an almost amusingly befuddled look on his face. "You weren't kidding."

"Of course I wasn't," Terese says, shaking out her hands, disquiet still running through her.

Still no sign of Daniil lurking in her brain, but now she's looking for it, and the lack makes her jumpy.

After making sure Izzy is well and truly in the middle of playing with the other dogs, she jerks her head to the gate, towards the coffee shop with the green sign.

"They have these everywhere," Melekai says, as if she didn't already know that, "you wouldn't have to go to a dog park to get to it."

"Did you barge in just to warn me I'm being sketchy with Axel?" Terese says, trying and failing to sound strict.

"Basically," he says without a hint of shame. "I'm going to guess you have never intentionally bonded with someone like that, you need to know the pitfalls."

"I didn't...mean to start whatever the Necromancer saw," Terese says as they cross the street, and Melekai looks as jumpy as she feels. They pass the convenience store, and there's a row of neon ball caps right next to the register, visible from the street. "It's just..."

"It's just he's the first person to show you concrete kindness and treat you like a person and not just a thing to be afraid of," Melekai interrupts. "I get it. I do. You just have to be careful."

"Is that what happened with you?" Terese snipes back, before rubbing her face as they get in line at the coffee shop.

"It's exactly what happened with me," Melekai says, and for once, his face is serious, serious and human. "That's why I'm telling you."

She mulls on that as they order, almost as if they are two actual friends out for coffee, and she gets both an extra milkshake for Axel and a cup of whipped cream for Izzy.

"So you're not trying to warn me away," she says, once they've left the coffee shop, and she's back where she can see Izzy tromp around in the park and the muscle in between her shoulders relaxes. "Not an actual threat."

"Not a threat, but I will threaten you if you're foolish and get him hurt," Melekai says gravely, and for a split second a bubble of laughter wells up in her throat, but she tamps it down. "Demons don't form friendships, and now I have several. I'd really like to keep them."

"I haven't even talked to him about this," she says, keeping her eyes on Izzy as they step back in the gate. She's not being insecure—she's not—but even she knows better than to assume that making out with someone makes up a lasting bond or relationship.

"Oh, I did," Melekai says, almost gleefully, and that doesn't help. "I care more about making sure my friend is safe and okay with whatever he does than making it easy for you."

"Thanks," Terese says, and a car passes a bit too close, and she flinches. "That was sarcastic."

"Somehow I gathered," Melekai responds, as they stare out at the dogs playing in the park. "I didn't tell him it was emotional. I told him that your magic was imprinting on him like a duckling."

"That's...not better," Terese says, and the dogs around them certainly don't care about her miniature breakdown. "That just makes me sound pathetic."

Melekai shrugs, like that's the point.

"And with Daniil..."

"Oh, he will not react to the idea of you having interests very well at all," Melekai interrupts. "If I were him, and I'm not, I'm nicer, I would kill the interloper and possess the body, make it confusing for everyone involved."

"Fuck," Terese says, and far across the park Izzy spots them and the cups from the store, her ears perking up.

"Only reason he wouldn't is because he wants to possess you," Melekai continues, "sees it as a waste of energy."

"What do I do if he wins?" Terese asks, and Melekai's eyebrows flash up again. "How do I get out? How do I stop it?"

He opens his mouth, then closes it, looking thoughtful. "You can communicate, you said? Even rudimentary?"

"I could scream at her," Terese says.

"Make it annoying," Melekai says. "It wouldn't matter how much power a body had, if it sincerely annoyed me, I would leave."

"The last demon couldn't."

"The last demon was also apparently tied in, I doubt Daniil would be," Melekai says, crossing his arms. "Annoy the shit out of him."

Despite herself, a smile tugs up on her lips.

"Mock him, annoy him, make him realize that whatever power you have isn't worth it," Melekai continues. "Most of us are prickly and don't like being insulted and not used to it at all."

Terese decides right then and there that she doesn't like him referring to demons as 'us'.

"He probably wouldn't make it fun for you," Melekai says with a shrug, "might try to kill you again, might leave you floating in the middle of the ocean, but it might get him to leave."

"You should make a plan," she says, the words falling from her lips as they watch the dogs play, "in case we aren't successful. In case he gets me."

"Oh, we have," Melekai says, dark, "we've had a plan since before you showed up."

Terese throws him a look. "I mean now. Now that Axel and I..."

"Oh, you mean one in case he refuses to accept it?" Melekai snipes back. "Yes, we have one of those."

"Good," Terese says.

"Though we all agree he'd be the one to notice it first,"

Melekai continues, "and if he survives the initial encounter, he'll activate the plan."

"Don't tell it to me." Because if they did, the demon could see it, read it like a book, and thwart it.

"Your life would be a lot easier if you didn't have another demon after you."

She swallows that down as Izzy bounds up for her whipped cream, tongue lolling out, and she watches her dog in the sun until the swell of panic recedes back into her bones instead of her gut.

Melekai's more than happy to watch the scene in silence, scowling at any other dog that comes remotely close.

"Any other pitfalls?" Terese asks, redirecting the conversation by sheer force of will. "In this apparently magic bond I'm forging without even realizing it or meaning to?"

This gets him to do a double take.

"What?"

"I thought you were being coy. You really had no clue?"

"None."

He shrugs again, his eyebrows raised. "Don't fuck it up."

And with that, their milkshakes starting to melt, and Izzy done with her whipped cream, Terese decides she's fucking done with the conversation and teleports them back.

23

T he moment their feet hit the ground next to the bramble and the giant spruce tree—it only takes two tries this time—both of their phones light up in a truly unholy screech of alarms.

"Well," Melekai says, silencing his phone without even looking at it, "the alarms work."

Izzy sniffs around the spot, as she always does, looking for something.

Terese's phone beeps.

THE HANDSOME ONE (1:59 PM): That you?

TERESE (1:59 PM): Yes.

THE HANDSOME ONE (2:00 PM): That's good, or else there'd be problems.

Her mouth still tugs up into a smile, despite herself, as they walk up the hill.

"Always that one spot?" Melekai asks, his nose wrinkling.

"Always," Terese confirms.

"So you got the shitty parts of being a demon, and none of the fun stuff," Melekai says, and he s grating against her nerves, like every moment out here is exposing more of herself.

"Yeah, well, not really my choice, was it?"

He shrugs again, scowling, before the compound comes into view and he visibly lightens, back straightening.

And the pit in Terese's stomach just grows larger as they make their way to the basement, past some runes obviously written by Alette more recently than the rest, and some vague outlines of magic from Zoel. Past more bare concrete and dead runes, down stairs with questionable hand rails and uncomfortable looking stains.

Her heart still flops over when she sees Axel, leaning casually against the wall, all long legs and idle motions, the coin flipping in his hand.

"So you went to Southern Washington, Romania, back to Southern Washington, then to the dog park, right?"

Even though they just left, Izzy's ears perk up.

"Yeah," Terese says, thrusting the espresso milkshake at him. "The alarms work."

"Oh, they work wonderfully," Alette says, and now she's holding a computer tablet, and she turns it to Terese.

On it is a single snapshot of Terese and Melekai the moment they landed under the spruce tree, Terese's hand still on Izzy's collar, looking over her shoulder.

And her eyes reflect light. Like a demon.

She recoils away.

"Do my eyes do that?" she blurts out, twisting to Axel and pointing at herself.

"Not that I've seen," he says, all fake casual, before he levels a glance at her, and she could swear that he can read her mind. "Are you okay?"

"Yes," she replies, automatic.

"You just teleported all over the world, after passing out for a bit."

"She's fine," the Necromancer pipes up, clutching onto the milkshake that Melekai brought her, "I checked when she was distracted."

And Terese hadn't even noticed.

IN THE END, Alette and Melekai stay and argue over the runes, with the Necromancer watching in bemusement, and Terese lets Axel bring her back upstairs, begging the need for rest.

Despite the faux confidence, a tension throbs underneath his skin, and no words come to her, either.

"Mel treat you okay?" he asks, after they pass by the giant wooden doors in the hallway, and Izzy stops to sniff. "He can be a dick."

She doesn't know what he's suggesting, what he's trying to get at, and it twists in her stomach. "No threatening this time, and he really wanted to teleport more." The words seem to have a gaping hole in them, stretching out far beyond what she can communicate, leaving her perched on the precipice with no way across. "I cannot imagine that he's pleasant to be around long term, and the Necromancer chose that."

He laughs, and the same gremlin self that wants to horde the sound springs back to her mind, and she swallows that down.

"They are so weird, you have no idea," Axel says, opening the door to his apartment with a grand gesture and a wink. "You should see his face when someone tries to flirt with Lyra, it's ghastly. And she likes it." He pauses, as if her words catch up to him. "Wait, did he threaten you before? Besides...besides the first day in the ballroom?"

"Yes," Terese replies, because if Melekai's going to throw her under the bus, she's going to throw him. "Woke me up to be all sinister and everything. Morning after the...the catatonic creepiness."

"Because that's what you needed then," Axel says, shutting the door closed with a click, and all of a sudden the enormity of the two of them alone together presses against Terese.

Izzy curls up into a ball on the sheepskin rug, tired from the park and the whipped cream, but the espresso buzzes in Terese's veins.

A quippy comeback dies in her throat as she glances up at Axel.

He seems unaware, tossing his phone on the table and shaking his curls out, like Melekai didn't actually tell him anything. Like there is nothing he has to worry about, not the bleak generalizations of her magic, or the demon after her, or whatever emotional bullshit she's developing.

"Lyra thinks that Mel's just real jealous you can still teleport—he misses that the most, apparently," Axel continues, like he didn't even realize she's stopped talking and is just staring at him. "If this is anything like when he discovered how music sounds on human ears, don't be surprised if he bugs you to teleport him somewhere again until you want to tear your hair out."

"And...and his whole...pulling you to the other room thing?" Terese asks, as gently as she can, standing stock-still in the center of his living room. "What did he say?"

The casualness cracks, and there's a brief glimpse of something much more raw underneath it, before it disappears.

"You know, the standard," Axel says, and she very much doesn't know, thank you very much, "normal bro things."

"Normal bro things," she echoes, disbelieving.

"What passes for normal for him, at least," Axel relents. "You know, dire proclamations that I'm being entirely too obvious about everything, coded language that I'm sure made sense to him and his demon mind, then some light encouragement that probably wasn't meant to be taken that way, but I will. You know, the usual." Then, deliberately, he takes a step towards her, stepping inside her personal bubble in a way that seldom do, and her heart jumps to her throat. "Why?"

Despite all the space in the tiny little room, he's so close she can feel the heat from his skin. Can smell the hint of his cologne, familiar from when she had been possessed and now from many car rides. Can see the freckles on the tips of his cheekbones.

"This is...abnormally stupid," Terese says, before she can stop herself, but she doesn't move away. "There's literally a demon after me, I'm not...I'm not really all that sane, I lose time, and you can't..."

She doesn't know where she was going with that, and the words die away, leaving just him looking at her.

And he studies her, just as intensely as anyone would, his brown eyes sharp.

"Mel didn't threaten you?" he says again, this time almost unbelieving. "Sounds to me he really wanted you to think twice about everything."

"That's a good way of putting it," she says, but doesn't move away. Even if it's stupid, even if the smart and kind thing would be to run away, get as far away from them as possible.

He sighs, and she hates that sound, she decides on the spot. "Do you want to think twice about this?"

Her lips part before words appear to her mind.

"No," she breathes, and her heart pounds, far more than it should, "no, I don't."

"Then I don't want to, either," he says, voice low. "This is beyond stupid, you're right. I should hate everything about you, every part of this whole thing is ill-advised, foolish, and risky."

She holds so still, she's not sure she'll ever move again.

"But you're...you're a lot better than your past, and we can stave off your future for as long as we need." He reaches his hand out, touching the edge of her sleeve with his fingertips and lighting her skin on fire. "And that's enough for me."

It's enough for him.

Before she can stop herself, she throws her arms around his neck, bringing him down and pressing her lips against his. With a groan, he holds her closer with one hand against the small of her back, until all she can feel is his body against hers. The other hand twists into her hair, sending a thrill down her spine that has never been matched.

He opens his mouth to hers, and she just presses up against him harder, like she can impress on the storm of emotions knotted up inside of her by just more touch.

It's more than just a fire dwelling underneath her skin, it's more than just an ache behind her throat, it's a swelling rage of confusion and want and softness and something far, far more vulnerable, to almost cross over into a need. It's more than her lungs denying her air, it's more than when her blood runs cold, it's more.

Hands shaking, she grabs onto the collar of his flannel shirt, pushing it off his shoulders, and he lets her go just long enough to strip it off, leaving him in just his undershirt tank top and jeans.

It's not enough, but she runs her palms over his shoulders, like she's just discovering them, and he hooks his fingers into her belt loops in some strange sort of possessive motion.

Strange how she really, really doesn't mind.

She should, some distant part of her brain tells her, she should object to someone holding her captive like that. She should stop, tell him to stop, get away, teleport away.

But she just leans into his touch, and his thumbs skim that strip of skin between her jeans and her shirt riding up, and it's a little more glory than she ever thought she could have.

And he wants this too.

"You're really okay with this," he breathes, breaking the kiss just enough to press his face against the crook of her neck, his hands holding her waist, "you're really—"

"Yes," she repeats, and in one smooth motion he twirls her around, leading her down the hallway of the apartment, towards the closed door she's never seen beyond.

It's a bit of his world she's never been, and her pulse thuds into her ears and her skin buzzes, but he opens the door without thinking, pulling her through.

The room is a cornucopia of details about Axel, from the neatly folded clothes, to the toolset on top of the dresser and the mirrored vanity. From the large computer system in the corner with three monitors, from the neatly made-up bed with many fluffy pillows, to the pile of books instead of a nightstand, the pages ruffled and well read.

She holds on to as many of the details as she can, as greedily as she can, until a single swipe of his thumb on the inside of her wrist crashes all her attention back onto him.

He's smiling, crooked, at her.

"I've never been in someone's room before," she says, almost shy, but she's smiling right back. "It's a...lot of information about you."

There's even a small collection of over-large coins on one side of the vanity, as if he practices every day in front of the mirror.

Given the smooth perfection in all his motions, she doesn't doubt it.

"Tell me, at any point in this, if you want me to stop," Axel says, and his voice is serious for once, the flippancy gone. "The moment you're not enjoying this, the moment you're not feeling great, tell me."

She nods, the lump in her throat, the idea of stopping whatever they're doing right now almost unbearable. "You too."

"Of course," he says, almost as if that's a given. "I'm not the one who's had almost no control over their life. I'm not worried about me."

It's true, and she lets herself absorb it for just a few seconds.

But this, this is something she's picking, something she's choosing to do, and every nerve in her body is prodding her to get on with it.

"I'm fairly certain I could stop you if I needed," she says, and it doesn't quite come across as joking as she wished it.

It's almost unbearably formal, but then he grins, and the moment's over, the palm of his hand sliding up her arm, all the way up to her shoulder.

She shivers, the pinpricks of sensation crowding out everything else, but then grins right back. "Or teleport away, that'd be definitive."

"Yeah, can't say that wouldn't stop things," Axel drawls,

pulling her close, and all of her attention shifts from his words to his touch, to the hand on her arm and the hand on the small of her back, on the bare skin where her shirt's ridden up.

And she gets to control this.

Warmth spreading to her fingertips, she pulls off her top, and the hand on her back presses her tighter to him.

She knows that whatever the first demon did to her body made her conventionally attractive, lean and tall, but she has had little need to contemplate her physical body's appearance much more than that. But his attention is like a laser, wire whip hot, burning against her skin.

"You have freckles," he murmurs, with a swipe of the pad of his thumb across her collarbones, a part of her body she most assuredly does not contemplate. "And...something here?"

There's a little scar, ever so slight, at the top of her rib cage, from obviously Before, or else it'd have been healed. She's marveled at it before, wondering where it came from, but has no answers. Something small enough the demon didn't magic it away, some small evidence of a life lived.

"Proof I existed before," she says, tugging at the hem of his shirt, then planting a kiss against his jaw. See if she can motivate him to move faster, to feel more of him, more of his body.

She knows she's had sex Before, this is too familiar, and the ache is too eager for this to be entirely new. But anticipation fizzles through her veins, so strong it's almost an emotion.

In a smooth motion that absolutely belies practice, he pulls his shirt over his head, and she lets herself admire the lines of his shoulders, the muscles across his chest, the trail of hair that disappears into the hem of his pants.

He offers her a crooked smile, almost embarrassed, and it takes her mind a few moments to realize why.

He used to look different. He used to craft his body to his wishes, mold his appearance until it fit exactly what he had in mind. And what he had in mind is almost certainly not what his body is now.

"You look amazing," she blurts out, before she can stop herself, then tangles her hand into his hair and pulls him into another kiss, teasing his mouth open, as if she could impress upon him how beautiful he is, how much she wants this, with just a kiss. As if she could pour all the emotions and want and need into that singular connection.

There's a frenzy underneath her skin for more of this. For more connections and more contact and more of him, buzzing throughout her.

As if he could read her mind right back, he wraps his arms around her waist and lifts her into the air, causing her to squeak, before he sets her down on his bed, leaning over her.

It's a new form of vulnerability, being so close to another person, and her heart beats a patter she has never known. That as he braces himself over her, that she could be there, that she could have that.

That as his hand trails up her stomach, and her hand against his back, that she, Terese, with the broken mind and broken sense of self, could have this. Could touch him all she wants, could marvel at the sensation from her fingertips to his skin, at the hundreds and thousands of nerves firing inside her body.

He pulls away, just long enough to peel her jeans off of her, and anticipation coats her veins as he gives her a smug smile. "I take it this hasn't happened since?" His voice is light, teasing.

"Not even remotely," she quips back.

He props himself up on his elbows, and the cunning glint is in his eye once more, and she really doesn't mind.

"So we get to figure out what you like?" he says, his fingertips making idle circles on the tops of her thighs. "Figure out how to make you happy."

Terese has an idea but doesn't want to derail whatever train of thought he's on. "This isn't just about me," she replies, meeting his brown eyes with her own colorless ones.

"Obviously, but this could be fun." He presses a kiss to the edge of her hip, and her breath catches. "Get to see your first reactions to everything."

His hand dips between her thighs, and she stills, as if she could will him to move faster by being as motionless as possible, before relaxing back against the pillow.

It's more than comfortable, with the soft sheets cool against her back and the multitude of pillows, and a small part of her mind marvels at the notion of her laying on an actual bed. With another person. And not being terrified.

She knows the previous demon had momentarily considered using her body to have sex but disregarded that idea in favor of hunting down the Necromancer, and for once, Terese is grateful that the demon didn't take that away from her as well.

"What's wrong?" Axel murmurs, his hands still just against her thighs with the promise of more. "You froze up."

"Just a bad thought," she says, even though that's the opposite of a sexy revelation, and she makes a face at herself. "Definitely don't want you to stop. If I stopped for all of those, I'd never get anything done."

His lips quirk up into a smile, and she wants years upon years more of that smile, before he presses a kiss between her thighs.

Her back arches at the sudden sensation, and nothing in the world could make her leave.

He hmms against her, and she can't open her eyes, everything's too intense and, at the same time, not nearly enough.

She breathes in, shuddering, as he opens his mouth against her, and somehow it's even more, and everything inside of her clenches with more anticipation.

"Come up here," she whispers, and he presses another kiss to her hip, almost a tantalizing tease. "Please —"

Before she can even blink, before she can think, he's on top of her, bracketing her in, and her breath catches in her throat. His curls fall over his eyes, unruly, and at some point he had shed his jeans, and she didn't even notice.

Instinct taking over, she reaches down and palms his dick, and he jumps at her touch.

She doesn't exactly remember her past encounters, but he feels impressive, and she raises an eyebrow up at him

"You good?" he asks, his voice husky, and she nods in reply, her hair spreading across the pillowcase. "Good," he whispers, close to her ear, and she shivers. "Because I want every moment of this to be good."

The tip of his cock brushes against her, and her breath hitches.

"And I," he continues, so quiet she can barely hear, "want you exactly like this."

"Please," she repeats, and he smiles, wide and heart-breaking, "please."

He gets a brief, contemplating look, and he's still pushed against her but not inside of her, and she shifts, something, anything, to get more sensation. "Apparently I also want you to beg."

He swipes the pad of his thumb over her nipple, and she

shudders again, arching her back to his touch and hooking one of her legs over his, and he pushes inside of her in one long motion.

And the world shudders to a stop. All that matters is him, inside of her and against her, so much and not enough. All that matters is the motion between the two of them, the sensation as it spreads through her fingertips and her body, the low groans he makes deep in his throat, the hand he fists in her hair to hold her in place.

Until she breaks apart in a way that is only good.

24

~

After, she lets herself snuggle up against him, shameless, her head tucked under his chin, and his hand plays idly with the edges of her hair.

His chest rises and falls with each breath, a metronomic pattern that soothes the shaky parts of her mind.

"You good?" he asks, soft, and she feels it more than hears it.

"Yeah," she responds, just as quiet, not wanting to move from him. Off in the distance of her mind, she wonders if she should worry, if she should panic about some new thing, but she can't bring herself to pay any attention to it.

The skin on his chest is just rough enough to be a contrast, and she spreads her fingertips across his collarbone. Something close to tiredness tugs at her eyelids, but not unpleasantly. Not the normal harshness that drags her to sleep, but a soft lull.

"This is definitely not the only time I want to do this,"

she says, still hushed, and he laughs, a perfect interruption to the rhythm of his breathing.

"See, this is why I like you," he says, running his fingers through her hair, until his nails graze her scalp, "you say things like that. Declarative. I don't have to guess or wonder."

Her eyes fully slip shut, and he softly scratches her scalp, and gets a thrill of success, a thrill of victory.

The last demon never got anything this good, and she did.

SHE WAKES SO LATE into the night it's early morning, and Axel's breathing is so deep it takes her a moment to recognize it. Somewhere in sleep, she shifted onto her side, and Axel's arm is draped over her waist, heavy, keeping her pinned down to earth.

For the briefest of seconds, her magic thuds before it, too, recognizes that she's okay.

But her eyes blink open in the dark room, with the light seeping in from underneath the door. Izzy sleeps, a dark mound on the rug, snoring ever so slightly.

So she exhales, past the almost panic of the unfamiliar, settling deeper into the bed. He had thrown the covers over them, and she marvels at the distinct comfort and domesticity of the sheer act of sharing a bed, at the lazy contact, until she falls back into sleep.

THE TWIN CHIMES of their phones wake them both, but she takes the opportunity to press more kisses against him, before Izzy plods back into the room and plops her head on the bed, giving Terese the most obvious of puppy dog eyes.

Axel laughs, an unguarded rasp this early in the morning, before he sits up, his curls rumpled.

Izzy pays him no mind as their phones beep in the other room.

"Are your friends going to be weird about this?" Terese asks, stretching her legs out instead of sitting up, lazily scratching Izzy between the ears.

"Weird? Yes. Bad? No," he says, pulling on a shirt over his bare chest. "Well, Mel might be snooty and Alette will be awkward, but not bad."

"Neither of them have any leg to stand on," Terese says, watching him as he putters through the room, wholly unwilling to get out of bed. "Mel slept with his necromancer while still a demon, he absolutely cannot talk."

"Weird that you know that, but okay," he says, combing his hair in the vanity mirror, and she could just watch him all day. Observe his little motions for forever. "Or is that a previous demon thing?"

"Previous demon thing, he was, apparently, super obvious about it," she says, taking one last stretch on the glorious bed, before pushing herself up.

Only a bit of residual head pain and neck snap—she's almost back to normal.

At her movement, Izzy perks up.

"Oh, alright," Terese murmurs to her dog, and Izzy wags her tail in response, sitting down as Terese pulls her clothes back on.

It's strange to do so, for no good reason, but Axel watches her in the mirror, a small smile on his lips.

And she knows it won't last. That Daniil will try again,

and soon. That there's a ticking time bomb inside her mind, a gaping weakness where any demon could take her.

But here, in this beautiful, quiet moment, where the world is soft and kind, she wants to believe it will.

Izzy noses her out the door, but Axel grabs her by the shoulders, kissing her with a fierceness she's never before felt before releasing her.

"How am I supposed to do anything after that?" she whispers to him, and gets an unguarded smile in return, before she grabs her phone off the table, following Izzy as she plods up to the solarium.

It's early morning sun through the panes of glass and disrupted magic, but she lets herself stand in it, still vulnerable to the world, before sighing and poking open her phone.

To her surprise, it's not the group text.

THE NECROMANCER (7:02 AM): When you have time, do you want to talk about what else I found with the scan?

THE NECROMANCER (7:05 AM): Not demon related.

Terese mulls it over like she would a piece of toffee as Izzy sniffs around. Non-demon findings edge into the territory that she's more broken than she believes, or that there's something else lurking in her brain.

But now that there's a bit of information out there, it almost seems irresponsible to not know it.

TERESE (7:21 AM): Sure, go ahead.

Maybe it's extra confidence from spending the night with Axel. Maybe it's the feeling that nothing could truly get to her, but she takes a deep breath, and sends the text.

It switches over to read almost immediately, like the Necromancer had been waiting.

THE NECROMANCER (7:23 AM): Beyond this still

residual bruising on your brain and instability in your neck —which by the way wtf—your brain has some trauma.

TERESE (7:24 AM): I thought we knew that.

THE NECROMANCER (7:25 AM): I mean, the trauma has rerouted how your brain processes chemicals.

Which again, isn't a surprise, but such clinical stating of it seems unusual.

THE NECROMANCER (7:28 AM): I'm still learning normal baselines, and it takes a long time for me to compare with med textbooks, but some things you're experiencing might be very fixable.

Terese blinks down at the phone, and Izzy tromps over and shoves her nose into Terese's hand.

The first question that pops to mind is immediately which things, followed shortly with how, then finally why. But none of those are easily textable, and none of those are things she quite wishes to examine, in the softness of the late summer sun.

THE NECROMANCER (7:34 AM): I don't have solid answers for you, but there is some possibility you might be able to take something for the panic attacks someday, once this has evened out and you're not getting repetitively hit in the head. Might make it easier to be you.

Easier to be herself.

It's an odd proposal, and Izzy leans fully against Terese as she contemplates it.

TERESE (7:38 AM): I don't know.

TERESE (7:39 AM): I'm not sure antidepressants would solve being possessed.

THE NECROMANCER (7:40 AM): Lol.

THE NECROMANCER (7:41 AM): I mean, your brain chemistry, not any of this magical bullshit that everyone keeps on insisting is a science.

Izzy pushes her snout so hard into Terese's extra hand that she almost drops her phone.

"I'm okay," Terese mumbles, past the thoughts swirling through her mind, "just...it's strange. I'm okay."

Izzy gives her such a disbelieving look that she can't believe even her own dog doesn't have faith in her.

So she sighs, climbing down until she's sitting on the dirt next to her dog, and throws her arms around her, burying her face into Izzy's fur.

Not that she's upset. It's a larger, more complex sort of emotion than that. The idea of living without the incessant panic actually sounds pretty excellent, all things considered.

But it's never something she thought she could have, and faced with the dizzying possibility that this could be over and she could be better is...a lot.

Izzy huffs, plopping to the ground in front of her, how she always does whenever Terese is like this. Gives Terese better access to hugging her, and more of a solid form to lean against.

And all Terese has to do is fight for this. Finish with whatever hell Daniil is attempting to put her through, make it through to the other side, and she might have a life. A tantalizing glimpse at a life, one where she's not on the run. Where she has people around her who can help.

And Axel.

She breathes wetly into Izzy's fur, but she's not crying, not really. More of a release of some tension, a letting go of something she wasn't entirely aware of.

And all she has to do is fight.

"I can do this," Terese whispers, and Izzy shifts, huffing out an agreeing breath. "I can do this."

∾

SHE LETS herself sit there for a few more minutes, before hauling herself up and dusting off her jeans. She's still in the clothes from the day before, so she stops by her little library room and showers quickly, finger combing her white blond hair back before shoving the neon green ball cap over it.

It's still pretty hideous, but she loves it.

THE HANDSOME ONE (8:31 AM): Alette has apparently made breakfast without knowing that Mel and Lyra didn't spend the night.

TERESE (8:32 AM): Is that a threat?

THE HANDSOME ONE (8:33 AM): No, but there's a lot of food and she's being intense.

TERESE (8:34 AM): How intense?

THE HANDSOME ONE (8:36 AM): Either someone told her she doesn't know something or she figured out she's missing some information and it's driving her nuts.

THE HANDSOME ONE (8:37 AM): She either cooks or goes crazy in a library when that happens.

A smile tugs up Terese's lips at the idea of someone being so put together, being so...human.

TERESE (8:39 AM): The moment she asks me demon questions, I'm out.

She picks her way back to the kitchen, only to find Axel and Alette sitting on opposite sides of the rooms from each other, both obviously not talking and staring at their respective phones. Axel even has his feet up on the table, ignoring the food.

In the center of the table is a pile of some sort of flatbread, still steaming, and a surprising amount of dips and fried potatoes.

Terese raises an eyebrow at Axel, who makes a quick, pained face where he thinks Alette can't see, before the disinterested mask falls once more.

Alette is, once more, practically glistening with magic, her fingertips dipped in gold power, but her pretty face is smooth and unmoving.

"Does all the untangling mean you don't have to sleep?" Terese asks, taking the seat next to Axel and bumping her elbow against him.

He responds with an equal pressure.

"Not entirely," Alette says, which isn't as declarative of an answer that she probably thinks it is. "But it makes it difficult to fall asleep if I untangle late at night." Almost fussy, Alette dishes up a plate for herself, the barest hint of a scowl on her lips.

Terese squints at her as Axel gets his own plate of food.

"Then what's wrong?" Terese asks, because she doesn't think she's ever been that much of a subtle person, and there's little reason for her to try now. "Something is."

She catches a hint of a hidden smile from Axel, but he says nothing.

Whatever this misunderstanding is between them, it somehow reared up in the small time she had taken to have a mini breakdown in the solarium.

Izzy sniffs curiously at the food, before plopping next to the collapsible bowl that Terese has taken to leaving in the kitchen.

Because she can do that. She can leave things for Izzy here, and know where they are and that they'll be there when she gets back, and Izzy loves it. Loves the small routine, loves the continuing location. Even the short few weeks of stability, and her dog seems to find glory in it.

Terese fills the silence of the kitchen by filling up Izzy's bowl a bit too much before turning back to the table.

Alette doesn't speak, instead staring down at her plate with a line of tension in her shoulders, so Terese raises her eyebrows at Axel, before grabbing a piece of flatbread. The other food doesn't seem bad, and she knows she generally likes potatoes, but there's a sinking sensation in her stomach that they'd take up too much concentration.

Maybe she has a thing with food.

Axel derails whatever thoughts she has, however, by resting a hand against her elbow, a tantalizingly light touch, his fingers lightly drumming.

He's always moving his hands, she's noticed that, but having the same motion against her skin takes up a good chunk of her focus, in how she never wants him to stop.

She glances up at him, and his brown eyes are watching her from underneath his lashes, like he wants to communicate with her but can't, not with Alette in front of them. He raises his shoulders into a hint of a shrug, like he doesn't know either.

"Zoel's found evidence Daniil is sniffing along the edges of his territory," Alette says, after too long of a pause.

It's not what's bothering her, that's for sure.

"We knew that," Terese says, when Alette isn't saying anything more. "I think that's fairly obvious."

"And," Axel says, languid, and all the hairs on the back of Terese's neck rise, "that's not what's bothering you."

How anyone could find him not-intelligent, she doesn't know, and it's gratifying to see him turn that on someone else. Especially someone as put together as Alette.

Alette gives him an honest-to-god dirty look, her eyebrows wrinkling. Which means she's just as uncomfortable, which is excellent. "Nothing's wrong. Axel just thinks there is because he always thinks something is wrong," she says, as primly put together as possible, which is objectively hilarious. "I didn't sleep well."

"Because of the magic?" Terese asks, resisting the temptation to press her side against Axel. It's impractical, they're eating.

"Because of the magic," Alette says, begrudging.

"And when this happens, Zoel made her promise to sit and rest," Axel says, smug, and while Terese doesn't understand all the backstory, this is vastly entertaining. "Because Alette"—he gives her a significant look—"overextends herself and puts herself at risk."

"Well, duh," Terese says, and both of them blink at her. "Have you not noticed that before the unraveling? She always had circles under her eyes, even the demon noticed them."

Axel cracks a smile, but Alette's eyes just widen, the argument forgotten.

"How much did you notice through her?" Alette breathes, sitting up and forward. "That should be theoretically impossible."

"Told you she was being intense," Axel says, almost a grumble.

Terese and Axel lock eyes, just a moment, and her heart soars. It's like they have a private little joke, just the two of them.

It's excellent. It's excellent and her blood fizzes and she wants more of it.

Terese considers telling her the worst thing possible for a few seconds, before sighing. "All of it, it wasn't fun." She snags another piece of the flatbread—it's good—before sitting back down.

Then, suddenly, like it's responding to the mention, her magic pulses, sharp, and Alette flinches back, recoiling as if she had struck out.

"Wha—" Axel starts.

"I'm okay," Terese blurts out, tamping down on the magic, though it thrums inside of her with the need to get away, to leave, go anywhere else.

Izzy jolts over to Terese, whining in the back of her throat, scrambling over the slick tile of the kitchen.

And the magic pounds in her veins, freezing her up, and she just has a chance to look up at Axel, eyes wide.

"Something's happening," she manages out, before her throat closes up, panic spiraling up her back.

Dimly, she can tell that Alette's shaken out some string, some sort of power threaded in her needle, but all she can do is still herself, blink up at Axel, as her magic swirls up around her.

Izzy raises her head and howls.

Something, a pressure, a panic, a physical thing, slams into her chest, skidding the chair along the tile.

Her ankle twists in the chair legs, a quick brilliant pop of pain, before she's standing, bracing herself against whatever this is, the chair clattering back away from her.

All sound melts away, the ringing in her ears rising. The commotion from Alette, spinning up her own magic. Izzy's howl. Axel's words. All gone.

Axel's in the room, Axel and Alette, but her eyes can't focus, can't tell where they are, it's all a Gaussian blur of fluorescent lights and vague shapes, and no matter how much she blinks nothing changes, nothing moves. Nothing.

This is less than ideal, in her mind Daniil whispers, *but this will do.*

She twists, as if he is just over her shoulder, but a thin fiery line of pain blossoms down her spine, unspooling her, freezing her in place.

Something drips down her cheek, dark and viscous, splattering onto her white shirt.

As if cut out in a different light and clumsily pasted onto her existence, stands Daniil, still in the same blood-specked body, though the ragged hole in his shirt shows smooth, unbroken skin. Deep shadows line his face, shadows that stick out in the fluorescents as being not correct.

He's not there, he's not in front of her, not really.

He looks up and around, like he's casually piecing together where she is, through the blur and the muffled noise.

I'm barely getting anything, he speaks into her mind, and though she can see his mouth move, it's not true noise reaching her ears. *Wherever you're hiding, it's bright.*

And even if he can't see them, Axel's still in the room, Alette's still here, and despite all the pain and the horror and the fury, they're there.

Liquid, thick, gurgles out of her ear. It's blood, it has to be blood.

She has to do something. She has to stop him or to distract him until they can leave, until they can get help or Axel's gun or get to safety or—

He turns the attention onto her, cutting through her thoughts like a knife. Deliberately, still lit from a dim light source in the bright room, he takes a step towards her.

Of course, her feet are frozen to the ground.

Good to know I can call you up for a chat, he muses, still in her mind, and he reaches out and swipes his finger through the blood on her cheek, his skin fury-hot and burning. *Good experiment.*

Slowly, with a smile unnatural on the blandly handsome face, he places the finger on his tongue, eyes never leaving hers.

Very good experiment. I'll see you soon.

And just as suddenly as it begins, he vanishes, and all the light and noise and sounds crash into her.

Her knees buckle underneath her, and she crumples to the floor, flailing a hand out to catch herself, and someone's screaming. Someone's screaming and—

Terese gasps, and she can hear it, she can hear things again, and hands grab at her, catching her by the shoulders before her head slams into the tile.

Pain, a roaring pain, burning around her, surges up, crowding everything else out. Another howl—it's Izzy, Izzy's in danger, Izzy doesn't make that sound—lifts through the haze.

"—an you hear me? Terese, can—"

"Let me see her, let me help—"

"Wait, she's—"

With another gasp, another greedy attempt at bringing air to her as her nerves spiral out of her control, Terese dies. Her heart stutters to a stop, her lungs flex, but nothing happens, and her throat closes up, choked out by something.

But.

She's still there. She's still conscious, despite the pain and the terror and the black crowding out everything else.

She didn't fall unconscious again.

A new spike of terror, as her eyes stare up at the tiled ceiling, as if they thought this was just another corporate building and this was just an office break room. She should be unconscious, she should be oblivious, until she comes back, better.

The hands at her shoulders move, and someone's cradling her head in a lap, gentle through the fire of pain.

"She's bleeding—"

Something soft presses against her ear, against the sludge leaking out, and she twitches. She's not breathing, her heart doesn't pound, but she twitches.

"Is she alive?"

"Go get the first aid kit, go." It's Axel's voice. He's close, and her eyes aren't focusing, but something moves between her and the ceiling. "Terese, can you hear me?"

He's close, she can almost feel the rumble of his words against her, so she blinks twice.

Her eyelids don't want to move.

A heavy exhale, and the same hand raking through her hair, a muted exploration. Looking for injuries.

"I got you, we got you, you're safe," Axel says, and his face swims into view for a brief second, before her eyes unfocus, against her will. "We got you, he's gone, there's no one else here, you're safe."

She tries to blink again, to clear her vision, but it doesn't work, everything blurry.

Footsteps skid up to them, before someone unrolls a bag next to her.

"Get the antiseptic and some gauze," Axel orders to the other person. Alette, it has to be Alette, unzipping pockets in deft motions. "Give me the towel."

A shiver races down her body, and she jerks. She's not breathing, not yet.

"I know," Axel says, then, "slide it under her neck."

In one brief, brilliant spike of pain, he lifts her head, then lays it back down, and the back of her neck meets rough terry cloth instead of...she's not actually sure what she was on before.

But it releases a bit of the pressure on her neck, and she shudders again.

There's a ripping sound, plastic sliding open, then something cool wipes through the sludge on her cheeks.

"Jesus Christ," Alette breathes, and she must be close, too, for Terese to hear her. "He only touched her once. What caused this?"

So Alette could see, at least. Could see it hadn't just been in Terese's mind, hadn't just been a specter from beyond.

"Fuck if I know," Axel says, and the tender motions continue against her face.

Her heart thumps, once, and her body jerks in response.

"Do we need to immobilize her? Is this like a seizure?"

Terese stares up at the impossible shape that may be Axel, and blinks once, hard.

"No," Axel says, and somehow, relief cuts through the wave of pain, that he understood her. "She just needs—"

All at once, her brain sparks up and back, her nerves slamming into place, and she jolts upright, gasping. One big, greedy breath after another, with Axel's hand on her upper back, holding her up.

Alette scrambles backwards, clattering through the first aid kit, and Terese gets one crystal clear impression of her face distorted in fear before everything blurs again in a reddish haze.

"I—" Something chokes through her words, and she coughs, hacking, and almost blacks out from the railroad spike of pain through her temples.

"It's okay, you're okay, we got you," Axel says, his large hand rubbing between her shoulder blades, and everything's not okay, thank you very much, but she leans into the touch, until she lists over to the side and thumps against his chest. "Okay, I got you."

Terese wants to answer, wants to say something, but

with each breath she just hacks out more, so she lets her eyes flutter closed and presses her face into him.

They're sitting on the floor, in the same kitchen where she's now taken many meals, the tile cool against her legs.

"Is that blood?" Alette asks, but instead of interested, she's horrified.

Understandable. Terese is horrified by herself a lot, too.

"I don't know, probably?" She feels Axel say through his chest. "I don't know, I didn't see it."

"Do we need to go to the hospital?"

Even though she's slumped against him, Terese blinks once, hard.

"She didn't last time." The hand, tender, in her hair again, until she has her breathing under control and each cough doesn't shake something loose in her chest.

Until her heart beats at a steady rhythm in time with the pounding in her head, loud and oppressive.

Carefully, she pries her eyes open, and her eyelashes clump together, before she pushes herself to sitting upright.

Her vision swims, but she just blinks hard, until the world comes into view again.

Dark red blood is splattered on the bright white tile, and her chair is crashed up against the wall. Izzy quivers, just feet away, her entire body trembling.

Alette's sitting back on her heels, her eyes wide behind her golden glasses, the needle in one hand and a torn open medical wipe in the other.

Terese pulls away from Axel, wobbling, and there's a smear of blood on his crisp shirt, the very shirt she saw him pull on that morning.

Her hand lifts to her ear, to the sludge slowly crusting on her neck, and her fingers come away damp.

"Did he hurt you?" she asks, letting her eyes lift to Axel's face. "I don't think he could see you. Did he hurt you?"

After a moment's hesitation, he shakes his head no. "I couldn't see a thing."

The glasses are, after all, most likely safe in his backpack in case they need to venture out. Because she didn't think, didn't realize, that it could happen here. That he could reach out to her, in the safest place she has, and still harm her.

Her vision blurs again, this time with tears, but she blinks as fast as she can to clear them, anger unspooling inside of her.

Izzy creeps close until she can rest her nose on Terese's leg.

"Well, I could see him, and that was terrifying," Alette says, before briskly pulling out the medical wipe and handing it to her. "He either couldn't see me or didn't notice, but I would very much like it if no demon ever gets in here again."

"Sorry," Terese offers, cautiously pressing the wipe to her ear, and the pain makes her head spin. "He shouldn't be able to, I don't know why, this place is safe—"

"I think you need to conclude that no place is truly safe," Alette says, unrolling some gauze, her needle still in her hand, like she doesn't know when she'll need it next. "Not if he could do that."

"A," Axel says, almost harsh, "not helping."

His face is pale, too, the freckles sticking out under the florescent lights.

"I'm okay," Terese says, even though she very much so isn't, and fear competes with the blood in her mouth for the prevailing taste. "I'll...I'll be okay."

Everything is heavy, keeping her head upright is heavy, and her hands shake, so she sits there for a second, letting herself take inventory of her body, see how badly he damaged her.

Her throat is raw, like something carved its way down her mouth. Her head pounds in time with the pulse of the overhead lights, but that's almost a given, and her eyes sting.

Now that her brain is back online, she can breathe, and other than the overwhelming feeling of something caught in her throat, her lungs are easy. No immediate injury in her gut or back, so he didn't hit her spine, not like last time.

"Did he melt my brains out again?" she asks, aiming for funny and missing it completely, her breath hitching in the middle.

"Jesus Christ," Alette whispers.

Axel, face still starkly white, shakes his head, then relents, nodding. "Maybe a bit. Not as...not as much as the first time."

"It was worse?" Alette whispers.

And she hadn't seen her the first time, hadn't been there the second time, and Alette's eyebrows draw together.

Terese just looks to Axel, locks eyes with him, as if she could will him to understanding something, something she still doesn't know. As if she could, by sheer force of personality, will the blood away from him, take away that terrified expression, and get him to smile again.

She hates the blood on him.

Something in Axel's gaze softens, easing a knot in her chest that has nothing to do with the fire in her head.

"Okay, let's get you some food," he says, and Alette makes a garbled noise behind them. "What, she just brought herself back from the dead, it takes a bit of power."

"Throat feels awful," she volunteers, "head hurts, so do my eyes." She briefly, ever so briefly, thinks about trying to stand, before remaining firmly on the ground.

It is, once again, very weird to be talking about this with another person, but something solidifies inside of her, something between rage and protectiveness and helplessness.

"Call Melekai back here," she says, and Axel blinks before nodding. "I need to ask how I killed him before."

25

They make her eat a bunch more of the breakfast, bringing the plate to her there on the ground, and as much as Terese hates it, she's way more stable than she used to be after dying. The pounding in her head is much more of a sharp throb than anything else, and the awful taste in her throat turned out to be blood, which was unpleasant to eat around but ultimately got washed away with a lot of tea.

As soon as she's done with a second plate of flatbread and fried potatoes, Axel unfolds himself from next to her, and she misses the contact the moment he steps away.

"I'll see about getting Mel back here. I know they went to a safehouse last night," he says, with a grimace of an apology. "Lyra will want to see what she can do to help."

Scanning sounds up there with the worst thing someone could threaten her with at the moment, but she keeps that to herself, instead accepting the second cup of green tea from Alette, who hasn't lost the horrified expression yet.

Still, when Axel steps out of the small kitchen, Alette turns to her, quick, as if the horror had just been a facade.

"Which runes kept you out," Alette says, fast, "which ones, and let's get them back up."

"I don't think I can do that right now," Terese says, dry, gesturing to the drying and crumbling blood splatter on the tile.

Alette nods to give her the point. "How long until you can?"

And while she's feeling better, the pain in her head doesn't give her an especially good idea of timelines. "I'm not usually conscious for this, so I don't know," she says, trying and failing to keep the snipping out of her tone. "Last time I was unconscious for fifteen hours, this isn't exactly a science."

In front of her, Alette looks like she very much so wants to debate that before she visibly pulls herself back, tucking the golden needle into her case. "You said you're in pain," she starts, and it takes Terese a few moments to realize that there's a question behind her voice, instead of just a statement. "Is there anything I can do?"

"I..." Terese trails off, at the enormity of someone who she once killed asking her that question, and she blinks down at the cup of tea in her hand. "I usually just deal with it until it goes away."

Which she doesn't have to anymore.

"I don't know if any pain medicine really works on me," she continues, pushing past the prickly sensation of telling her this. "Last demon experimented, it didn't go that well."

"From what we can tell from Mel, that tracks," Alette says, and almost worse, her voice is analytical. "With how he was projecting himself, he had to be more vulnerable than he appeared, I'll teach you how to attack when he's like that."

"He takes away my ability to grab at magic," Terese says,

rubbing her hand on her eyes and coming away with more blood. "The only thing that worked is the death bubble when he's already inside me and Axel's gun."

"Good data," Alette says, handing her another wet wipe. "That just means we need to give you some tools."

Alette sweeps herself up to her feet in one smooth, graceful motion, then holds her hand out for Terese. And Terese is still a bit more than wobbly, so she just stares at her.

"Let's get you up and to the table," Alette explains, "so you're sitting on a comfortable chair instead of a pool of your own blood when Axel comes back."

"Sure," Terese manages, then grabs her hand to haul herself up.

Immediately, a wave of pain sparks through her head, black crowding out the edge of her vision, and Alette's grip tightens, keeping her upright, until she can breathe through the initial wave. Magic drips off of Alette's hand, an almost distracting sensation against the hurt. Terese almost stumbles, and her ankle gives her a warning throb, but before she can even say anything, Alette guides her to the padded chair and dumps her in it.

Izzy follows, a whine in the back of her throat.

"What the," Terese mutters, pulling up the leg of her jeans.

Right at the pain, there's an already deepening bruise, her ankle puffy over her shoes.

Without even needing to be asked, Alette drags over another chair and props Terese's ankle up on it, then hands her a bag of ice from the freezer.

"You probably don't need this, but it can't hurt," Alette says briskly as Terese clumsily unties her shoe and pulls it off. "We can't do anything about the brain bleed, but I know how to treat sprained ankles."

"I'll be fine tomorrow," she mumbles, flexing her foot, and it still hurts.

She's still bleeding out of her ear, and the trickle derails her attention, so she leans her forehead against the table. It's cool to the touch, which is almost nice against her skin but hovers right on the edge.

Fear still coats the back of her throat, so she focuses on breathing and the sensation of the chill of the ice and the table.

She's vulnerable like this.

She's vulnerable like this, and now Alette is in the same room as her, with an evaluating tint in her eyes.

"I wasn't okay for a week when I came back, and a Necromancer healed almost all of my injuries," Alette says, sitting down across from the table to her. "Maybe you just need to rest."

Terese leans her head over so she can blink at her without removing herself from the table. "Didn't you almost burn out by grabbing too many Ley Lines a few months ago?"

"Did Axel tell you that?" Alette says, quick, before she makes a face at herself. "I mean—"

"Remember the whole time around when you two shot me and then you somehow started dating Zoel?" Terese asks, unable to filter her words into something nicer. "It was pretty obvious around then."

"Right," Alette says, shifting uncomfortably, and even in all the hurt and fear, there's a small part of Terese celebrating that she actually could make an insightful statement. "You're not wrong, but I'm...trying. To learn to not do that."

There's an undercurrent there, and Terese actually debates lifting her head to stare at Alette. Then, "I don't think Axel would do anything to betray your confidence."

Because even with whatever tension, whatever thing they're not communicating about, Terese can't imagine him doing that to Alette.

A quick series of complicated expressions flash over Alette's face, before settling on something a little sad.

"He still calls you his best friend," Terese continues, not knowing if she's helping or hurting, but wholly unable to stop. "So even if he's...whatever...I don't think he'd tell me anything you wouldn't really want him to."

Alette takes a deep breath, then another, then gives her an almost perfunctory nod. "Thank you," she says, voice almost controlled. "It's been hard, without us talking all the time. We grew up together."

It's not new information, but Terese nods, then immediately regrets the actions.

"He's probably freaking out to Mel on the phone right now, that's why he's not back yet," Alette says. "I don't think he enjoyed seeing you die."

If Terese had been feeling better, she would shrug. "I get better. Just takes some time."

Axel steps back in the tiny kitchen, phone in his hand, and obviously avoids looking at the pool of blood. His cheeks are wet and his eyes shining.

He locks eyes with Terese, and Terese wishes she could take away all the stress, all the helplessness in the lines of his shoulders.

But instead he just drags another chair to sit next to her and lays a hand on her back, and the simple contact wells up tears in Terese's eyes.

He's here.

"And it's okay," Alette continues, "to take the time you need to rest, even when the world seems like it's going to end."

The world has seemed like it's going to end too many times for Terese's tastes.

I T TAKES a little less than an hour for Melekai to make it to the compound with Lyra, so wherever they were hiding it's definitely not far enough, but Axel and Alette sit with her, forcing awkward banter with each other that even Terese can tell they don't want to be making. Zoel joins them at between one blink and the next, and Terese is too tired to even be happy to see him.

Terese doesn't even bother to hide her flinch when the Necromancer looks at her, blazing through her meager defenses.

"He's definitely trying to weaken you," the Necromancer announces, instead of saying hello or anything that even Terese would call civilized. "He hit the part of your brain that controls your blood and your lungs, he's trying to weaken you."

"Ow," Terese says, without any heat, in regard to the scan.

Melekai stands in the back, awkward with his hands in his pockets, almost a lost scowl on his face.

"You have bruising on the inside of your skull and blood pooling right at your neck," the Necromancer continues. "Your head must be killing you."

"It's not great," Terese says, pushing herself to sit upright, and even with the time and the food, she wobbles a bit. "And I apparently sprained my ankle."

"It's just a muscle twist, not a sprain," the Necromancer says, almost instinctively, then makes a face at herself as she sits at the table, grabbing a now-cooled piece of flatbread. "Those heal faster on normal people than sprains, who knows about you."

Zoel nods at Terese, and if anyone has witnessed her first bumbling healing times, it's him, so it's a nice bit of confirmation.

Melekai's still standing, his shoulders hunched.

And all at once, Terese realizes she probably asked him a rather uncomfortable question. A question full of trauma and change and everything weird that's happened in his life.

She wouldn't want to answer, either.

"Hey," Axel says, noticing as well, "wanna come join us?"

Melekai looks like he very much so does not, and he turns the frown on Axel, before sighing dramatically and flopping on the chair next to the Necromancer.

Axel leans forward towards his friend, only a smidgen more put together, and he didn't even bother to change out of the bloody shirt. "Just think, after all this time, you get to get revenge on her by boring her with this story."

"Thanks," Melekai says with a lewd gesture.

"I'm not asking for a play by play, I just want to know the theory of how she did it," Terese says, unsure if that will help whatever it is going on in the former demon. "I don't remember much of that day, just being freezing and the demon screaming."

"I'm glad she screamed," Melekai says, with more force than she would have thought, "I'm glad she hurt."

Terese doesn't have a response to that.

"Short answer, a lot of power," Melekai says, as the Necromancer passes him a chunk of flatbread, which he unthinkingly takes, "she was completely letting loose with everything in her, not conserving anything. That's how she did things like kill Dr. Bitch and take away his power with just a single graze." Melekai jerks his thumb to Axel.

Alette sits back and crosses her arms at his phrasing but says nothing.

"It's stupid," Melekai emphasizes, "if she somehow won, killed us all, unless she consumed some power"—this time, he jerks his thumb to the Necromancer—"she'd be unable to do anything, unable to teleport away, unable to heal anything. She'd be a sitting duck, until she regained it, and the rate people—demons—regain power without being jumpstarted would not be fast enough for her to get out of any trouble coming her way."

It needles a memory loose, deep from the part of Terese's mind she tries not to think of.

"Like on that street, when I wrecked your car," she says, pointing at Axel, who raises his eyebrows at her. "You got a head injury, you had some cuts but also shot me, and you got a bunch of scrapes and took power back." She points to each of them. "And I think she almost got you bad."

Melekai crosses his arms and looks like he'd rather be anywhere else. "She did," he says, begrudgingly.

It had been pretty awful of a time, not gonna lie, but Terese turns the memory over in her mind.

It had been slushy, and the demon had a jolt of terror that bled over into Terese the moment the Necromancer stepped out of the wrecked car, not wanting a repeat fight with her protector.

And instead of thinking of her power like a thin stream of sand from her fist, she flashed it everywhere, as if she could pour from a pitcher with no end in sight.

"Sorry about wrecking your car," Terese says, leaning her head over to glance at Axel. "And the head injury."

"Noted," he says, lips twitching up. He's still pale, his fingers tapping against the back of Terese's chair.

"Well, that makes Daniil's actions make sense," Alette says, clinically, and everyone looks at her. "What, he can tell she's powerful, so he's trying to bleed her power bit by bit so she can't fight him off. Annoying tactic, simple tactic."

"And he doesn't quite understand how fast you heal," Axel says, catching Alette's idea with an ease that Terese marvels at, "so he's testing different things, until he finds out a good way to do it."

Melekai leans back, silent.

"And he has a decent understanding of things he can do, from your first interaction," Alette says, and the pit of doom grows in Terese, "he knows how much he can harm you, he knows how you can kick him out and how much power it takes, so he's skirting on the edge of that to make you weaker."

"And skirting away from my territory, so he can't be cornered into responding to me," Zoel speaks, finally.

Terese watches Melekai, whose face doesn't move, and the plan forms loosely around the pounding in her head. Alette and Axel continue to talk, almost too fast for her to keep up, obviously born from years of knowing each other and doing exactly this.

And Daniil had gotten to her here.

Izzy wiggles her way in between Terese and the table, shoving her nose into Terese's hand with the insistence that this must at least look like a severe panic attack, at least to her dog.

"Should we ask the college for help, both with taking down a demon and so they stop looking for her?" Alette asks and immediately gets Zoel and Melekai shaking their heads at her. "What, it'd eliminate one complication."

"I think...I think it'd just create more, A," Axel says, light, but his eyes are sharp. "They've mostly given up, it's just Gurlien out there being annoying."

"And what do you think he'll do when he finds out we have her?"

Terese just glances between the two of them, at the almost practiced volley of debate.

"He's cried wolf so many times, I doubt the college would believe him," Melekai chimes in, and there's a dark undercurrent to his voice. "They've all but turned their backs on him."

After the break. After Terese saw the man go into the Ley Line break, somehow surviving. "What happened to him in there?" Terese asks.

A series of quick emotions flash over Axel's face, before he shrugs, glib. "He lost all his powers, now has to live like a normal human, you know, like me."

"Except he's an asshole," the Necromancer chimes in, "and accepted no help from any of us."

That explains the expression on Axel's face, that's for sure.

Alette whispers something to Zoel, and it distracts Terese enough to miss the next few statements, and she resists the urge to close her eyes as the words wash over her.

"So first thing," Terese starts, and the rest fall quiet, "would be actually making a safe place for me to recover, get everything back, not just a place I feel safe."

Slowly, Alette nods.

"Then would be storing up enough energy until I could take him on," Terese continues, and she doesn't like this, she doesn't like this at all, and she can see it in Melekai's face that he's reached the same conclusion. "Then we bait him somewhere, use that circle, and I...detonate."

26

The rest of the group debates, and Terese quickly makes the executive decision to tune them all out and close her eyes to the pounding in her brain. Izzy lays down at her feet, curled up on the tile.

Detonating certainly doesn't sound too pleasant, and her mind immediately spins off in all the different ways it could go wrong, and she rests her head in her arms on the table again, and the group immediately falls silent.

"What?" she mumbles, not even opening her eyes.

"You're, uh...still bleeding a bit," Axel says, and the trickle in her ear could have told her that.

"Yeah, you should go rest," the Necromancer says, her voice embarrassed. "You have active brain contusions, we shouldn't be yelling around you."

Terese agrees. Every part of her feels vulnerable and new, so she just nods, keeping her head against the table.

One by one, they leave. Melekai stalking off to go do some research, Alette and Zoel off to some hidden place in the building that Terese doesn't want to contemplate, and the Necromancer following some pathway that only she can sense, until Terese's awareness of her dims.

Leaving Terese with just Axel, under the florescent lights and the drying bloodstain on the tiles.

"I don't want to lie down," Terese says, even though she probably should, she'd feel better if she could sleep, but everything is too sharp, too pointed, for her to feel safe resting that deeply.

Axel just traces a pattern on her back, halfway between soothing and distracting.

"But also..." Terese gestures at all of herself. "Don't really feel great."

"I can't help with that," Axel says, after a few moments of silence, like he's searching for something to say or do. "Do you want to help me repaint the car?"

This makes her pop open an eye to look at him.

"Do you want to sit there while I repaint the car?"

HE HELPS her to one of the camp chairs haphazardly set up around the car, still in a blazing circle of power. He stares at the car, an unhappy twist on his mouth, before he stalks through the circle and pops the trunk, pulling out a fresh shirt and stripping off the bloody one.

It helps, seeing the blood come off of him.

"I know that sanding this all down isn't exactly going to remove all the power and shit, but it's going to feel real good," Axel says, filling the silence and the dread left behind by the view of the spiky words.

And she's supposed to be resting. Her head pounds and her eyes throb, but she squints at the car, at the still tepid level of demonic energy threaded through it.

Izzy flops over next to the chair with a huff.

"Do Alette and the Necromancer need the power intact to track him?" she asks, resting her hand over the arm of the chair to dangle in Izzy's fur.

"Nah, once we get a sample we have it forever," he says easily, "unless he pulls a you or a Melekai and fundamentally changes the very core of his being, then it's useless."

"You totally tried with an old example of the demon's magic, didn't you?" Terese says, and somehow, despite herself, she's smiling.

"It did nothing," he confirms, pulling over a cart of tools and supplies. "First thing we did when everyone was out of the hospital, tried that. Then Lyra tried something based on some residue or something you left on her brother, and all that showed was you were...somewhere."

She scrunches her face at him, and the motion hurts. "Residue."

"All it showed us was that you were probably still alive which, you know, totally useful," he says, selecting a tool that Terese's mind recognizes as a belt sander, plugging it into the wall. "We tried to get another sample—well, A tried to get another sample, I was too busy freaking out—when we found your tunnel, but it didn't work. Probably because you're, you know, actually a human and not a demon." He fixes a pair of safety glasses on his face—normal ones, not any trace of magic on them—before giving her a thumbs up.

It's a nice thought. Then his words catch up to her.

"You freaked out?"

Instead of answering, he powers up the belt sander, and the soft whirr fills the air, and there's something familiar in the noise. Like she's been around it before and associates it with something kind.

She pokes at the memory, and it's another one of her on

a stage, sitting with her legs dangling over the edge, watching as someone uses it on a piece of scenery.

"Not to be weird, but I've never actually killed someone," Axel says, as if that's a bad thing. "So I had the freak out about shooting someone in the head, that's traumatic, and then the person still said a few things with blood all over her forehead. It's up there with the strangest experiences in my life, and I've seen people brought back from the dead with magic and I used to change my own face."

She pulls herself from the vague remembrances of a stage and the smell of pine.

"So yeah, little bit of a freak out. A literally collected everything she thought we could use, and all but pushed me out of the cave," Axel continues, "and either she chose the wrong things or you're too human."

"You know, I like that you haven't killed anyone," Terese says, the words falling from her mouth before she thinks twice, and his eyebrows flash upwards. "It's not a great feeling, so it's...good you haven't had to have it."

He gives her a sideways smile before fitting a mask over his face, then begins to sand the paint off the car in an easy, practiced motion. Like he's done this hundreds of times, not just because of Daniil.

"Are you in your 'blurt-out-things-without-a-filter' stage right now?" he asks, voice muffled by the breathing mask.

"Probably," she answers.

"Because unless you took control back from the demon, you haven't killed either," he says, and she watches as the words fall away from the front door of the car, the shiny black paint evening out and smoothing to an off-grey dullness. "What do you say to that?"

"You're mostly correct," Terese replies, going with her

immediate gut reaction instead of anything more advanced, "but I still experienced it happening and felt it."

He nods to give her that.

It's a warm feeling, to be curled up in the camp chair with her legs underneath herself, watching him sand away the threatening words. To contemplate the familiarity of the sound, and the soothing that even after all of this, Axel doesn't consider her a murderer.

The belt sander skids over some words, and there's a sudden little kick to her stomach, some sort of pull. To see them disappear, see such a threat literally vanish in front of her.

It's almost as cathartic as the shots of vodka.

"Will you paint it black again?" she asks, after a few minutes of lulling sound.

"Oh, yeah," Axel says, flipping up his glasses to look at her. "Always end up painting it some sort of glossy black. Classy, you know?"

"Yeah," Terese says. "I love you."

Once more, the words spring forth, unbidden, but her head hurts too much for her to want to pull them back, despite how simplistic and incomplete they are. Despite how inopportune of a moment it is in her life to say something like that, despite all the drama and the direness of the morning.

He pulls off the mask just enough so he can grin at her, and her heart turns.

"Hey, you too," he says, and there's an easy affection in his voice, one she marvels at, before he sets the sander down long enough to stride over to her and gently press a kiss to her lips, bracing himself on the fabric arms of the chair. "We'll get through this."

She curls her fingers on the hem of the clean shirt, and despite the pain still racking her brain, believes him.

TERESE ENDS up dozing off in the chair in some blessed sleep, and when she comes to, there's no more spiky words carved into the car, instead a fine settling of paint dust on the ground and some spent sandpaper. The belt sander is on the ground, unplugged.

She blinks, muzzy, and Izzy's in just as deep of sleep, snoring loudly.

Axel's sitting on the ground with a piece of sandpaper, working on something in the wheel well. Paint dust covers his shirt and sweat drips from the back of his curls.

She doesn't know how long it's been, but her eyes hurt less, and her ears aren't as blocked up. Her head still throbs, insistent, and she'll probably need to eat more at some point if she's truly going to rest up and regain strength.

But there's a bit of peace in watching him move, the evidence of the demon all brushed away.

She extends her legs in a stretch, the fabric of the camp chair creaking, and Izzy opens one eye to glance at her before closing them again.

"It looks good," she says, and Axel startles, almost dropping the sandpaper. "More like a car, less like a hate letter."

He blinks owlishly at her from behind the safety glasses, then takes them off, setting them on the hood of his car.

"I hyper focused a bit," he says, pulling off the mask, and there's a line of paint dust around where the masks sat against his skin. "You feeling better?"

She nods, and it's less hostile than before, though her brain still feels sloshy.

"Not sure how anyone could sleep through a belt sander against a car," he continues, pushing himself up to standing, using the car to support himself, then checks his phone. "Jesus, it's been hours."

Like the time caught him unaware, too.

Carefully, she stands, and the ankle gives her a pang but supports her weight. She flexes her toes, they all move.

The blood in her hair sticks against her cheek, and she's going to have to wash the ball cap before it stains.

"Noise isn't too bad," she says, stretching her arms over her head, and the motion disrupts nothing new, which is nice. "I desperately need to clean this up." She shows him the inside of the ball cap, the mottled brown-red splotch against the neon green.

Axel looks back to the car, to the sheer amount of work he got done and the dust on his hands, then nods, still looking a bit lost. "Yeah, me too."

HE LEADS her to his apartment, grabbing an extra towel on the way to his bathroom, before they both crowd into his little shower.

It's not quite sexy, as they're both equal amounts of gross —her with the copious amounts of blood in her hair and him covered in grime—but there's something nice in that moment, seeing him whole and healthy, the strong muscles of his chest, the evidence of Daniil's words getting rinsed down the drain.

Seeing the almost comical hickey she gave him on his neck the night before, and his wink when she points it out.

It's a casual sort of intimacy, she decides, as they dry off afterwards with more of his fluffy towels, the humidity of the shower fogging up the mirror. Where she can see his body and see him uninjured, and he can see the same.

"You can stay here," he says, as she towel-dries her hair, loosely dressed in a pair of his extra sweatpants again. Like she had worn her first night here. "Sleep on an actual bed."

"You really felt bad about that, didn't you?" she asks, more curious than anything else.

All he's wearing is a towel slung low around his hips.

"Well, obviously," he starts, but there's a smile on his face, one she hopes to see many, many more times, "but it was...nice. Waking up next to someone. It's been a while since I've had that."

With how vulnerable she's been that day, bleeding literally on the floor, it's strange to see that side of him, opened up for her. Like if she chooses wrong, it would hurt him, leave him ready for pain.

She doesn't want that.

"Sure," she says, and it's not even that much of a decision, "I'd like that."

SHE WAKES in the middle of the night with him curled around her, and despite the throb that takes her breath away behind her ears and the ache in her ankle, she's warm, and she's safe.

THE NEXT MORNING, despite all her protests, he drags her to a semi-cleared section of the forest. There's a chewed-up log on one end, and a table on the other, ivy growing thick along the ground.

Axel heaves his bag onto the table, and curiosity worms its way through her.

"I offered my gun. Now you get to learn how to shoot," Axel says, almost surly.

Terese casts a slightly more critical eye over the clearing.

"Beyond those trees"—Axel points—"is a dirt mound that will effectively stop any bullet from reaching further than we want. I made this place a few years ago, it's excellent."

"So you bring everyone here to teach?" Terese asks, drifting closer to Axel as he unloads some foam cases from his bag, then neatly lining up a few boxes of ammo.

"Not everyone," he amends, "I tried with Lyra, she hated it, Mel thought it was fun."

He selects the now familiar pistol.

"Do you learn from explaining or from seeing?" Axel asks, which is a good question.

"I think from example," Terese says, unsure, her gaze drawn to his hands. They're strong hands, with a few callouses, and her mind derails her focus.

"Then here."

He goes over the motions of loading the clip, putting it into place, the proper stances, general rules of safety. It's odd to be on this side of a gun, and a part of her hind brain still shies back from it, remembering the pain of the tunnel.

He shoots a few times, after securing eye and ear protection for the both of them, knocking a few tin cans off of the log with ease, before offering her the gun.

She quickly shakes her head, not confident in it yet, so he lines up more bottles and cans on the log.

"I'm surprised that Mel didn't insist on Lyra learning this," she ventures after watching his clean efficiency.

"Lyra has dead hidden all over, now," Axel says, after a

few more rounds of shooting and her watching, and it's almost alarming. "Now she knows how to ignore the death, she can hide dead things—I'm talking bugs, mice, not people—and put them where she thinks she might need them."

"Comforting," Terese says, watching as he aims down the gun again, knocking the bottle off the log.

"I think it comforts Mel more than anything," Axel says, scowling at the perfectly good shot he just made. "Mel likes the idea she'd be able to do something big anywhere."

"Of course he does."

Another shot and another can off the log.

They had left Izzy back on the rug on account of her ears being way more sensitive than either of theirs, but the warm breeze and the gentle sunshine would have been great for the old dog.

"When did you learn how to do this?" Terese asks, watching the long line of his shoulders. "I know Alette shot me, before, but—"

"I taught her how to shoot," Axel says, popping out the magazine with one smooth motion. "Dr. Frisse aside, all of her family members are Quebecois Canadians who have a rather dim view on guns."

"Well, you certainly taught her well," Terese says, absent-mindedly rubbing her sternum, right where Alette had shot her and the demon that one time. "Certainly pissed off the demon."

The corners of Axel's lips twitch up. "But I got this from my dad," he says, showing her the gun as he slides the magazine back into place. "The asshole didn't teach me much, but he instilled a rather firm belief in self-defense."

And as much as Terese's background is a mystery, she realizes she knows just as little about Axel's.

"He would have to, giving you a name like Blake," she remarks, and gets a full smile, before he sets the pistol on the table with a click.

"It's not going to bite you," he says, as she eyes it. "Just a jolt to your wrist and arms when you shoot."

He fits his warm hand around hers, showing her how to wrap her fingers around the textured grip. "First rule, never point it anywhere you don't want to hurt."

She rarely wants to hurt anything, so she nods.

"The safety is here," he says, moving her thumb to the button, "never press it unless you're about to shoot."

The gun is hot in her hands, vivid against her palm with magic, the careful and precise kind that comes from Alette.

"Nifty bit of work," she says, as he adjusts her stance with a small touch to her hips, her mind derailing to focus on him. "Fairly certain this was made directly for me, right?"

"Well, yeah," he says, and he's standing so close that if she leans back a little, she'd be pressing against him. "Well, demons in general, but with the specific goal of incapacitating you if we needed, after you shrugged off the other shots."

"Shrugged is a strong word," she says, squinting down at the cans on the log. "Little bead in the sights?"

"Brace yourself with your knees bent," he says, right into her ear, and despite the heat of the sun, she shivers. "Bring it up a bit more." He prods her arm upright more with a gentle touch to her wrist. "Closer it is to your eye line with both arms, better of a shot you are."

"You shot him with just one arm," she points out, but complies anyway.

"That's because I have way more practice," Axel says, soft and oh so close to her ear, "you try to get me to shoot with my left arm and I'm useless."

She shivers again and throws him a look, which he returns with a cheeky grin.

"Here, focus," he says, propping up her arm, "focus, know it'll kick back at you, and squeeze the trigger."

He claps on the ear protection over her head, muffling the world just a little bit, before taking a step back.

The gun is heavier than she anticipated, even so, she squints again, taking a deep breath and then pulling the trigger.

The world shatters apart at her fingertips, the gun kicking her wrist back, before within a blink the world is back to normal, the gun still hot in her hands, all the cans still on the log.

Carefully, she sets the gun on the table, then shakes out her hand. "Yeah, that's not for me."

27

They spend the rest of the week and into the next few in an odd sort of fugue: where the Necromancer insists Terese takes it easy, where Alette skirts around them both like she's afraid of breaking them, and Melekai firmly avoids her.

She knows he's around, catches him talking with Axel but quickly leaving before Terese can ask a question, but it doesn't bother her as much as it probably would have at the beginning of this.

It's a time of eating more than she has for at least the last eight months, of sleeping deeper than she ever thought possible while being alive. Of pestering Alette to give her reading research, and hearing Axel's cackle when Alette looks startled. Of taking Izzy on meandering strolls through the forest around the compound, of the occasional throb of magic telling her to whisk herself away, run away while she can.

It's a lot easier to breathe through those when she's around them. When she's around Axel.

It's quick kisses when she thinks other people won't

notice, it's leaning her head against his shoulder and dozing off as he fixes something small, it's learning how he takes his coffee when he's not hungover and which TV shows he likes. It's the way his hand lingers against her hip when she walks past, gentler than anything she's ever encountered. It's squabbling over pet toys, of all things, which apparently Axel has strong feelings about and apparently she does as well.

It's losing time, once, for a few hours. Blacks out while standing next to Axel cleaning the dishes, then comes to sitting on the damp dirt of the solarium, Izzy's head on her lap, Axel aggressively taking a screwdriver to the inside of a computer speaker.

It's accidentally staying up late, devouring a book he had on the nightstand next to his bed, still naked. It's another trip to the seedy dive bar with the tacky painting, where they get less drunk but make out way more. It's catching Izzy actually thump her tail at Axel once, when his back is turned and he doesn't see.

It's the most peace she's ever felt, and Daniil does nothing. Not a word, not a whisper, nothing.

AFTER AT LEAST THREE WEEKS, after she's read all the research Alette's given her and gets tired of Melekai avoiding her, she wakes up one morning with something like resolve settled inside of her.

Axel's curled around her, a leg thrown casually over her hip, and Izzy's fast asleep on her new favorite blanket next to the bed, but Terese blinks up at the wall.

"Okay," she whispers to herself, and it feels proper. "Let's do this."

Carefully, with the practice of only these last few weeks, she wiggles out from the cuddles, and Axel dramatically flops backwards on the bed, still asleep. It's easily late morning, but they stayed up late watching the most ridiculous movie Axel could find.

She pads barefoot to the table where she left her phone, flicks it open to the group text.

TERESE (10:22 AM): Okay, it's time to practice now.

THEY SPEND one day meticulously combing through the wards, activating the ones Zoel identifies won't impact him, buttressing ones specifically against demons. Making the building as impregnable as imagined until the very stones and bricks gleam with magic that reads as the biggest 'fuck off' in history.

It's prickly work, and despite not extending much energy, sweat drips down Terese's neck by the end, before she tests with a simple teleportation.

The alarms go off, it's like moving through peanut butter, but she's still able to leave and the entire compound now breathes with power, bristling with protections, and something in her heart settles even more as she strides up the hill to the compound, through the forest and blackberry brambles.

And still not a whisper from Daniil.

THEY ALL COALESCE on the cracked helicopter pad once more, where the dent from her previous death bubble still collects dust and, now, the first few leaves of fall.

"I take it you actually don't use this for very many helicopter visits," Terese says, scuffing her foot along the largest of the cracks.

"We've had a helicopter here all of once?" Axel says, and the same shiver of excitement seems to run through him as well. "Back when Dr. Frisse had some other magicians over and one had a stroke?"

"Fairly sure it was a heart attack," Alette murmurs, and this time it's her turn to write the rune circle, and the lettering flows from her with a practiced ease.

"Either way, road's too thin for a proper ambulance to get through, so helicopter," Axel continues, bouncing on his toes. Izzy's leash dangles from his hands, but Izzy's content to lay on the concrete, panting from the walk up. His military backpack is slung over his shoulder and the glasses over his eyes, and everything about him is covered in a thin sheen of anticipation.

Between one moment and the next, Zoel appears besides Alette, but she doesn't startle, like she expected him. Like she knows him well enough to know—or sense—when he's arriving.

It's never something Terese ever got the hang of in all of her interactions with him.

"How are you feeling?" Lyra asks, just on this side of being intrusive. "I don't think you want me to scan you."

Somewhere in all of this, her name slid in front of the title Terese's mind had given her, and the name Lyra no longer sticks out as being wrong.

"Yeah no definitely not," Terese says, watching Alette paint with magic. "No sign of Daniil."

"Hmm," Melekai says, noncommittal, and they all look at him for that one. "What?"

"That's your 'I have a suspicion' sound," Lyra says, but she's smiling, a soft expression at Melekai.

He sighs. "I worry," Melekai starts, his eyes flickering between Terese and Axel, "that he's biding his time, and we're all going to be slammed when he makes another attempt."

"If he can," Axel says, and there's a hint of pride in his voice.

Like he's proud of her.

Melekai stares at him, then shakes himself loose and rolls his eyes.

"I'm going to put up a block," Zoel says, drifting over to them like he had been paying equal amounts of attention to the frankly extreme amount of power Alette is putting off and to their inane conversation. "So for as long as it is up—which will be minutes—he cannot sense you."

He had reassured her of that before, but the reminder is nice.

Minutes, until the spell will break, and it will be close to twenty-four hours before Zoel can cast it safely again.

Not for her safety, of course, but for the safety of the magic in the area. Because if there's any constant in her life, especially now, it's that she is way more of a danger to everyone else.

"Too bad that's not a permanent thing," Melekai grumbles, and Zoel gives him an unreadable look that just might involve a hint of a smile, "then we wouldn't have to worry about any of this."

"Pretty sure I'd still worry," Terese says, but shakes out her hands anyway as Alette finishes the circle.

The first step over the spray paint pops Terese's ears, and her own magic briefly pulses inside of her to run away, but she stills herself, keeps herself on the dusty concrete.

Izzy lifts her head, then cranes her neck to give Axel a wounded look, the same thing she does whenever she discovers that Axel—or anyone else—holds her leash.

Deliberately, Terese turns their back to them, and looks at the dummy Alette had set up. There's no real safe way for her to practice against another person, when the only person who's immune to her death bubbles is also the only person who can bring someone back in case of an accident, and even Zoel is wary of her aiming something at him.

Especially if they want her to let loose.

Alette had talked her through the theories of different techniques until she mentally matched them up with ones the previous demon had done.

A wave of power, borne from restlessness and whatever else she had in her.

Lyra lets slip a slice of a scan, dulled by the surrounding circle, and it buzzes through Terese.

"You shouldn't be impaired by anything," Lyra calls over, "your power levels are fine, you're not tired, you're not blood sugary."

She could have told her that, but Terese just eyes the dummy.

Behind her, she hears Izzy whine, and the telltale sound of Axel thumping her on the side to calm her down, and she knows, she just knows, that Izzy's going to be fucking distressed by this. Going to hate it, hate the separation and hate the effort.

Every bit of magic she's tried since getting unpossessed, with the glaring exceptions of the struggles with Daniil, have been a chaotic struggle to keep things tamped down. Restrained. Let her not cause as much damage as she already has.

A glimmer of movement, and Zoel's nebulous power

settles over her, and for a moment it's like she can't breathe, before the sensation slithers off of her, like a pile of slippery fabric.

And that is her signal. Once that is cast, she has at most four minutes before the protection fades.

"Okay," she whispers, closing her fist on a thread of magic Zoel had isolated out for her, so she did no lasting damage. "Okay."

Then, with no care for finesse or for scale, she rips it apart.

Immediately, wind snaps through her hair, the air racing away, detonating out from around her in one breathless moment.

Her eyes sting, and reflexively she lifts a hand to shelter them, but the wind isn't coming from any one place, just around her, so she forces herself to exhale. To calm her heart, until she can look out to the dummy, keeping the strange, nebulous power close to her chest.

The entire space glimmers with a strange coat of gold, like her death bubble is so thick it's almost opaque, and no noise reaches her ears. Nothing from Izzy, who must be howling up a storm, nothing from Zoel and Alette, nothing from Lyra and Melekai, and nothing from Axel.

Just her, in this golden storm, neatly corralled by the lines of the circle, and the dummy.

She only has four minutes to practice this.

She takes a second to unclench her hands from the magic. To envision it as a stream flowing from her, to feed from the well of terror all the emotions the demon had tapped into. All the pain, all the twisted knowledge of what is fair and what is right and how it no longer applies to her, all the emotions that let the demon strike out with such fury. All the things that drove the demon to madness.

And let them go.

The fury blasts out from her hand, and between one blink and the next, the dummy evaporates, threads tearing to pieces and wood splintering and—

Terese jerks the power back, cutting it off, and the gold vanishes, leaving her ears ringing and her eyes watering.

"Well, that was good," from behind her, Melekai drawls, "definitely don't feel bad being taken out by one of those now."

She shakes out her stinging hand, until no trace of the magic remains on her fingertips, before turning.

True to form, Izzy's hunched into a crouch, her ears flicked back and her tail between her legs, a steady small whine at the back of her throat.

Behind the glasses, Axel's brown eyes are wide, the whites around all the edges showing clearly, even from the distance.

"Was that it?" Terese asks, then makes a face at her own word choice. "I mean, did that look like what happened?"

Axel's mouth opens, like he's about to say something, before it closes again.

"Not exactly," Alette says, and there's fear behind her voice, fear she's hiding behind something clinical. Zoel hears it too and rests a hand on the small of her back.

And no matter how far she's come, no matter how close she's gotten to them, she still scares them.

"The demon was more focused," Lyra says, but instead of fear it's thoughtful. "Same general shape, but more directed. Like a spear, not a cone."

"And she didn't hold back," Melekai says. "You did."

Terese shakes out her hands again, then takes a step towards the edge of the circle, a step towards Axel, and

Melekai takes a step back. Alette flinches, an ever so slight motion, and Zoel's face is grim.

But Izzy thumps her tail, still in her crouch.

"Safe for me to leave?" Terese asks, holding up her hands.

"Yes," Zoel says, then at the same time—

"Maybe?" From Alette, and—

"No." From Melekai.

Disquiet grows a thorny knot in her chest, before Axel's lips twitch up into a smile, and it settles into something familiar inside of her.

"Not like conflicting information is ever fun," he says, before winking at her from behind the glasses.

"Don't do any magic and you should be safe," Melekai amends with a scowl.

And Terese doesn't feel wrung out, but she definitely doesn't feel like she wants to go around spraying power everywhere, so she nods, stepping over the painted runes.

Izzy slinks along the ground until her nose meets Terese's ankle, then she springs up, wriggling all over her, and Terese sits down, right on the edge of the magic circle, and lets her dog climb huddling into her lap.

"Good news, your heart's still beating," Lyra says, like that's a comforting statement, and Terese pauses in her petting of Izzy to give her a blank stare.

"Did it stop?" Axel asks, and somehow, he isn't alarmed.

"It didn't feel like it stopped," Terese says, and Izzy wiggles enough to lick her face, "I can usually tell when it stopped."

"It's the 'usually' that gets me," Axel says, and they share a brief, mad grin.

"Well," Lyra says, then looks up, like she's suddenly realizing that everyone's staring pretty intently at her, "no, but you were...uh...reading as dead against the necromancy. For about ten seconds. But you were standing and blinking and breathing."

Terese should feel a lot weirder about that than she currently does, but her eyes are only now stopping stinging, so she scratches Izzy in between her ears.

"Will it kill a demon?" she asks, and doesn't miss the helpless look Zoel and Melekai exchange with each other. "Do I need to go back and try again—"

"No," Zoel interrupts her, which is unusual by itself, but Alette's shaking her head in agreement.

"Food first," Lyra says. "And probably sleep. You look wiped out."

"I don't feel wiped out," Terese protests, but her hands haven't stopped tingling yet, despite tangling them in Izzy's fur.

So she glances to Axel, who shrugs, and she knows him well enough now to know when he's faking being casual, but something inside of her is a little grateful for that grace.

ALETTE AND ZOEL stay by the circle, their heads bent together and their brows drawn, discussing in whispers how to fix what she broke. Melekai loops his arm in Lyra's, pulling her back towards the compound, and Axel and Terese follow at a more sedate pace.

"Feel weird?" Axel asks, the moment they could possibly not be overheard. "Your face did a thing."

"Yeah, look weird?" Terese asks, tapping the side of her head, where glasses would be if she wore them. Axel still wears the glasses, and it's a little fun to see him so easily distracted by all the runes woven into the very lands he's lived on.

"Dazzling," he says, conversationally. "You're a bit terrifying. It's great."

"Great," she echoes, but he grins at her again.

"What, it's pretty great to have someone who can just unload a massive amount of power at a moment's notice, not gonna lie," Axel says. "Before, our best bet with that was Lyra because nobody knew how powerful necromancy could be, now we have you, it's nifty."

"Nifty," she says, but feels herself smiling despite it all.

"I mean, beyond all this," Axel continues, and he drapes his arm over her shoulder.

She likes this, all the casual touch, and Axel is full of it. Gives it away like there're no strings attached, like he would be forever happy to brush up against her, to lean her against him, to hold her hand.

"Besides Daniil, once he's dealt with"—he's also started planning for beyond, casually— "it'd be silly to expect that we won't always have some sort of threat against us. Having a superhero on our side just sounds great."

All at once, the blanket of Zoel's protection slithers off of her, and she shudders at the sensation, before shaking it off.

"I guarantee you're the only one who thinks of me like a hero," Terese says, even though she really doesn't mind.

"Anyone who can survive against a demon counts as a hero in my mind."

From in front of them, Melekai turns and throws Axel the finger, and Lyra laughs, a bright, joyful sound. And here Terese thought they were being quiet enough, that the other pair were far enough away, but the easy lines in Axel's face still suggest it's not actually an issue.

And despite the oddness still in her limbs, the weird

sensation that her ears are going to pop once more, she's happy.

But...

Izzy stops dead, digging in her heels, and howls.

"What—" she starts, before there's a sudden punch in the air, a sudden shift of pressure, and—

With only that split-second warning, she jerks back, a hand closing around Axel's shirt, pulling him out of the way.

In one long clean motion, Daniil appears in front of them, already moving. There's a glint of something, a metal, before a bright hot slash of pain blossoms across Terese's stomach.

A knife. He has a knife, a normal human pocket knife, the one that's been forever on his belt, and he just tried to gut her with it.

Her knees buckle, but she shoves Axel back, stumbling him away.

Axel needs to get away. He needs to be away.

Daniil makes another slash at her, but misses, catching on the edge of her jacket and ripping there, before he jerks the knife down across her arm, tearing the leather and the skin underneath it, spraying blood.

From behind them, Lyra screams, and Daniil freezes, awe and hunger racing over his face, before he straightens and turns.

"No," Terese grits out, and lets her knees stumble so she crashes into Daniil, the palm of her hand to the side of his face.

The body he's in jerks at the sensation of her bloody hand hitting his face, and with that one little split second of timing, the split second of distraction, she pours as much of her power into him as she can.

Black blood wells from the eye sockets, cascading out of

the body's ears, but he shoves her off, sending her limp into the blackberry brambles.

"Fine then," Daniil says, past the blood bubbling from his mouth, then crowds into her head.

Her entire body convulses, and this time he tears through her defenses like they're tissue, tossing them aside like a child unwrapping a gift.

What the hell was that, he demands, in her mind, and she can't answer, she can't, pain shuddering through her stomach and her arm.

There's a twist of weakness. A mental limb held curled against him. She hurt him.

Stop, he demands, and opens her eyes for her, and she's staring at the bright blue sky above the trees.

He inhales through her body, sharp, at the vividness of the sky. The last demon had done so, too. Gotten so distracted by the sensation that it stopped in the middle of whatever action it was performing.

So Terese tries again.

Tries to pull all that energy, what little she has left, into herself, into her mind.

A hand closes over hers, brilliantly hot, and there's still screaming outside, and she just has the capability to jerk her body before she blacks out.

28

The lull of the waves brings her back, and the sea mist against her cheeks flutters her hair.

For a single, gut dropping moment, she can't open her eyes, can't twitch her fingers, like she's possessed all over again. Like she's possessed and Daniil's just sleeping, keeping her hostage in her own body.

The wave ends, and the ground tilts slightly to the left, a gentle lift.

The boat. She's on the boat.

She breathes in through her nose, and salt tickles down her throat. But she could control it, she commanded herself to breathe.

With one more breath, to steel herself up, she lets her eyes flutter open.

It's barely dawn, pink streaking across the sky, and the teak floor of the boat is slick with mist.

And sitting on the deck across from her, pistol laid across his lap, is Axel.

There's a flush over his cheekbones, like a sunburn.

He stares at her, hard, and his hand tightens around the pistol.

"What..." she manages out, before he very calmly puts the glasses over his face again.

She's slumped against the hull on the deck, where she always teleports to on the boat, and blood—both black and red—stains against the white of her tank top. A blanket is thrown over her lap, another loosely tucked around her shoulders.

As if remembering itself, pain slams into her, and she squeezes her eyes shut once more.

"Terese?" Axel asks, and there's a rough edge to his voice.

"Yeah, I'm here, it's me," she manages out, clutching her stomach.

"Open your eyes," he says, and underneath the roughness there's a pleading note. "Just open your eyes for me."

It takes her a second, but she does, and he stares into her, as if looking for something, waiting for something, before he too slumps against the opposite hull in relief, setting the pistol down with a click.

"What happened?" Terese croaks out, and everything hurts, each word pulling on the jagged edges of her stomach.

Axel pushes himself up into the little cabin of the boat and returns with one of her stock of water bottles.

She rarely ends up on the boat, but it's so remote she keeps it stocked.

It's a small boat, with fishing poles attached to the side, sun-bleached. The paint on the hull spiderwebs in cracks, and the plastic awning has long since torn to pieces.

But the cabin is still waterproof, with a bench that converts into a bed and a working microwave.

As far as the eye can see stretches the sea, just the water and the sky above them, and despite coming here before, she still has no idea where the boat is located. She's never seen another person, never seen an airplane fly overhead, nothing.

"Here," Axel says, crouching next to her and holding the water bottle.

Her hands shake, still slick with blood, but she takes a sip, and her throat is dry, much dryer than it should be.

"He got you, for a few seconds, I think," Axel says, helping her with the bottle of water, "then you did something else, and we were here, and you've been unconscious since."

She blinks at him, at the red across his cheekbones.

Izzy's not there, Terese realizes with a terrifying drop, Izzy's not with them, she's still back—

"There's no cell signal here," Axel continues, before he gently, very gently, brushes her hair away from her face, "you've been out for...for almost a day."

His voice breaks at that.

Terese closes her eyes against his touch, and he rests his hand on the back of her neck, a soothing weight.

He hadn't known if she was still possessed; he had needed to look into her eyes and see if there was any trace of the demon. He had been here for most of a day, in the middle of the ocean, and didn't know if it was her or a demon in the body in front of him.

She can't really pull together words, so she just leans into his touch a bit more, like she could impart her feelings at that alone.

He folds himself so he sits next to her, his leg pressing against hers, and she tilts herself so her head rests on his shoulder.

Her head is one of the few things not hurting right now.

But if she's been unconscious for most of a day...then her gut wound should feel far better than it does.

"So this is one of the safety spots?" he asks, and she nods against him. "Nice and remote. Outstanding collection of snack food, but there's way more dog food than human food."

"Where's Izzy?" she asks, and her voice sounds quiet even to her ears.

"She was further away," Axel says, and it's still terrifying. "I think she's still at the compound."

He shifts, so he can put his arm around her, careful over the still painful gut wound, but she pops her eyes open anyway, makes herself look down at herself.

The wound itself is pink and puffy, not even halfway through the healing process, but she knows if she stands or moves wrong, it'll open all over again.

"Did I—he—hurt you?" Terese asks, her voice reedy.

"I don't think he had a chance," Axel says, and she never wants to be without this touch, without this contact. "Whatever you did to him, I think it got him a bit."

He holds out the water again, and she takes it, dumping a bit on her hands to wash the blood off.

"There's another three pallets in the hold," she says, at his alarmed look, "more food, too."

There's enough that she and Izzy could stay for a few weeks, but she's never tried. Never stayed longer than two days.

The silence of the waters and the boat put them both on edge after too much longer.

He sighs, then slowly, ever so slowly, presses his lips against the top of her hair.

"I'm sorry I scared you," Terese says, after another few gulps of water, "this place is alarming alone."

"That's an understatement," he says, and she can feel his mouth moving against her hair. "I peed off the edge of a boat. I've never done that before."

"It loses its charm really quickly," she mumbles, and he laughs, small.

She suddenly, viciously, wants to go home.

And suddenly, viciously, home means the compound. The fluffy rug and the table with the tape grid and the bed with many pillows. The kitchen with three coffee machines and the smattering of libraries throughout the entire building.

She's never had a home before.

"There's beef jerky in the silverware drawer. Get me some?" she says, after wallowing in that for a few seconds. "Then there are some energy drinks, and some chips."

She'll need more energy if she's going to get them back.

"I absolutely found the energy drinks already," Axel says, already unfolding himself to stand back up, "they are vile lukewarm."

Terese thinks they're vile cold, too, but they do the job of getting her to feel better.

Carefully, she sheds her ripped jacket, and examines the slash down her arm. Red and black blood crusts along the side of it, but the edges are neat, already itching their way back together.

The black blood means she bled while he controlled her, just a little.

Axel appears back with the snacks, and the sun lightens the sky around them, and in the dawning glow he's beautiful. He's beautiful and tall and strong, and her heart breaks at just the sight of him.

"You're amazing," she blurts out, and he gives her a

crooked smile. "You're amazing and handsome and I'm so sorry."

"I'm just glad you're alive right now," he says, serious, but something in his eyes softens. "You're alive and you're you."

"I'm me," she says, accepting the bag of chips and tugging it open.

They sit there in silence, as the sky brightens to blue, turning the water a deep turquoise.

She's long thought this must be somewhere almost tropical. The water is too perfect, but she has no idea where. All the books in the cabin were in a language she didn't know and couldn't easily identify, and all the instructions on the long since dead equipment in an entirely different one. She never saw birds, and only once saw dolphins way off the bow, but they were so far away they might as well have been a mirage.

"I never want to see that again," Axel says, quiet, after so long with just the soft lull of the waves and the crunching of chips for noise. "I could tell he was possessing you and I thought we lost you."

She drops the bag of chips to grip his hand, as tight as she can despite the pain in her arm.

"I thought I'd have to shoot you, and even if it wouldn't kill you, I don't want to," he continues, "or I thought I'd be left here until I starved or killed if you woke up and you were him. I didn't know what would happen."

She didn't know, either, so she just reaches up to cradle his face, where the barest beginnings of stubble prickle against her hands.

He shuts his eyes at her touch, like he's stopping himself from crying.

"I think I love you," he says, and his voice cracks, right in the middle of his words, "I think I love you and I don't want to lose you."

She leans her forehead against his, and the position is quite uncomfortable, but she would sooner chop off her arm than move away.

He rests against her, his eyes squeezed shut for a few moments, until his breathing evens out.

"I can't send you to the store to get me snacks to stop the panic attack this time," Terese says, and he coughs out a wet laugh.

"Was that what that was?" he asks, but at least he's smiling, despite the furrow in his brow.

"At least partially," she replies, and without moving from their contact, he grips her hand right back. "I only had a chance to strike him because he got distracted by the sky."

This pops his eyes open enough so he can squint at her.

"The other demon did, too, when we first...she got distracted. Everything's more intense with the human eyes, apparently."

"That explains some things about Mel," Axel says, but his voice is still wrecked. "Though apparently his body is severely short-sighted, which doesn't stop being amusing."

"I'm not sure the distraction will work again," she says, and his face drops. "I don't know what I'll do next time."

He says nothing, instead pressing against her, leaning up in the boat's hull, and handing her the energy drink again.

It's just as vile as she remembers, but she sips slowly, waiting for the revulsion from her stomach.

Her stomach that had been cut open.

She glances back down at her mid-section, and bile rises in her throat at the sight of the black blood. The other blood she can deal with, the carnage and itchy pink skin she can deal with. The black blood, the proof and parcel that she had ever so briefly been possessed again, threatens to choke her out.

"Can you get me another shirt?" she asks, and her voice is small, way too small. "If you lift the bench, there are some extra clothes."

He nods, pulling himself up on the hull, and surveying the water for a few moments before heading inside the cabin.

She thunks her head against the hull.

For the briefest of moments, Daniil had won. Had succeeded.

"Fuck," she mumbles, viciously wishing Izzy is in the boat with them.

Izzy's probably refusing to eat, probably scratching the hell up out of any carpet or flooring they've put her on. Probably terrified, probably sick to her stomach.

Much like Terese.

Axel comes back, holding a long-sleeved shirt of hers, one she keeps for the nights she spends on the boat when the wind blows cold.

"I didn't see any sunscreen, so put this on so you don't get burned."

"Sunburns do nothing to me," she informs him, but slowly, carefully, peels the slashed tank top off her skin.

The crusted blood sticks to the fabric, giving the sensation somewhat akin to ripping off a Band-Aid.

He blanches at the sight of the wound, at the ragged edges and the re-growing skin, but she takes the moment to dab some water along the edges, rinses off the worst of the black blood, then does the same to her arm.

"I'll be okay," she mumbles, "the first time you saw me was worse."

"Still not great," he replies.

"At least I was unconscious this time," she says, then makes a face at herself. "I mean, less good that you were alone and worried, but nice that I didn't have to...experience all of this in real time."

"No yeah, I can see that," he says, picking up the stained shirt. "Want me to burn this?"

She curves an eyebrow at him, fitting the long-sleeved shirt over herself. It tugs unpleasantly at the rip in her arm, but nothing's going to feel good against it for a bit.

"I say, let's burn it, then throw the ashes in the water. Get rid of it, so we never have to see it again."

"Burning it's not going to make the problem go away," she says. "There's a lighter and a camp stove under the sink. The sink doesn't work."

"Even if the problem doesn't go away, it's going to feel good," he says, scrambling up and reemerging with the lighter.

"Just don't burn down the boat, I can't teleport yet and I don't want you to drown."

"Have you ever drowned?" he asks, and she shakes her head.

He's still pale underneath the sunburn, and the guilt worms its way against the wound in her gut, but she watches as he flicks the lighter against the cotton fabric.

The flames flicker up the ruined shirt, past the blood-stains, and he holds it over the edge of the boat.

For a few moments, she thinks the blood is going to dampen the fire, before the flames surge up and around it, and he tosses it in the ocean with a fling of his hand. It disintegrates into ashes as the wind catches it and pulls it away from the boat.

"That'll confuse some fish," Terese says, and he gives her a smile, such a smile, tinged with desperation. "I'm sorry."

"Stop apologizing," he says, sitting next to her again, "it wasn't you that caused this."

She resists picking up his hand again to eat a few more chips, to gain more energy back so she can bring him back home.

"Let me apologize," she says, after figuring out why his words bother her so much. "This entire thing is awful and distressing and I want to apologize because it sucks."

"Yeah, well, I've always wanted to go on a boat ride... wherever we are."

He leans against her, almost like he needs the comfort, and she lets him, eating in silence.

It takes another few hours before she can stand up without ripping herself open, and she wobbles when she does, but he braces her by the shoulders and helps her up.

By then it's fully day, the sun beating down on her head, and her green ball cap is probably on the forest floor half a world away, and sweat dripping over a still healing wound is always unpleasant.

Axel shoulders his pack, then nods to her, and she reaches a hand out to him.

"You sure you're okay?" he asks, taking her hand, then extravagantly kissing the back of her hand like a prince from a storybook. "I'd hate for you to misjudge and drop us in the middle of the ocean."

She'd pull him in for a proper kiss, impulsive, but her arm aches too much to effectively do that, so she just focuses on the idea of safe. On the sensation that nothing could get to her, nothing could reach her.

It's much harder to do that with vicious proof on her own body that that idea is wrong.

But the lull of the wave is replaced with the rough-hewn wood of the cabin, and Axel exhales.

"I wouldn't drop you in the water," she says, and at least the cabin looks untouched. They have a split second of getting used to the solidity of the ground, before both of their phones beep, then again, one right after the other.

She throws a glance at him.

"No signal on the boat," he repeats. "I guarantee you everyone was freaking out."

"I'd freak out, too," she says, then squeezes his hand to give him a warning and teleports again.

This time the puff of cool air of the cave, and the paint has dried and flaked away, so she wouldn't have even known it was there.

Their phones are still beeping, still accepting messages from when they were gone.

She doesn't bother warning him again, before their feet meet the leaves and the moss underneath the giant spruce tree.

It's dark out, disorienting after witnessing a dawn so recently, but it's the quiet dark of a peaceful night despite the alarms ringing on their phones, with nary a breeze rustling the brambles.

Axel squeezes her hand twice before releasing her and pulling out his phone, dialing instead of bothering to check his messages, flicking it onto speaker phone as they slowly make their way up the long, sloping driveway.

Walking hurts, each step horrific against her gut.

It rings twice before—

"Axel?" It's Alette's groggy voice. "Axel, are you okay?"

"Yeah, we're both here, we're walking up," Axel says, his

eyes flickering to her in the light of the silver moon. "We were in a safety spot with no cell signal."

The phone abruptly clicks off, but Axel shrugs anyway.

"That just means she's walking down this way and grabbed her phone too hard," he says, offering the explanation easily and freely. "A side effect of all the untangling she does, technology doesn't always like her."

Terese nods, concentrating on stepping one foot in front of the other.

It hadn't been too early to teleport, but maybe a smidge too early to walk uphill.

Axel taps on his phone. "Yeah, everyone was panic texting," he says, idly, and she's certain he's going to have to deal with the panic he had the last day because right now he's not. "Huh. It's four AM here."

Her phone beeps again.

"I'll read all of them later," Terese says, weariness seeping into her voice. Half of her expects concern, and then a little of anger, then some fear.

She doesn't know what they saw in the split-second possession either.

"Everyone's probably asleep, I'm gonna have the weirdest jet lag ever," Axel says, then slows himself down, seeing her lagging, "I don't feel bad waking up Alette, she'll fall asleep midday if she needs it."

"And I'm sure she's concerned," Terese points out, and he shrugs, loose. "No, she cares, I'm pretty sure."

"Of course," Axel says, the discomfited look over his face, then he sighs. "We had a bit of a falling out. She's like my sister, still, but it's weird."

That seems to be an accurate description of what she's pieced together, so she nods, neutral.

"Gurlien, the guy...the guy from the college told her he

could fix my...lack of magic bullshit, but only if she basically committed genocide to all the spirits of the land and such."

"I can't see her agreeing to that," Terese says, blinking.

If what he described happened, then no ordinary magician could fix him just like that, but something deep inside of her knows better than to just blurt that out.

Wounds from demons run deep. She's enough evidence of that.

"Exactly, it's a no brainer, obviously," he says, spreading his arms wide, "but she didn't tell me. Just kept it a secret. Like she thought I'd tell her to pick genocide just for me."

Terese keeps herself silent, as the filtered moonlight plays over Axel's sunburn and a breeze rustles the trees.

"And then she almost got herself killed with the Ley Line and things are...weird," Axel finishes up, lame. "We've talked about it so much it's exhausting but it's still so awkward and I'm tired of it."

She leans against the bark of a tree, for just a second, and he stops, curving an eyebrow at her.

"Walking is more difficult than teleporting," she says, and he laughs, awkward. "I'm trying to not pass out, I don't think you'd like to carry me up the hill."

"I mean I could, but yeah," he says, then wrinkles his nose at her. "I feel a bit like an ass being flippant, but—"

"Please be flippant," she says, a hair too sincerely, and he smiles at her, handsome in the moonlight. "Flippant is way better than all of this."

All of this. All of her pain, all the terror he must've felt on the boat, all the horror that Daniil had succeeded, if only for a few spare seconds.

Instead, he leans against the tree with her, almost a parody of suaveness, until the telltale sound of a very large dog crashing through the underbrush interrupts the silver silence.

Terese pushes herself to standing straight, as Izzy's grey fur streaks down the curve of the gravel driveway, a blur too fast for the human eye to track.

Behind her, Alette hurries down the hill, wearing pajamas and a hastily wrapped dressing robe, her long hair a frizzy mess.

Izzy stops dead a few feet away from Terese, eyeing her frozen for a few solid seconds, and Terese's heart drops. What did her dog see, what's wrong—

But then she bounds over to Terese, wiggling at her, dancing around her legs, but thankfully not jumping.

Terese isn't quite sure she could handle the entire weight of her dog jumping on her right now, so instead she sits down on the gravel and lets Izzy lick her face enthusiastically.

"You're okay!" Alette calls, as soon as she's in earshot, then rushes over and wraps Axel in a giant hug, messing up his hair. "We couldn't find you. Zoel couldn't tell where you were, you weren't answering your phone—"

"Sorry," Terese says, as Izzy pushes her face into hers over and over again, licking the side of her neck. "It has no cell signal, and I was dead for...most of the trip."

Alette gives Axel another squeeze, then abruptly lets him go and faces Terese. "Are you okay?"

Terese locks eyes with Axel for a few seconds, because how the hell does she answer that question. "My stomach's still a bit ripped up."

Izzy sits on the ground next to Terese, leaning her entire weight against her, thumping her tail on the ground, before she plops over on her side to get belly rubs, covering her coat in the dust of the gravel road.

"Right," Alette says, unsteady. "I don't know how to respond to that." Still, she regards Terese, eyes wide. "The demon didn't win."

It's a statement, but Terese can hear the question.

"Nope, she's not possessed, I checked," Axel says, re-shouldering his bag. "All I've had to drink in the last however long it's been is lukewarm energy drinks and equally tepid water."

He holds his hand out to help Terese up, making a show of it, but she grips on, anyway, pulling herself up without wobbling the best she can.

Izzy dances in front of them, tail held high.

"Zoel tried to find you, where were you?" Alette asks, hugging the dressing robe closer to her. "You were nowhere in his network of Wights."

"Near as I can tell from navigational equipment I can't read, somewhere in the middle of the ocean," Axel says, dry. "It was warm, and day when we left."

Alette steals another wide-eyed glance at Terese, and this may just be the most unguarded she's ever seen her.

"The demon didn't hurt him," Terese says, and Alette's shoulders sag in relief, just a bit. "Apparently I kicked Daniil out pretty much as I passed out, which is nifty."

They start back up the long gravel driveway, with Izzy crashing around them, and Terese can see Alette pull herself back together, until by the time they're back at the compound, swinging open the creaky metal door, she's every bit imperious as she usually is, wearing the dressing robe as a coat of armor.

"You must be tired," Alette says, with a cold certainty that now seems as manufactured as anything else, "but I need to do a reading on you before you sleep."

Terese nods. She would do the same.

"A, she just came back from the dead and then teleported around the world," Axel starts.

But Alette turns to him, too. "You as well," she says, and for a split second her face falls, before piecing it back together. "I want to make sure you're okay."

There's something fragile there, like the rebuilding of trust.

"Good idea," Terese says, and they both start with surprise. "What, make sure nothing sneaky was done."

29

The linen Alette picks already has gold woven into it, a familiar, soft gold, and it stirs when Terese pokes at it.

It's familiar in the way an old shirt feels, like how the phone felt her first few days with it. Like how the first safety spot she disappeared to felt right, felt correct for her to be in.

"Is this from me?" she asks, flopping into a chair. They're in Alette's room, which is mostly a larger library with a sewing alcove attached, and it very much so looks like a fabric store exploded over every spare surface.

It's almost eerily similar to what the previous demon had internally mocked a different spell weaver for having.

"Yes," Alette says, after setting a teakettle to warm up some water.

Axel plops himself onto the couch with a familiarity in the room that she envies. "With the whole magic exploding thing, she gathered a lot."

He rubs his face, though, and Terese wishes she could

take all the stress away from him, all the anxiety and horror he has felt the last few days.

"Was anyone else hurt?" Terese asks, watching the gold glimmer. "Did Daniil turn on anyone?"

There's a barest flicker of a glance over to Axel. "No."

"That's good," Axel says, blinking blearily. Like now that he's actually sitting somewhere comfortable it takes all of his attention to not fall asleep.

"You damaged the body he was in enough that he had to leave it behind," Alette says, brisk, "so you won't know what he looks like next time."

"Pretty sure I'll be able to tell," Terese says, before sparing a thought to the businessman who had come out when he thought someone had needed help.

"Mel insisted we burn the body," Alette continues, and a shiver crawls its way down Terese's spine. "He thinks you bought us a few days, at least, until a normal demon would recover."

It's good to know, some part of her rationalizes, though dread drips through her as Alette sits down across from her, steaming mug of tea on the table, and gestures for her hand.

"But Zoel thinks it'll be good to test this," Alette says, deftly tying it around Terese's wrist, knotting it in a way she's not familiar with. "Are you sure you're feeling alright?"

"She could show you the really gross stomach wound if you like," Axel drawls, and Alette wrinkles her nose.

"I would categorize myself as not really alright," Terese says, staring down at the familiar gold magic glimmering through the linen. "But I want to know whatever this is more."

Axel raises his brown eyes to her, and she can't make herself look away, not as Alette focuses on the linen, stitching with the curved needle that still smells of power, and nerves worm their way into her stomach.

Because what if Alette finds something? What if she finds something and then everything is ruined once more?

"Are you okay with me being here?" Terese asks, almost without meaning to. "If he found me before, he can find me again."

Axel frowns, the furrow forming in his brow.

Alette's lips tighten. "We've been tightening defenses," she says, surly with the early morning lack of sleep, before she glances, obvious, at Axel. Like she's trying to convey something to him, trying to speak telepathically, and Terese knew they were close but not that close. "And…"

Axel sits up at her tone. "And?"

"Mel might have found something," she says, and the set of her shoulders is grim. "I'm certain he'll tell you tomorrow."

"Something," Terese repeats, more fear settling in her stomach.

"Yeah, good way to be vague, A," Axel grumbles, worry pulling at his forehead.

Alette just nods, sitting back and giving the linen a critical glance.

On her wrist, the gold threads suddenly constrict, snapping against her skin, and Terese jumps.

"That's what I thought," Alette says, and Terese can't read her well enough to know if that's a good thing or not, but when she unknots the linen, the gold remains.

There's no pressure, not like the sudden feeling of a hair tie, but the gold glows against the nearly translucent skin of her inner wrist.

"That's what you thought what?" Axel drums on his leg, but even she can tell it's a tired motion.

Terese doesn't know if he slept at all on the boat. Or if he had just been waiting for her to open her eyes, to see if she is possessed.

The moment they finish with the readings, she's going to drag him to the bed and make him sleep. She doubts she will sleep, but she silently vows to remain next to him for as long as he needs.

"That regardless of what Daniil did to her, enough of her still remains that her magic intrinsically recognizes her," Alette says, and that all sounds good, all sounds normal. "Zoel thought he might've tried to change a part of your biology, which would rend that...not as nice."

"Oh, like how the other demon changed all of this," Terese says, gesturing at her face.

Alette has a moment of looking unsettled, but she covers it well. "Yes, probably, but I didn't know your appearance changed."

"Yeah, it's another list of reasons that demon sucked," Axel says, then plops himself down on the table next to Terese, dragging a chair over and holding out his wrist. "Go ahead and check me."

Deft and much more comfortable, Alette wraps a different strip of linen around his wrist. "What did you look like before?"

"Not a clue, besides vaguely not this," Terese says, running a hand through the shock of white blond hair. "I think I might've been a brunette, maybe."

The strip of linen glows, and Axel's eyebrows shoot up into his curls.

Alette gives the linen a frown, then raises an eyebrow at Terese. "You did magic on him?"

"I teleported," Terese says, before blushing, "that's all the intentional magic."

Without smiling, though, a dimple appears on Axel's cheek. He knows what she's talking about.

"Have you talked to Mel about that?" Alette asks, and just looks like she's about to die from embarrassment as Terese nods. "Then I'll let him tell me if I need to be concerned."

Quick, as if it'll burn her, she unwraps the linen, folding them both neatly into tiny squares.

"I can tell you're both you, you're both relatively psychically unharmed"—Terese doubts that but isn't going to say anything—"and there's no additional obvious tracking." Her eyes flicker to the door, like she's waiting for something. "Don't teleport out of the building tonight—we reinforced it."

LATER, after he drags her back to their room and she lays, exhausted, on the bed with many fluffy pillows, he watches her, something lost and soft in his eyes.

"Did you sleep?" she asks, not entirely sure she can get up to do anything about it if he doesn't crawl into bed next to her. "On the boat?"

Instead, he leans against the doorjamb. "I dozed." He shrugs, and there's a bit of black blood on his shirt collar and she didn't even realize it before. "Like I said, I found the energy drinks."

"I'm not one to talk," she starts, and he flashes her a grin, "but energy drinks aren't a proper substitute for healthy sleep."

He takes the moment, stripping off the shirt and tossing it directly into the garbage can, which she can't blame him because demon blood is gross.

"Is there...is there anything you need?" he asks, and his voice trembles, for just a second. "Anything I can do to help this? Besides the food, besides the rest, anything?"

She doesn't know. She doesn't know, and at the same time, what he's offering seems insurmountable. Seems so much, so incalculable of help, that he has given her.

"Come to bed?" she asks, and his lips twitch up. He's not letting himself smile, but it's close. "We...we will see. I don't know."

Slowly, he climbs into bed next to her, slotting himself around her so he doesn't jostle her stomach.

"Maybe whatever Alette was alluding to, that Melekai found, maybe that's something," she says, and he's warm against her back, a contrasting sensation to her stomach, as the skin itches with newness. "Maybe it's a magical fix, maybe it'll solve everything."

He presses a kiss to the back of her head, but she can feel the weariness in the motion, the stress and horror still held in the muscles of his neck.

"What about you?" she asks, even though exhaustion slips her eyes closed and pulls at her consciousness. "What do you need?"

He hmms in the back of his throat, and doesn't answer, and before long sleep tugs her under, wrapped in his arms.

SHE WAKES before he does the next morning, and lets herself lie there, cozy underneath the blankets, and hopes this moment never goes away.

BEFORE LONG, of course, the world summons them, and they get just a moment of sipping coffee in the kitchen together with Izzy lazily chowing down food before the rest of the world comes crashing in.

Lyra breezes in first, then, in one brief blaze of power, scans Terese so hard Terese almost spits out the espresso.

"You're you," Lyra says, once it cuts off and leaves Terese gasping. "Okay, you're you."

Axel just stares wide-eyed between them, and Izzy glances up from her food before continuing to eat.

"And your gut lining is still not in place, so I don't understand how you're eating, but okay," Lyra says, and Melekai slinks in behind her, a conflicted look over his face. "And your arm has to be stinging."

"It's not great," Terese says, blinking the tears out of her eyes, "but that was worse."

"One of these times I'm going to have the glasses on for that, and it's gonna be great," Axel says, but he still rubs Terese's back as she regains herself.

Melekai throws Axel a nod before helping himself to another chair at the table. "Glad you're not possessed," he says, gruff. "Glad you stopped him from getting Lyra."

So they had seen the turn, too.

"A says you found something?" Axel says, and the discomfited look just grows on Melekai's face. "Any good news?"

Lyra and Melekai glance at each other, like they're weighing the words, and Terese's gut drops.

"That's a no," Terese says, at their expressions. "What is it?"

"Remember the thing I promised you, at the beginning of all of this?" Melekai asks. "I found it."

"What?" Axel asks, and Terese sits back.

The thing he promised. A way to kill her, so that she wouldn't come back.

"How?" she breathes.

"What is it?" Axel asks again, and his brow furrows.

"I told her I would find a way for her to die, without coming back," Melekai says, clinically, and it's not helping, "so if she is possessed, if that happens, she won't be aware."

And she sees it dawn over Axel's face. Sees the blood drain from his lips, sees his jaw loosen. Sees him set the coffee mug on the table with a thunk.

"No," he says, dumbly, then he twists to face Terese, "no, I don't...we can fight this."

Melekai slouches in his chair, and he doesn't look as happy as she would have thought. "It's the knife. He left it behind. He bespelled it, I don't know exactly how, but he was trying to kill you, so you couldn't fight him. It just would've taken a strike to your heart, not...not slashing you around like that."

"No," Axel repeats, and worse, there's something like anger across his jaw. "All that would happen is you'd die. We'd still have to fight him, he'd still try to destroy the world, this isn't an option."

"That's not your decision," Melekai says, surly, and numbness steals over Terese's limbs, leaving her fingers tingling.

"I worry that it's already weakened you," Lyra says, with an obvious flicker of her eyes towards Terese's stomach. "The wound doesn't feel right, even for you."

"And if something happens"—Melekai gestures at Terese—"we'd have a way to stop the worst."

A way to stop the worst.

All of a sudden it's too much, and Terese doubles over,

breathing hard out of her nose, until her forehead reaches the table.

She wouldn't need to have that eternal consciousness, trapped for forever. She wouldn't have to scream, unheard, wracked with pain.

With a click, Melekai sets the knife on the table, and it's the plain pocket knife that Daniil had worn on his belt.

"Or Lyra can rip the demon out of her again," Axel says, his voice spiraling up in pitch, "or we can trap her until we figure it out. We have options, Terese, no—"

She sits back up, and he's blurry behind her tears.

"Terese," he says, and panic hitches his voice, "Terese, you can't."

"Axel," Lyra says, and the gentle voice is directed at him this time, not Terese, and it's surreal, "Axel, we aren't making any decision right now, we just have...another tool."

Another tool. And this one just might save her.

SHE DOESN'T BLACK OUT, not really, but time blurs out, and by the time she blinks back to herself, Lyra and Melekai are gone and it's just her and Axel in the kitchen.

He's brewed another couple of shots of espresso, but he's still, so still, staring down at the table next to her.

"I don't want to die," Terese says, and even the words feel like a little lie.

He doesn't start, doesn't move.

"But I don't want to be possessed more."

"When did you ask him?" Axel asks, and there's something awful in his voice. "When did you ask him to find this?"

"The...the second or third day here," she says, and she

rests her fingertips against his elbow, but he doesn't react. "The day after...after I lost time for the first time here."

Something small unwinds in him, and he breathes out, a little taste of motion. "Before we..."

"Yeah," she says, and he nods, swallowing.

"I don't like it," he says, "I don't like it and I won't. I'll figure something else out." In a jerking motion, he grabs the knife off the table, shoving it in his pocket. "We have Lyra, we have so much more knowledge, we have Zoel. I won't let you die."

"It would be so much better than being possessed," Terese says, and he flinches. "It would be so much better, I've been both, I know."

His jaw ticks, and he stands, jolting upright. Izzy woofs, low.

There's a wild look in his eyes, full of hurt and anger, and something horrifically vulnerable. Something so new and exposed that she just wants to take it, to shelter him, to stop any of the harm.

But Daniil had succeeded, for just a few brief seconds,

He stands there, like he's expecting her to say something, but no words come to her lips for far too long, and he turns on his heel, striding out of the kitchen, and the door closes behind him with a final, loud click.

30

For a few blessed moments, everything is still against her skin. The air doesn't move, her clothing lays motionless against her body, and when her eyes slip shut, she can pretend she doesn't exist.

There could be a way out. There could be a way out and she wouldn't have to go back.

She allows herself a brief, exhilarating breath, where she absorbs that fact, absorbs that it's not inevitable. That she might not have to suffer like that again.

Then...

That would mean she wouldn't ever see Axel.

Her brain skips over that, then circles back, obsessively poking at it.

She couldn't spend more time with Axel, no more slow mornings waking tangled in bed, no more walks in the shade of the forest, no more brushing up against him. No more heart-stopping moments of happiness, no more joy so intense she thinks she's going to cry.

And it hurts him she would ever think of this.

A remote part of her understands. That she'd kick and

scream and fight it, too, if the positions were reversed. If Axel was the one offered a way out, but only if it removed him for forever.

Her phone beeps, loud on the table, bringing her back into the body she inhabits.

THE GRUMPY ONE (11:01 AM): I'll talk to him.

And Terese marvels at that, too. That she has friends now who would go up against Axel for her.

Friends who hate texting but still give her the space to say this like that instead of to her face. Because if anyone tried anything emotional with her right now, she'd probably black out for real.

THE GRUMPY ONE (11:02 AM): Though Lyra would like me to remind you that this should be a last case scenario and not something to just do immediately.

TERESE (11:03 AM): I know.

She stares at her phone, at her small list of contacts, then thumbs over to the chain with Axel, and hesitates.

The other times he's been angry at her, when he stormed off, he needed space, and following him immediately wouldn't help. Would just make it worse, make him feel worse and her horrible.

Still, she taps out a text.

TERESE (11:05 AM): I love you.

When he feels better, when he doesn't shake apart with anger and wants to come back, he'll read it and appreciate it.

Last time he said he did.

She settles into herself even more, then tucks the phone into her pocket, pushing herself up, and Izzy springs to her feet, tail wagging.

"Yeah?" Terese murmurs to her dog, who points her nose towards the door. "You need to go out?"

Everything's draped with unreality, but she meanders

with Izzy down the hall, up the long familiar path to the solarium, a path that she and Izzy know by heart and by step by now.

Having a steady home has done Izzy good, she decides, and another pang goes through her, at the idea of leaving Izzy behind. Izzy, who hates pretty much everyone else, would flounder if Terese died or got possessed. Izzy, who sticks her nose in Terese's face if she panics, and Izzy, who would like nothing more than to lay on the fuzzy rug in front of the couch.

As Izzy sniffs around the one spot with the broken glass, the spot where mice and stray bits of magic sneak in with the breeze, Terese leans over and scratches her on the shoulders, right in the spot she can't reach.

And then, several things happen at once.

One, the alarm on her phone shrieks, splitting the quiet summer air, and she jumps.

Two, Izzy raises her head and howls, fur fluffing.

Three, something slams Terese into the soft dirt, and for a second she sees stars.

"Wha—" she manages, then—

Hands close around her neck, and there's something above her, a glimmer of red eyes, before—

Now.

She jerks back, head cracking against a bench, and in between one moment and the next her mind is no longer her own.

She takes a breath, past the pain and the fury sparking down her spine, and when she exhales, it's not her controlling the motion.

There, Daniil says, cozy in her mind. *I thought this would work.*

31

Terror spikes through Terese, and there's magic all around her, magic even next to her hand, but she can't even twist her fingertips to break it. Can't shred it, can't pull it towards her.

"I don't think I'll let you do that, this time," Daniil says, aloud through her voice, laying back against the dirt and marveling at the sensations against her legs. At the soil pressing up against her, at the breeze soft on the small hairs on her arm, at the brilliance of the light and shadows of the overgrown plants.

Terese screams, shrieking up to the sky, but her body does nothing. Daniil just glances around, almost lazily, lolling her head from side to side, testing the motions.

And her eyes fall on Izzy, cowering in a corner, growling, her teeth bared.

No, Terese begs, as he stuffs her further and further into a corner of her own mind. *No, don't do anything.*

"I'm not stupid," Daniil says, and she never wanted to hear someone else talk in her own voice ever again. "If someone finds a dead dog, we know they're going to know."

Slowly, he climbs to her feet, unsteady, flexing her toes in her boots, flicking her fingers.

"This is entirely different from a dead body," he says, working her jaw, and pain spirals down her neck at the motion, enough to give him pause, before he shakes it off, taking a deliberate step towards Izzy.

Izzy growls, backing up further, and she's shaking. She's shaking so hard Terese can see, even when the demon is directing her eyes.

"Shh," Daniil says, then reaches out Terese's hand and flicks the tip of Izzy's nose.

Almost immediately, Izzy's eyes flutter shut, and she lists to the side, before falling over in a way that would hurt her joints. Would hurt her legs getting back up.

It's a trick Terese saw from the previous demon many times. That, with a touch and some effort, can instantly make another creature fall asleep.

Daniil stares down at Izzy, long enough to see the steady rise and fall of her breath. "You have more power than I thought."

The words from her own voice sends Terese into a shudder, but Daniil remains still. Hyper aware of every breeze against her skin, of the pressure her feet give on the ground, of the still lingering itch of pain on her arm or stomach.

Before her phone beeps in her pocket, and he quick flashes through her memories to figure out the reason for the noise, what it means, and what he should do about it.

ALETTE (11:36 AM): Was that you?

He spends a few seconds swiping her finger against the slick glass of the phone, marveling at the sensation, before he pieces through her memories, pulling up the one of the alarm, of the test, then clumsily taps out a response.

TERESE (11:37 AM): Yes, sorry. Got overwhelmed.

"That seems like you," he remarks calmly, then flicks through more of the texts. Of her developing friendships, of the flirty ones with Axel, the gruff ones with Melekai.

You're trying to act like me, Terese pushes towards him, from where she's huddled in a corner of her own mind. *Why?*

Instead of answering her, he flashes one of her own memories at her, from when the last demon had control. Of her standing in the snow, watching as Lyra looks at her with pity.

That won't work, Terese says, more confident, and he retaliates by slapping a hand on the wound on her arm, sending a jolt of pain directly to her.

Enough of it hits him that he pauses, mid-step.

"So this will take getting used to," he murmurs, then, confident, steps back into the compound, leaving the sleeping Izzy alone in the solarium.

HIS FIRST STEPS are to the practice rooms, still bitter-bright from Lyra's power, and he cracks the door open, then slides inside, breathing deeply, and the punch of hunger hits him just as harshly.

"Oh, you feel that," he marvels, aloud to the padded room, before rifling through her memories, settling on the one of Terese willingly being scanned. The time she passed out, out of apparent fear. "I wonder if you would have felt that before...the other one."

Gently, as if still not knowing her body, he trails her finger along the ragged foam, the traces of magic still imbedded in there, and the nerves spike at the motion.

I don't want you to kill her, Terese says, and he ignores it.

He takes one more long, lingering breath, before he steps back out, and she can feel her fingers tingling even through the possession.

I do wonder what else you can feel, he says, this time silently in her mind, as they move through the hallways. He's distracted, flashing through her memories at every hallway and junction, looking for where to go. *Shall we find out?*

If she was in control of her body, she'd be shaking, she'd be trembling, but underneath that something iron hard forms in her stomach.

I can tell when you're planning something, he chides, *you're not hiding anything.*

He pauses in the hallway, quickly searching to see if she had any special code, any special password, to establish she's been possessed.

So the Necromancer can tell, and the Alchemist when he's wearing the glasses, he muses to her, standing stock still in the middle of the hallway, before he presses harder on the memories of Axel.

Terese cringes back in her mind, not wanting to share, not wanting anything to touch those, but he leaves through them, easily, all of her mental barriers like paper in his hands.

A spike of anger bleeds through the two of them, and she can't tell who it came from, before it twists to amusement, and he alters their steps.

Heading to Axel's apartment.

"Think he's still mad?" he murmurs out loud.

~

AXEL'S not in the apartment, but Terese is hardly surprised after he stormed off earlier.

Daniil hesitates, staring at the rug, at the couch where she slept the first night, at the table with the grid, like he's just as overwhelmed with emotions as she is.

But he shakes himself loose, crossing and sitting on the couch, spreading her fingers on the textured fabric and marveling at it, before kicking off her shoes and burying her toes in the fuzzy carpet.

And he relishes in it, in the physical touch of the items around her, almost removed from her. Almost not even paying her any mind, just existing in her body. Experiencing.

Terese takes the time to regroup, the best she can. To pull deeper inside her mind, as if she could construct a wall around herself that he couldn't tear down with a thought.

She needs to get some word out, some way of communicating. Some signal, something.

This is wonderful, Daniil remarks idly, and all he's been doing is touching the couch. *How do humans avoid becoming overwhelmed?*

He searches through her memories, pulling up many where she was, in fact, overwhelmed, and he smiles, pulling her lips in a motion that's unfamiliar. *I see.*

Fuck you, Terese thinks back.

He hmms deep in her throat, and she can feel his amusement between them. *I had thought this would be powerful, but this is going to be fun.*

And then, the telltale sound of someone turning the handle, and he freezes.

Quickly, Daniil finds the memory of Axel explaining how she is when she loses time, and sits bolt upright, staring at the wall.

Axel steps inside, and Terese shrieks again, but Daniil holds her still. He's not looking over at Axel, barely moving, but Terese can still see him out of the corner of her eye.

Even the sight of him hurts.

Axel hesitates in the doorway before he sets his keys on the table, and Daniil doesn't move.

For a long moment, it's still, with Axel staring down at her, a hand still on the doorjamb, before he sighs, heavy.

"Aw, you're creepy catatonic," he murmurs, before he sits next to her on the couch.

The fabric dips, tilting her towards him, and Daniil almost reacts. Almost startles.

But instead, Axel just leans against her, like they have so many times before, and if it was under any other circumstance, Terese would rejoice. Relish the touch and the contact and the acceptance.

But all she gets is a vicious stab of joy from the demon inside of her.

Axel wraps his arms around her, pressing his face into Terese's hair, and Daniil barely suppresses a shudder of pleasure from that simple contact.

Daniil keeps her still, an almost perfect replica of Terese's lost time self.

"I'm still mad at you," Axel mumbles against her hair. "I'm still mad and you're still wrong."

Daniil has an agonizing moment of curiosity but doesn't split his attention away from the physical contact. From the pressure of Axel's arms against their skin, from the sensation of her hair moving with his breath, from the heat radiating off of him.

I see why you chose this, Daniil speaks, finally directly at her. *I see why you attached on, if this is what you get with every touch.*

Axel shifts, tilting her so she's leaning against him, a cuddle they've shared so many times, and now it's sullied by Daniil.

If I pull this off, and nobody ever finds out, Daniil muses to her, *then I think I might keep this.*

He won't let you, Terese says, though something's shifting inside of her, some sort of new horror. *He'll figure it out, he'll figure it out, and then never touch you again.*

Then I will find new people, Daniil responds lazily. *He's hardly the only human in the world.*

Axel sighs against her hair, a deep, weary sigh, and a small remote part of her, the part that's not shrieking in terror, knows that it's because of her.

"Where's Izzy?" he mumbles, looking back around the room, as if he just now notices that the giant fluffy dog isn't on the rug. He pulls away from her, and Daniil almost breaks again at the lack of contact. "Did you leave Izzy somewhere?"

Why is he talking to you when he's not expecting an answer? Daniil asks, poking with some honest curiosity, before pulling up memory after memory of Axel chatting at her, even when she's not losing time. *Ah.*

And Daniil shudders her body, as if coming back to, and Axel raises an eyebrow at her as she blinks up at him.

He is handsome, Daniil says, coy.

"Lost time?" Axel asks, and the softness is still there, but guarded.

"Yeah," Daniil says through her voice, and he even nails the intonation, the inflection. "I was in the garden, then...here."

Axel's brow furrows, ever so briefly, before it smooths out. "Last time you ended there, so I guess that works," he says, before reaching out and tugging on the edge of her sleeve, in the idle touch he does whenever he's upset by something.

"I'm sorry," Daniil says, through her own voice, and he doesn't even know what he's saying. Terese can taste the impulse, taste the risk he's taking, taste the exhilaration at the reactions.

"Yeah, well, it sucks," Axel says, and Daniil catches her eyes on the muscle ticking on the edge of Axel's jaw, before Axel consciously relaxes his face. "Mel talked to me, called me a dick."

Mel, Daniil demands, then flashes through the memories, finding the double vision of the last time she was possessed, then seeing him as a human later on.

Daniil pauses, caught on the implications. Of a demon in a human body, living a fully human life.

I'll have to ask him for tips, Daniil muses. *He doesn't seem to care for you too much.*

He won't help you if you kill his Necromancer. This time, Terese throws up a memory of him helping Lyra from a chair, adoration clear in his eyes.

Why? He can't benefit any longer.

Axel's talking, he's been talking, but Daniil's absorption in her memories means Terese misses it.

"—and Lyra said I shouldn't judge too harshly, and that you're more reasonable than that," he says, as Daniil focuses back in on him. "Alette said you're being unreasonable, which means I then had to argue with her on your side and I hate that, but..." The idle motion on the edge of her sleeve gentles, as he swipes his thumb against the inner part of her wrist.

It's abruptly too much for Daniil, and he shudders, and Axel cuts off his words, watching her.

"You okay?" Axel asks after a long moment of silence.

"Yeah, still...still out of it." She hates hearing her voice like that, hates hearing believable words come from her lips that she didn't say.

For a split second, Axel's face breaks, and he leans forward, resting his forehead on her shoulder, and Daniil almost panics at the contact again.

Now who's getting overwhelmed? Terese snipes at him.

"Losing time isn't gonna solve every argument," Axel mumbles, "but I'm sorry for storming out, I really am."

Daniil scrambles in her memories for something to say, but takes too long, and Axel pulls back with a sigh.

"Where's Izzy?" he asks. "She's probably upset you're gone."

"Sleeping," Daniil says, finally, piecing together a reply almost too slowly. "Before I was...here...she was sleeping in a sunbeam in the garden. I didn't want to disrupt her."

Axel sighs again, and his brow is still furrowed, and he pushes himself up to standing, and Daniil sucks in a breath at the lack of contact. "I'll go get her, you should rest a bit," he says, and Terese can feel the distress rolling off of him, before he steps back out of the apartment.

Leaving Daniil stock still on the couch.

I would have gone with him, Terese snipes, the best she can, *I would have gone with him and he knows it.*

He's not that observant, no human is, Daniil snipes back, before standing, dusting off her clothes, and almost teleports off, before catching himself with the memory of the alarm.

That's inconvenient, he says, shoving the boots back on her feet.

This is all inconvenient, Terese replies, as loud as she can, a hard well of anger bubbling up underneath all the panic and the fear. *This will never stop being inconvenient and painful and frustrating and you will wish to just leave.*

I would never leave you to another, Daniil says back, vicious, and a wave of harsh jealousy slams into her, staggering her body in its intensity, as Daniil himself gets swept away in the strength.

If she was in control, she'd be gasping.

And if your 'Axel' tries to take you back, he flashes the memory of them looking at each other, in the bar, with the neon signs and the tacky painting and the soft look in Axel's eyes, *then he'll die, too.*

He narrows her eyes, deliberately straightening her shirt. *It's believable that you're emotionally compromised,* he says, and it's so petty she wishes she could kick him, but before the thought is even fully formed, he teleports.

And lands her in front of Lyra's house.

Terese hasn't been back, not since the last demon, avoiding it as best as she can, but Daniil toes the old, aging lines of runes that Melekai had put into place all those months ago.

I could probably take these down, he muses, but instead focuses their attention like a knife onto the small mobile home.

Someone's planted flowers along the pathway, and in general the entire thing looks to be in better repair. More cheerful. New curtains hang in the windows, and a cat with black and white spots pokes its head out of them to peer at Terese before disappearing.

The neighbors still have a yard full of rusted cars, and another mobile home lays empty, wood nailed over the windows.

Why would a Necromancer live in such a horrible place? Daniil asks, and Terese has no answer.

Still, Daniil closes their eyes, then opens them to a world of gold. A world where walls melt away and all that remains is visible magic.

The cat shines brightly, curiously so, and with a jolt Terese realizes Lyra brought the cat back from the dead.

Besides the cat, there's no living creatures in the house.

Daniil scowls at the empty house. "That would be too easy."

A ball of satisfaction wells up in Terese, that this will be all that more difficult for Daniil. That he wasted some of his advantage by teleporting out.

"Those runes only stop from teleporting inside the boundaries," Daniil says aloud, and she flinches deeper inside. He can still read her mind, even if she's not directing it at him.

Then he teleports back, only a few feet from the boundary, on the gravel road, the giant spruce tree she laid under further away than she's used to seeing.

Without any alarms, Daniil tromps over the boundary, peering down at the base of the spruce tree. Rain has long ago rinsed the evidence of her death there, but the air still tastes strange to his senses.

"I wonder which came first, the healing or the demon," he murmurs, before shrugging her shoulders and tromping up the road.

Whatever body he had been walking in recently has a different stride than her, and her toes pinch by the time he ducks into the trees.

Her gut aches, the cut on her arm pulls at her awareness, but he doesn't stop, funneling all the pain to her instead.

It's a trick the last demon used, but it only works for so long.

What are you doing? Terese asks, and a tiny part of herself recoils away in horror at the idea of demanding answers. Of provoking the being controlling her.

"I'm investigating," he says aloud, surly, then closes her eyes briefly, before opening them up to a world bathed in gold.

Bathed in gold and dulled along the edges. Viewing it how demons do, instead of humans.

If you do that too much you'll see it everywhere, and my eyes will hurt and you'll be unable to see properly, Terese thinks to him, then cringes back deeper into her mind when he slaps the hand against the cut again.

"Maybe I'll get the necromancer to kill us, then they'll bring me back in the body instead," he says, then rests her hand against a strip of magic fluttering along the forest.

It's a familiar jolt of power, one Terese hates.

If you break this, they'll know immediately, she cautions, still sitting in that well of anger. *If you break this, your chance at the Necromancer goes away.*

"I know that," he says, then follows the strip of magic down the wandering game trail.

Leading them right up to the split boulders. Where Axel had sat and showed her magic tricks to distract her.

The memory provokes another wave of envy from Daniil, a twisting, ugly thing.

"But I want to try some things, see if you're actually powerful or if it's a ruse," he says, then grabs the strip and pulls it towards him.

The ground beneath them shifts, and the boulder splits further apart.

And Daniil is silent, but a little bubble of satisfaction twists through the two of them.

Alette will know what that is, Terese says, and she's not even sure what she's trying to do at this point, if she's goading him to run or goading him to get caught. *Alette and Zoel.*

"Then we kill them, easy."

The memory of the last demon ending Alette flashes up, unbidden by either of them, and Daniil pokes curiously at that.

"The last one was stupid, wasn't she?" he says aloud. "If she didn't catch on that someone coming back from the dead means a Necromancer." He rifles through her memories, searching for something, then, "Wait, her name was Terese?"

Terese doesn't want to answer that again, so she doesn't, but he pulls up the memories nonetheless.

"And you just have no name?" Glee coats her own voice, at her own misfortune, before he pieces through the moments of possession, the terror and exhilaration she felt, and the fogginess before it, before a chunk of it clears away like mist to the wind.

A memory of her, with nut brown hair down to her waist, carefully putting on eyeliner in a dirty dressing room mirror. Her eyebrows are different, her cheekbones are different, her nose no longer looks like that. She's wearing a dress—a short one that she hates—and waiting for her band to finish vamping.

"You...just sang at bars," Daniil says, dismissive, like he's not revealing a part of her she didn't know, before tossing her another memory.

This one, she's laughing with a group of people, all of them covered in sawdust and sitting in a small community theater. In between laughing and chatting, she catches the eye of a handsome man with blond curls sanding something near the edge of the stage, and smiles back at him, open and deliberate in a way she never is. She's flirting, flirting in the way normal people do, normal people without the heaping mound of trauma she has.

Your Axel isn't even all that special, he mocks, then grips the strip of magic in her fist and shatters the boulder in front of them.

Shards of rock splinter around them, but Daniil just stands in the middle of it, satisfaction deep inside of him. Satisfaction at the power and might that he's been missing for years. Centuries. At eagerness of potential, at calculating old faults and feuds and how he could win them now. At the ability to change the world around him now, and with more power than he even knew.

Terese still reels from the memories, but the magic around them shifts. Aches. Twists and frays at the edges, warping beyond recognition.

Her phone beeps in her pocket, but Daniil's too absorbed by the stone around them to bother pulling it out and checking.

They felt that, Terese says, *they felt that, and they know.*

"You just don't want me to hurt your friends," Daniil says, her own voice thick with mocking. "Your own friends, who want to kill you, and plot behind your back."

Because I told them to.

"Pathetic," Daniil says. "Now, let's go kill a Necromancer."

32

With a finesse she can only dream of, he teleports them back to the compound, waiting for the sound of the alarm.

Nothing.

"Must've only been for teleporting from outside the boundaries," he muses aloud.

They're deep in the bowels of a basement, where the partially reconstructed runes pile on top of each other, and he tilts her head, looking at them.

"Nice," he says, appreciative, "you're not that much of an idiot when it comes to these."

Fuck you, Terese thinks back, and her fingertips itch to reach out, to pull on one of them, alert everyone to what's happened.

Instead, Daniil reaches out to another one, some sort of tracking spell, and it snaps against her hand.

It didn't do that when it was just her.

He shakes out her hand, and a small part of Terese marvels that he's the one feeling the pain, not her.

Anti-demon. Not Anti-Terese.

Daniil concludes at the same time. *So they're going to be like that*, he muses, looking through the runes.

Filtered through his mind, through his knowledge, Terese can parse out more. Parse out what Dr. Frisse must've meant to do, all the different layers of security and paranoia she built into the very structure.

The one Daniil had tried to reach to specifically tracked Lyra, and it's obviously built into the fabric of the magic. At some point, between the magicians meeting Lyra and Dr. Frisse's death, Dr. Frisse decided she needed to keep track of her.

Melekai would have hated that, if he knew.

He's the one who slept with a food source, Daniil chimes in, from where he had obviously been following along on her thoughts. *He gets whatever foolish results he deserves.*

He pokes and prods her memories to figure out if Lyra's within the building, but unless Lyra does magic, she'd have no way of knowing. They could have left when she and Axel were talking. They could have left right after giving Axel the knife. They could have meandered down into the research basements, completely unaware of everything.

I don't want to pretend for forever, Daniil complains, and her phone beeps, completely derailing his train of thought.

This time, he pulls it out of her pocket.

THE HANDSOME ONE (12:01 PM): Hey something weird is going on, where are you?

"You have him listed as the Handsome One in your phone?" Daniil says aloud, tapping out an answer.

TERESE (12:03 PM): Pacing around. Ended up in the basement. What's going on?

That's not how I would talk, Terese thinks at him, and he lashes out, shuttling her into a smaller part of her mind, sending wave after wave of pain her way.

THE HANDSOME ONE (12:03 PM): Alette noticed something going on in the forest, her and Zoel are distressed.

THE HANDSOME ONE (12:04 PM): Izzy was, in fact, sleeping in a sunbeam.

I also would have asked about that, Terese says, from her little corner. If she had control of her body, she'd be shaking, she'd shut her eyes away from the pain.

"If you weren't so powerful, I would leave this body dead in a ditch," Daniil grumbles, swiping on the phone.

You can still do that, Terese says, and there's a hint of pleading in her own mental voice.

TERESE (12:06 PM): What about Mel and the Necromancer?

THE HANDSOME ONE (12:07 PM): They're fine. Come up right quick?

Probability that this is a trap? Daniil asks her, turning the phone over and over in her hand.

High, Terese says, desperate. If she could get him to get away, give them a bit more of a warning that this happened, then it'd be worth it.

You're a shit liar. Between one thought and the next, Daniil teleports them to the hallway outside Axel's apartment, not even rocking on her feet. Just...able to teleport. Without thinking. With accuracy.

It's all the technique that Terese has wanted this entire time.

If I had the Necromancer, I could do more, he goads, *we could do more, we could be unstoppable.*

You realize she killed the last demon, Terese says.

Who was an idiot, Daniil retorts, turning the handle to the door.

It's empty, no sign of Axel, which takes Daniil aback, and he scowls through the area.

He probably is on his way back, it takes a while to walk up from the basement, Terese says, as if she could push in a needle and make Daniil feel foolish. *He'll be startled to see us here so quickly.*

Stop talking, Daniil snaps as he strides in, momentarily getting distracted by the carpet again. The military bag's still on the extra dinner chair, the snack bag half opened, and a screwdriver sits next to another pair of those geeky glasses, one that doesn't yet have any traces of magic.

Why even bother to try here? Terese asks. *If something strange is going on, he's not going to tell you where Lyra is, he knows better than that.*

I could always go camp out at her house, he muses back to her, which is not the direction she wants him to think at all. *Wait for her to come back to feed that cat.*

Terese cringes back.

Or I could torture your Axel, Daniil continues, *everyone breaks under torture, he's no different.*

You wouldn't dare, Terese responds, and for a split second of anger, she twitches her own fingers, cutting off Daniil's train of thought and derailing it into fury.

I could fuck him, and then tell him after, Daniil says, vicious, *I could kill him so no necromancer could ever bring him back, and the last thing he'd see is your face, ending him.*

Terese tries again, tries to flex her fingers, anything, but Daniil shuts them into a fist.

I could cut you open and make him watch. We could break his heart, then break his spine. You could hurt him so deeply that he could never recover.

"Oh, there you are," Axel says from the doorway, and Daniil spins to look at him.

His brow is still furrowed, but this time out of confusion, which makes sense because there's no way she could have made it up there that quickly, and Terese sends a jab of smugness to Daniil.

"What's going on?" Daniil says, studiously ignoring her, crossing until they're standing close, so close, and Terese's stomach drops.

The frown pulls further on Axel's face, like he's not sure he's forgiven her yet. "Strange shit," Axel says, guarded. "Something in the forest, Zoel's worried you pulled on something while you lost time and destabilized it."

With a stab of viciousness back to Terese, Daniil reaches out, hooking Axel on his belt loop to pull him closer.

His eyebrows flash upwards.

"I don't think I did," Daniil says, modulating Terese's voice down. "I'm...I'm still sorry. I didn't want to distress you, just..."

"Is your arm doing better?" Axel asks, and both Terese and Daniil can't follow his train of thought, until Terese realizes Daniil reached out to him with the hurt arm. "It looked rough earlier."

"I'll be okay," Daniil says, then, with an intentional push of anger towards Terese, tugs Axel down into a kiss.

Terese shrieks, motionless inside her own body, and Axel stills, before pulling back, his face wooden.

"What?" Daniil asks, coating her voice with desperation. "What did I do?"

Axel pushes past them, breaking the contact, and Daniil feels the lack almost as sharply as Terese. "Do you know if you ever destabilized while losing time before?" he asks, unloading his pockets on the table, like he's looking for something.

"Zoel said once, when I first got free," Daniil says,

completely fibbing, not having time to reach into Terese's memories.

Axel opens his mouth to respond, then Izzy plods around the corner of the doorframe and howls.

Axel flinches, half turning to Izzy, then snaps his eyes back up to Terese, and Daniil just tilts her head at him, watching him.

"She's been doing that," Daniil says, and Izzy growls, a deep snarling sound, "ever since—"

Staring at her, Axel freezes, a hand on the military bag. "Since when?" he asks, and his face is pale underneath the sunburn

He can't buy this, he can't, and Terese rails against Daniil's control, and her finger twitches again.

"Since I lost time, but she growled at me last night," Daniil says, somehow instilling some of Terese's confusion into the words. "I woke up in the middle and she was growling."

Axel's shoulders relax, just a hair, and Terese's stomach drops. Like normal, Axel fiddles with his phone, tapping something out.

"She seems really distressed, but she calmed down when..." Daniil turns them towards Izzy, who's backed herself into the corner of the living room, hackles raised and teeth bared, and it guts Terese, strong enough that Daniil gapes as well. "I don't know."

Once I have the Necromancer, I'm killing that dog, Daniil snarls at her, as if she's not already upset enough, as if her heart doesn't pound with Axel buying it and Izzy growling and—

"Hey Terese?" Axel says, but Daniil keeps her eyes on Izzy, forcing her to stare at her dog, the dog he's promised death. "Sorry about this."

"Sorry about what?" Daniil says, automatic, as Izzy backs away even more, teeth snapping. Izzy would bite her like this, and another drip of anger makes its way from Daniil to Terese, blurring and warping her own emotions until she can't tell where the anger begins and the terror ends.

There's a click, metal on metal, and it fishhooks Daniil's attention back to Axel, turning her body towards him. "Wha—"

In front of her, his grip unwavering, Axel holds the bespelled gun up to her chest, and Daniil has a paradoxical split second of wonder, of confusion, of gaping at him, before Axel pulls the trigger.

Pain slams into her, rocketing her back, but Daniil's shrieking. He's shrieking, in her mind and through her voice, and black blood sprays across her vision.

Her body clatters to the ground, head hitting the fuzzy white carpet, and Izzy howls.

Daniil screeches in her mind, pulling at the well of magic in her to teleport away, anything, but nothing happens. He scrabbles at her mind, looking for something, anything, to get her away, but it doesn't work.

What? He yells, so loud it echoes inside her head, scratching and tearing apart, anything to get away.

It doesn't work.

"Fuck," Axel breathes, and she can't see him, her head's tilted away, but the gun ratchets again, and he steps over her, pointing the gun at her head.

Daniil lashes out, or tries to, but her limbs don't move, the magic slipping through her fingertips.

Some point in all this, Axel's put on the glasses again, and runes race across the lenses, as he stares, grim, down at her.

"Move and I'll shoot again," he says, and his voice breaks. "It won't kill you, but it will hurt."

I'll kill him, Daniil swears to her, still unable to move, unable to do anything. *I'll kill him and anything he holds dear.* He tries to flex her lungs, force her to breathe, to jolt her heart back to working, but nothing.

He's as helpless as she is when she's dead.

Panic pulses through Daniil at the thought. He's never been restricted, he's never been unable to do something, and she almost blacks out from the terror bleeding over into her.

There's blood seeping through her chest, black blood, viscous and thick, staining the fluffy carpet.

"Okay," Axel says, then kneels on her, a knee into the wound on her chest, keeping her body down, and his hands are shaking. His hands are shaking, and she can't calm him, can't help him, can't reach out to him—

Her body shudders, her heart beating a few lone beats, and blood bubbles out of Terese's throat.

Pain wracks through her, wracks through Daniil, and he shrieks again, still unable to move.

This is what I mean, Terese thinks, as vicious as she can, the hurt hitting her just as hard. *This is what I mean by the pain.*

Daniil screams, strident, and finally, finally, Terese blacks out.

33

She comes to with wind hitting her face, her hair whipping around her eyes, her hands tied behind her back.

Daniil blinks her eyes groggily, disoriented. The last demon was rarely this disoriented, this off guard, and he jerks her arms...

...Only to find them tied behind her back, upright on a chair.

He flashes them both to painful, painful awareness, color blooming in front of her eyes, color and sunlight and magic and—

They're in the circle, spray painted on the cracked helicopter pad, and Daniil scrabbles to teleport away, as instinctual as breathing.

They remain in place.

There's still a gaping hole in her chest. She can feel it with each breath that Daniil pulls, and her arms ache from the angle they're pulled back in.

"They're awake."

It's Axel's voice, miserable and wrecked, and Daniil jerks up her head.

On the other side of the circle stands everyone. All the people in Terese's little circle; Lyra and Melekai, Alette and Zoel, with Axel standing in the back, a hand firmly on Izzy's leash.

Her eyes stick to him, until Daniil drags them away, focusing on Lyra.

Lyra pales at her gaze, and Melekai makes an aborted motion, as if he could protect her.

They should have run away. They should have run far away until there was no hope of finding them.

Daniil takes the moment to savor the brilliance of the Necromancer, before he glances at the circle. There's something close to trepidation in him, bleeding over to Terese, at the runes and the bronze paint.

He prods, hard, into her memories, and in one searing moment, she's back in the circle with the other demon, full of fiery pain and panic and snow, before he shakes her head to clear out the image.

Interesting tactic, he says, and there's a tinge of bitterness in his mental voice to her. *They can't hope to duplicate the results.*

The last demon had fixated on revenge, and Daniil has none of that.

Beyond the panic, beyond the terror and the disorientation of not being in control of her own body, a tiny part of Terese is pleased. *I knew they'd have a plan.* They had a plan and despite everything intertwined, Axel was able to put Daniil down before he could hurt him.

All without power.

Daniil ignores her, casting her eyes to the individual

runes, reading them as easy as breathing. Analyzing. Looking for a way out.

It's more advanced than the one they used on the previous demon, somehow, and Terese can spot the runes cast with jerky necromancy, the smooth ones of spell weaving, and a strict band of natural power all throughout it.

Even Daniil can't interpret all of it, and he puzzles over them, tilting her head.

"Why are you in my territory?" Finally, someone speaks, and it's Zoel, his voice a frozen wasteland of strictness. For once, he wears his overbearing nature like a cloak of power, instead of making himself small.

Daniil opens her mouth to speak, but all that comes out is a croak, so he makes a face.

Axel flinches, and she doesn't know if it's because of the injury or the noise.

Or the fact that he's seen that face on her many times, and now has to see it through someone else.

Her heart hurts, just watching him, and Daniil refuses to focus on his face.

"You don't have the authority to block me," Daniil says, finally, and each word sears through the chest wound. Whatever bullet they put in that gun, whatever spells they put on her while unconscious, it's good. It's good, it's smart, and it speaks to months of planning, long before she reentered their lives.

She twitches a finger behind her back, and Daniil doesn't notice.

If she was in control of her breathing, she'd hold her breath, but he's too focused on the threat around him.

"Terese is under my protection," Zoel continues, and her skin prickles at his words. This can't possibly work, he won't be able to talk the demon out of her, it's a formality in the face of power.

Daniil thinks so, too.

Tugging at her magic—it's slow inside this circle—he focuses a burst of power on the ropes holding her to the chair.

It detonates, shattering to splinters, and he stands, swaying on her feet.

The body doesn't like to stand after such an injury.

The chunks of wood hit the band of power of the runes, bouncing harmlessly off and clattering to the concrete ground.

So it's a shield as well. Preventing what happened last time, getting hit by stray bursts of power.

Prevent what happened to Axel from happening again.

What humans are even this smart? Daniil muses, shaking out her hands and eyeing the group.

He tries to teleport but goes nowhere. Lashes out a strip of power, tearing it apart and slamming it into the shield in front of Zoel.

Zoel doesn't flinch, but next to him, Alette does. It was far and away enough power to kill them both.

You don't even like her, why would you care? Daniil thinks, rolling the torn strip of magic in her fingers.

And Terese can feel him shift tactics, evaluate whip fast.

"So you trapped me," Daniil says, and it's Terese's matter-of-fact voice, the voice she pulls out when she doesn't want people to know she's upset.

In the back, Axel raises an eyebrow. Of course he heard it.

"The last demon tried to end the world," this time, it's Melekai speaking, and his face is grim, unmoving. "I saw it firsthand, I will not watch that happen again."

It's clever for Melekai to phrase it like that, but Daniil refuses to acknowledge that.

"Well, I promise not to do that," Daniil says, carefully, very carefully, pacing around the circle. He wants to appear powerful, he wants to appear in control, but the pain wracks her body with every step and hits him all the same. "Though what would a demon stuck with an eternity of being human care about the world?"

Mistake, Terese pushes at him, hope settling deeper in her, and he flashes the pain over to her in retaliation.

Melekai rolls his eyes, and a spike of anger slams through Daniil at the casual dismissal.

"Necromancer," he calls out through her voice, and Lyra doesn't move, doesn't flinch, like she had been expecting this the entire time. "If you come in this circle, I'll leave you and your friends alone, including this one." He raises Terese's hand, fluttering her fingers in the wind.

"Really," Lyra says, her voice calm, "that'd be astoundingly stupid of me."

"Worth a try," Daniil says, with a shrug that sends agony through her chest, leaving him breathless.

Terese pulls at the control, in that brief vicious moment, and jerks her hand into a fist.

Izzy growls, deep, at that motion, drawing Daniil's focus to her instead.

"All that this body cares about is the dog, anyway," Daniil says nonchalantly, and her heart goes cold. "If you all died and the dog remained, she'd still cooperate with me."

As if she's cooperating right now.

Fuck you, Terese shoots at him.

Something strange is happening on Axel's face, just outside of her field of focus, but Daniil refuses her the ability to look. Refuses to give her that glimpse.

The moment stretches on, with the group still, as if waiting for Daniil's next move, and Daniil casting around their mind for ideas, something, anything.

A glimmer of motion, in the back of the group, of Axel handing Izzy's leash to Alette, and Terese's breath hitches.

Izzy hunkers down to the ground, ears back, very much not liking any of this, Terese in the circle, the demon, or someone strange holding her leash.

"How's the pain?" Axel calls out, and there's anger in his voice, an anger that draws Daniil's attention back to him. "We know you feel it."

"I don't," Daniil bluffs, "the body does."

Axel's face doesn't move, doesn't buy it. "The thing is, we've been around Terese enough to know when she's lying."

Daniil quick flashes through her memories, trying to find what that expression could be, to twist it and use it, but even Terese couldn't tell him what it was.

"Axel," Alette murmurs, some sort of warning, but Axel clearly ignores it.

"How long do you think you could manage with that?" Axel says, and he takes a step forward, towards the circle, and Daniil jabs through Terese's mind, trying to figure out Axel's plan. "The last demon went insane within a month."

"The last one was foolish," Daniil shoots back.

In Axel's hand is the gun, and the want to avoid that injury again pulls strongly at Daniil.

And the beginnings of a plan worm their way into Terese's mind, and Daniil chases after it, so Terese jerks back, minutely, a physical distraction for Daniil.

"You should have used the knife," Daniil goads him, and Axel doesn't quite flinch, but it's a near deal. "You should have used the knife. You have no idea how much she's suffering right now."

Axel ratchets the gun, and Daniil raises one of Terese's eyebrows at it.

"That won't kill me, just hurt her," Daniil says. "You know that."

"Oh, I'm aware," Axel says, and there's a smile on his face, a grim, cocky smile that sits poorly on him. "How long were you in her?"

She can feel Daniil weigh lying, then weigh how easily disprovable it would be. That they had the necromancy scan right before, glimmering proof that he hadn't been possessing her then.

Feels him piece apart what would be the most hurtful to Axel, what would wound him the most.

"I could give you your powers back," Daniil says, instead, drawing Axel up short. "It'd be easy. Demon took away, a demon can give back."

It's not a lie.

It's not a lie and Terese's stomach drops. It's not a lie and Axel can see it written across her face.

"Terese could, too, but she didn't," Daniil continues, with a glee that bleeds through to her, poking at the memories and the way to do so, so obvious that it hurts. "I think she liked the idea of a powerless man."

"In exchange for what?" Axel asks, and Terese squints at him, and it's enough of an action Daniil wants to do anyway that he lets her. "You're saying that in exchange for something, you wouldn't give us something for nothing, you're not stupid."

There's no way it's not a trap, and Daniil pulls back his hope, pulls back his glee, mixing it with Terese's confusion.

Letting me out would be too much, he wouldn't give the

Necromancer up, what is it? Daniil demands, and Terese doesn't know either.

She's exhausted, and it hits her suddenly. Too many emotions, too much pain, too much back and forth between hope and despair and struggling for control. Too much confusion, too much trying to guess what's going to happen, too much focus.

She doesn't know if Daniil will let her sleep, ever.

Axel takes another step closer to the circle, and just like that, they're back at fully aware, all of her attention on him.

He's still sunburned from the time on the boat. From the time where he stared at her until she woke up, not knowing if she'd be herself when she did.

He's had too much despair, and now he's looking at her with his eyes ablaze in anger and stiffness in his shoulders.

She doesn't know why anyone's not stopping Axel, as he stands on the very edge of the circle, and Daniil doesn't know why either. He doesn't know why Axel's doing this, doesn't know why he'd put himself at such risk, doesn't know why they didn't just leave him trapped in the circle until he gives up.

Daniil doesn't like not knowing things.

He stalks her body towards the edge of the circle, on the other side of the shield and the runes, until they are barely an arm's breadth away. Until she can count the freckles on Axel's cheeks, many more now than just a week ago.

"Axel," Daniil pitches her voice low, so that only he can hear, and Axel's eyes tighten, "if you let me go, I'll leave Terese to you."

It's such a lie that Terese jerks at her hands again, curling them up into a fist, and Daniil doesn't notice, too obsessed with the man in front of them.

There's something spelled on him, some sort of protection, which relaxes the hard ball of anxiety in Terese. They weren't just sending him in here, there's some plan, something.

But what is it? Daniil asks, still staring unblinkingly at Axel's beautiful face. This is a stupid risk for him, there's no reason for it.

There's a long moment of watching as Axel stares down at them, before he smiles, wide and heartbreaking, and strides across the rune barrier.

Terese's ears pop at the sudden shock of magic, and Daniil steps back, keeping a hand on the strip of magic, pulling it towards them.

"What—"

Axel opens his arms wide, like he's challenging Daniil, and there's something smug in his face. There's the open charisma, like he's putting on a show, just for her. The wild magnetism, the thing that draws people to him with no effort, all focused down on her and Daniil.

The gun dangles from his fingertips, loose in his left hand. His not dominant hand. The hand he can't shoot from.

"What are you doing?" Terese breathes, and it takes both her and Daniil a moment to realize it's her who's saying those words.

"You said you'd give me back the powers, go ahead and try," Axel goads, and from somewhere behind them, Izzy whines. "I want to see if you're good for it, then we can bargain."

"You're planning something," Daniil accuses, and Axel just shrugs. "You're planning something and I'm not buying it."

"You're the one with all the power here," Axel says, then, with another smile, the soft look just for her, he winks.

Cold floods through Terese, just enough of a warning that Daniil jerks back.

Right as a vicious slice of necromancy slashes through them, staggering Daniil with hunger and distraction, and he turns. Turns back to the others, to the ravenous brilliance of power, and for a moment Terese sees double. Sees the Necromancer twice, Melekai next to her, Zoel and Alette moving to the other side of the circle, and—

Pain blossoms along her side, shattering Daniil's control, and her legs buckle, but Daniil's still looking for the Necromancer, instinctively towards the source of power for him, and Axel catches them before they hit the ground, as another slice of the necromancy hits them.

It's like she's flying apart, pieces shaking off of her, and Daniil shrieks. Lyra's advancing, she's in the circle, and Daniil reaches towards the magic with Terese's hand, but too much of him is focused on her, focused on reaching Lyra.

There's a knife sticking in her side. The same pocket knife, wedged between her ribs, radiating terror and fury and cold.

"I got you," Axel whispers, almost inaudible over the din, and there's magic swirling around them, the Necromancy spiraling inside of her, picking apart the very core of her being, and for a split second it's familiar. It's familiar, it's how they won the last time.

And Daniil yells again, a vicious screeching and tearing of Terese's voice, clawing himself back. He's going to win this, he's going to overpower the Necromancer, and—

Terese grabs Axel's hand as tight as she can, then takes the strip of magic so close by and shreds it, blasting it into herself.

Daniil wails, and the bubble pops, bright golden around

them, and she's gripping Axel's hand but the rest of her collapses, thudding against him.

What— Daniil manages, just for her, then Lyra's on top of them, through the bubble, and there's a strip of death in her hands, some magic she summons and Terese didn't see where from, and she slams her hand on Terese's shoulder.

The demon jolts from her, like a rope snapping in two.

The Necromancer exhales, and for a moment, a heartrending moment, Terese thinks they've lost, thinks that Daniil's still there.

Then the presence of him evaporates.

Gone.

Terese sags back, and there's a beautiful crystalline moment of quiet. Where nothing happens, where nothing's moving, where nothing hurts, and her head tilts up to see Axel, staring in wonder at the gold around them.

She tries to exhale, tries to do something, anything, before everything plunges into black.

TERESE AWAKENS, slowly, and there's still wind on her face.

It's quiet. There's no swirling undertone of magic, there's no fury or fear or pressure in her brain, just the soft susurrations of the breeze fluttering her hair.

Everything hurts.

There's a brilliance of pain in her side, her chest still a gaping wound, and her head thuds. Everything is muted, like her ears are plugged, and when she tries to open her eyes, her eyelashes stick together, gummy.

She's leaning against someone. Arms loose around her, holding her up.

She struggles with her eyes, blinking them open, and

ALESSA WINTERS

she's still in a world of gold, glimmering and warping threads around her.

Her bubble. Still too thick for her to see out of, still somehow upright despite—

Despite Daniil.

She jerks upright.

"Woah, it's okay."

It's Axel. He's inside the bubble with her, and there's blood on his face, black blood smeared from her. The glasses are askew over his eyes, the runes not moving.

"You got him, it's okay," he says, then gestures outside the bubble.

He should be dead. Nothing else can be in the bubble, nothing.

"Where is he?" Terese wheezes, and everything fucking hurts. Her side, where the knife—

She jerks herself to look down. The knife is out, clattered to the side, and fresh red blood leaks from the wound. Not a wound to the heart—he had missed.

Axel makes a soft noise, like the air gets punched out of him. "You got him, he's dead," he says, like he can't believe the words he's saying. "You won."

Terese blinks at him, through her gummy eyes and the agony in her head, and the words hit her like a brick.

"You're okay?" she asks, and her voice breaks.

"Yeah, I'm good, haven't tried to walk out of the bubble, but yeah I'm okay, I'm fine, I'm..." He ducks his head, leaning against her, and there's blood in his scalp, red blood. "You're okay, you won, it's done."

EPILOGUE

After, recovery is messy.

With a gunshot to the chest, a mid-abdominal stab wound with a knife designed specifically to hurt her, and the resulting mind scramble of having a demon stuffed inside her brain for a few horrific hours, not even Terese's ability to bounce back within a day or so can catch up.

Once they determine that yes, Daniil the demon is in fact dead and that somehow Terese's death bubble didn't also kill Axel, the entire team quickly moved Terese and Axel to the makeshift infirmary inside the compound, where Lyra gets to watch in horror as Terese dies a few times from a few different injuries and Axel gets to be completely fussed over by Alette for a concussion that he somehow received in the mess. Izzy huddles in the corner, entirely unwilling to leave, but entirely too spooked to get closer.

And Axel's hand never leaves Terese's, even when Alette's checking his pupils with an annoying pen light and even when Terese loses consciousness again for what might've been a few minutes or might've been a few days.

But when she comes to, Axel's hand still tightly grips

hers, and he's sitting in a plastic chair next to her medical cot, his head tilted back against the wall and his eyes shut. There's a bandage around his temple, holding gauze against his skin.

Terese takes a moment, takes as many as she can, just watching the rise and fall of his chest.

Izzy snores, and from her position on the cot, Terese can barely see the rise and fall of her dog's shaggy fur.

Terese's still in pain — massively so — and it tugs at her awareness with something vicious, and even she can tell that her mind's not all the way back. That the demon wrestling his way in did damage, damage that'll take her some time to heal.

But Axel's next to her, breathing in the way he only does when he's restlessly asleep, and all she can do is just blink up at him, before her brain catches up to her.

"Hey," she whispers, and it's a croak, and she squeezes his hand back. "Concussions. Not supposed to sleep."

He twitches, then blinks his eyes open, long lashes fluttering from sleep.

At some point, someone must've washed Terese's face, for her own eyelashes don't stick together anymore.

"M'not sleeping," Axel mumbles, which means he absolutely had been asleep, and it tugs at something deep inside Terese that she knows this. "Just thinking."

The lights are dim, but she makes a face at him and crooks his lips into a smile before checking his phone.

"You've been out for about...seven hours? I think?" Axel says, "Alette and Zoel are getting food. They'll be back soon."

"I don't think I'm hungry," Terese says, and Axel's hand twitches in hers. "I know I should eat, but I don't think I'm hungry."

There's something unbearably soft in Axel's smile, something so gentle that tears prickle at her eyes as the only sound is Izzy's deep, sleepy breathing.

"I'm sorry he hurt you," Terese says, and the soft look doesn't vanish, doesn't go away. "I tried to fight him." At his silence, Terese settles deeper into her words, deeper into her mind, parsing out images and flashes and pain of the last day.

Her brain shies away from thinking about it directly, but she blinks her way through it.

"I did fight him," she corrects herself, thinking of finger twitches and breathing and the final blast of power. "I did. It wasn't just an attempt."

Axel uncrosses his legs, so he can lean close enough to the cot to brace himself against it, gently resting his forehead against hers. "I would say so, though I'm hardly an expert," he says, but there's some of his old confidence in his voice. "We could see it. Flashes of you in your face, traces in your words."

He's so close that she can see the freckles in the dim light.

"He showed me some of my memories," Terese says, then shifting so he can lean against the cot easier, sending a fiery line of pain down her side. "Saw magic so much easier. This time it was like...reading a book once you already knew letters."

Out of her control, her throat closes up around her words, like the panic of the time bleeds into now.

"And he fell for the same stupid tricks," Axel says, after she struggles to find her voice for a few moments. "Fell for the most obvious bluff of all time."

The fear of Axel crossing the line of runes flashes into

Terese's mind, but she breathes through her nose and instead looks up at him.

"Talk to me," he starts, "tell me about the memories. Anything fun, anything juicy?"

It's so remote, in this infirmary with a cot and dim lights, so far away from all of it, but she does. Tells him of the nutbrown hair, of singing on a stage and at a bar. Of actually flirting with someone. Of the sensations and the immediate nature of all of it, unfogged by any of her issues.

And he holds her hand through all of it all, and she can feel herself drawing to say something, divulge everything.

"He looked at you and knew how to fix you," she finally blurts out, after exhausting everything else in the story, after all the horror and all the lies and pain. "He knew what to do, and I saw it."

It takes a moment before it dawns on Axel's face, and his beautiful brown eyes widen, before he squeezes them shut, bending over the cot and resting his head against the sheets.

His hand still holds hers.

"I don't know if I can, I don't...but I know how," she continues, as he obviously breathes through whatever he's feeling. "I could see the theory. I could see what he was thinking of doing."

"You don't have to," Axel says, voice muffled by the bed, like the very words are torn from him. "Whatever it is, you don't have to. You don't ever have to think about it if you don't want."

Terese attempts to prop herself up before quickly thinking better of it.

"But I can try," she says, after she's back laying down and blinking the stars away from her eyes. "I can try."

He takes a few more moments before he sits up just

enough to push some of her hair out of her face for her, and his cheeks glisten with tears in the dim light.

"It might take a few attempts," she says, suddenly shy, but he smiles at her. A proper smile, even through all the emotions and the tears and the head injury. "But..."

He leans in and softly, ever so softly, presses his lips to hers, like he's afraid the kiss will break her apart.

"I love you," he mumbles through the kiss. "I love you, you just went through something insanely traumatic, and your first thought is to help me. I love you."

"Oh, I'll have to recover first," she says baldly, and he breathes out a wet laugh. "I don't think I can do anything right now."

"Yeah," he says, then strokes her hair back and her eyes slip closed at the touch. At how tender it is, at how it pulls her mind away from the pain in her side and the confusion in her mind. "I think I can wait as long as you need."

As long as she needs.

She exhales, keeping her eyes closed, and lets the gentle contact pull her back to a more restful sleep.

THE END

ALSO BY ALESSA WINTERS

The Magic of the Living and the Dead
The Girl Who Brings The Dead
The Girl Who Has Already Died

The Ghosts of Riverside County
A Ghost of Her Own
A Ghost to Haunt Her

Summer Merman Series
The Man of the Lake: A Merman Romance
The Man of the Isle: An Alaskan Merman Romance

The Paranormal Organization Series
Marked By The Demigod
The Succubi's Choice
Katya and the Young God

Follow her on twitter at @writerLyn
Want a Free book? Sign up for her Newsletter here and receive a
previously unreleased Novel!

Printed in Dunstable, United Kingdom